Praise for the Wor

"An absolutely witty, swoon-wo
Delightful from beginning to en

—Julie Murphy, #1 *New York Times* bestselling
author of *Dumplin'*, on *All the Feels*

"Joyful, clever, and full of heart, with two irresistible characters whose connection is both gorgeously sweet and wildly hot. Mixing riotous humor and aching tenderness, *All the Feels* is all the things I love about romance. Olivia Dade has jumped to the top of my auto-buy list!"

—Rachel Lynn Solomon, nationally bestselling
author of *The Ex Talk*

"Olivia Dade is so gentle with her characters, giving them each the space to become their best selves while also being loved for all their flaws. *All the Feels* is hilarious and poignant at the same time."

—Cat Sebastian,
author of *The Queer Principles of Kit Webb*

"If you're a fan of romances that feature nuanced protagonists, whip-smart dialogue, scorching chemistry, and sidesplitting humor, look no further than Olivia Dade's books. This author is an absolute gem!"

—Mia Sosa, *USA Today* bestselling
author of *The Worst Best Man*

"*All the Feels* leaves you swooning and eager for more!"

—Denise Williams,
author of *How to Fail at Flirting*

"I adore *All the Feels*. This slow-burn romance had me falling in love every step of the way."

—Meryl Wilsner,
author of *Something to Talk About*

"Olivia Dade once again delivers a book as sexy and charming as it is cathartic. Her books speak to my soul as she deftly tackles complicated subjects with humor, heart, and infinite kindness. I adored *All the Feels* and can't wait to see what she writes next. Olivia Dade is an auto-buy author!"

—Jessie Mihalik, author of *Chaos Reigning*

"Olivia Dade is consistently one of my favorite authors. Her writing is warm and witty, frequently funny, and often achingly poignant. She has a knack for creating sympathetic characters who leap off the page with their vulnerable hearts and relatable struggles."

—Lucy Parker, author of *Act Like It*

"Olivia Dade writes with such compassion and kindness for her characters, and, in the process, makes you want to live in the world she creates."

—Jenny Holiday, *USA Today* bestselling author

"With richly drawn characters you'll love to root for, Olivia Dade's books are a gem of the genre—full of humor, heart, and heat."

—Kate Clayborn, author of *Love Lettering*

SHIP WRECKED

Also by Olivia Dade

All the Feels
Spoiler Alert

Love Unscripted Series
Desire and the Deep Blue Sea
Tiny House, Big Love

There's Something About Marysburg Series
Teach Me
40-Love
Sweetest in the Gale: A Marysburg Story Collection

SHIP WRECKED

A NOVEL

OLIVIA DADE

AVON

An Imprint of HarperCollinsPublishers

This is a work of fiction. Names, characters, places, and incidents are products of the author's imagination or are used fictitiously and are not to be construed as real. Any resemblance to actual events, locales, organizations, or persons, living or dead, is entirely coincidental.

SHIP WRECKED. Copyright © 2022 by Olivia Dade. All rights reserved. Printed in the United States of America. No part of this book may be used or reproduced in any manner whatsoever without written permission except in the case of brief quotations embodied in critical articles and reviews. For information, address HarperCollins Publishers, 195 Broadway, New York, NY 10007.

HarperCollins books may be purchased for educational, business, or sales promotional use. For information, please email the Special Markets Department at SPsales@harpercollins.com.

FIRST EDITION

Designed by Diahann Sturge

Emojis throughout © FOS_ICON/Shutterstock, Inc.

Library of Congress Cataloging-in-Publication Data has been applied for.

ISBN 978-0-06-321587-0

22 23 24 25 26 LSC 10 9 8 7 6 5 4 3 2 1

To everyone searching for a true family. If you weren't given one from birth, may you find it out in the world, and may you know down to your bones that you're understood and loved. Always. Even when you're lost. Even when you don't feel lovable. No matter what.

1

WHEN MARIA'S HAZY BROWN EYES BLINKED BACK OPEN after her orgasm, Peter held her gaze for another dozen thrusts. Then, braced on his forearms, fingers tangled in her hair, he pushed deep one last time and groaned into her mouth.

Rolling them to their sides, he held her tightly as they both recovered.

Despite the steady hum of the hotel room's AC unit, her forehead was damp, her disheveled blond hair darkened with sweat at the roots. Which was only fair, since their energetic fucking had his own skin slick and his chest heaving. After a minute, he mustered the energy to dispose of the condom, but that was all he could manage before crawling back to her and tangling their legs together once more.

His thoughts took even longer to gather, probably because she'd blown his damn mind. Then again, that had been true from the second he'd entered a Hollywood sauna earlier that evening, accompanied by some of his former castmates, and seen her lounging full-length along a cedar bench, her ample breasts and lush hips barely contained by her damp red bikini.

Crimson. A power color for a powerful woman.

Once his companions had left, she'd crooked her finger, and he'd come to her. No questions asked. No hesitation. He hadn't balked at renting a new hotel room instead of going to hers either. If a woman like her wanted him, he didn't intend to quibble with his good fortune. And as long as she was willing to stay in his arms, he'd keep her there.

Soft as velvet beneath his fingertips, the salty skin at the crook of her neck throbbed with her pulse and smelled herbal and musky. Like rosemary. Like sex. Like sex with *him*. He couldn't get enough.

Unfortunately, once her breathing slowed, she nudged him aside with a gentle push, and he reluctantly let her go. Raising her arms and pointing her toes, she stretched her lengthy limbs on top of the rumpled white sheets, entirely naked and entirely unembarrassed by that nakedness.

Like him, she was fat, with a rounded belly and a soft chin. Like him, she was strong too, those endless legs of hers curvy and muscled, her biceps evident when she'd opened the heavy sauna door for him on their way out. He already knew she packed a figurative punch, and he suspected she'd pack a literal one too.

With all that softness and strength, all that confidence, Maria Unknown-Last-Name was the sexiest woman he'd ever met. Bar none.

And now that they'd fucked—stupendously—it was past time he learned more about her than her first name. Even though he was possibly the worst conversationalist in LA.

So when she sauntered back from the white-tiled bathroom and knelt on the edge of the mattress, her stare bold as it swept his sprawled body, he sat up, propped himself against the headboard, and finally put together enough functional brain cells for intelligible speech.

"You're . . . European, right?" The smile felt odd on his face. Unfamiliar. But he was trying, and hopefully she wouldn't notice his awkwardness. "I'm not great with accents, despite the best efforts of various dialect coaches."

Her tousled waves glowed like a nimbus in the golden light of the bedside lamp, and he had to catch his breath all over again.

"Swedish." It was a brisk response. Unadorned by extraneous . . . anything.

He'd like to believe her brevity stemmed from a laconic nature, or Scandinavian custom, or discomfort with English. But he knew better.

It was him. It was always him.

"Okay," he said, then stalled out, his synapses refusing to fire. "Uh . . ."

Dammit. After fifteen years in Hollywood, he should be better at this. He wasn't a naive twenty-one-year-old fresh out of college anymore, and he'd grasped long ago how the industry worked. Talent alone wouldn't get him the roles he wanted, the roles he deserved.

Good luck played a part. So did good timing. But connections with power players and influencers, the ability to schmooze—those would almost definitely score him better, higher-profile jobs. Which was why his inability to generate genial small talk, even when it would goose his career prospects, was unfortunate.

Playing the lovelorn or bumbling best friend, the comic relief, the unnamed murder victim, the character whose entire arc revolved around his weight, had grown old more than a decade ago, and he needed more. A role that would challenge him and stretch his acting skills. Professional recognition. A steady income. The sort of success even his father couldn't deny.

Tomorrow, maybe he'd earn that role, that recognition, that income, that success.

Tonight, he wanted to earn more time with Maria, so he was going to have to find the right words and soon. Because she'd already glanced once toward the door, and he wouldn't forgive himself if he let her leave so quickly, with no way to keep in contact.

Clearing his throat, he tried again. "Is that why you were at the sauna? Because you're Scandinavian?"

Weren't Swedes into saunas? Or was that Finns? Shit, he didn't remember.

"Yes, exactly." Her wide mouth curved in a smile, and an immediate surge of triumph swelled in his chest. "I was curious what a faux-Swedish sauna in Hollywood would look like."

"It *is* kind of an odd business to plant in the middle of sunny, palm-studded LA." His shoulders loosened as he let out a slow, relieved breath. Finally, *finally* he was gaining some conversational traction. "Were you impressed? Disappointed?"

She considered the question for a moment. "Both, I'd say? The sauna itself was lovely, although we don't use cedar much in Sweden. More aspen or alder or spruce. And, of course, we're usually naked, at least in private saunas."

Just as she was naked now, her breasts round and heavy and gorgeous, those plush thighs slightly parted. Not wide enough so he could see between them, sadly.

"Is that right?" Now he was smiling too. At the sight of her. At the sudden ease of their exchange. "I'm sorry they didn't faithfully follow Swedish custom, then."

To be fair, her bikini hadn't hidden much anyway. Not how stiff her nipples got after he'd toyed with them. Not the seam of her pussy when she'd stood before him and he'd traced that tempting line with a light fingertip, the brief, teasing touch a promise. A promise he'd made good on as soon as they locked the hotel room door and he slid his hand between her legs.

When she came that first time, his fingers deep inside her, his thumb on her clit, her hair wrapped around his left fist, she'd moaned so loudly he'd expected a call from the front desk.

Holy shit. At thirty-six years old, how was he getting hard again this quickly?

"At the very least, I should have been able to go topless." When he concentrated on maintaining eye contact and thus failed to respond, she elaborated. "Everyone has nipples, Peter. Why only some people get to display them without police citations, I have no idea."

This was entrapment. She was kneeling on the bed naked and talking about nipples, for fuck's sake. No jury of his peers would convict him for his wandering gaze.

He cleared his throat. "Uh—"

"No, that's a lie. I know why."

He blinked at her.

"Patriarchy," she declared.

Well, he couldn't really argue with that. "Ah."

That explained a few things. Including why, unlike every other woman he'd bedded, she evidently didn't shave or wax. Not that he cared. That blond hair between her dimpled thighs, under her arms, on her legs—it hadn't turned him off. It was yet another sign of the confidence that so aroused him, and it had made the whole encounter feel . . .

Primal, maybe. Honest. *Intimate*, in a way he hadn't anticipated.

Disregarding the modern conveniences of the hotel room, she could have been a woman from almost any point in time. Painting an antelope on a cave wall. Marching to battle alongside Joan of Arc. Boarding a Viking war vessel, a shield-maiden armed and pitiless in the face of danger.

It was all way too dramatic for a simple hookup. Foolishly over-romantic, especially for the taciturn, plainspoken sort of man he was. But to him, in that moment of sexual connection—tangled together, heat against heat, his body inside hers—they'd felt like lovers out of time.

The feeling had shaken him. Left him floundering and uncertain in a way he'd never experienced after sex. He needed to know if it would happen again. He needed to know whether that tectonic shift was a fluke, or . . . not.

But Maria was still talking, and he also needed to listen. Because at some point it would be good to know, just for example, her *fucking last name*.

"Plus, I've heard Americans have more hang-ups about nudity and sex than Swedes," she said breezily. "Which seems to be correct, from what I've seen so far."

The cultural differences between Sweden and the U.S. interested him. They really did. But right now, he intended to steer the conversation toward more basic information.

"So, I was wondering." His beard had left the delicate skin between her breasts pink, and he could barely drag his eyes away from that telltale, viscerally satisfying flush. "Do you live in LA, or are you just visiting for fun, or . . . ?"

Her kiss-swollen lips compressed for a moment. "I'm here for a job opportunity."

Which meant she might live in Sweden still. But where? And what job was she applying for? Did she think she'd get the position?

Shit, he was terrible at this. With anyone else, literally anyone, she'd say more, elaborate on her answers, give them the context he—

Suddenly, he was on his back again, her palm firm on his chest, her hair tickling his face as she planted a hard kiss on his mouth. Before he could catch his breath, she was moving down his body, then down again, dragging her open mouth over his neck, his chest, his belly.

Oh, fuck. *Fuck.*

Her strong hands spread his legs, and she crawled between them.

Then she proceeded to blow his damn mind—again—with that wide, talented mouth of hers before riding them both to another orgasm.

After that, he had no words left. None. She'd taken them all, just as she'd taken him.

And by God, he wasn't complaining. Not even a little.

THE CHIMING ALARM on his cell woke him, and he stretched with a quiet groan, enjoying the brush of cool hotel sheets against his skin and the lingering ache in his well-used muscles after a long, hot night.

Shit, he hadn't felt this relaxed in years. Maybe ever.

Maria had wrung him dry. And after he'd made her come the fourth time, she'd seemed pretty damn exhausted too, her long, generous thighs quivering, those gorgeous brown eyes heavy-lidded. But they'd both slept, and he still had an hour or two before he needed to get ready for his audition, so he'd be more than delighted for her to wring him out again.

Already grinning in anticipation, he rolled onto his back and looked to the other side of the bed, where he found—

Nothing. No one.

He sat up abruptly, the easy laxness of his body gone in a split second.

The door to the bathroom stood open, and the space was dark and empty.

Her purse was gone from the nightstand.

Her clothing, once strewn across the thick carpet, had disappeared too.

If it weren't for the two used condoms in the bedside trash can and the smell of sex in the sheets, he'd have wondered whether he'd dreamed the past twelve hours.

Throwing off the bedcovers, he lurched to his feet and prowled around the room, hunting for the inevitable pad of hotel stationery inside the top desk drawer.

It was blank.

Another minute of searching, and he knew. There was no number scrawled on a sticky note. Not even a quick goodbye on the back of a receipt.

She'd left without a word, and fuck knew he remembered what *that* felt like. Four years might have passed since Anne had left him exactly the same way, but some memories didn't fade over time.

The irony was bitter as lemon pith. He could barely remember the sound of his mother's voice most days, but he could re-create the exact moment he'd realized his fiancée was gone for good, down to the unlaced sneaker on his right foot and the dust motes dancing in the sunlight as his world collapsed around him.

He should have known Maria would leave too. Goddammit, he should have *known*.

In the sauna, they'd been too busy making out to swap personal information, and that was partially on him. But in the hotel lobby, when he'd handed over his driver's license so she could text a friend with his full name for safety's sake, she hadn't bothered to share her own surname. And when he'd attempted to talk with her after the first time they fucked, she'd kept her answers frustratingly brief and vague.

He'd blamed that on his own lack of social skills. In retrospect, though, she'd deliberately withheld any identifying information.

And after their second bout of sex, he hadn't been able to gather his thoughts sufficiently for further conversation. Which—again, in retrospect—she'd clearly counted on.

He'd wanted to fuck her again this morning. Wanted to learn more about her, because even after such limited contact, he could tell she wasn't just spectacularly confident and sexy as hell, but also sharp-witted and funny. He'd hoped to find out over a room-service breakfast together how long she planned to stay in LA and whether she might move to the area.

Instinctively, he'd *liked* her. Connected with her to a foolish degree, even knowing next to nothing about her.

So, yeah. Maybe it was stupid to feel used after a blazing-hot night of no-strings sex with an irresistible stranger, but he did. Used, discarded, and angry.

It didn't matter. They'd had a good time together, and she was gone. He'd never see her again. Now he needed to calm the hell down and channel all that turbulent emotion into his performance later that morning.

In his entire acting career, he'd never had an audition this important for a project this high-profile. The role of Cyprian on *Gods of the Gates*—a show that was already a worldwide hit, even though the first season hadn't finished airing yet—could transform him from a character actor into something else. Something more.

A leading man.

Best of all, the role was meaty. Cyprian's story encompassed survival and grief, anger and fear and lust, as well as a reluctant, burgeoning romantic connection with Cassia, a shield-maiden and the sole other Viking who'd survived being shipwrecked by Neptune.

Why the showrunners had decided to move the story from ancient Rome to medieval Europe but kept all the Roman gods and goddesses, he couldn't say, and he didn't care. Muddled mythology be damned: As Cyprian, he could—for once—be a love interest and a goddamn *hero*.

But only if he performed to the satisfaction of the casting director and showrunners, as well as the other execs and creatives who'd be evaluating him today, and only if he had good chemistry with the actors they were considering for the role of Cassia.

He was one of maybe two or three men still in contention to play Cyprian. In this final audition, he'd have to prove himself and outshine his competition.

And he would. Because, in the end, Maria and her decision to leave him behind without a second glance didn't matter. Not as much as his career.

If he ever saw her again—and he wouldn't—he'd thank her for reminding him of that.

APPARENTLY THE CASTING director had a certain physical type in mind for Cyprian. Peter and the other two men were all white, all tall, all burly dudes with some extra heft to them, and they were all sitting in the same chilly, impersonal waiting area outside a conference room full of decision-makers.

One woman had already arrived for her audition too, and she was almost as tall as the men. Like the potential Cyprians, she was white and built along generous lines, and her long, light brown hair, glowing skin, and a crooked, charming smile made her undeniably pretty. No doubt he'd be performing with her shortly to determine whether they had sufficient chemistry, along with any other women in the final running for the character of Cassia.

As they waited to be called into the conference room, all four of them checked their phones and tried not to fidget. And once his cell indicated two minutes before the hour and no one else had arrived, Peter figured the showrunners had already decided on the pretty brunette for Cassia.

Then, precisely on the hour and not a second beforehand, the door to the waiting room swung open again, and—

Shit. *Shit.*

There she was, all tits, ass, belly, and long legs. She strode confidently toward the nearest empty seat, wearing some sort of expensive-looking patterned blouse, skinny jeans, and polished boots with low heels, her shoulder-length hair rippling with waves and shining under the fluorescent lights.

Maria Whoever-the-Fuck.

The woman who'd fled from their hotel bed without a single word.

She sat gracefully, deposited her purse in her lap, and glanced around in bright-eyed curiosity, smiling.

Until she saw him, anyway.

Then that easy smile died, and her brow puckered for a moment. Finally, she nodded at him as if they were friendly acquaintances who hadn't seen each other for a few weeks.

"Peter," she murmured, and tried with limited success to resuscitate the once-cheerful curve of her lips. "Good to see you again."

Last night, he'd found her slight accent charming. Sexy, even. Now it grated. So did everything else about her.

And unless he was mistaken, he was going to have to act alongside her soon. Luckily, Cyprian and Cassia did nothing but argue in their early scenes together.

That worked for him.

In response to her greeting, he simply looked at her, expressionless. She met his eyes without flinching, and held his gaze until the door to the conference room opened and the casting director poked her head out.

"Peter and Maria, please join us," she said, fuck it all.

Apparently he wouldn't have any time to reconcile himself to this clusterfuck. So he rose to his feet, offered the casting director a respectful dip of the chin, and walked through the doorway without glancing back at Maria.

The conference room was large and filled with various people, some he recognized and others he didn't. The showrunners he spotted right away, as well as a director with whom he'd worked previously. Then he and Maria were ushered toward the front of the room and given an excerpt from a script, and he immediately dismissed everything but the role. Nothing existed but the dialogue, the expressions, the gestures. The emotions he was meant to display and evoke.

If he could, he'd dismiss Maria too, but in this task, she was his partner.

Though not a particularly accomplished one, as he soon discovered.

She delivered her lines well. He'd give her that. But her expressions and gestures were too exaggerated for television or film, especially in a show like *Gods of the Gates*, where the cameras would pull in tight and let the audience read every subtle shift on her mobile face, every twitch of her fingers or infinitesimal tilt of her head.

After a minute or two, Ron Acheson, one of the showrunners, interrupted her in the middle of a key bit of dialogue to give feedback, and he didn't mince words.

"This is your first time auditioning for a television show. Is that correct, Ms. Ivarsson?" Ron asked, slouching back in his cushioned chair and steepling his fingers.

Maria didn't hesitate before answering. "Yes."

"Then let me offer some advice. This isn't a dusty stage in a small Stockholm theater, and you're not playing for the yahoos in the last row." He glanced toward his fellow showrunner, R.J. Nullman, and rolled his eyes. "Take it down a dozen notches, will you?"

When it came to television and film, to Hollywood and its power players, she was an amateur. And thank fuck she clearly wouldn't be chosen for the role of Cassia, because he wasn't wasting his best—and possibly his final—real shot at professional respect and success on someone who didn't know what the hell she was doing. Not when the actors playing Cyprian and Cassia would be performing together, one-on-one, without other cast members and on an isolated set, potentially for years. Not when his gut churned acid at the mere sight of her.

Maria didn't argue with Ron, but she also didn't appear embarrassed or cowed by his criticism. Her chin tipped high, she waited calmly for further guidance.

"Fantastic work, Peter. Continue everything you're doing." In theory, R.J. was complimenting Peter, but he was staring at Maria. Twisting the knife a bit, maybe to see how sensitive she was. How she'd react. "Let's start again from the top."

Peter had to give her credit. She didn't flinch at R.J.'s jab, and in their second go-round, he could tell within moments that she'd adjusted her performance in accordance with Ron's direction. In fact, she adjusted so well that Peter abruptly fell into the scene with her.

"I told you to save Erik," she cried, angry and broken at the loss of her Viking lover to the roiling ocean. "I *told* you. I told you I could swim, and he *couldn't*."

He kept his face stony, only the merest hint of his mingled

grief and relief evident in his expression. "You were tiring, and you were nearer to me than he was. I had a choice. I made it. Now we'll both live with it."

When he held her tear-glazed eyes just a moment too long, the audience would realize, even if Cassia didn't: Cyprian had secretly wanted her. And if there was a chance she'd drown, he couldn't leave her. Not even if that meant dooming his closest friend, the man she loved. Not even if that meant hating himself for what he'd done.

She shoved his chest, hard enough that he rocked backward. "May all the gods damn you, Cyprian. And even if they forgive you, I vow to you: I never will."

He dismissed her with a sneer. "So be it."

Her snarl of heartbroken rage in response was perfect. Just loud enough, just obvious enough. Maria was no longer playing to the cheap seats.

Still, this take was probably a flash in the pan. Most likely she was a moderately talented theater actor not meant for either film or television, one who'd briefly gotten lucky and given the best performance of her life at a crucial moment.

She was a fighter punching above her weight, and that would become evident soon enough. Any minute now.

But by the time she and Peter finished their scene, then did a cold read of another script excerpt, Ron's smirk had entirely disappeared, and R.J. had turned to the casting director for what appeared to be a whispered, extremely intense conversation. Various execs looked thoughtful, and a few were even smiling.

It shouldn't have been a surprise, not after their pleasurable but ill-fated night together, but somehow it still stunned Peter: He and Maria had undeniable chemistry. Worse: After her disastrous start to the audition, she'd recovered. More than recovered. At least for this one morning, this one audience, she'd *shone*.

Before the showrunners finally dismissed them back to the waiting room, R.J. complimented both of them on their performances, then urged them to clear their schedules for the rest of the day and have their agents or managers on call.

The decision-makers in the room still needed to put two alternative Cyprians and another Cassia through their paces, of course, and maybe those other actors would slay their auditions. Maybe their performances would demonstrate such towering chemistry and acting ability, Maria and/or Peter would find themselves shunted aside.

That said, the showrunners weren't exactly being subtle.

"I think it would behoove both of you to have your teams waiting in the wings," Ron told Maria with a wink even Peter considered smarmy. "Just in case."

That was the moment Peter realized.

Even if he landed the role of a lifetime today, he might still have a serious problem. One he had no idea how to solve.

And her name was Maria.

2

LATE THAT AFTERNOON, BOTH MARIA AND PETER SIGNED their contracts after due consultation with their agents and—in her case—her brother Filip, a lawyer.

It was all a bit surreal, frankly. A couple of months ago, she'd sent in her audition materials on a lark. Eager to get far, far away from her family's concerned scrutiny and her own wounded heart, itching for a new professional challenge, she'd taken her shot but hadn't expected much to come of it. Because yes, despite her talent, she wasn't actually an experienced film or television actor, and no one in the United States knew her work.

But now she'd somehow landed a plum role on *Gods of the Gates*, the biggest show on television. Not just in America, but around the world, including in Sweden. She couldn't be prouder or more excited, and she couldn't wait to tell her family.

Only one cloud currently darkened her delightfully sunny skies.

Peter. Tall, dark, sexy, surly Peter Reedton.

Her closest colleague would be the man she'd fucked and left without a word last night.

It wasn't optimal, frankly.

All afternoon, she'd tried to catch his eye and get him alone for long enough to smooth things over. To offer what explanations she could, whether or not he found them satisfactory. To diffuse any awkwardness between them in a private conversation. Maybe even to tell him how unexpectedly hard leaving him behind had been, how often thoughts of him had entered her mind that morning, and how much she'd not only wanted him but also . . . *liked* him.

Enough to frighten her. Enough to make her run.

From the moment Peter walked into that sauna, she'd wanted to fuck him. But she'd seen no possible future for them, and these days, she allowed herself no intimacy of the nonsexual variety with short-term lovers. She did entirely casual or fully committed. Nothing in between.

There was no point to it, and she wouldn't waste her time, her energy, or her heart. She'd learned that lesson early and well, and suffered through a refresher course on the topic only months ago. When it came to their one-night stand, liking Peter hadn't been a bonus but a threat.

So she'd insisted on a hotel room—and hadn't offered hers as an option. When they were finished, she didn't have to persuade him to leave. She could simply go, and that was exactly what she'd done.

Now he was avoiding her. Which was quite a trick, given her centrality to the day's proceedings.

No matter. She could bide her time.

Hours later, her opportunity finally came. After various rounds of congratulations and discussions about their next steps, the two of them were allowed to leave the studio. Peter didn't hesitate, and he didn't offer her a single unnecessary moment of his attention before heading toward the parking lot.

He wasn't an especially chatty soul. That had been evident from almost the first moment she'd spotted him across a steam-hazed sauna.

She hadn't cared.

The other men in his group she could take or leave. They were tall and tanned and impeccably groomed. Lean. Ripped. Their bodies were hard, top to toe, and good for them, but that wasn't what she most wanted in her eyes and in her bed.

The big guy in plaid swim trunks at the end of the bench, though . . .

He was tall—*very* tall—and tanned too, but rougher around the edges. Maybe midthirties, about a decade older than her, with intriguing little lines fanning out from the corners of his eyes. His wavy near-black hair, slicked back from his face, fell to his broad shoulders. His beard was thick and well maintained, but just a little too long for the cover of *GQ*, unless they had an annual Big Hottie Lumberjacks issue she hadn't yet encountered on newsstands.

And best of all, he was clearly strong, but not lean. Not ripped. He had heft over those muscles, softness over that strength. A belly that told her he liked his food as much as she did. If he held her, he'd envelop her with that broad frame of his. As a woman with her own tall, generous body, that didn't always happen, but she loved it whenever it did.

If she was built like a Valkyrie, like an opera singer in a horned helmet and molded breastplate belting out her final aria, he was the dark, thick-thighed Viking striding onstage, bent on plundering her, and she would gladly welcome her ravishment.

"Anything happening with you, Peter?" the guy with sandy-blond hair had asked her Viking. "Did you get a callback for that mobster movie?"

In response to his companion's question, the Viking had given a single, definitive shake of his head. "Nope."

And that was it. Nothing more.

As she'd discovered, such a laconic response was fully in character for him. He'd sat quietly for fifteen minutes with his back against the side wall, his knees bent, his feet flat on the bench. In that time, he interjected with his rumbly, deliciously deep voice once or twice, but otherwise listened to his companions, his face calm to the point of expressionlessness.

Except when he looked at her. His eyes were as dark as his hair, and they flicked her way frequently. Eventually, she'd caught his gaze and held it. Smiled at him, a slow curve of her lips, and his expression hadn't been so difficult to read then. He hadn't looked away until the guy to his right called his name and started yammering about a role in some sitcom pilot.

At that, he'd broken their prolonged eye contact and turned back to his group, his thick brows pinched in irritation.

But he hadn't spoken another word until the other men had finally departed.

So yes, based on what she'd seen last night and today, Peter Reedton did not enjoy small talk, and his baseline temperament in a group setting could not, in good conscience, be termed *jolly*. Even in a moment of professional triumph, his sharp-eyed intensity hadn't softened, and he hadn't offered more than a fleeting smile in response to praise and good wishes.

As far as she could tell, he was reserved with nearly everyone.

With her, however, he was now—unlike last night—absolutely silent. And unless circumstances forced him to acknowledge her, he didn't.

She got it. He was pissed at her, and maybe he had reason to be, even though she'd made him no promises and done her best not to mislead him.

Apparently he hadn't understood, and he was angry. Fair enough.

But very soon, the two of them would be spending nearly every workday in close, unavoidable proximity, and unnecessary animosity was a luxury they could no longer afford. Not if they wanted to excel in their performances, because that kind of one-on-one acting required a certain level of trust and teamwork.

He didn't have to like her. He did need to cooperate with her.

So she followed him to his car, determined to clear the air. With each stride, he covered an absurd amount of ground, but luckily, her legs were almost as long as his, and she was motivated to hustle.

She was also motivated to stare at his fine ass in those dark-wash jeans and the breadth of his shoulders testing the seams of his untucked pale blue button-down. He wouldn't welcome that kind of attention and admiration from her anymore, though. Which caused a pang of—something—near the vicinity of her heart, but she couldn't let that bother her.

"Peter!" she called.

He didn't even glance her way.

His SUV was parked halfway across the expansive lot. By the time she caught up with him, her heart was thumping with exertion and seemingly lodged in her throat. The rapid tap of her footsteps on the pavement must have warned him of her approach, but if so, he chose to pretend otherwise.

"Peter." As he searched his pockets for his keys, she laid a hand on his lower arm and tried to catch his eye. "We need to talk."

Beneath the sleeves rolled to his elbows, his forearms were thick, and the LA sun on his skin nearly seared her fingertips. Not for long, though.

Within a heartbeat, he'd shaken off her touch and taken a step away, but at least he turned to face her. At least he made eye contact, however begrudging.

He raised his dark brows. "Do we?"

Such stony displeasure for so little cause. She'd never understand men, at least men who weren't members of her family.

And upon further reflection, he really *didn't* have good reason to be pissed at her. She'd offered him a fuck, he'd accepted, and they'd both gotten off safely and repeatedly. What precisely had he expected after one night spent with a stranger? An appointment to choose wedding announcements?

She hadn't even given him her last name, and if he hadn't picked up on *that* rather obvious clue, she didn't know what to tell him.

"I think we do." Hands on her hips, she studied him for a moment. "Is last night going to be a problem? Because if so—"

"Nope." His tight smile didn't reach his eyes. "No problem at all."

In her opinion, an actor of his talent and wide-ranging experience—because yes, she'd used her phone to check out his IMDb page back in her own hotel room that morning—should really be a better liar.

"I see." She tipped her head to the side, her skepticism obvious. "Then why do you look so unhappy after landing the biggest role of your career?"

With laudable insouciance, he leaned that fantastic ass against the side of his hybrid SUV, crossed his arms over his broad chest, and met her gaze head-on. "You sure you want to know?"

The question was a warning of ugliness to come, but so be it. Better to lance the wound now and give it time to heal before their first day on set as castaway castmates.

And luckily, her knowledge of American cinema provided the perfect response.

"Bring it on," she told him, her smile wide and full of genuine amusement.

He didn't ask her twice.

"You're right. This is the biggest role of my career." Still leaning against his vehicle, he carelessly slung one foot over the other, the very picture of unflustered composure. "Which is why I'm displeased to be cast opposite a total amateur. One who's likely to drag down my performance and stop me from getting the recognition I deserve."

Wow. *Wow.*

Once more, she'd proven her inability to choose men who weren't assholes. Which was why, when her friends had asked why she wasn't dating again months after the breakup or hurrying to move out of her parents' home, she'd told them men would come and go, but family was forever.

Her brow furrowed in feigned confusion. "I hadn't realized one could still remain an amateur after years of performing onstage in one of Europe's most sophisticated cities and earning the most prestigious theater awards offered by her country."

"Ah." He nodded thoughtfully. "Out of curiosity, what's Sweden's population?"

Oh, she knew where he was going with this. "A little over ten million."

His chest shook with his laughter. "That's even less than I thought. Shit, it's about the same population as Los Angeles County. Still, congratulations on your very prestigious awards. I'm sure your family is extremely proud."

Her hands on her hips curled into fists, but she bit back the vicious swipe tingling at the tip of her tongue. *At least I've won acting awards, unlike my new castmate. His roles were never prominent enough to garner that sort of attention.*

Instead of lashing out, she told him the simple truth. "They are proud."

For some reason, that was when his fake little smile died.

"I'm sure Stockholm's great, honey, but it's no Broadway." The endearment was so acidic, it should have stripped the finish from his vehicle, his condescension so thick it could choke them both. "And theater experience doesn't always serve film and television actors well. As I believe you learned during our first go-round today."

"True." Her own smile was sweet enough to give him a toothache. "But one thing theater experience teaches you is how to adjust your performance quickly, as needed, so the production can shine. As I believe you learned during our second go-round today."

He didn't argue that point, probably because he couldn't without outright lying. Again.

After one long, slow breath from the depths of her diaphragm, then another, she softened her tone and offered him the best olive branch she could. "I may not have much experience in film or television, but I'm a talented, hardworking actor, and I'm excited about this role. I don't want to fuck up your career or my own, and I won't."

He regarded her silently, his narrowed gaze guarded.

Then he sighed and dropped his arms to his sides. "I guess that's something."

Maybe it wasn't the sturdiest of olive branches to get in return, but she'd take it. Take it and run with it, especially since she had a question for him.

"I was wondering . . ." She paused, waiting him out. Forcing him to engage.

It took him a minute, but he finally sighed and grunted, "What?"

Ah, the taciturn sound of victory.

"Isn't it . . ." Her nose wrinkled. "Isn't it a little odd that the showrunners chose fat actors for characters not specified as fat in the source material? As far as I know, neither Ron nor R.J. has ever expressed an interest in body diversity, and they don't seem like natural champions of fat acceptance in Hollywood. But maybe you know something I don't?"

After she'd seen the other actors up for the roles of Cassia and Cyprian, certain suspicions about the showrunners' intent had crept into her thoughts. As a Hollywood insider, though, Peter would understand the dynamics better than she would. And hopefully, asking him to share his experience and wisdom would flatter his ego enough that he'd stop being a dick.

But he only lifted a shoulder. "I don't care why they did it. I'm just grateful they did."

Well, that was remarkably unhelpful.

"And you should be grateful too," he added. "A lot more grateful than you seem to be."

Also patronizing.

Maybe he simply needed time to get past his wounded pride. She'd give it one more try, and if he didn't respond to this attempt at reconciliation, she'd let it go for now.

"Peter." Keeping her voice calm and quiet, she moved a step closer to him. "I know you're unhappy with me. But from what I understand, we'll almost always be the only two actors shooting on that island. And throughout E. Wade's books, Cyprian and Cassia remain stuck there, so we could be filming together for years. *Years.* I'll have to rely on you, and you'll have to rely on me. Otherwise—"

Before she could even finish her thought, he was *roaring* with laughter. Bent over at the waist, he actually slapped his knees in merriment before looking up at her and laughing harder.

"I'll have to . . ." Shaking his head, he wiped his eyes with the collar of his shirt and calmed himself. "Jesus Christ almighty, I'm not going to rely on *you.*"

If anyone ever handed him an actual olive branch, he'd probably snap it over his knee and use it as kindling, then extinguish the resulting flames by urinating on them.

He gave a final, rude little snort. "Have you ever filmed on location?"

"No." A lie might be easier, but she wasn't ashamed, and she wasn't backing down.

"What about working with a camera crew? Have you done that before?"

She pressed her lips together. "Sometimes my performances got filmed for television."

"How often?" he pressed, his eyebrows raised in mocking inquiry.

"Not that often."

Three times, maybe? And she hadn't been asked to alter her performance for the cameras, although she didn't intend to volunteer that tidbit of damning information.

"Hmmm." In a singularly infuriating gesture, he stroked his beard, as if in deep contemplation. "Have you acted in front of a green screen before?"

Skit, he was obnoxious. "No."

"I see." All at once, he dropped his hand and his curious-professor act. "So how the fuck could I possibly rely on you? You know next to nothing about what we'll be doing."

Given the shooting location and circumstances, she genuinely didn't see how he'd have a choice in the matter. He'd only rarely be performing opposite anyone else, and people who shared one-on-one scenes necessarily leaned on their acting partners.

Clearly, though, he was going to try to find a way. His unyielding obstinacy would almost be impressive, if it weren't so short-sighted and self-defeating.

Also stupid. Very, very stupid.

"I'm just going to do my job to the best of my ability and try not to let your performance harm mine." Pushing away from the car door, he stepped closer and ducked his head to make certain she could see nothing but his face, hear nothing but his derision. "We're not on the same side here. We're not a team, we're not going to stand united, and you're no longer in a socialist country. Welcome to unfettered capitalism, Pippi."

What an ass, she thought, and unlike last night, she wasn't praising his actual, physical ass.

He straightened and produced his keys from his pocket. "Besides, even if I could rely on you, there'd be no point in trying."

She smiled at him, ready for whatever barb he intended next. "Why would that be?"

"Because I figure they'll realize their mistake well before we ever make it to that island, and you'll be replaced by our other possible Cassia." A casual toss of his keys high in the air, and he caught them in his broad palm without even looking. "Amber, I think her name was. I look forward to working with her. She's very talented, as I found out today. Very experienced. Very pretty. I expect the camera will love her."

Her smile didn't waver, even though a startling lick of rage had stiffened her entire body. "I suppose we'll see."

"I don't have to see." He threw the words over his shoulder as he unlocked his car and climbed inside. "I already know."

He shut the door before she could respond. And as his engine roared to life, she walked away, thinking she would gladly give him the last word.

In fact, he could have all the last words he wanted.

Because she'd enjoy watching him eat them.

3

AFTER A DEEP, FORTIFYING BREATH OF SALTY OCEAN AIR, Peter carefully stepped off the ferry and onto the windswept chunk of limestone near the western coast of Ireland where he, Maria, and a very small crew would be filming for—years, potentially. As long as the characters of Cyprian and Cassia remained alive and stranded there.

After slinging his huge duffel over his shoulder, he walked to the end of the pier and waited while everyone else disembarked. The assistant director, line producer, boom op, camera op, hair and makeup artist, grip, and a handful of other crew members: one by one, they ventured off the wave-rocked boat and took a moment to look around and get their bearings.

Maria was one of the last to disembark, probably due to her truly absurd number of huge suitcases. To be fair—although fairness wasn't generally something he cared all that much about—she did wrestle them onto the pier with a startling amount of vigor and without complaint, so at least she had that going for her.

Darrell, their production assistant, well-muscled and lean in his low-slung jeans and long-sleeved tee, gave her a big, gleaming smile and leaned in. Way too close, in Peter's opinion.

"Need some help with your bags, Maria?" the PA asked.

Did the kid even have enough experience to participate in such an important shoot? He looked like he was twenty-five, max. Barely old enough to rent a—

Wait. Wasn't Maria twenty-five too?

Peter scowled. Then immediately cleared his expression in order to prevent further wrinkling across his forehead and at the corners of his eyes.

Dammit, thirty-six was *not* old.

"I wouldn't say I *need* help." Her wide grin plumped her cheeks and lit the cloudy afternoon. "But I'll certainly accept some, especially when it's offered so kindly. Thank you, Darrell."

After she rolled two of her suitcases closer to him, she briefly touched his shoulder in seeming gratitude. Within seconds, he was capably wheeling those bags alongside his own suitcase and matching his stride to hers as they easily chatted about . . . whatever other people chatted about.

The colony of twenty-odd seals they might spot on shore, evidently. Also a cranky local dolphin known, for whatever bizarre reason, as Dolphy McBlowholeface. Not that Peter was listening that closely.

"She apparently slaps away overfamiliar tourists with her fins," Darrell noted with another obnoxiously bright smile. "Or sprays blowhole water in their faces."

Maria's snort was audible, even over the constant *swoosh* of wind. "I've met actors like that."

Peter refused to check whether she glanced in his direction after saying that. *Refused.*

"Anyway, I'll bet the island's year-round residents enjoy the show," she said as she easily rolled her remaining bags off the pier and onto the flat, fissured, pavement-like slabs of limestone that covered much of the island.

Clints, those grass-edged slabs were called.

Freaking Darrell wasn't the only one who'd done his damn research.

"Yup." The PA nodded. "Especially since visitors are warned to leave her alone. If they get slapped around by a disgruntled dolphin, they're just getting what they deserve for disturbing local wildlife."

"So what you're saying is that she beats up importunate, handsy admirers and drives them away without mercy or consequence." She tapped her chin thoughtfully, her lips twitching. "I think Dolphy McBlowholeface should be my new life coach. Or possibly my future waterlogged wife."

When Maria and Darrell chortled together, Peter turned away to hide his frown before hurrying toward one of several horse-drawn carts waiting by the harbor—jaunties, the locals called them. Passenger cars weren't allowed on the hilly, startlingly green island's few roads. The production had received special dispensation to use transport vehicles for necessary equipment, but otherwise, everyone would be walking, riding a bike, or taking a jaunty wherever they went.

Unlike his agile triathlete of a father, Peter didn't have a great sense of balance, and he couldn't see himself forcing beleaguered equines to cart him everywhere, so he figured he'd mostly be hoofing it. Which he didn't mind, honestly. He enjoyed walking, and exploring the sparsely inhabited island on foot might distract him from potential boredom and . . . other issues.

When Maria's voice came from too close behind him—"I'm issuing a seaweed-eating challenge to you and the entire crew, Darrell, because if I'm dying of iodine poisoning as we film this season, I'm taking all you bastards out with me"—he quickly picked up his pace.

Very soon, though, avoiding her would require more effort than turning his back and breaking into a near-jog. Even more effort than he'd expended during their initial stints filming in the production's Canadian studio and that huge, high-tech Belgian water tank.

Almost every remaining scene in the second season featuring Maria and Peter featured *only* Maria and Peter. Always together. Just the two of them.

Amber certainly wouldn't be replacing her, despite all his bravado and his idiotic taunts.

Yeah. He was shit out of luck, and deservedly so.

When he was a kid, his mom had called him a champion grudge-holder, and not much had changed since then. Other than, of course, her presence in his life, since she'd died while he was in middle school, and he missed her every fucking day. But apart from that crucial difference, over two decades after her death, he was still her same sturdy, surly son, more than capable of remaining pissed at someone indefinitely.

Even when, upon further reflection, maybe he didn't have all that much actual cause to be pissed.

Maria might be a television amateur, but she was game and she was *good*.

Alongside two dozen other actors, they'd first spent endless days in the studio surrounded by green screens. Their reconstructed knarr, a Viking cargo transport ship, had been mounted on a gimbal, and everyone hung on for dear life and attempted to remember their lines as the hydraulic system tossed them from side to side and up and down as if they'd been caught in a terrible storm, while water sprayed in their faces.

Some of the extras had eventually vomited. Others had quietly bitched about staying cold and wet for hours at a time. Peter had kept his mouth grimly shut and huddled under a blanket near a space heater during halts in the filming.

Maria had treated that bucking boat like a goddamn roller coaster, eyes bright with enjoyment whenever she didn't need to look scared or fiercely determined. Between takes, she'd laughed with the crew and extras, and when the camera was rolling, she'd acted her delectable ass off.

Then they'd all flown to Belgium and filmed at an enormous water tank, where high-tech equipment created vicious waves to buffet all the actors. Everyone except Peter and Maria pretended to drown horribly, and Cyprian and Cassia had their first on-camera fight. And sure, they'd had safety equipment, stunt actors, and various professionals ensuring their well-being, but that fucking tank was over thirty feet deep, and those waves were frightening as shit.

He knew for a fact she'd never faced anything like that on a Swedish stage. Hell, during his fifteen years in Hollywood, he hadn't experienced anything remotely comparable either. To say the conditions were challenging was a vast understatement.

Somehow, though, she'd managed to convincingly convey absolute devastation at the death of her lover and teeming rage at Cyprian, the man she blamed for Erik's drowning. All while coughing up mouthfuls of water whenever a wave surprised her. All while looking hot as hell as she struggled in his protective hold and fought to discard her wet clothing, piece by piece, before the added weight dragged her to the ocean floor.

All while remaining pleasant and civil to him between takes, even though he barely said a word to her or looked at her off camera. At least, not when she could see him looking.

Suffice it to say, he wasn't too worried anymore about her ruining his biggest, best chance at fame and professional recognition.

He might not *like* her, but he could definitely work with her. At this point, he was avoiding her mostly out of habit and partly out of shame, because he'd been a real dick to her in that LA parking lot. And, yeah, partly out of some lingering animosity too, because he'd admit it: She'd hurt his stupid fee-fees by not wanting more than a single night with him, especially when he'd been so damn hungry for as much of her as he could get.

Sighing, he slung his duffel in the nearest horse-drawn cart as their line producer, Nava Stephens, indicated he should, and tried not to grit his teeth at the sound of Maria's cackling laughter behind him.

Right now, the crew probably thought his reserve in her company was due to method acting or some shit like that. Eventually, though, they were going to realize his behavior toward her could in no way be considered professional. Which was ironic, since he'd derided Maria for her ostensible inability to meet his own lofty standards of professionalism.

Again, he was thirty-six years old. He should be better than this.

Maybe after a few more weeks of filming, he would be.

WHEN HE'D BEEN told he would be staying in a local hotel, Peter had pictured something like a typical American chain. Nothing too fancy, but a building with two or three floors of rooms. Lots of guests, and lots of space to avoid anyone—cough *Maria* cough—he might be avoiding out of sheer obstinacy.

Turned out, very few tourists stayed overnight on the island, and the local fishing community didn't require turndown service. The only actual hotel on the island, as opposed to a few rented rooms in private homes and a handful of small inns, usually stayed open only from April through September. It was now June, but filming would take place during the winter too, and the couple

who owned the place had been persuaded to return anytime filming did.

Upon first glance, the all-suites hotel was nicer than Peter had
anticipated. Elegant in its simplicity and not at all generic. One
story constructed of local stone, with panoramic windows everywhere. Gleaming wooden floors and thick rugs. Fireplaces. King
beds. Granite bathrooms. A private outdoor seating area for each
spacious suite.

Living there, even for months at a time, shouldn't prove a
hardship.

The older half of the couple, a fiftysomething Black man named
Fionn, had cooked for Michelin-starred restaurants around Europe
before coming home to run the hotel's small, well-regarded restaurant. His pale, freckled husband, Conor, dealt with their guests'
other needs, so far with impeccable politeness and easygoing charm.

But the damn place boasted five suites. Total.

Five.

Those suites went to him, Maria, the director, the producer,
and the cinematographer. Everyone else was scattered around the
island, staying in those tiny inns and rented rooms.

Maria had been given the suite right next to his, fuck it all, and
all five of them would be eating the included breakfast together
every morning in the hotel's small dining area, just like one big,
happy family.

Speaking of which, Maria apparently spoke to her family daily.
Even now, she was chatting with them in rapid Swedish as she
began to haul her luggage to her door one-handed, piece by piece,
her other hand occupied in clamping her cell to her ear.

From all indications, she and her family got along great, and
today's call proved no exception.

"*Ja*, Mamma," she said, then unsuccessfully tried to drag a particularly heavy suitcase over the threshold to her suite as she laughed. "*Fem. Fem!*"

He'd heard her talking with her *pappa* on their charter plane in the minutes before takeoff, as well as someone named Vincent, who seemed to be her brother. Her easy, cheerful tone never changed during those conversations. At the end of every call, her wide brown eyes softened with warmth and affection as she said she loved them—his best guess; he didn't fucking know Swedish—and disconnected.

He had no idea how it would feel, being in a family like that.

He did know that watching it from the outside hurt.

Her one hand clearly wasn't up to the task of wrangling such oversized luggage. She'd paused in her attempts to hoist her bags over the threshold, probably intending to wait until her call ended. But she needed to get inside her suite and away from him ASAP, and he knew exactly how to hurry things along.

He set his enormous duffel along one side of the hall. Then, placing his hand on her shoulder, using the least possible pressure and dropping the contact as soon as he could, he nudged Maria out of her doorway. Her rapid flow of words faltered for a moment, and her confused stare licked at his skin like a flame, but he kept his own eyes elsewhere.

With two hands and one heave, he deposited her largest suitcase five feet within her suite. Then the next largest, and so on, until all her luggage was resting on that pale wooden floor, against the wall. For good measure, he wrestled the heaviest suitcase, one she'd evidently filled with bricks, or possibly lead weights, onto the waiting luggage rack.

It wasn't an apology, but at least it was . . . something.

And fucking hell, he didn't want to hear those fond family farewells again, even in a foreign language. So without a word, he urged her into her suite using the same glancing, minimal contact with her shoulder as before, paying no attention to her sudden silence. Then he shut the door firmly behind her and set out for a walk that would last until their team's first official on-location meeting later that afternoon.

He'd admire the panoply of late-spring flowers growing in the grikes. Study the austere stacked-stone walls dividing the island's tiny green fields and avoid making eye contact with the cattle and sheep grazing on the grass within those walls. He'd wander down to the golden-sand beach on one side of the island and climb up to the cliff tops overlooking the pounding surf of the Atlantic on the other side. If he got tired after a long day of travel, a couple of the local horses were out of luck, because he'd be hiring one of those jaunties to keep him moving.

Then, if that didn't do the trick, he'd wade into the freezing surf and encourage Dolphy McBlowholeface to slap him around a little, or whatever else it took to get a handle on himself and the way he reacted to Maria. Because this was the first of countless days in close quarters with her, and he needed to keep his shit together.

Worst-case scenario: Seals might not have fins, but they did have flippers optimized for effective slapping. He was pretty certain he could alienate them too, as needed.

He was good at that.

4

DURING THEIR FIRST WEEK OF FILMING, MAKING MARIA AND
Peter look like absolute disasters took well over two hours every
morning, and Maria enjoyed every minute of the process.

"At first, he didn't believe me," Jeanine said, twisting and plait-
ing one side of Maria's hair. "Then he asked whether it was a Ben-
jamin Button situation, because he wasn't the brightest bulb in the
chandelier, if you know what I mean."

It was just so *interesting*, listening to Jeanine and watching her
weave all those little braids, then backcomb them so Maria's hair
looked ratty and big and ocean-ravaged and—frankly—like post-
club sex hair. Then the hairstylist–slash–makeup artist–slash–
costumer would smudge kohl around Maria's eyes and smear dirt
on her face until, in the end, she resembled a well-fucked raccoon
who'd recently spent quality time in a dumpster.

When she got back to Sweden, she was totally re-creating the
shipwrecked shield-maiden look one night, doing the same for
her friends, and hauling everyone to an expensive Stockholm bar,
just to freak out all those urbane, besuited business types there.

Peter required less makeup and fewer braids. Getting his beard
the right degree of unkempt took extra time, though, and so did the
daily application of the prosthetic scar on his cheekbone and the
swirling temporary tattoos on his strong arms and broad chest.

Those tattoos, while slightly blurry and monochromatic, suited him far too well. As did his costume. Or rather, his lack thereof, because he spent those early days of filming shirtless, his chest bare, his shredded leather pants exposing more than a hint of his powerful thighs.

Too bad he was a jerk, because she wanted to lick him like an ice cream cone.

And once Maria donned her own tattered leather pants and torn woolen tunic . . . well, it was pretty amazing. Somehow, Jeanine had made the castaway Viking thing both realistic *and* sexy. The woman wrought miracles daily for Maria and Peter.

Plus, Jeanine was delightful company. At over fifty years old, she looked thirty. And her greatest joy in life was bedding men in their twenties without either lying about or revealing her own age ahead of time, then—afterward—savoring their reactions as they found out.

It was Jeanine's version of sports, Maria had concluded.

"Anyway," Jeanine added, "then he called his mother while still in my room and apologized to her, for reasons I can't quite comprehend?"

"Wow." Maria didn't want to consider the Freudian implications too deeply. "Awkward."

After ten days on the island, Jeanine had already received two marriage proposals from local fishermen. If what she did *were* a sport, the trophy would deservedly be hers.

One last tweak to a braid, and the other woman stepped away from Maria's chair. "Done. Enjoy scrounging for seaweed and hauling rocks, both of you."

Maria and Peter got to their feet and headed for the shoreline, primped for another day of filming that would leave her staggering, sore, and exhausted on her way back to their hotel.

Maybe Peter's own exhaustion could explain why he'd lingered in a chair at the other end of the trailer and thumbed through a dog-eared paperback while Jeanine had worked on Maria today, instead of going outside and finding an isolated spot near the filming location. It wasn't raining yet, so that wasn't his motivation for staying. Besides, the island's frequent drizzle—nippy even in June—hadn't prevented him from fleeing her presence before today.

So, yeah, this was odd.

She and Peter had made it through their first week of on-location proximity without further hostilities, although the chill between them remained. Before today, he'd still avoided her whenever possible, and she'd remained civil but hadn't pushed her company on him.

To be fair, he kept his distance from everyone. But with the crew, as opposed to her, that distance seemed more due to blanket awkwardness than specific dislike. He might appear unfriendly in their presence, but she'd come to suspect he simply didn't know how to make casual conversation or find common ground with people he didn't know. Both of which she would gladly help him with, if he'd only thaw enough to let her.

Which he might not, and so be it. She wouldn't let his iciness bother her. In fact, she'd been using it to enhance her performance. Because the unspoken tension that coalesced between them, thicker than the island's frequent fog? It helped her get into character. Cassia was an independent, determined woman marooned alongside a man she didn't like and didn't trust and to whom she found herself unwillingly attracted.

Maria could relate.

They'd almost reached the semicircle of crew surrounding the area where Cassia and Cyprian were hauling rocks from the shore and stacking them into an initial shelter. More a wall than any-thing else, really. A windbreak that would suffice for the summer, as they built more permanent shelter and preserved food in prepa-ration for the long, dark winter ahead.

To her absolute shock, Peter cleared his throat and—spoke? To her?

"Jeanine's mistaken," he muttered, looking straight ahead. "No more hauling rocks today."

Maria glanced around, but there was no one else in hearing distance.

Weird.

"Okay," she said cautiously.

He tilted his head toward Ramón, their director, who was studying something near the shore. "This morning at breakfast, Ramón said we were moving on to the food-gathering scene."

Even before he'd hated her, during their one night together, she wasn't certain Peter had strung this many words together in a row. Had an Irish witch cast a chattiness spell on him? Or, alternatively, removed a Curse of Manful Silence from his very soul?

"So . . ." When he didn't fling himself away from her in disgust after a single syllable, she continued slowly. "We'll be doing some fishing, then."

He halted just out of hearing range of the crew, all of whom were eyeing them curiously. "And foraging for other things. Wild leeks from the grikes. Seaweed and shellfish from the shore. He said they'll plant fake birds' nests and eggs for us to find too."

Fy fan, this conversation was agonizingly boring, especially since she already knew what was going to happen, so did he, he knew she knew, and she knew he knew she knew.

She could only assume his newest version of an olive branch

involved a tedious recitation of previously acknowledged information. Which—fine. She'd take it.

Okay, what else did they both already know? "We'll be preserving the food next week, then. Sun-drying the seaweed and so forth."

"Smoking the pollack." He nodded. "Salting and drying it too."

She supposed she shouldn't tell him that *smoking the pollack* sounded like an unfortunate euphemism for oral sex.

Whatever. Time to up the ante, because she was done talking about pollack.

Turning toward him, she smiled and waited to speak until he made reluctant eye contact. "Eager to choke down more dulse today?"

When they'd filmed their half-drowned first scene on the island, they'd eaten fronds of the reddish-purple, leathery seaweed in take after take, picking it directly from the rocks while the tide was out, washing off small snails and pieces of shell, and consuming it like the starving Vikings they were pretending to be.

It was a delicacy. She got that. When dried, no doubt it was delicious as a flavor enhancer, and maybe even as a snack. She could even admit to having enjoyed the first few mouthfuls of the fronds, fresh and still dripping with ocean water.

But she was relatively certain another dulse-filled day of filming would require a vomit bucket just out of camera view, readily available between takes.

"Choke down?" He blinked at her. "Eating endless dulse was the highlight of my week. I can't get enough."

Her brow pinched in a confused frown. "Really?"

Because she could have sworn his face had begun turning as green as Ireland's famous shamrocks late that Tuesday afternoon.

"Fuck, no," he said. "And if all our seaweed consumption puts me off sushi, I'm suing the damn show and having them write a formal letter of apology to California rolls."

Before he strode away, she spotted the slightest hint of a grin through that thick beard. Which meant . . .

He was . . . teasing her?

That had to be a good sign. Still, she wouldn't push things. Until she knew for certain the hostilities were over, she'd let him come to her.

She intended to treat him the same way she'd treated the stray moose who'd accidentally wandered through the garden of her family's summer home. In other words: with great caution. Because moose might be gorgeous and majestic, but they were also wild creatures. Unpredictable, sometimes cranky, huge, strong as fuck, and liable to lash out whenever anyone got too close.

That said, if he called her Pippi again, she would be forced to beat him over the head with a jar of pickled herring in an act of extremely Swedish revenge.

Suiting actions to intentions, she didn't continue their conversation as they prepared for the first take of the day, and he didn't either. Not until the countdown to action was about to begin, and his gaze, dark and clear and studiously neutral, caught hers.

"Ready?" he asked.

To begin filming? Yes.

For them to finally work together in harmony?

"*Ja*, Peter," she said, smiling, and watched the faint smile he offered in response.

Embarrassingly, she almost missed her cue.

AT SUNDOWN, CASSIA and Cyprian were crouched by the shore. Using a knife salvaged from the shipwreck, they gathered sea urchins from the cold, rock-strewn shallows, then deposited the creatures onto a swath of leather she'd torn off the leg of her pants.

Slowly, reluctantly, the Vikings were becoming a team, because they had no other choice if they wanted to survive. Also because they were beyond horny for each other, and no wonder. Jeanine's work had only improved upon the bounty nature had already provided both of them.

"Cassia, dry off by the fire," Cyprian ordered, his eyes lingering on her naked thigh.

Crouched low, she shook her head. "Not until we're done here."

Maria's feet, bare and bruised from the day's activities, had gone numb, but this was most likely the last take of the evening. She didn't mind a few more minutes of discomfort. Besides, if she complained, Peter—still distant, but markedly more pleasant all day—might revisit his previous accusations of unprofessionalism, and she wanted all that behind them for good. Years spent in such intimate, unavoidable proximity with a colleague who didn't respect her might not break her heart or her will, but it would be a pain in the *rumpa*.

Cyprian took Cassia's arm and hauled her upright. At that point, Maria was supposed to shoot him a narrow-eyed glare and stomp back toward their primitive shelter, her anger obvious, her unwilling pleasure at his protectiveness hidden from him but not the camera.

But she could no longer feel the craggy rocks beneath her soles, and she'd been crouching far too long. As soon as he released her arm, she lost her balance, slipped on a seaweed-slick chunk of limestone, flailed, and began to fall.

Only to find herself slammed against Peter's chest, her breath squeezed from her lungs by the unforgiving pressure of his arms around her.

Gods above, he was big. Big and blessedly warm, and so strong.

It took him a moment before he loosened his grasp and let her lean back far enough to look up at him. Far enough to see the severe line of his mouth, the angry concern in his gaze, and the stony set of his jaw as he held her tight and safe in his embrace.

She opened her mouth to say—something. She didn't exactly know what. Maybe an apology for ruining the take. Maybe a heartfelt *Thank you, Peter* for saving her from a painful fall, because she'd been headed for some very sharp rocks.

The cameras were still rolling, though.

What would Cassia say in this situation?

Maria had no clue. The heat of Peter's body pressed against hers had burned away all her higher-level reasoning abilities. And he didn't say anything either, just kept staring at her with those hot, dark eyes. His arm braced her back, his big hand gripping the nape of her neck. His other palm clamped low on her hip, his fingertips biting into her leather-covered ass, and *fuck.*

How did she still want him this much? Why?

She swallowed. Hard.

Slowly, his mouth dipped toward hers. A millimeter. Two.

Then he jerked up his head with a rumbling snarl and essentially dragged her off the rocks and up toward their inadequate shelter. Strong as he was, he couldn't carry a woman of her size. But he was supporting a startling amount of her weight without visible strain, and there was zero chance he was letting her fall. None.

Near the rock wall they'd built, he lowered her onto the grass, the firm press of his palm on her shoulder a mute order to *stay.* Still stunned and numb, she did, unable to look away from that giant, capable body silhouetted against the falling light, the play of shadows over his grim face, the stalking grace of his every stride.

The fire had turned to embers. Without a word, he added dried grasses, followed by splintered chunks of their knarr that had washed ashore—eventually, Cyprian and Cassia would discover the wonders of peat, but not yet—until the leaping flames began to thaw her frozen feet.

Then, after one final, lingering look at her, sitting sprawled and speechless before the fire he'd rebuilt, he turned and prowled toward the shore once more.

At long last, Ramón shouted, "Cut!"

"I'm almost certain that's the one we'll use," Nava said as she approached Maria. "Good job almost taking a header onto various sharp rocks, Ivarsson."

Even amid her confusion, Maria had to laugh.

"She's nothing if not committed, Nava." Grinning, the director high-fived Maria. "Great work, everyone! We're done for the day."

It took a long, long time before Peter returned from the water and rejoined the group. For the rest of that night, he avoided her again. Sat as far away from her as possible at dinner.

He didn't speak to her. He didn't even glance her way. And if she claimed not to know why, she'd be lying.

What lay between them—the undeniable chemistry, the brief but fraught history—was . . . inconvenient. Much as it might sting, maybe avoidance truly was the smartest path forward.

Still, the next morning, when he talked to her again, the relief almost brought her to her knees.

Gods of the Gates Cast Chat: Sunday Night

Summer: Maria and Peter, welcome to the chat! You probably already know this, but I play Lavinia. I'm so glad you're part of our Gates cast now. ♥

Mackenzie: Yes! Whiskers is so excited!

Mackenzie: I knew that even before he said so, because he cleaned himself with unusual vigor after we got the email

Mackenzie: Just went to town down there

Mackenzie: Didn't you, Whiskers, didn't you

Marcus: . . .

Mackenzie: Oh, and I play Venus!

Ian: Oh Christ, more costars, just what we needed

Ian: Some episodes, Jupiter's barely on-screen as it is, which is a travesty

Carah: IAN, I'M FUCKING WARNING YOU

Ian: I'm Jupiter, obviously, king of the gods

Alex: No, you PLAY Jupiter, which is NOT the same thing

Alex: And don't be a dick to our new castmates or I'll find your main tuna stash and donate it to local sushi places

Alex: Every

Alex: Last

Alex: Goddamn

Alex: Morsel

Ian: You wouldn't DARE

Asha: He definitely would

Asha: And if he didn't, *I* would, so either be kind or be quiet, Ian

Asha: Welcome, Maria and Peter! I'll say more later, when I'm back from Ibiza, but I'm delighted you're part of our group. And I play Psyche, the mortal who's way too good for Cupid!

Asha: No offense, Alex

Asha: (he plays Cupid)

Alex: Offense! Offense, I say!

Carah: MARIA MOTHERFUCKING IVARSSON

Carah: YOU GORGEOUS SWEDISH BITCH, WELCOME

Carah: PETER "NEVER MET A ROLE I COULDN'T FUCKING SLAY" REEDTON

Carah: WELCOME, YOU TALL GODDAMN DRINK OF VIKING GOODNESS

Carah: I play Dido, the infelix regina herself, who's also way too fucking good for her boy toy du jour

Marcus: I would dispute that, but we both know it's true.

Marcus: I play Aeneas, BTW, the boy toy in question.

Alex: ZIP IT, EVERYONE, IT'S MY TURN TO OFFER GRACIOUS GREETINGS

Alex: Just letting you know, Peter, if you end up dethroning me in Fan Thirst's "Celebrity Beard We Most Want to Ride" poll, REVENGE WILL BE MINE

Alex: And it'll be a dish served piping hot, because I'm an impatient son of a bitch

Marcus: Dude, you realize he doesn't know you, and doesn't know you're joking, so that could be construed as a serious threat, right?

Alex: Whatever, he'll eventually learn to appreciate all the glory that is moi

Ian: Don't count on that, newbies

Ian: After almost two years working together, Jupiter still thinks he's an asshole

Carah: Ian, don't you have gross tuna smoothies to make, somewhere way the fuck away from your phone

Ian: Yup, my two-hour tuna timer just went off, Jupiter OUT

Alex: I will never forgive that smelly bastard for ruining poke for me

Alex: Anyway, glad you're with us, Peter, you're an amazing actor

Alex: Just work on making that beard a bit less lush and enticing, thanks in advance

Alex: And Maria, I Googled the living hell out of you after we got the announcement, and the casting director scored huge when she found you

Alex: Also, all that body positivity and fat acceptance stuff?

Alex: LOVE IT

Alex: Anything I can do to help, let me know, my vast array of scintillating talents is at your disposal

Alex: Also my beard

Alex: My very thick and soft and lustrous and poll-topping beard

Maria: Thank you, Alex, and everyone else too

Marcus: I'm happy you're part of our cast now, both of you. Maria, I watched your performance as Nina in The Seagull on YouTube. Your acting was masterful and heartrending.

Maria: Thank you, that's very kind

Marcus: Peter, I've seen so many of your movies. You're very subtle and incredibly skilled at disappearing into a character.

Maria: Marcus, didn't Peter guest-star on a series of yours years ago?

Marcus: Oh, lord. Which one?

Peter: Maria, I have no idea how you knew this, but: Creekwatch

Marcus: OH LORD

Peter: I played Drowning Guy #2, clearly a key character on the show

Peter: You ran into the creek in your Speedo to save me after making a speech about avenging your murdered sister

Marcus: Oh, fuck, I remember that now

Marcus: You were great, unsurprisingly

Marcus: The script was . . . less great

Peter: Hey, the paycheck cleared, right? Good enough.

Marcus: Exactly. EXACTLY.

Maria: I'll bet you both appeared on the same show other times too

Marcus: Yeah. Maybe even shows that weren't terrible!

Marcus: But probably not, given my acting CV

Marcus: Maria's right. We should grab a meal and compare roles at some point, Peter. Next time you're in LA?

Peter: . . .

Peter: I'd like that.

Peter: Thank you, all of you, for being so kind.

Alex: . . . with one exception

Carah: Fucking Ian

Maria: Please don't put that image in my mind, Carah, I don't need sexual nightmares involving tuna

Carah: OH SHIT, I LOVE YOU ALREADY

Carah: WE'RE GOING TO BE BEST BITCHES FOR LIFE, AREN'T WE

Maria: ☺

5

SHE MADE IT LOOK SO EFFORTLESS.

Peter didn't want to be watching Maria from across their plate-choked dinner table at the hotel, but he couldn't help himself. Seated between Nava and Darrell on the long upholstered booth lining one wall of the hotel's small but elegant restaurant, she glowed in a way that owed nothing to the candlelight and very little to her undeniable beauty.

No, that glow was *her*. Her charm. Her vivacity. Her humor. Her interest in others.

They'd only been on the island for three weeks, but from her easy chatter and seeming comfort in the crew's presence, she might have known everyone for years. Right now, for instance, she was speaking to Nava as if the two women had attended elementary school together, helped each other move into their first apartments, and recently reunited after a too-long separation.

"So how did Carlie survive her first year of college?" After swallowing a healthy bite of butter-drenched local lobster, Maria took a sip of white wine. "Back in Belgium, you said she was worried about how she'd done on her finals."

Nava smiled. "She aced them, to the surprise of absolutely no one but her. Now she's already fretting about her fall classes, even though it's only July, and Dottie took her to the Wisconsin Dells for a week to help the poor kid relax."

Before his parents separated, his family used to visit the Dells. At least once a year.

Until this moment, he'd had no clue Nava was from Wisconsin too. And who the hell was Dottie? A friend? A partner?

He pinched the bridge of his nose, frustrated with himself.

Why couldn't he do this? Why hadn't he somehow managed to get past his social awkwardness after more than three and a half decades of suffering for it?

"She's attending the University of Wisconsin, right?" When Fionn came to collect their plates, Maria patted him on the arm. "I meant to tell you, Fi, that scallop tartare is going to be starring in my dreams. There may well be a ménage à trois with the lobster, so please ignore any sounds of ecstasy coming from the suites tonight."

When Peter's brain helpfully provided a picture of Maria in the throes of a non-shellfish-induced orgasm, he pinched harder.

Both Nava and Jeanine chortled, and Fionn snorted loudly. "Thanks, love."

"Thank *you* for all the incredible food, Fi. I can't wait for dessert." Maria turned back to Nava. "Sorry, Nava. What were you saying?"

"You're right. Carlie's going to college in Madison. Just like Dottie and I did"—she made a show of mumbling—"*mmphmmm* years ago. Although I suspect Carlie consumes way less beer than we did, probably because she'd never think of getting a fake ID. I truly have no idea how we ended up with such a sweet, responsible kid, Maria. It's bizarre."

Unexpectedly, Maria turned her head and made direct eye

contact with Peter, and he flinched a little in surprise. Had she caught him staring?

"Peter," Maria said, her wide brow creased in thought. "That's where you went to university too, right?"

He cleared his throat. "Uh, yeah. Theater major. Born and raised in Madison."

"I had no idea!" Nava leaned toward him. "I grew up in Janesville. I was a theater major at Madison too, although there's no way our times there overlapped. You're way too young for that."

Most days, he didn't feel like it. But saying so wouldn't keep the conversation going, so he needed to find something else to discuss. Something to ask. But what?

He pleated the napkin in his lap, let it flatten, then folded it again. "Did—did you raise your daughter in Wisconsin?"

"Nah." Nava's nose wrinkled. "Dottie and I fled to LA as soon as we graduated. But after the divorce, she moved back to Janesville. When it came time to pick a college, Carlie wanted to stay near one of her moms and both of our families, especially since I'd be out of the country so often, so she chose Madison."

"A fine choice, clearly." Maria gestured toward both of them. "Just look at the exemplary graduates the institution has produced."

"Honestly, we should be on all their brochures." Nava reached across the table with her hand raised, and it took Peter a few awkward seconds to realize she wanted a high-five. When he gave it to her, she grinned at him. "I expect them to rename a building for us any day now."

"Undoubtedly," he said.

Why was Maria smiling at him like that?

"It's a great place to go to college," Nava said. "Although I think Carlie's diet is eighty percent cheese curds during the school year."

The fried version was his favorite, personally. Melty and excellent with ranch dressing.

He grinned. "I assume the other twenty percent is brats?"

"Ten percent brats, ten percent frozen custard." The producer tapped her chin. "Although that doesn't account for her consumption of butter burgers."

When he laughed, so did Nava. Even Maria looked pleased, even though she likely had no clue what the fuck they were talking about.

Without warning, Darrell and the other crew members erupted in loud laughter of their own, and both Nava and Maria turned their attention to the PA.

Peter sipped at his water, still smiling to himself.

There. That hadn't been so hard. He'd had a friendly conversation with a colleague, and now he knew a lot more about her, which would make later conversations easier. They could reminisce about the Dells, or compare their favorite State Street restaurants, or praise the glory of balmy summer nights spent listening to music on the Terrace overlooking Lake Mendota.

To his surprise, he actually *wanted* to talk with Nava again. She was interesting and funny and good at her job, and she seemed . . . warmer than he'd expected. He . . . liked her?

Yes. He liked her. Which was good, since they'd be working together for years to come.

"I put up my fifth video last week," Darrell was saying. "Some people still haven't realized I'm trolling them. Even after I enthusiastically praised the innocent romanticism of 'Every Breath You Take' and said Sting intended it as a guide to healthy relationships."

Peter choked on his water amid more cackling.

Somehow, Ramón managed to groan and laugh at the same time. "Jesus."

From across the table, Jeanine leaned toward Darrell, her bright gaze trained unwaveringly on the younger man. "Despite my best efforts, one of my closest friends danced to that song at her wedding."

Darrell didn't look away from Jeanine. In fact, he set both forearms on the table and canted his body forward, lessening the distance between them even further.

"Has either of them been arrested for stalking?" A smile played at the edges of his mouth, and Jeanine's gaze dropped there for a split second.

"No." Her voice had turned husky. "Not yet."

He raised a single dark brow, and the gesture was so damn smooth, Peter had to fight the urge to applaud the young man. "I assume they're divorced?"

"Yep," she said, and they both snickered.

With a slight shift of her shoulders, Jeanine's top dipped lower. So did Darrell's eyes. And for the first time, the PA's too-bright grin didn't bother Peter in the least.

"Next week, I'm reacting to Ginuwine's 'Pony.'" When Jeanine bit her lip, Darrell's grin widened. "I intend to discuss how refreshing I find his interest in equestrianism."

That time, Peter sprayed his water across the table, and Jeanine thumped him vigorously on the back as he coughed.

"Thank you," he wheezed.

"You okay?" Nava looked concerned and ready to leap across the table to his rescue. "Do you need more water?"

"I'm fine." Another couple of coughs, and he could breathe again. "Just took a drink at the wrong moment."

At Jeanine's urging, Darrell was talking about his ideas for future videos. "I have a whole bit planned about how 'Down Under' extols the merits of cunnilingus. Also why I believe the phrase 'Vegemite sandwich' is a filthy metaphor. But after that, I'm not sure what song to do."

Thank fuck Peter hadn't taken another gulp of water, because *damn*.

"Peter." Maria's voice wasn't overly loud, but it carried clearly across all the chitchat. "I know you listen to music between takes. Do you have any suggestions for Darrell?"

He did, in fact, listen to music between takes, mostly because it gave him a valid reason for not interacting with everyone else. With earbuds affixed and his cell in his hand, no one expected him to demonstrate sparkling wit or even basic sociability.

And once more, Maria had put him on the spot, dammit.

"Um . . ." With everyone turned toward him, his mind emptied of all musical knowledge. But he tried his best to push past the blankness, because there was something . . . Ah. Perfect. "Have you already done a video about the unabashed go-America patriotism of 'Born in the U.S.A.'?"

Darrell nodded approvingly. "A classic of lyrical misinterpretation. That's a great suggestion, Peter. Thanks."

"If . . . if I come up with anything else, I'll let you know," he offered.

For the first time, Darrell's absurdly charming smile was directed at Peter, and it nearly blinded him. But in a good way.

Absently, he touched his belly. He hadn't had any wine, so he couldn't explain that odd sensation of warmth in his gut. It was pleasant, though.

When Jeanine captured the PA's attention once more, Peter picked up his fork and prepared to address the delicious-looking apple crumble in front of him. Which was when Ramón nudged his arm.

The director stretched his neck to whisper near Peter's ear. "Do you see what's happening?"

That was vague, but Peter was pretty sure he knew what Ramón meant.

"Between Jeanine and Darrell?" When the other man nod-ded, Peter pressed his lips together, unsure what to say. "It's their business, of course. I just . . . I just hope Darrell doesn't get hurt. He's so damn *young*."

Because Jeanine was fantastic—why hadn't he acknowledged that to himself before?—but she tended to like her men dispos-able. At least, that was what he'd gathered from what she told Maria every morning in the hair and makeup trailer. And Peter knew all too well exactly how it felt to have someone he cared about dispose of him without warning.

Even if he didn't like Darrell, he wouldn't wish that on the PA. But he did, so—

Peter frowned down at the crisp streusel atop the steaming tart-sweet apples.

Huh. He *did* like the kid. Not something he would have said before tonight.

"Don't worry. Darrell knows exactly what he's doing." Ramón offered him a sly smile. "He's been eyeing Jeanine for a while now, ever since they worked together last season, and she loves music from the eighties and nineties. This new venture is his big bid for her attention. And besides, he's not actually that young."

"Really?" Ducking his head, he tried to keep his voice as quiet as possible. "Because he looks like he's in his midtwenties. Thirty, tops."

"Brace yourself." The director looked smug.

Peter's brows rose. "Consider me braced."

"Darrell is forty-three years old, and Jeanine has no idea." When Peter's mouth dropped open, Ramón laughed. "Paul Rudd Syndrome, dude. The man doesn't age."

"Wow." Setting his fork back on the table, he contemplated the PA's unlined countenance and reconsidered his skepticism about sorcery. "That's . . . impressive."

"Like you said, it's not really our business, but . . ." Ramón flicked a glance across the table to where Maria and Nava were snort-laughing at some private joke. "It's hard to keep anything secret in a group this small."

Did the crew know he and Maria had slept together?

Did they suspect how desperately he still wanted her? How often he dreamed about her?

Unwillingly, he glanced in her direction too, and there she was, watching him again. Offering him that pleased, beaming smile again for reasons he didn't understand.

"I'm glad to see you looking more comfortable with the group," Ramón said, clapping him on the back. "Everyone would love for you to have dinner with us more often, you know, instead of eating in your room. I thought you understood that, but Maria said you probably didn't, so I'm telling you now."

Maria. Again.

And then—then he understood her smile. Mentally replaying their dinner together, he understood *everything*. What she'd discreetly done for him without seeming to do much at all. What she'd wanted to facilitate. What had her looking so . . . proud, almost.

Of him. She looked proud of *him*.

No wonder he hadn't recognized the expression. He hadn't encountered it often in the last two decades, had he?

Ramón was still talking. "You're not obligated to join us, obviously. It's your choice. Whatever makes you happy, Peter."

Eating in his room had never been about what made him happy. Just what felt bearable.

He swallowed hard. "If you want me at dinner, I'll be at dinner."

And not as an outsider, apparently. Not anymore. Not after Maria's intervention.

"Good," Ramón said firmly.

Peter smiled at him in gratitude.

It didn't even feel like an effort.

WHEN MARIA'S PHONE buzzed, all five people with hotel suites—including Peter, who stood only centimeters away—were clustered in the hall outside their rooms, chatting after what she considered an extremely successful dinner.

A candid photo of her older brother appeared on the cell's screen, and one glance at the time told her why. Normally she called him for their weekly FaceTime chat on the hour, but she'd run late, unwilling to end the evening's festivities. Also, possibly, slightly drunk.

He would understand. He always did.

Tapping the display, she stepped away from the group and answered the call.

"*Hej,* Filip," she said, then briefly apologized and asked if they could talk later. When he agreed with his typical amiability, she ended the call and turned to rejoin the crew.

Only to come within a millimeter of bumping into Peter, who was, for some reason, *right there.* To her shame, she emitted a shrill little squeak of surprise.

His lips twitched once before returning to their customary severe line. "Who was that?"

"Filip, my older brother." Not that it was any of his business, especially when he asked in such a gruff way. "I'm late for our weekly chat."

"Oh." Peter seemed to—deflate somehow. Or at least become less loom-y. "He doesn't . . . uh . . . never mind."

And now he was back to looking ill at ease, poor thing.

She took pity on him. "He doesn't look like me. I know. We're both adopted, and so is my sister."

Filip from an orphanage in South Korea, Astrid as a Swedish newborn, Maria following the death of her Swedish birth parents and several failed attempts at finding her a permanent home. Her other older brother, Vincent, was Stina and Olle Ivarsson's biological child, but her adoptive parents had never treated him any differently from Maria or Filip or Astrid.

Her family was everything to her. *Everything*.

That was true in Stockholm, and it was just as true in LA or Ireland. Her siblings and her parents were the foundations upon which she'd built her life, as solid and immovable as the granite boulders that studded the landscape around Stockholm, and she missed them all terribly.

Over the past several weeks, though, she'd begun to think that she might be able to create a sort of family for herself here on the island too, and she didn't want to leave anyone out. Not even Peter. *Especially* not Peter, a man who already seemed far too accustomed to being an outsider.

"Oh," he said again. "I didn't realize."

Of course he hadn't realized. The night they'd met in LA, she'd been unwilling to share personal information, and since then, he'd mostly been avoiding her. Although he seemed to be getting over that now, and she had high hopes for their future as scene partners and—maybe even friends?

Ja, she'd definitely had more than her share of wine with dinner, because she heard herself declaring in a too-loud voice to everyone in the hall, "I feel really lucky to have such a talented castmate and such an amazing crew on the island. I'm so glad you're my colleagues."

"You *should* feel lucky." Nava raised her chin high in feigned hauteur, even as her cheeks creased in a smile. "We're fucking incredible."

"So we are." Ramón laughed. "And if you'd hated us all, it would have been pretty damn awkward."

"But you'd still be stuck with us," Peter noted with his usual cynicism. "So, yes, count your blessings."

"Nope," Maria cheerfully told him. "That's not true."

Now she was really feeling that final glass of wine, so she edged around Nava and drifted toward her suite. When she stumbled, a strong hand grasped her elbow and kept her upright.

Peter, inevitably. Of course it was Peter.

Tall, strong, sexy Peter. *Fy fan*, he smelled good.

Face creased in confusion, he steadied her all the way to her door. "What do you mean?"

"What do you mean, what do I mean?" Giggling, she patted him on the chest, then dug her key out of her dress pocket. "You need to be more specific, Peter."

He closed his eyes for a moment, probably in an effort to muster his patience.

When he spoke next, every word was slow and pristine in its pronunciation. "I said you'd still be stuck with us even if you hated us all, and you said that wasn't true. What did you mean by that?"

Their colleagues were calling out good nights and disappearing into their own suites, and she waved hard enough to wobble in Peter's hold. Then it was just the two of them, and she stretched up closer to his neck and inhaled deeply.

They were nowhere near that LA sauna. How he still smelled like cedar, she hadn't the faintest idea.

Wait. Had he asked her a question?

"Oh. Yes. I remember." The keys almost fell, but she managed to catch them. "That's easy. I meant exactly what I said. If I hated all of you, I wouldn't be stuck. I'd leave."

He went very still. "You'd just . . . quit?"

"Exactly." She smiled at him, pleased that he understood her now. "I'd go home and get back to the theater. Or try to find other film and television work. Or whatever."

"You'd just quit," he repeated quietly to himself.

When she waved a dismissive hand, she came very close to smacking him in the face. Luckily, he managed to dodge in time. "It's a job, Peter. Only a job. Not worth my happiness."

It was past time to call Filip back, wash up, and get to bed, but the lock was being terribly uncooperative tonight. She gave it a second attempt, then a third, before that same strong hand—gods above, she'd *loved* Peter's hand between her legs—leaned her against the wall by the door and took her keys.

For some reason, the lock worked for him right away, which was very unfair. He swung open the door but didn't move out of her way for a long time.

"Why are you looking at me like that?" she finally asked.

He shook his head, jaw stony. "You wouldn't understand."

"Are—" She swallowed. "Are you mad at me? Again?"

He didn't hesitate. "No."

"Really?" Moving closer, she squinted at him. "Because you look kind of mad."

"I'm not. I mean it." His chest deflated as he let out a long, slow breath. "Drink some water before bed, Maria. I'll see you tomorrow."

"Okay," she said. "Water. Got it."

His smile twisted around the edges in a strange way. "Enjoy your talk with your brother."

Gently but implacably, he steered her into her room. And before she could gather her thoughts enough to say her own good night, he was gone, the door firmly closed behind him.

Texts with Peter: Friday Night

Maria: We're streaming a movie in Nava's room, so get over here, Peter

Peter: What movie?

Maria: Australia

Peter: ???

Maria: The Baz Luhrmann film from 2008 with Kidman and Jackman

Maria: Nava worked on it, so she can tell us any sordid behind-the-scenes gossip

Peter: Oh, yeah

Peter: Didn't that movie have a lot of

Maria: A lot of what

Peter: Cows?

Maria: . . . I guess?

Maria: I mean, the story's apparently about a cattle station and a cattle drive, so I'd assume a certain number of cows are on-screen

Maria: Why?

Peter: Maybe I'll skip this one

Maria: Do you . . . have an issue with cows?

Peter: Of course not, don't be ridiculous

Maria: Let's explore this, shall we

Peter: No

Maria: Did cows kidnap your daughter, and you had to track her down using your very particular set of skills, which make you a nightmare for cattle like them

Peter: Maria. Really.

Maria: Maybe a bovine temptress left you at the altar, heartbroken and heiferless

Peter: MARIA

Maria: Perhaps a bull wrongfully accused you of a crime you didn't commit

Maria: When the murderer was really the One-Hoofed Holstein all along

Peter: . . . I knew we shouldn't have watched The Fugitive last week, Taken was bad enough

Maria: Did you lose your life savings because you invested in a cow's pyramid scheme

Maria: Bernie Moodoff

Peter: Are you done now

Maria: Depends on whether you're coming to Nava's room

Peter: I'm staying in mine, so have a nice night

Maria: Nope

Peter: Nope?

Maria: You owe me, Reedton

Peter: Oh, really?

Maria: Really

Peter: Enlighten me, Ivarsson

Maria: Today, when Cassia and Cyprian stripped down to wash their clothing in the shallows, I rescued you from that big wave before it dragged you under and you were forced to meet Ariel's entire dysfunctional family and sing songs with talking crabs

Maria: I basically saved your life, even though it meant flashing the crew

Maria: Not that I really care who sees my nipples, but still

Maria: You were so into the scene, you didn't notice the wave coming, so yes, you owe me

Peter: . . .

Peter: Yes

Peter: That's why I didn't notice the wave

Peter: I was just completely into the scene, you're right

Peter: Fine

Peter: I'll watch the damn movie, as long as you never bring up today's incident again

Peter: I'm trying very hard to forget it

Maria: ???

Maria: The wave traumatized you that much?

Peter: . . .

Peter: Make like Elsa and let it go, Maria

Maria: Fine, but only if you get here in the next two minutes

Peter: On my way

Maria: ☺

6

"THE THATCH IS LOOKING A LITTLE THIN THERE, REEDTON."
Maria pointed toward a particularly sparse spot on the roof. "I
thought you were all about professionalism and doing the job right?"

Hahafuckingha. Peter's scowl didn't noticeably discomfit her,
but maybe further exposure would do the trick. He'd persevere.

"I didn't see you perched on top of that wall and wrestling
straw, Ivarsson, so shut it." He pinched his thumb and forefinger
and mimed zipping his mouth closed. "That scene was a pain in
the ass."

In fact, anyone in their right mind would find the *entire* roof-
thatching process miserable. Ye Olde Thatchery Enthusiasts might
resent that conclusion, but they'd be fucking *wrong*.

Exhibit A: the endless goddamn threshing with a primitive flail
to remove grain from the straw. Exhibit B: the afternoon spent
twisting grass and straw into ropes, ones that would secure the
roof to the stones of the permanent shelter they'd built. The task
left Maria's hands blistered and so stiff she'd barely been able to
hold a fork at dinner that night.

But Maria hadn't bemoaned those blisters, and she didn't mind
physical labor. He didn't either. The weather maintained enough
coolness and cloud cover, even in the middle of summer, that they
didn't sweat to death. And working side by side with her was—

Anyway, yeah, those parts weren't so bad. They were actually kind of . . . enjoyable?

But they shouldn't have been. If, to reiterate, he'd been in his right mind, rather than trapped in Maria's Tractor Beam of Charm and Fun.

Which brought him to Exhibit C, because attempting to attach various dried grains and grasses to a layer of sod while perched high in the air on a famously windswept island? Yeah, that *did* blow. Literally and figuratively.

He could only hope the locals' various horses, cows, sheep, and goats appreciated the free all-you-can-eat straw buffet that descended on them from the heavens for an entire fucking week.

"You've been bitching about your stupid windblown straw for days, Peter." She shook her head at him, a bemused smile curving her wide mouth. "I don't understand why that part of things got under your skin so badly."

He knew one thing for certain: His displeasure had nothing to do with how he and Maria had filmed separately all that week.

In the script, while Cyprian struggled with the damn roof, Cassia walked the perimeter of the island in search of more salvageable goods washed ashore from their shipwrecked vessel. They hadn't needed to be on camera together, and that was fine. A welcome break from several months of close proximity, actually, and some much-needed time off from work when the crew tackled her scenes.

So her absence during filming definitely wasn't the issue. His ill-fated attempts at installing the roof were simply frustrating, and that would've been true even if she'd helped him.

Very, very true.

So true. The truest.

Hmmm.

Lying to himself had grown easier over time, what with all his recent practice, but he'd never gotten better at believing the lies. A shame, that.

He crossed his arms over his chest, eyeing her balefully. "Keep taunting me about the roof, and I'll force-feed you seaweed, Pippi."

Maintaining a threatening demeanor became significantly more difficult at that point, since Maria produced a glass jar of herring, seemingly from midair, and shook it approximately an inch from his nose.

No closer, though, because she didn't touch him off camera, and he returned that favor.

"So help me, *skitstövel*, if you call me Pippi one more time . . ." *Shake shake shake.*

After three months with Maria, he knew what *skitstövel* meant.

Shit-boot. Swedish insults were fucking bizarre.

He bit his lip, then regained his composure. "You'll do what? Dye your hair red, sling it into two weird braids that defy the laws of physics, and sleep with your feet on your pillow?"

There wasn't much to do at night on the island, so revisiting Astrid Lindgren's stories hadn't proven a hardship. Not when Maria's irritation rewarded his efforts so handsomely.

"I will brain you with herring and dethatch the shit out of that roof, Peter." Her eyes had gone squinty, but her cheeks were quivering as she tried not to laugh. "Don't test me."

"Too late." He swept an arm around them, indicating the day's setup. "We're past the point where thatchery hooliganism would cause problems for me. And if you give me a concussion now, with the last day of filming incomplete, you'll keep the crew away from their families for longer than necessary."

She fake-glared at him, which he found very enjoyable.

Not too enjoyable, though. Not *unusually* enjoyable. Just a normal amount.

"*Fine.*" Her jar of herring—*sill*, she called it—disappeared once more, into whatever convenient black hole she concealed on her person. "But sooner or later, I'll have my vengeance, Reedton."

"I'm all aquiver," he stated in tones of unmitigated boredom, then yawned widely.

She couldn't hold back any longer. Her inimitable cackle nearly deafened him, and he couldn't help but laugh too.

Ramón waved them back to their places with an indulgent smile, and the two of them reentered the house they—and the crew—had built together.

This last day of filming before their lengthy break was a celebration, on camera and off. The shipwrecked Vikings had put together a feast for their first evening in their new home, the stone structure they hoped would see them through a harsh winter. Another, presumably less seaweed-intensive feast was waiting for the entire crew at the hotel, because they wouldn't return to the island or see each other again for several months.

This should be their final take of the day, because otherwise they'd be letting Fionn's food go cold, a near-criminal act. Their final take for some time to come.

Suddenly, he didn't feel the slightest urge to smile.

Side by side, he and Maria sat at a simple table Cassia and Cyprian had pieced together from yet more salvaged wood, its surface crammed with all the bounty the island could provide in late summer. The countdown to action began.

And he decided that tonight, at long last, he'd say what needed to be said.

AFTER DINNER, HE waited until everyone else had disappeared into their suite or left the hotel for their own lodgings. Then he knocked at Maria's door for the first time ever.

It swung open a moment later, and her brow furrowed at the sight of him. "Peter? Are you all right?"

He had no idea how to answer that question. "May I come in?"

Without hesitation, she ushered him inside her suite. Where, he could immediately see, she'd been packing for her return to Sweden the next day. Half-filled suitcases littered the floor, including one with—

Dammit, he did *not* need a reminder of what her panties looked like.

"If you're thirsty, I have sparkling water in the minifridge," she said, waving him toward her low-slung couch. "Or—"

"I'm sorry."

There. There it was, finally.

She closed her mouth and blinked up at him.

He shifted his weight but forced himself to maintain eye contact. "I said a lot of shitty things to you in that LA parking lot, and I want you to know that I was wrong, and I apologize."

A slow smile of malicious glee dawned on her expressive face.

Even though he'd remained standing, she lowered herself onto the sofa and stretched out lazily. Like a satisfied cat. Or, more aptly, like a queen claiming her space, confident of her own power.

Her chin tipped high to watch him. "Wrong how? Please be specific."

Yep. She intended to milk every last drop of penitence out of his long-overdue apology, and he couldn't even blame her. He'd been an asswipe.

"You might have been new to television when you got this role, but you weren't an amateur when it came to acting. There is no conceivable way filming alongside you could ever hurt my career, and I knew that by the end of our first day in the studio together." He sighed, then told her the rest. "I looked up the theaters in Stockholm where you worked before, and they're impressive. So were the recordings of your performances available online, although I obviously didn't understand all the Swedish."

That was more evidence of his obsession with her than he'd wanted to share, but she deserved to hear it.

Propping her elbow on the sofa's arm, she rested her cheek in her hand and raised her brows. "You cyberstalked me. How flattering."

He wouldn't say *cyberstalked*, exactly. He'd simply . . . researched her. Extensively. Via her website, all extant YouTube clips of her work and interviews, and her social media accounts from five years ago until the present.

Which was, clearly, very different from cyberstalking.

With enough practice, surely he'd believe his own lies someday. Today, however, was not that day.

Whatever. Better to abandon the topic of cyberstalking and cover the last bit of the speech he'd been mentally rehearsing all evening.

"Your talent is undeniable, and you work hard." He swallowed over a dry throat, suddenly longing for that sparkling water. "You make the set a better, happier place every day."

Her face softened at that, her smile gentling. "That's a lovely thing to say. Thank you."

He firmly believed he was an asset to any production that cast him. That said: On most sets, when the cameras stopped rolling, he remained entirely himself—in the worst of ways.

Quiet to the point of surliness. Unable to fit into the group. On the outside looking in, and so used to the view that he didn't bother trying anymore.

Maria, though . . .

She was a midnight sun, drawing everyone into her orbit. She *shone*. She brightened everything around her. Including him.

Maybe because she was entirely comfortable in her own skin, she seemed to *enjoy* herself so damn much, always. And with her casual ease and good cheer, her inexorable magnetism, she'd repeatedly drawn him into conversations with the crew. And she'd been doing it for months, so now those conversations didn't feel like small talk anymore, even if he was chatting about the fucking weather, because he *knew* the people involved. He *liked* the people involved.

And he could almost . . .

No, he *would* swear that they liked him too. That they'd become not just friendly acquaintances or professional contacts, but his . . . friends?

Even without Maria present, he spoke to them now, and he did so easily and often. She'd cheerfully bullied him into joining the cast chat as well, which was sometimes an absolute shitshow— Ian Dromm was a total asshole and apparently reeked of tuna?— but also entirely hilarious. He was actually *looking forward* to meeting his costars in person during various press junkets and at cons.

She'd made it impossible for him to remain petty or distant with her, and impossible to deny her the heartfelt apology she should have received months ago. And now he'd given that apology, so he could take an easy breath in her presence for the first time in a long, long while.

"Fortunately, that lovely thing to say is the truth." He offered her a faint but genuine smile. "This show is lucky to have you."

Her brown gaze watched him closely. "Even if I'm not grateful enough for the role?"

Well, damn.

For all her good cheer and social ease, Maria was as sharp as sea urchin spines and as relentless as the tides. She forgot nothing. And as always, she was right. He admired her talent and her hard work, and he was unequivocally glad to be her costar, but . . .

She wasn't *hungry* in the same way he was. She didn't *need* this job, or maybe any job, the way he did. From what she'd said that night in the hotel hallway, she would walk away from the show if she decided the role no longer worked for her. Without a backward glance or a single regret.

Even without *Gods of the Gates*, even without an acting career, her life would remain full and happy. Her loving family and loyal friends would surround and embrace her. Her government would financially support her until she found different work, and he suspected she'd be good at whatever she chose to do.

But this show, this opportunity, was everything to him.

The showrunners were lucky to have her, yes. Definitely. But even so, being cast on a big-budget, blockbuster show was a privilege the vast majority of talented actors would never receive, and one she didn't seem to appreciate sufficiently. Not the opportunity. Not the professional recognition. Not the money. Not the fame.

So, no, she wasn't grateful enough. About that, he hadn't budged.

Which meant he wasn't answering her question, because he wasn't a fool.

"You certainly seem to take your packing seriously." He glanced around the room. "Have you somehow acquired more suitcases since we arrived? Or did they simply procreate in the depths of your closet?"

Her narrow-eyed stare told him she'd noticed his subject change. But after a moment, her shoulders dropped a fraction, and she let it go.

"Since you were the one who hauled my suitcases over the threshold of this room, you know very well that I have the same number now as I did then." She smirked. "Also, Swedes receive very comprehensive sexual education in schools. I wholeheartedly believe in luggage control and always practice safe packing."

He pointedly glanced at the nearest suitcase. "If you believe in luggage control, why the hell did you bring so many bags?"

"Snacks," she told him, unembarrassed. "Lots and lots of snacks. Three suitcases' worth."

What the fuck?

"You realize this isn't an actual deserted island, right? And that the production will make sure we get fed?" He peered down at her, befuddled. "What were you thinking?"

"I suppose I thought we might have food supply issues," she said vaguely, then waved her hand in dismissal. "Anyway, care to sample the contents of Sweden's candy aisles?"

He'd prefer to taste other things belonging to Maria, but snacks were certainly safer. "Sure."

With easy grace, she rose from the couch and disappeared into her bedroom. When she returned, she held a small yellow plastic bag with cartoon animals on it. The bag was full of some sort of unidentifiable black candy and covered in Swedish text, and she ripped it open.

When she held it out to him, he eyed its contents with caution. "What is this?"

"Don't be a baby, Peter." She shook the bag impatiently. "It's one of the most popular candies in Sweden. Take a piece."

Well, ten million Swedes couldn't be wrong. Without further argument, he popped a vaguely round bit of candy in his mouth and chewed.

Then he promptly spat that piece onto the floor, because—

"*Holy fuck!*" he shouted. "What the hell, Maria?"

"The l-look on your f-face." She was bent over and cackling uncontrollably. "Oh, shit, the *look* on your *face!*"

There wasn't enough sparkling water in the world, but he snatched a bottle from her minifridge anyway and drained half of it in a single guzzle. When that didn't do the trick, he hurried into her bathroom and rubbed a dollop of stolen toothpaste over his tongue.

Normally, he'd spit out the toothpaste, but not today. He wasn't risking the return of that candy's particular flavor to his taste buds.

"What was that—that *abomination*?" He pointed accusingly at the half-chewed lump on the hardwood. "Did you *poison* me?"

She rolled her eyes to the ceiling, but she was still chortling. "It's salty licorice. Lots of Swedes love it, but most people from other countries . . . not so much."

"You live in a nation of monsters," he informed her.

"What did I tell you earlier today, Reedton?"

Her smile bright enough to blind him, she leaned in close. So close he could smell a hint of the raspberry dessert she'd savored at dinner and count the golden flecks in her brown eyes.

He stared, too swamped by fierce, damnable *need* to answer her.

"Vengeance is mine," she whispered, then chucked him under the chin. "As you Americans say: Mess with the Pippi bull, you get the Pippi horns, *skitstövel.*"

She was insane. Adorable but insane.

And it didn't matter how much he wanted to touch her. He couldn't.

Even disregarding his other very serious concerns, she'd already rejected him once, and once was enough. So before she could further decimate his self-control, he gathered up the disgusting wad of candy from the floor with a stray tissue and headed for the door.

"I'd better get packing myself, especially since my flight leaves so early," he said. "I imagine I won't see you tomorrow, so . . ."

He didn't reach out for a hug or a handshake, because he wasn't stupid enough to touch her. Not when they were alone at night in her hotel room.

"Goodbye, Maria." Exiting her suite with all due haste, he stopped a generous distance outside her door. "Safe travels. I'll see you in November."

Her knuckles bulged white where she gripped her doorframe, but her smile was as cheerful as ever. "Same to you, Peter. *Hej då.*"

Farewells safely accomplished, he turned and left without another word.

He'd managed not to say that he'd miss her terribly. Good. She didn't need to know that.

He'd rather not know it himself.

The Hottest Magazine About the Hottest Celebrities

Curvy and Confident, New *Gods of the Gates* Star Maria Ivarsson Reveals All!

When showrunners Ron Acheson and R.J. Nullman began to adapt author E. Wade's bestselling fantasy series two years ago, they chose to excise a few key characters.

"Without cuts, we were concerned the show would become too sprawling," Nullman says. "We knew some fans would protest those decisions, but we definitely weren't prepared for Cyprian and Cassia's cult following among Wade's readership."

As soon as the first season began airing and the shipwrecked couple's absence became evident, that following reacted. Fans of Cyprian and Cassia—original characters created by Wade, not to be found in Roman mythology—wrote petitions. They picketed the production studio in Canada. They started very popular social media campaigns calling for the inclusion of the book series' favorite enemies-to-lovers storyline.

In response, Acheson and Nullman added two more cast members for the show's second season: longtime character actor Peter Reedton and Swedish theater ingenue Maria Ivarsson. That casting choice reverberated throughout Hollywood, and not simply because the showrunners had bowed to the demands of the outspoken Cyprian/Cassia fandom.

"Ron and R.J. cast two fat actors for characters not originally specified as fat in the books," Ivarsson explains. "That never happens, and the showrunners deserve an enormous amount of credit for their decision. It's a real step forward for body diversity in Hollywood. I'm especially delighted because fat acceptance is a passion of mine, as followers of my social media accounts can attest. And, of course, it's an honor to be cast alongside an actor as accomplished as Peter and to join a show already so beloved by its viewership."

That viewership hasn't yet seen Cassia on-screen—the production is filming its second season right now—but Ivarsson has already become a social media darling, with millions of followers on her various accounts, as well as an overnight symbol of body positivity.

She embraces that role wholeheartedly, and with total confidence in her own plus-sized, all-natural sex appeal. When *Fan Thirst* approached her to model for our October cover, she didn't hesitate . . . even when we asked her to bare everything for our readers.

"'Just don't get me arrested,' I told them," she says with a laugh. "Otherwise, I had no concerns. I'm not shy, and I love my body. Also, I'm happy for the attention the cover may receive, because I really want to ensure that Ron and R.J. get all the kudos they deserve for such a forward-thinking casting choice."

The authorities won't be beating down her door anytime soon, not with the way our photographer carefully posed Ms. Ivarsson. At least, they won't be beating down her door to arrest her.

They might, however, request an autograph, and for good reason. Maria Ivarsson is a sultry, statuesque star on the rise, as this month's cover shows so nakedly.

Check out our website for alternate cover images and our top-ten list of Ivarsson's funniest and most incisive social media posts!

7

"WHO ELSE IS HERE ALREADY?" MARIA ASKED CONOR WITH studied casualness as she accepted her heavy, old-fashioned room key. "Ramón? Nava?"

The hotel proprietor's freckled nose crinkled charmingly when he smiled. "You're the last to arrive, Maria-My-Dear. Same rooms as last time."

"Good." She tossed her room key in the air, caught it with a flourish, and winked at Conor. "I like an audience when I make a grand entrance."

He chuckled and waved her toward her room, after reconfirming that she didn't want help with her bags. Of course, she did actually want help. But not from Conor, and not because she truly needed assistance.

She simply needed an excuse to see Peter immediately.

After several trips down the hall, she had all her luggage stacked outside her suite. Ten more swift steps brought her to his door, and she knocked firmly.

It took him a minute to answer, long enough that she started bouncing on her toes in impatience. But once his door swung open, she feigned calm like the talented thespian she was and offered him a brisk wave.

"Peter!" Her greedy gaze devoured him, from wavy dark hair

to broad, bare feet. "Could you possibly help me put my suitcase on the luggage rack?"

Normally, Maria was not a fool for men. Not anymore.

But they'd been on separate continents for far too long. After Cassia and Cyprian's late-summer feast, the show didn't pick up their story again until winter's merciless chill had turned their island desolate and bare of food, so filming had stopped for three endless months.

And she'd missed him each day of their time apart. *All* of him. Those wary brown eyes. That wall of a chest. His rusty laugh. The endless strength powering his every stride, and the quick wit sharpening his talented tongue. And now, now . . .

There he was. Her sexy monolith of a Viking.

Only not hers, of course. Even though she'd turned down a dozen potential hookups in their months apart, unable to erase his image from the backs of her eyelids anytime she closed her eyes to kiss someone. So, in the end, she hadn't kissed anyone. She hadn't hooked up. She'd spent her time among friends and family and taken care of her own sexual needs with the very competent help of her various LELO toys.

Given more time, she might get over this uncharacteristic burst of sentimentality concerning him. Just . . . not yet.

"Well, hello to you too, Maria." He leaned against the doorway with a lazy smile, feet and arms both crossed. "I'm doing great. Thanks for asking."

She raised her brows. "So you're a fan of small talk now? Good to know."

"In your absence, I've become a paragon of politeness and good manners." His brows beetled in feigned confusion. "For some reason, it's much easier to be nice to people when you're not around."

In deliberate provocation, she snapped her fingers. "Less chit-chat, more lifting of my luggage, *skitstövel*."

"Brat." He pushed off from the doorframe, shaking his head. "Let me rephrase: For some reason, it's much easier to be nice to people who don't call you a shit-boot."

But his shoulders were shaking with suppressed laughter as he brushed past her, so close she could sense the heat of his skin, and he gripped the handles of her two largest bags.

She unlocked her door with a grin, the exhaustion from a day of travel suddenly gone. "I missed you too, Peter."

After testing the weight of the heaviest suitcase, he sighed. "More disgusting snacks?"

"You know it," she told him cheerfully.

With a sort of grunting noise, he heaved the suitcases over the threshold. After she rolled her carry-ons inside, he brought in the final bag and placed all the suitcases on the couch and the luggage rack, so everything would be within easy reach as she unpacked.

He held out his hand, palm up, and she stared at it in confusion.

"Do you . . ." She tilted her head. "Do you want a handshake? Or a low-five?"

His fingers wiggled in mute demand. "I'm waiting for my tip."

She snorted. "Here's my tip, then: Always ask for the money up front. Otherwise, unscrupulous foreigners will take advantage of your unparalleled politeness and good manners."

That did it.

His laughter filled her suite. She watched his face crease in mirth and wondered—as she had repeatedly during their filming break—whether he might be able to offer her a real future together someday. If not now, then next month or even next year.

From what she could tell, he'd devoted his life almost entirely to his profession before now. That could change, though. He could change, and so could his priorities.

A career was all well and good. But it couldn't make him laugh like she did.

And if he let her, she intended to show him that. Starting now.

THEIR FIRST DAY back on set was a blast.

Everyone seemed fresh, eager to return to work, and delighted to coalesce once more into their tight-knit little crew of friends and colleagues. They quickly fell into a familiar rhythm, even as they shot at a new location, one they'd likely revisit often over the years.

In this episode's script, Cassia and Cyprian finally encountered the island's gate to the underworld, and they did so while perched on a craggy cliff more than a hundred meters above the pounding Atlantic waves. The late-November wind howled. The cold rain lashed.

Sure, shooting there was uncomfortable as hell, but it was a pivotal moment. Dramatic. Maria's favorite type of scene.

In reality, the ostensible gate to Tartarus was a small blowhole that tunneled all the way from the top of the cliff to the ocean below, and it sprayed a new puff of shiver-inducing water with every vicious crash of surf against the towering limestone. After the SFX people got through with the scene, though, that hole would be larger and more ominous. The puffs of ocean water would become steam. She imagined there would be a spooky-as-fuck soundtrack accompanying Cyprian and Cassia's discovery.

And despite their shivers, she and Peter were acting the hell out of their script.

By the time Ramón and Nava were satisfied, everyone was shaking with cold but bright-eyed with accomplishment. Given the weather conditions, they'd even gotten permission to use a

van to return to their various lodgings, and they were basking in
the vehicle's warmth as they made idle conversation and dropped
crew members off, one by one.

Then Ramón got a call on his cell. After a few seconds, his smile
died.

"Are you certain—" he began, but whoever was on the other
end cut him off.

Discreetly, Peter caught Maria's eye and gestured toward their
director in mute question, and she shrugged and spread her hands.

After another minute, Ramón nodded, his forehead deeply furrowed. "Okay."

He disconnected the call, then studied the van's nubby carpet
for a moment as the vehicle trundled toward their hotel. Finally,
jaw tight, he looked at Maria and then Peter.

"When we get back to our suites, the two of you have a virtual
meeting with Ron. As soon as you arrive." With a sigh, he raked
a hand through his dark, wet hair. "I would accompany you, but
I can't."

Peter frowned. "What's going on?"

"I'm not supposed to tell you this, but . . ." Ramón trailed off,
lips thin and white around the edges. "You should be prepared."

That wasn't ominous at all.

"I thought Ron and R.J. had dropped the idea. For the record, I
argued against it, and so did Nava." The director and line producer
made eye contact, and her chin fell to her chest as she sucked her
lips between her teeth. "The showrunners want to dramatize how
Cyprian and Cassia would have starved over the winter."

Oh. *Oh*. So *that* was what this meeting was about.

Not a huge surprise, really. Part of her had understood it was
coming from the day she was cast. And when Peter inhaled
sharply a moment later, she knew he'd worked it out too.

He'd once told her he didn't care why the show had chosen to cast fat actors as Cassia and Cyprian. Then, only moments later, he'd said they weren't a team and wouldn't stand united on the set.

Well, if she'd wanted to learn whether Peter's priorities had shifted since that venomous conversation in an LA parking lot, she was in luck.

"I would say more. I really would." Ramón pinched the bridge of his nose. "It's just that Ron ordered—"

"It's okay." She reached over to give him a consoling pat on the arm. "We get it."

"That makes two of you," Nava muttered, her face hard. "*Fuck.*"

The rest of the ride, Peter didn't speak or look at her, but that was fine. The decision ahead *should* make him think hard. She was thinking hard too, marshaling her various arguments and reviewing the groundwork she'd been laying for months to prepare for today.

Any battle she chose to enter, she intended to win.

When they entered the hotel, Ramón put his hand on her shoulder, squeezed, and gave it a little shake, then did the same to Peter before disappearing into his suite. Nonverbal support, and she appreciated the gesture.

Halfway down the hotel hallway, Peter unlocked his own suite door and shoved it open so hard it thumped against the wall.

"We can use my phone," he said brusquely and held the door for her without making eye contact. "I'll bring you a towel and start a fire."

Did he actually intend to talk to Ron *right now*? Was he really trotting to obey the showrunner's unreasonable edict like a whipped dog summoned by its master?

"Peter—" Her short bark of laughter contained no humor. "Peter, we should talk before we meet with Ron. Besides, we were outside *all day*, and I need a hot shower before we do anything else."

His jaw ticked, and he didn't move from his doorway. "Ramón said we had to call right away."

"I am literally shaking with cold right now." She spoke clearly, enunciating every syllable. "So are you. And we both know this meeting can wait twenty minutes."

When he didn't respond, didn't budge or concede her point, something in her withered.

She closed her eyes for a moment, then nodded. "Fine, then. I won't shower. But we still have to talk first."

They entered his room, and she sat on his sofa and waited as he built the world's speediest, most inadequate fire. When he offered her a towel, she dried off as best she could. Almost immediately, though, her wet hair resumed dripping down onto her quilted parka, and she gathered the sopping strands into a single rope with unsteady fingers.

He sighed and sat next to her. "Maria, let's just—"

"You knew they were going to ask us to lose weight sooner or later, right?" Twisting the towel, she wrung out her hair and swiveled to face him. "I mean, why else choose two fat actors for characters stranded on a chilly, desolate, windswept island for years? The only fat actors, I'll note, in the entire cast, even though our characters aren't described as fat in the books. They wanted us fat for a purpose, and since we're not Hansel and Gretel, it wasn't serving us for dinner."

Peter closed his eyes, the lines bracketing his mouth deepening moment by moment. "Of course I knew they'd want us to lose weight. I'm not an idiot."

He'd understood from the beginning what would eventually be

asked of them, then. So had she—but he'd had no way of knowing that. So why hadn't he warned her? If not in LA, then later, when he'd gotten over his animosity toward her? Once they'd become friends?

"I can't believe you didn't—" She gave her head a violent shake, her hands trembling with cold. "Never mind. We don't have time for that now. The important thing is this: When my agent and Filip looked over my contract the day we were cast, I had them check whether anything in the language would oblige us to lose weight if we were asked to do so. They said weight loss is not legally enforceable according to my contract. Probably not according to yours either, though they couldn't know for sure without seeing it."

His dark eyes blinked open, and he gazed expressionlessly at the fire.

Fine. If he didn't want to speak, she had more to say anyway. "When Ron asks us to starve for the sake of drama, I'm going to refuse. I imagine he won't be thrilled, but if they choose to fire me over the issue, fine. I'd rather that than the alternative."

Slowly, he turned toward her. Brows drawn together, he was staring at her like she'd just announced her intention to eat nothing but *surströmming*—fermented herring; a famously smelly Swedish delicacy with a truly disturbing texture—for the rest of her misguided life.

"That's why you packed all those snacks," he said. "To defy them if they tried to fuck with our food supply."

She inclined her head. "Of course."

When he didn't say more, she set aside her towel, laid a hand on his forearm, and made her appeal.

"That day in the parking lot, you told me I was on my own. But

Peter, we'd have more power if we stood together on this issue," she told him, gently shaking his arm. "If we both refused—"

"I'm not going to *refuse* the showrunners anything." There was no indecision in his voice. No hesitancy. "I need this role, and I'm willing to make sacrifices to keep it."

Astounded, she opened her mouth but found herself speechless.

He jerked his head toward his phone, mouth firm. "Can we call Ron now?"

She paused before speaking again. Finding the right words in English took longer than she'd prefer, but her point was too important to leave unclear.

"Peter. Listen to me." She leaned in until his face was a mere handful of centimeters away from hers, because he needed to pay attention. "Don't you understand the long-term effects of what they're asking us to do? Haven't you read about the contestants on those awful weight-loss TV shows and the irreversible harm they did to their bodies?"

The creases at the corners of his eyes deepened in a tiny, nearly imperceptible flinch, but otherwise, his face might have been carved on a Viking runestone.

"You should know, Peter. You *have* to know what'll happen." Brows furrowed, she fought the urge to shake his arm again, this time much, much harder. "Your body will scream at you to eat more and get back to your original weight. You'll be hungry all the time. *All the time.* And while you starve yourself, you'll fuck up your metabolism, and it'll never be the same. *Never.* Because your body will think you're in a famine and slow everything way the fuck down, permanently."

For those reasons and so many more, she'd resolved long ago to stay healthy and strong at her current size, rather than focusing on weight loss. Back home, she'd even given occasional talks about the issue. And if the role of Cassia raised her public profile and allowed her more of a platform, she would gladly take advantage and spread the word to as many people as possible.

Starting, apparently, with her sexy idiot of a castmate, Peter Reedton.

"If you lose weight too quickly, you can damage your internal organs, including your heart. If you don't believe me, I'll send you links to various articles written by trustworthy sources." She squeezed his arm for emphasis. "You can't switch bodies the same way you switch roles, Peter. If you do this, you'll harm yourself for life, and no job is worth that. None."

To his credit, he appeared to be listening. He even took a minute before replying.

Then he said simply, "I'm sorry, Maria, but I disagree. For smaller roles, I wouldn't do it. For this one, though . . ."

His shoulders lifted in an eloquent shrug, and apparently that was it. Everything he had to say on the topic.

Ah. Now she truly understood.

He cared about work above all else. As many Americans supposedly did, probably because they didn't have much of a safety net if they lost their jobs.

But she'd suspected that about him already, hadn't she?

The part she hadn't realized, though, not until this very moment: It wasn't going to change. He wasn't going to change. Not now, not next month, not next year.

Work was what drove him. What mattered most to him. What he lived for, and what he might very well die for. Not friendship or love or good deeds. Not happiness. Not even his own physical well-being.

Now she knew: Her initial instincts hadn't led her astray.

Peter could never make her happy, because he'd never make her his top priority. Her needs, her well-being, would always come second—at best—to his career. And unlike him, she cared about her own happiness, so she wasn't settling for less than the sort of relationship she wanted. Even if that meant never having Peter in her bed again. Even if that meant potentially staying single for the rest of her life.

Carefully, finger by finger, she removed her hand from his arm.

This conversation hadn't proceeded as she'd hoped, but that was fine. She'd learned valuable information anyway.

When she shivered at the loss of his body heat, Peter's frown deepened. "I've changed my mind. Go take a shower before we call Ron."

"I'm fine." Every limb felt weighted with disappointment, and she couldn't bring herself to look directly at him anymore. "Let's get this over with."

"Stubborn," he muttered, his voice gruff and unhappy, but he set aside his own towel and had them connected to Ron within moments.

The showrunner, of course, wanted them to start losing weight. Rapidly.

"Because Cyprian and Cassia would have so little to eat over the winter," he explained breezily. "This is an excellent opportunity to dramatize the severity of their conditions on the island and the extremely high stakes of their partnership. If they don't cooperate to the fullest extent, they'll starve, and seeing the two of you become thinner and thinner will sell that story to the audience in the most powerful way possible. Starting tomorrow, you'll—"

"No," said Maria.

When he was startled, Ron's chin jerked back toward his neck, and he looked like a turtle. A very dickish turtle. "Pardon me?"

"I've already had both my agent and my lawyer study my contract, and there's nothing in there that would legally obligate me to diet or lose weight."

She didn't wait for or watch Peter's reaction. Her response was her own and didn't depend on his, and its consequences were hers to bear alone. Even if she still hoped he might have altered his stance on this issue in the last, say, thirty seconds.

Ron's pale eyes had turned hard. "Maria, you certainly have the right to refuse my directive. Just as I have the right to recast the role of Cassia. Immediately, as necessary."

"Of course you do." So predictable, that response. So predictable, and so disappointing. "That said, your memo from last week indicated that this season's filming is already running late and over budget due to issues at your other shooting locations. Can you truly afford the time and money it would require to stop everything here while you found another actor for my role, got her to the island, had her outfitted, and adequately prepared her for the part?"

"I'm certain . . ." He visibly swallowed, an angry red tide of color rising from beneath the collar of his button-down. "I'm certain we could make it work."

She inclined her head. "All right. Then let me ask you another question. Haven't you noticed the amount of positive publicity you've received for casting fat actors on your show? Do you really think you can ask those actors to visibly starve themselves and not expect a terrible, extremely public backlash? I'm a symbol of the body positivity movement, with a substantial social media platform, and if I'm fired because I refused to diet, there will be hell to pay, Ron, and I won't be the one paying it. You will. The show will."

Peter was still and quiet next to her. Very, very quiet.

If he was going to speak on her behalf and his own, this would be an excellent time.

A vein began visibly throbbing at Ron's temple. "It would make no fucking sense for you and Peter to remain your current size, Maria. Cassia and Cyprian are on a fucking deserted island with almost no vegetation, and it's *winter*. They'd lose weight. They'd *have* to lose weight. If they *don't* lose weight, our show will lose all credibility."

"*Gods of the Gates* is a fantasy television series that features Roman gods, fissures to the underworld, and—if what I'm hearing is correct—a pegasus." The cast chat had been chortling over that upcoming episode for weeks now, actually. "The story already doesn't adhere to reality, and the fantasy aspect of the show gives you a great deal of freedom to explain away the choices you make."

When he merely stared at her in seeming befuddlement, she realized she'd need to describe possible directions he could take, because apparently he wasn't too great at coming up with ideas on his own. Gods above, the show was going to be a fucking *disaster* once they moved past the completed books, wasn't it?

She spoke slowly, pleased that she'd previously considered the matter. "Neptune already cast them ashore with a violent storm so they could guard the gate to the underworld. Why couldn't he intervene again to keep them fed and prevent them from dying and leaving the gate unattended? Cyprian and Cassia could find some sort of enchanted fruit that would magically keep them fed all winter. An apple, maybe, given the importance of apples in both Roman and Norse mythology."

Any time now, Reedton. Feel free to speak up whenever you'd like.

But she knew. She knew.

He wasn't going to advocate for her. He wasn't even going to advocate for himself. If he was going to be saved, she'd be the one making the rescue attempt.

"Let me be clear, Ron. As I've just explained, you have choices.

But forcing me to lose weight for your show is not, and never will be, one of them. If you try to restrict my food, I'll quit. And just to clarify, if you try to restrict Peter's food, it won't matter whether you do the same to me. I'll still walk away."

At that, Ron—all flared nostrils, red-striped cheekbones, and white male privilege—finally turned to the man sitting motionless and silent at her side.

At her side, but not on it. Just like he'd promised.

"Please tell me you don't agree with Maria, Peter." Ron stabbed a finger in her direction, the gesture near-violent. "You know better."

In that parking lot, Peter had claimed unfettered capitalism offered no solidarity, but he was mistaken. Solidarity was precisely what Ron wanted right now. Confirmation that the two men in the conversation would remain united against the hysterical demands of the woman shivering on Peter's couch.

At long last, Peter spoke, his voice quiet but firm. "I respect Maria's opinions and decisions, but they're hers. Not mine."

A bit of welcome news: She no longer had to worry about being a fool for him.

"Good." Ron rolled his shoulders, and that angry flush hadn't faded. Probably because he knew she was going to win this particular battle, but his injured ego wouldn't allow him to admit it yet. "I'll discuss the issue with R.J. and get back to both of you shortly."

Peter dipped his chin in acknowledgment, and she did the same.

"One more thing, Maria." The showrunner's lips curved, but it wasn't a smile. "Let *me* be clear. You're right that replacing you now would be difficult. Replacing you between seasons, however, would be much, much easier."

Then he immediately ended the virtual meeting, because—just like Peter—he needed the last word.

She took one slow, deep breath. Another.

All her adrenaline began to dissipate, leaving her exhausted and so fucking cold she could cry. But she didn't, because there was no reason for tears, and no one in this suite she trusted with that kind of vulnerability.

"They're going to cave." She stood without looking at Peter. "And since I threatened to walk if either of us lost weight, you should be safe too."

When she took her first step toward the door, he wrapped a hand around her upper arm. "Think about it, Maria. He's right. They could replace you between seasons really easily, and that would be a huge loss to everyone involved. If you call him back right now, maybe—"

She stopped listening.

He sounded worried, and his voice was all gentle reason and persuasion. The skin of her cheek prickled under the intensity of his stare, but she didn't turn her head. Didn't meet his eyes.

When it came to Ron and Peter, she was done for the night. Beyond done.

With one fierce shake of her arm, she threw off his touch. "As long as I maintain my popularity and keep bringing the show so much positive publicity, they won't kick me off. And even if they did, I'd be fine. I could find other parts or go back home and return to the theater. Hell, I could work alongside my parents on the production line, and I'd still be happy."

"Somehow, I—I didn't think you would actually do it." It was a stunned, hoarse whisper. "But you weren't bluffing. You meant it. You could just . . . walk away from this and be fine."

Apparently he hadn't believed her the first several times she'd told him so. Lovely.

"Yes. That's correct."

"I can't . . ." His reply came as she wrenched open the door. "I can't fathom that."

He sounded—lost somehow. But finding him wasn't her responsibility.

"I know," she said flatly, and let the door swing shut behind her.

This time, the last word was hers.

8

THE SHOWRUNNERS CAVED.

Neither Ron nor R.J. had the good grace to concede their position face-to-face, or even in a phone call. Instead, they sent a very terse email to inform Peter, Maria, and Ramón of the change in plans and had a courier deliver a new script for their upcoming scene.

Cyprian and Cassia, nearing despair at the onset of winter and the accompanying scarcity of their remaining food supply, would share a magical apple. A gift from Neptune, left at the very precipice of their gate to Tartarus. Pretty much exactly what Maria had suggested, although the showrunners didn't openly acknowledge that.

Peter couldn't believe it. A fucking *magical apple* and a bit of CGI work, and suddenly he wouldn't have to starve or fuck up his body after all, and neither would she.

Maria had won her high-stakes gamble and made it look— easy.

But, of course, that ease was only possible because the stakes actually *hadn't* been that high for her. Not in the same way they were for him. As she'd told him, she could walk away from this role or even her career and be fine. He couldn't.

She didn't understand that, though.

It was obvious, at least to someone who watched her as closely as he did. She still laughed and chatted with him, still made an effort to include him in group conversations and activities, but when she looked at him, some of the warmth in those lively brown eyes had cooled. Some of the growing ties of trust between them had been severed.

He'd never thought he'd miss Maria calling him a shit-boot, but he did. The Swedish obscenity hadn't passed her lips once since the night of Ron's meeting.

Which was ironic, since he'd never felt more like a shit-boot than that night. When he'd sat beside her during that awful meeting and seen her hands pale and shaking with chill, her lips blue around the edges, all because he'd jumped to obey Ron's command and urged her to do the same. When he'd heard her save not only herself, but him too. When he'd left her swinging in the cold, cold breeze to preserve his own professional future, exactly as he'd told her he would.

He'd had his reasons. But still: *skitstövel*.

They remained friends, and he valued that. More than she probably understood. Any hints that she might feel more than friendly toward him had vanished, though.

The loss hollowed out something within him, a void he hadn't even realized was full—for maybe the first time in his life—until it emptied once more.

Another bizarre, hilarious phrase Maria had taught him to recognize that summer: *Nu har du verkligen skitit i det blå skåpet.* Now you've really shit in the blue cupboard.

Essentially, the phrase meant: *You fucked up.*

He'd protected his own interests, and that wasn't the same as fucking up.

But somehow, it still felt like he'd fucked up. Badly.

IN MID-JANUARY, A stupefyingly powerful winter storm churned toward the island.

The day before it hit, the Atlantic itself seemed alive and angry, lurching and dipping in nauseating churns, whipped along by roaring winds. The towering waves smashed against the cliffs so viciously that the spray soaked anyone standing on top of those cliffs, the staggering power of each impact elemental and frightening.

Peter knew. He was there, and he was frightened.

Not for himself. For Maria.

"Action!" Ramón shouted, a severe frown creasing his weathered face.

On cue, there she went again, wandering near the edge of the cliffs with her face in her hands, blond hair tangled in wet ropes, her sobs drowned out by rain and howling gusts of wind.

Darrell, positioned next to Peter with his hood cinched tight over most of his face, was—for once—not smiling. His whispered *shit* was barely audible, and Peter had never appreciated the man more. Even Jeanine stood grimly watching, with one wet, gloved hand covering her mouth and the other clutching Darrell's arm.

No one was happy, although Maria was probably the most sanguine of them all about the situation. Apparently she considered today's awful filming conditions an *adventure*. Which would normally be charming as fuck, if only she couldn't end up *dead*.

He didn't understand her reasoning. Not even a little.

Dieting? No fucking way. Taunting the Grim Reaper? No problem!

Hell, even their hotel proprietor had registered his disapproval. That morning, when the group had left for the day, Conor had asked where they were filming, in tones that implied a silent addendum: *And* why *are you filming, you absolute plonkers? Have you lost your bloody minds?*

When he'd heard about Maria's scene, for some unknown reason he'd immediately turned to Peter. Stared at him, as if waiting for . . . something, with lines of worry and disapproval carved deep across his freckled forehead. Then, when Peter hadn't responded, Conor had swiveled in place and trained his glare on Ramón and Nava instead.

To be fair, the director and line producer hadn't wanted to keep filming either. Their requests for a delay in production had been promptly and firmly refused, however, because the foul weather would actually save the over-budget show some of its postproduction costs.

In a bit of awful serendipity, the script that week had already called for a fierce Atlantic storm to come ashore, Neptune's punishment for Cyprian and Cassia's unwillingness to make the exhausting trek to the cliffs during the harshest winter months. The shipwrecked Vikings had left the gate to Tartarus unattended for far too long, and the god of the sea intended to make the cost of their negligence personal and unmistakable.

The wind would destroy part of their home, and Cassia would despair. As Cyprian restlessly dozed after a sleepless, miserable night, she'd travel to the gate on her own, unwilling to risk him as well as herself, and beg for mercy. And when the storm continued unabated, she'd contemplate ending her misery for good in one leap from those unforgiving heights.

Cyprian would wake and find her gone. Panicked, he'd race after her and persuade her to return from the edge of ruin, and they'd embrace. Kiss for the first time, to the horror of both.

It was a great scene, all high drama and intensity. Peter had been looking forward to it for weeks, and not only because he'd get to kiss Maria again without having to justify it to himself.

But the storm was supposed to be the creation of postproduction and the skilled efforts of the VFX supervisor, not an extremely pissed-off Mother Nature. It wasn't supposed to be real, and it wasn't supposed to be dangerous to the cast or crew.

Above all else, Maria wasn't supposed to be standing that close to a fucking cliff's edge when a stray gust of fifty-mile-per-hour wind could send her hurtling three hundred feet down and plunge her into the merciless, agitated ocean. The ocean where, if she somehow managed not to die on impact or drown—and to be clear, she'd *definitely* die on impact or drown—the pounding waves would simply crush her body against the cliffs and grind her to pieces.

A single moment of carelessness, a single misstep, and—no more Maria.

The storm hadn't even officially arrived yet, which was maybe the most terrifying thing of all. Current forecasts called for torrential rain and wind gusts of up to ninety miles per hour the next day, and Fionn had told them what to expect afterward: flooding, washed-out roads, scattered stone walls, and possibly no phone service or electricity.

And yet, filming was scheduled for tomorrow too. Unlike today, Peter and Maria would be acting together. Cassia would remain near the cliff's edge for a long, long time while Cyprian pleaded for her to stay with him, to stay among the living.

With a larger crew, with a more generous shooting budget for their location, with different showrunners, they'd have various people watching to ensure the safety of all concerned. But their crew and their budget were tiny, and their showrunners were cutting corners wherever possible to save time and money. What

Ron and R.J. were telling various authorities, Peter couldn't even imagine.

Toward the end of the take, a particularly brutal gust of wind sent Maria swaying, and she stumbled sideways, closer to the edge, as the crew gasped.

Peter tasted metal. Fear and blood.

The lightning jolt of terror stopped his breath, and he didn't think his heart beat again until she regained her balance and subtly moved farther from the precipice.

"Cut!" It was a snarl, and Ramón immediately strode in her direction, his jaw as stony as the island itself. "Get away from there, Maria. That's our last goddamn take for the day."

Oh, thank fuck. Another go-round might very well break Peter.

Given how much the crew loved Maria, it might break all of them.

"Tomorrow, should I have a leash or something?" she asked Nava, who'd turned paler than he'd ever seen her. "I don't know what's standard under these conditions."

The women walked past him, yet he still couldn't seem to move, not even to hear the producer's response. His legs shook, and not from the wind. He kept swallowing, kept dragging his trembling hands through his hair.

In the end, Darrell had to set him in motion and steer him away from the set. The PA's hand on his shoulder was firm but supportive, his eyes full of more understanding than Peter was comfortable with.

On their miserable trek back to the van, Ramón continued muttering under his breath. Peter couldn't make out most of it, except for the word *OSHA*.

And that was when he knew what to do.

After they'd arrived back at the hotel, while everyone else

trudged silently down the hall toward their suites and hot showers, Peter lingered near the front desk. When the hallway had
cleared, he leaned close to Conor. The proprietor looked up from
his computer monitor and jumped a little at the sight of his waterlogged guest looming over him.

"Sorry. Didn't mean to startle you," Peter whispered, recalling
the teasing affection in the other man's voice whenever he spoke
to *Maria-My-Dear*. Yes, Conor was definitely the right person for
the job. "I have a big favor to ask."

"Tell me," Conor said quietly, and Peter did.

THE WEATHER WAS swiftly turning from ugly to hideous, so
the local doctor evaluated Peter's condition via a virtual appointment that evening. The determination of his ill health required a
startlingly short amount of time. Or at least it *would* have been
startling, under other circumstances than these.

"It's good Conor sent you my way," Dr. Fitzgerald cheerily said,
tapping out a few quick notes on her tablet. "Otherwise, the consequences might have been disastrous. Deadly, even."

Should he cough again? It wasn't strictly necessary, but . . . was
he or was he not an actor committed to his role?

One racking cough later, he nodded at the physician. "I appreciate your time and help."

"From what I understand, I'll need to share my findings with
your director and producer." The doctor rearranged her round, lively
face to convey the appropriate solemnity. "Why don't you call them
in? Or, rather, text them, so as not to tax your limited strength?"

A quick message, and both Ramón and Nava arrived outside
his door.

He greeted them with a wan smile and a limp wave toward his
couch. "Thanks for coming." Mouth in elbow. *Hack hack hack.* "I

had the hotel contact their doctor on call when we got back this afternoon, and she wanted to talk to you about my illness."

"I'm so sorry, Peter." Nava's broad brow had puckered, and she shook her head. "I had no idea you were sick. Why on earth did you come to the set this afternoon if you weren't feeling well?"

Ramón scanned Peter from head to toe, paused, then looked down at the thick rug for a moment. "Oh, I'm sure he had his reasons, Nava."

"But—"

"Anyway, we should listen to what the doctor has to say. You don't want to risk the health of our cast member, do you?"

"Of course not," Nava snapped, running an agitated hand over her buzz cut. "That's why we were both so damn angry when they forced us to—"

Enlightenment dawned midsentence.

She bit her lip. "Ah. Yes. Right you are, Ramón. We should definitely listen to the doctor, who so kindly took time out of her busy schedule to help our endangered star."

"Step one toward sainthood: check," Dr. Fitzgerald murmured.

Without further ado, Ramón and Nava perched on the edge of Peter's couch and positioned his phone's screen so the doctor could see both of them.

"Without seeing Peter in person, it's hard to make a definitive diagnosis, but all the symptoms he described to me correspond with the flu. A severe enough case to prohibit working for several days, but not so severe that he needs to seek medical attention elsewhere." The doctor phrased each sentence delicately, word by careful word. "I don't see any reason why someone with those symptoms shouldn't be able to recover at the hotel. Unless his health were to take a very sudden, very steep downward turn, I'd recommend that he simply rest. Drink lots of fluids, eat nourishing foods, take over-the-counter fever-reducing medicines if his temperature were to spike. Once the storm is safely past, if his symptoms haven't lessened in severity, I'd be delighted to see him in person. But otherwise, in another"—she tapped her chin thoughtfully—"oh, let's say three days, he should be just fine."

"That is . . . excellent news." Nava gave her own little cough. "That he should be better soon, I mean. Sadly, the rest of this episode's scenes feature Peter, so we'll have to stop shooting entirely until he recovers. But we certainly wouldn't want to risk our stars by forcing them to film when they shouldn't be on set."

"No. Of course not," Dr. Fitzgerald said soothingly. "Luckily, you don't have to."

"Thank you, doctor." Ramón's voice was low and fervent, and he let out a slow breath. "*Thank you.*"

"It was my pleasure." Her smile was wide and impish. "Trust me on that."

After offering a few cheerful goodbyes, as well as a promise that the production would receive her bill in due course, she ended the virtual appointment.

The silence in the hotel suite suddenly seemed very, very loud.

Peter sneezed lustily, if dryly, into a convenient tissue.

"Reedton." Ramón stood, stretching his arms upward with a satisfied yawn. "I can't tell you how delighted I am that you sought medical intervention."

Sagging into the back of his chair, Peter rasped out, "Anything for actor safety and good health."

"Indeed." Once she'd risen from the sofa, Nava walked to him, bent down, and kissed him on the cheek. "We'll check on you tomorrow. Hopefully you'll feel well enough for our usual breakfast, even if your health takes a sudden downturn immediately afterward."

"Uh . . ." *Hack hack hack*. "I heard some weird rumors earlier, by the way. Just . . . around the internet. Don't remember exactly where."

Arms crossed over his chest, Ramón raised a single eyebrow. "Is that so?"

"Apparently some entertainment blogger received an anonymous tip about filming conditions here on the island, and she may be making inquiries with the actors' union?" Peter shrugged in pretend befuddlement. "What's weird is that the tip came from somewhere in Boston. How could the tipster even know anything about our production from an ocean away?"

"Wow. What a mystery." After a pause, Nava added, "I imagine a bit more supervision on set wouldn't be such a terrible thing, if it ensured the safety of our cast and crew. Even if additional filming delays and budgetary requirements angered our showrunners."

"Well, if they get angry, no one on this island is to blame. That much is clear." As he passed by the chair on his way to the door, Ramón ruffled Peter's hair affectionately. "Enjoy your much-deserved rest, kid."

Kid. As if Peter were sixteen instead of thirty-six.

Maybe he *was* running a fever, ironically enough, because he suddenly felt very . . . warm.

Then they were gone, and Peter called the front desk to arrange a bit of room service for dinner. After all, it wouldn't do to give anyone the wrong impression about his health, right?

That night, for the first time since November, he fell asleep easily.

He dreamed of Maria.

She called him a shit-boot.

It was the best night's sleep he'd had in ages.

9

PETER REEDTON WAS A *KNÄPPGÖK*.

By yesterday afternoon, all his scenes for the day were done. He could have gone back to the hotel. Hung out by the fire. Read in bed. Taken a really long, really hot bath. Trimmed his toenails. Learned how to dance the merengue via YouTube videos. Anything, really. Literally *anything* other than spending several unnecessary hours outdoors in the freezing wind and rain.

But noooooo.

Instead, he'd come to watch Maria film that scene on the cliffs. And now, as Nava had informed her at dinner last night, Peter was ill due to sheer idiocy. As well as either a virus or bacteria—or possibly a fungus? Oh, or an amoeba!—but also, definitely, idiocy. Which was why she was taking charge of his health, starting now. Clearly he couldn't be trusted to do the job adequately.

By the time dinner had ended, it was too late to yell at him. If he'd gone to bed early, as he should have—as she'd make certain he did tonight—she'd only have disturbed his much-needed rest. But it was morning now, even though everything outside the windows was extremely dark and apocalyptic, and she intended to lecture him before she ate a late breakfast in the dining room.

She hoped Peter wasn't napping, because she needed to explain her newfound authority over his immune system and the protection thereof without further delay. He could nap later, after she bullied him into good health once more.

By, say, forcing him to nap.

And if that didn't entirely make logical sense, who cared? Neither did spending all fucking day outside in a fucking Atlantic storm for no fucking reason.

If ever someone had literally shit in a *blå skåpet*, he was the obvious culprit.

Her knock on his door could have woken the dead—and according to Conor, Peter was halfway there already.

He answered her summons with surprising swiftness.

Oddly, he didn't look half-dead. And when she hooked an arm around his waist and hauled him back to bed, his body against hers didn't feel any warmer than normal. He also wasn't staggering or miserably infirm in the way Conor and Nava's descriptions of his condition had led her to expect.

Turning his head away from hers, he coughed as she sat him down on the mattress. She paused, crouched by his bedside, and listened to him hack and hack. And after she straightened, she studied him for a minute. Hard.

That cough . . . that cough, she recognized.

She'd heard it in late November, when Cyprian had fallen terribly ill from hunger and his makeshift home's inexorable chill, and Cassia had cared for him with reluctant tenderness. The big Viking had hacked and wheezed and groaned, his voice hoarse as he reassured her he was fine. She didn't need to fret.

Peter's current cough had the same sound, the same cadence.

Maybe his actual cough exactly matched his fake cough.

Or maybe—

"Show me." Bending down until he had no choice but to meet her eyes, she stared at him in open challenge. "Show me what medicines you've been taking. Given the weather, I can't go to a pharmacy, so I intend to collect whatever you need from everyone at the hotel, and I don't want to grab duplicates."

If he was faking, if he'd cost her a night's sleep due to needless worry over his health, she was going to make certain a moose trampled him whenever he visited Sweden for publicity purposes.

"Uh . . ." His gaze briefly dropped, and his brow—which was, yes, cool against her palm, as she'd suspected—furrowed. "I forget where I put them. Maria, thank you for checking on me, but maybe you could come back later. I can tell you then what I've been tak—"

"No need. I'll look myself."

About-facing, she scanned the room. No medication or crumpled tissues on his bedside table. A half dozen strides put her in the bathroom, where . . . again, she found nothing to indicate illness. Not even a thermometer. Same with his coffee table and the little nook that held his coffeemaker and minifridge.

Another turn on her heel, and she marched back to the bed, where he appeared to be cringing. For good reason.

She stabbed a finger into his perfectly healthy chest. "*Faker.*"

The wind's roar, the slight rattling of his windows, the near-violent lash of that endless downpour against the glass were the only sounds in the room for a long, long time.

"Let it be, Maria." With a sigh, he nudged her accusing forefinger aside. "I don't want you involved in this."

"Involved in . . . what?" She frowned at him, fists braced on her hips. "Why are you pretending to be ill? Did you not want to film our scene today, given the conditions?"

But that wasn't like Peter at all, was it? His health, his body, and his convenience meant nothing to him. Not when weighed against the dictates of the showrunners and his desire for professional success. So if this damnable farce wasn't about his own comfort and safety, then what in the world would prompt such an underhanded, secretive . . .

Fy fan. Fy fan.

She knew. She knew precisely what he was doing and why. And the source of that anonymous tip about shooting conditions on the island—the one various media outlets had already emailed her agent about in a request for her commentary—wasn't such a mystery anymore.

She preferred face-to-face confrontation, and she didn't mind risk.

Peter, though . . . he would want to minimize any threat to his future, and he had. But he'd still taken a risk, however contained.

And he'd taken it for her.

Whether he knew it or not, she'd glimpsed his expression after that scary little bobble at the cliff's edge yesterday, seen him white-faced and frozen with horror at the end of the take.

She never wanted to see that expression again. It hurt to witness, almost as much as it seemingly hurt him to watch that near-miss on camera.

So yes, she'd known he cared about her safety, cared about *her*. What she hadn't known: He cared enough to actually *do* something about it. Not as she would have, but in his own extremely cautious but undeniably effective way.

He'd made certain her next cliffside adventure wouldn't involve wind gusts of 150 kilometers per hour. He'd ensured that the set would have increased scrutiny from now on, so she'd never be put in a similarly precarious position again. And he didn't want her to know what he'd done, because her ignorance meant plausible deniability if everything went to shit despite his precautions.

Even his lies were an attempt to protect her.

"Um . . ." His fingers plucked at the fluffy duvet on the bed. "If I don't seem ill right now, the doctor said my condition might, uh, vary from moment to moment, so . . ."

He paused, still fumbling for an explanation. After licking his lips, he started to say something else, no doubt another lie, and she didn't care what it was, she didn't care whether he ever told her the truth, because she understood now.

"Come here, *skitstövel*," she said.

Then she ducked down again, cupped his bristly cheeks, and kissed him. Hard.

His lips were already parted, so she teased his tongue with hers, then delved deep and reclaimed her territory after far too long an absence. He responded like a starved man at a feast, a low groan rumbling deep in his chest as he seized control of the kiss—and of her.

Within moments, he'd stood, but only to push her onto the bed, onto her back, crawling between her legs and trapping her in the cage of his big body. The bruising pressure of his lips against hers eased, but only so he could nip and suck a hot, open-mouthed trail along her jaw and down her throat.

His hands delved under her sweater, and then her bra loosened, and her breasts were cupped in his hot palms. She rounded his hips with her legs and slid her own hands beneath his jeans, beneath the soft material of his boxer briefs, to squeeze his ass greedily.

Gods above, she loved his body. No man had ever made her this hungry to stare. To touch. To take.

Shoving her sweater up to her neck, he dove down to suck her nipple, while he plucked and twisted and rubbed the other, and she was done with foreplay.

Unbuttoning his jeans took a heartbeat, and her fingers moved swiftly to his zipper.

At that moment, his entire body shuddered against hers. Shuddered and stilled.

"No," he ground out hoarsely, lifting his head from her breast. "No."

Her knuckles pressed against his sizable erection, she immediately stopped unzipping him. "Peter?"

"We're not doing this." His face flushed, his gaze still devouring every inch of her bare flesh, he slowly tugged her sweater down. "We can't."

Removing her hands entirely from his body, she laid them flat by her sides as he clambered off her, his jaw like stone. Nostrils flared, breathing ragged, he sat at the edge of the bed, his jeans still unbuttoned, and gripped white-knuckled fistfuls of the duvet. He stared across the room blankly.

She was lost. Frustrated and bewildered.

"I thought . . ." After a pause, she sat up. "You don't want to fuck me?"

It certainly looked like he did, at least on the most basic physical level. She was surprised his zipper was holding up so well under the strain, frankly. But desire wasn't consent, and neither was a hard dick.

His bark of bitter laughter shook the bed, but he still didn't turn his head and meet her eyes.

"It doesn't have to be serious, Peter, and it doesn't have to be public." Thoughts fuzzy with her own arousal, she tried to think through his possible reasoning, then find the right phrase in English. "We could be costars with secret benefits, if you wanted."

Because she was giving up, at long last. She'd burned like an inferno for him from the moment they'd met, and now she also *knew* him. Liked him. Trusted him, at least a little. Enough to offer that much of herself, even if he couldn't offer her everything she needed in return.

When they were done, it might crack her heart around the edges, but she'd try her best to keep the core intact. And maybe she'd fail. Maybe she'd grow too attached. That was a risk she was willing to take, as long as she got to take *him* in the bargain.

"Shit, Maria." He scrubbed his hands over his face, then lowered them to his sides again and twisted his upper body toward her. "You know I want you. I couldn't hide it if I tried."

Without thinking, she dropped her gaze to his lap.

His laugh—no longer bitter, merely rueful—sounded tired. "And to be clear, I *have* tried. My need to fuck you isn't the issue here, though, and neither is my . . . uh, affection. How charming and smart and funny and talented I think you are, and how much I just—*like* you."

Absently, she rubbed at her chest, which seemed to be . . . melting somehow?

"Okay." After such lovely compliments, now she *really* didn't understand. "So what *is* the issue, then?"

Those dark eyes of his were solemn and steady. "If we got involved that way, and things went sour between us, we'd have nowhere to hide. Nowhere we could lick our wounds until we got over whatever happened. Instead, we'd be forced to confront each other day after day, week after week, no matter how angry or hurt we were. It would be terrible for us, and it would be terrible for everyone on the crew forced to endure the awkwardness and tension alongside us."

He wasn't wrong, of course. But wasn't it worth a gamble?

She opened her mouth to ask that very question, but he wasn't finished.

"Maria, we may spend years together on this island. *Years*. We're the only two actors on the set, and we both know you're the center of everything here. You've made us a team. Hell, you've made us a goddamn *family*, and you're what holds our family together. But if things went bad between us, the community you've built, all the camaraderie you've nurtured, could disappear"—he snapped his fingers—"like that."

He'd never strung so many words together at one time in her presence.

Funny. After months of wishing he would talk more, express his thoughts and feelings more clearly, she now wanted him to shut the hell up, because his words hurt.

"It would be unbearable." Gods above, he was still fucking *talking*. "And the work would suffer too. You know it would. All the strain off camera would bleed into the footage, and I'd have ruined this once-in-a-career opportunity for what? Sex?"

For me, she wanted to tell him. *You'd have risked everything for* me.

Instead, she swallowed past the burn in her throat and pointed out the obvious. "Peter, you've already endangered your career for me. Today, as a matter of fact."

"That was potentially a matter of life and death." With a decisive shake of his head, he dismissed the only good argument she had left. "The state of my dick isn't."

If this was just about his dick, he probably wouldn't be so worried.

But that didn't really matter, did it? He'd said no.

And despite the faint prickling in her sinuses, everything was fine. She and Peter might have fucked, but they'd never been lovers. Now she guessed they never would be.

That was fine too. Or at least it would be, once her stupid chest stopped aching.

After all, she'd still have him as a valued friend and colleague, and nothing he'd said changed what he'd done for her today. For a man like him, risking his career even that much was a testament to how deeply he truly cared about her.

So she would make things easy on him. She would make things easy on them both.

"Very well," she said. "Friends?"

Her hand rock-steady, she extended it toward Peter. But because he truly was a fucking *skitstövel*, he didn't shake it. Instead, he raised it to his mouth and brushed a kiss over her knuckles before letting go.

The brief, glancing contact might as well have blistered her.

She needed to get the hell out of his suite.

The soft curve of his lips was bittersweet. "Good friends."

"The best of friends," she confirmed with an answering smile that stretched her cheeks painfully, then hopped off his bed.

Just as she was set to leave as quickly as possible, the silver-framed photo on his nightstand caught her attention. Unable to stop herself, she paused and studied the only real decoration he'd added to his suite.

The picture's colors had faded slightly, and no wonder. It had to be over two decades old.

In the photo, a boy of maybe eleven or twelve, indisputably Peter, stood next to a woman who looked almost exactly like him. Long-limbed and solidly built, she had wavy, deep brown hair, dark eyes snapping with intelligence, and a smile that somehow encompassed both genuine, affectionate joy and wariness.

A blue expanse of water sparkled in the background, and fiery autumn leaves on the trees bracketing them seemed to rustle in an invisible breeze. She had her arm wrapped around his shoulders. His smile echoing hers with eerie similarity, he'd cuddled close to her side.

There was no mistaking the photo. "This is you and your mom."

Any trace of softness in his expression, however conflicted, disappeared in an instant. He grunted out an affirmative sound, mouth now grimly shut.

"I suppose I don't have to ask whether you're adopted too." Because maybe a little ironic humor would help relax that now-stony jaw. "She's lovely."

Not delicate or ethereal, but undeniably striking. If Maria fully understood Nava's explanation of the term a few weeks back, *handsome.*

Another low, rough sound of agreement as he stared at his childhood self, at his mother.

When he finally responded with actual words, though, they were bland. Stripped of any inflection or emphasis. "She was."

Oh, fuck. She'd hoped it was simply a favorite photo among many others taken over their years together, not a memento of a parent gone too soon.

"Peter, I—" she began.

"She died the next year."

Each carefully neutral word landed in her heart like an anvil.

She bit her lip. "I'm so sorry."

What else could she say, really? The pain of death, of loss, wouldn't be eased by any facile words she might offer. Only time and love could do that—and he'd had plenty of the former and wouldn't let her offer the latter.

"It's fine," he told her in casual dismissal, and it wasn't just a brush-off and an obvious falsehood. It was an impenetrable wall constructed between them in the space of a heartbeat, tall and solid and entirely unnecessary.

If he didn't want to talk about his childhood, she—of all people—understood. She certainly wouldn't force him.

"Okay." With firm resolve, she turned away from the photo. From him. "Well, I'd better get going, friend. It's time for breakfast. And of course, I shouldn't linger in your suite. I wouldn't want to catch your *terrible* illness, would I?"

After directing a breezy wink in his general direction, she put a bounce in her step as she headed for his door and offered a jaunty wave before leaving.

"See you—" he started to say, but the door shut behind her before he could finish.

As she started down the hall, she kept smiling until the expression didn't feel forced anymore, and she could greet Conor and Fionn and her crew with the good cheer they deserved from her.

Honestly, she couldn't imagine why she felt so unsettled. Because, really, all was well, and nothing much had altered between her and Peter. Even good friends didn't share everything, and even close friendship and mutual attraction didn't guarantee a romantic or sexual relationship.

He *was* a good friend, and those didn't come along every day. That was definitely something to appreciate. *Nej*, to *cultivate*. Also, the next time someone tempting offered a potential hookup, she knew not to turn them down, which was certainly useful knowledge to have.

As he'd noted, they had years ahead of them.

She'd make the best of those years. In a variety of fun ways.

And if she now had a new set of words she'd like to watch Peter eat, that was no one's concern but hers.

Con of the Gates Panel Transcript

Moderator: Maria and Peter, you're the two newest *Gods of the Gates* cast members, but you've managed to make quite a splash during the second season of the show. You've quickly become fan favorites, and we're glad you could both join us today.

Maria: That's very kind of you to say. Thank you.

Peter: If we're truly fan favorites, that's entirely due to Maria. No one can resist her Nordic wiles.

Moderator: Did you get along well from the beginning? Because otherwise, finding yourself stuck on an island together could have been *awkward*.

Maria: [laughs] Yes. Very awkward.

Peter: Incredibly awkward.

Maria: I can honestly say I liked Peter the first moment I saw him.

Peter: Same here.

Maria: And fortunately, filming together on the island allows us plenty of time to work through any disagreements that might crop up.

Peter: Yes. For example, disagreements about the appropriate number of times one actor should threaten to beat the other with a glass jar of pickled herring. I.e., none.

Maria: Stop calling me Pippi, and I'll stop menacing you with herring, *skitstövel*.

Moderator: What does that mean?

Maria: It means Peter deserves a fistful of salty licorice shoved down his throat.

Peter: Even after *The Girl with the Dragon Tattoo*, I don't think people realize the startling amount of seething violence buried beneath those bland Swedish facades.

Moderator: Um—

Peter: Just ask the Norwegians. They know all about unprovoked Swedish aggression.

Moderator: Let's—

Peter: Also the Danes.

Moderator: —go to—

Peter: Iceland moved halfway across an ocean to get away.

Moderator: —our next—

Peter: Finland has been cowering for centuries now. They hide in their saunas.

Moderator: —panelist, shall we?

Peter: Can an entire country take anger management classes? Because—

Maria: I should have kidnapped you, put you in a boat, dumped you in the water in front of Dolphy McBlowholeface, and watched her smack the shit out of you, Reedton.

Peter: Again with the shit. Another thing I don't think people realize about Swedes: their unswerving obsession with—

Maria: Keep talking, *skitstövel*. Keep talking, and good luck digging out your blue cupboard.

Moderator: His . . . blue cupboard?

Peter: If you know, you know.

Maria: And believe me, he *knows*. From very personal, very smelly experience.

Moderator: I . . . think we should move on to Marcus Caster-Rupp now. What can you tell us about the upcoming third season?

Marcus: I think fans will be absolutely delighted by my new hair care routine!

Alex: We should talk about beards. Specifically, whose beard was fuller and more becoming over the course of the second season. Because it's clearly mine, and I want that publicly acknowledged.

Moderator: [mumbles] Jesus Christ.

10

"NOW THAT WE'VE TALKED THROUGH THE BASIC SEQUENCE
of events, I want to revisit the beginning of the scene, if that's ac-
ceptable to you both." When Peter and Maria acquiesced with a
nod, Delia—the production's intimacy coordinator—continued.
"Once their years of repressed lust boil over—"

Six. Six years of repressed lust.

Not that Peter was counting.

"—Cyprian will shove Cassia against the wall and tear off her
tunic, leaving her naked from the waist up. Then he'll push a thigh
between hers and kiss her passionately while squeezing her breasts."

Liquid nitrogen, he thought. *The North Pole. Wisconsin in Janu-
ary. Meat lockers.*

Delia looked up from her notes. "In other words, the encounter will start near-violently, before transitioning into more gentle
lovemaking. Does anything about that part of your scene worry
either of you?"

In retrospect, he definitely should have jerked off before re-
porting to the set.

It was just choreography, he'd told himself upon reading the
script. A simple series of heavily scripted movements accompanied by the display of whatever emotions were relevant. What
he and Maria filmed this week might turn on viewers, but in the

end, it was only a job. Only another scene, no different from a battle sequence or all those hours spent harvesting seaweed at the shoreline.

It wasn't romantic. It wasn't private. It wasn't about the two of them but their characters, and they had nothing to worry about. *He* had nothing to worry about.

But in reality, now that they'd reached this—literally—climactic scene between Cassia and Cyprian, the scene for which their fandom had been clamoring since their first episode aired, the scene that would surely launch thousands of startlingly filthy fics on AO3 and reams of NSFW fan art . . . so much about the situation bothered him.

First, there was Cyprian's sheer sexual aggression at the start of the encounter, aggression that Cassia welcomed. But Maria wasn't Cassia, and he refused to hurt or frighten her, however inadvertently. As Delia had repeatedly emphasized, even though the scene expressed their characters' sexual preferences rather than their own, Maria's comfort and safety still mattered. So did his, obviously, but after six fucking years of unassuaged desire for her, he figured she could do just about anything to him and it would feel good.

More than good. Like a benediction. Like oxygen to a man slowly, painfully suffocating.

Second, Maria would no doubt jump into character with her usual enthusiasm . . . but with significantly fewer items of clothing blocking his view and preventing skin-on-skin contact. Other than a few key barriers for modesty, they'd spend most of the scene entirely naked—and they'd stay that way for almost a week of filming, because constantly changing angles and lighting meant even short sex scenes took forever to shoot. And this was *not* a short sex scene.

Maybe that still wouldn't have been an issue, except that he hadn't bedded another woman after meeting Maria. Even knowing she'd had occasional dalliances between seasons, as various tabloids eagerly documented. The knowledge had stung—of course it stung; it more than stung, it *burned*—but she'd offered herself to him, and he'd said no. And he was a bastard, but not enough of a bastard to expect her to remain celibate for over half a decade to spare the feelings of a man who'd refused a sexual relationship with her.

Over time, he'd expected to find consolation in someone else's arms too. Since that fateful day in an LA sauna, though, even flirting with someone else felt like cheating, for some asinine reason. So now, primed by six endless years with only the dubious consolation of his left hand, he was essentially an SFX fireball ready to explode, only hotter and less controlled. Fuck, if even this relatively dry conversation was making him hard, the actual scene itself might very well kill them all in some sort of boner-induced cataclysm.

And third—shit. He tried not to think about it. He'd been trying not to think about it for weeks now. Possibly months. But he couldn't avoid it any longer.

This was his last scene with Maria. Ever.

Last week, they'd separately filmed their deaths, because of course Ron and R.J. couldn't abide the thought of a hopeful ending for anyone.

After Cyprian and Cassia's lovemaking, the triumphant roar of the undead told them their gate had been breached, and their destiny was upon them. They both knew they wouldn't survive the battle ahead, not as mere humans. So he sent her away for her safety, although she initially refused to leave him. But when he reminded her that she could, even then, be carrying his child—his legacy in the living world, and the only proof of their love that might survive—she agreed to go, sobbing brokenheartedly all the while.

He helped her into the frail currach they'd painstakingly assembled over the course of endless isolated, lust-choked, pining-filled years and pushed the boat as far into the storm-tossed ocean as possible before marching, numb with despair and terror, toward the gate. Toward the cliffs.

And that was where, in the scene they'd shot last Tuesday, Cyprian had watched the woman he loved to the point of agony remain atop the towering, churning waves only a few precious minutes before she foundered and drowned within sight of the shore.

Then he'd battled the undead from Tartarus and had his ass handed to him. Or, more accurately, his head, removed from his shoulders by some terrible creature—the VFX folks were going to have fun with that—as he shouted Cassia's name with his final, tortured breath.

It was depressing as fuck. But however grim, at least their character arcs made sense, which was more than could be said for many of his colleagues.

Maria had returned to that enormous Belgian water tank for her death scene, while he'd remained on the island for his. But since productions like theirs didn't always film sequences in order, the two of them had this one scene left to shoot together. Their lone love scene, after all this time.

Then he was leaving the island forever. Leaving her forever.

Portraying Cyprian's devastation as he watched Cassia sail away, as he watched her die, hadn't been a challenge. Peter had essentially been dabbling in method acting.

So, yeah, this entire situation kind of blew.

Which was, incidentally, something else Cassia dropped to her knees and did.

He scrubbed his hands over his face. *Professional, Peter. Remain professional.*

"Maria?" Delia apparently required words in response to her question, which was fair. "Does anything about the opening of the scene make you uncomfortable?"

Maria kind of jerked in her seat, blinking rapidly.

"Oh," she said blankly, then seemed to recall her surroundings. "No, I'm good."

Delia's ponytail swayed as she tilted her head. "Are you certain? Because you have the right to express and impose physical boundaries, Maria. In scenes like this, agreement and consent are paramount."

"I'm absolutely certain." Slowly, a wicked grin crept over Maria's flushed face. "In fact, I look forward to Peter throwing me around a little."

When he choked on thin air and reached for his mug of ice water, she reached over and slapped his back.

"I consider it an irreplaceable opportunity to watch how an experienced actor approaches scenes like these," she added, her tone suspiciously prim.

Once he'd stopped coughing, Delia turned to him. "How about you, Peter? Are you comfortable?"

No. Not in any possible sense. But only one of his reasons for discomfort was something he'd share with a near-stranger.

"I just don't want to do anything that might scare or harm Maria." He paused. "Actually, let me rephrase that. I *won't* do anything that might scare or harm her, no matter what Ron and R.J. might want. That's my priority and my only concern."

At that, Delia shot him a look of warm approval and leaned over to give him a lingering pat on the arm. "Beautifully stated,

Peter. That sentiment is rarer than you'd like to think, and exactly what I want to hear."

For some reason, Maria was scowling at him now. Which made zero sense, because why the hell would his declaration that he considered her safety more important than the showrunners' demands piss her off? Shouldn't she be sending him melting glances of admiration too?

Although, of course, he hadn't said it for her approval. At the end of this scene, he had to live with himself. If he frightened her, hurt her, he couldn't. Period.

"Don't worry, Peter." She was smiling again, but her jaw remained oddly tight. "I trust you not to hurt me that way."

His brows drew together. Something about that phrasing—

"Let's talk about what you'll both wear." Delia turned her tablet's screen to face them. "Eventually, both your characters are meant to appear naked to viewers. Postproduction can take care of a lot, but we try to make their jobs as easy as possible while still preserving your comfort and safety. For your scene, I'd suggest that you both wear strapless thongs like these, ones that adhere to the body and match your skin color. Maria, you'd wear a silicone guard underneath, so there wouldn't be any direct genital-to-genital contact, even through fabric. And on top, pasties would provide nipple coverage."

Oh, jeez. He knew precisely—precisely—what Maria would say in response to the whole pasties thing.

Peter tunneled his fingers through his hair and tugged at a handful. Hard.

"Oh, I don't need pasties," Maria breezily, predictably proclaimed. "I don't care who sees my nipples. After all, Peter won't be wearing pasties, will he?" She paused. "On-screen, I mean. What he does on his own time, for recreational purposes, is none of my concern."

Discreetly, he angled his raised middle finger so only she could see it.

At her muffled snort, he found himself fighting a genuine smile for the first time all day.

"You're certain, Maria?" Delia's forehead creased as she typed a note to herself. "Remember that you can change your mind at any time during filming."

"That's good to know, but I don't expect to." Maria tucked a stray lock of blond hair behind her ear. "Can you tell me more about how the thongs adhere?"

He'd been wondering about that himself. "Yeah, wouldn't the adhesive, uh . . . cause some issues?"

"You mean, when you remove the thongs?" Judging by Delia's beam, she considered him a prize pupil for asking the question. "That was my next suggestion. Before attaching them, it's better to shave or wax your bikini line, so taking them off doesn't cause depilation and discomfort. Same with your genital guard, Maria."

He winced. Then winced again, because he knew. He already knew what Maria—

"That won't work for me." Her statement was cheerful but firm. "I don't shave, and I don't wax. Peter?"

The tips of his ears went hot. "Um, the same."

Although he'd be willing to do so for the cause. Maria, on the other hand, wouldn't.

"So what's the alternative?" Maria drummed her fingers on the surface of the little conference table Darrell had squeezed into a production trailer. "Just a regular nude thong?"

"For you, yes. It's one option for Peter as well." The intimacy co-ordinator cleared her throat delicately. "But he could also wear a—"

"Cock sock!" Maria swiveled toward him, face alight with glee. "That's what it's called, right?"

At the moment, he envied Cyprian, whose acute suffering had at least ended, and who never had to hear Cassia utter the word *cock* with that agile tongue of hers.

"I believe so." He knew so. "At least, that's the unofficial term."

"Correct." Delia let out a tiny, near-silent sigh. "The choice is up to you two, obviously. Whatever makes you both most comfortable."

Honestly, he'd prefer not to rip out his pubic hair or experience stubble near his groin, and he didn't particularly want to floss his butt crack for a goddamn week, so . . .

"If Maria is fine with it, I'll go with, uh, the"—*cock sock cocksock cocksockcocksock*—"latter option."

Stuffing his dick and balls into a drawstring pouch couldn't hurt him any more than this discussion already had, he supposed.

"Ah. A wise choice for a wise man." Maria turned back to Delia. "And I'm good with a thong. Or nothing at all, for that matter."

"A thong, then." With another infinitesimal sigh, the other woman made a note. "All right, let's discuss what happens once Cyprian and Cassia move to the bed. First, he'll kneel on the floor and perform cunnilingus on Cassia while they maintain eye contact. We should map that whole sequence out, step by step, then determine in advance exactly how long their eye contact will last and where he'll be touching her during the act."

Slowly, Peter closed his eyes and prayed to the god of thwarted lust for deliverance.

"I figured he'd be spreading my thighs with his hands, but I suppose he could be holding my ass or playing with my breasts instead." Maria sounded thoughtful. "What are your thoughts, Peter?"

Holy fuck. Before their next discussion with Delia, he was jacking his dick raw.

With a concerted effort, he managed to choke out, "I have no thoughts."

Not ones he could share, anyway. So it wasn't even a lie.

Gods of the Gates Cast Chat: Three Years Ago

Alex: Maria and Peter

Maria: Yes?

Peter: ???

Alex: You better watch out

Marcus: Dude, I have no idea what you're doing, and I can't count how many times I've already told you this, but: You realize that can be construed as a threat, right?

Alex: You better not cry

Carah: What the Christmas fuck, Alex

Alex: You better not pout

Peter: I don't pout

Peter: I brood manfully

Alex: I'm telling you why

Maria: Yes, a bit more context would be welcome at this particular juncture

Maria: Weirdo

Alex: CUPID MAN IS COMING TO TOWN

Alex: And by TOWN, I mean your tiny-ass island in the middle of fucking nowhere

Peter: You have a scene with us?

Maria: I'd been hoping we might get company at some point!

Alex: You've had the rest

Alex: Time for you to have the best

Alex: THE BEST = ME

Alex: Obvs

Peter: Am I . . . supposed to be the rest here

Peter: Because if so, I'm not saying I'm pouting

Peter: But I will admit there may be a certain amount of manful brooding in progress

Alex: Cupid is coming to sweep you off your feet with his inimitable charm, dashing good looks, and the extremely brief loincloth thingy the wardrobe department gives me

Alex: Also some very phallic arrows

Alex: ::waggles brows::

Maria: Tell you what

Maria: If you can literally sweep me off my feet, you can have me

Peter: ...

Marcus: Maria, please don't encourage him

Peter: Wouldn't it make more sense to film Cupid's scenes in a studio, in front of a green screen, and fix things in postproduction

Peter: Because travel is very expensive, and this season is already over budget, so

Maria: BUT

Maria: Only if you can manage to *stop talking* for an entire night, Alex, because I'd prefer not to wear noise-canceling headphones in bed

Alex: UNFAIR, WE BOTH KNOW I CAN'T DO THAT

Maria: And we also both know we don't feel that way about one another

Alex: I don't brood manfully

Alex: I fucking POUT

Alex: ::pouts::

Peter: Anyway, Maria's right, it'll be great to have company

Peter: Couldn't be happier you'll be here with us, dude, can't wait

Carah: Forget our show, this is fucking ENTERTAINMENT right here

Maria: ???

Peter: ???

Alex: ::continues pouting::

Marcus: . . .

Marcus: Fine, we can listen to Mötley Crüe on our way to the studio if you'll *stop pouting*

Alex: BEST DAY EVER!!!

Marcus: Just FYI, I don't brood, manfully or otherwise, and I don't pout

Marcus: I sigh

Marcus: ::sighs::

Alex: DON'T SIGH, OR I'LL SING ALONG TO DR. FEELGOOD

Alex: To be fair, I'll do that anyway

Marcus: ::sighs again::

11

"CUT!" RAMÓN PEERED DOWN AT HIS CELL. "GOOD WORK, you two. Let's take a half-hour break while Ron and R.J. glance over some of today's footage. And for our next take, unless they have a different suggestion, we'll start at the point where Cyprian rolls Cassia onto her back and kisses her neck. Okay?"

Peter nodded his agreement, then carefully—oh so carefully—removed his hips from the cradle of Maria's thighs without dislodging the pillow placed there. The blessed pillow that had prevented utter disaster and epic embarrassment on his part as they humped away at each other for what seemed like millennia, even though it had only been two days so far. Two days of glorious torture, all caught on camera.

With a quiet thank-you, he shrugged on the robe Jeanine handed him, shoved his feet into flip-flops, and directed his gaze somewhere, anywhere, other than Maria's gleaming, near-naked body as she got up and donned her own robe and slippers.

Don't look at her bare breasts. Do not, *Reedton.*

It wasn't as if they weren't already burned onto his retinas anyway. For life, most likely.

At various points, the scene had called for him to stare at those stupendous tits, to cup them as they shone in the firelight, slickened by the rosewater-glycerin spray meant to simulate coital sweat. After six years, they were maybe a little fuller than they had been, a little lower on her ribs, and more gorgeous than ever.

Seeing them again was a gift. So was seeing the rest of her long, curvy body.

Their first night together—their only night together—he hadn't known. He hadn't known that would be his one time in Maria's bed. He hadn't known to slow the fuck down and savor the sight of her beneath him, her hair tangled around his fist, her cheeks flushed, her body naked and open.

Due to his newly rigorous masturbation schedule, he'd kept things professional on set. But that didn't mean he couldn't admire her in those moments when the script directed him to look at her, to touch her. That didn't mean he couldn't draw from his own passion and tenderness to fuel Cyprian's, and find a bittersweet joy in doing so.

And since the filming was drawn out over a long week, since he wasn't lost in a haze of mindless lust as he'd been their one night together, he'd had ample opportunity to imprint every moment in her arms on his memory. Which he'd done, gratefully.

But seeing her again, near-bare and unashamed, wasn't only a gift. It was also a torment.

For six years, he hadn't had her in his bed, and after this week, he never would again.

Unless she still wanted him.

Because yes, the show was almost over for the two of them, and the pain of that realization practically leveled him every time he let himself consider it. And yes, no future role would ever offer him the sort of extended time in her company this one had. But once they'd finished shooting their last scene, they were free. *He* was free.

From that moment on, their relationship couldn't endanger the set's camaraderie or put his career at risk in any way. Which meant, if she longed for him the way he pined for her—and sometimes he could swear she did—they could be together. Finally. In all the ways those dirty, dirty fics on AO3 had envisioned, and also as a committed couple.

Not yet, though. Not until they were entirely done filming. Which they weren't, so he really needed a snack and some water before their next take.

The early-spring air remained nippy, both inside and outside Cyprian and Cassia's little stone home, so he grabbed what he needed from the craft services table and retreated to his usual seat in Jeanine's trailer. Maria followed him inside, closing the door behind them with a muffled thud.

"This is Ron and R.J.'s first time actually checking the footage, right?" Plopping down onto the mesh-backed chair at Jeanine's workstation, she peeled a banana. "I'm curious what they're going to say."

"Since we've already spent almost two full days shooting this scene, I can't imagine they'd want to make any major changes. Especially when they're over budget again, and reshoots cost time and money." He chewed and swallowed a mouthful of his granola bar before continuing. "Besides, as Carah would say, we're fucking amazing—"

"Literally." Maria chortled and took a painfully suggestive bite of her banana.

"—so I have no doubt our performances are stellar."

After having watched a few minutes of the raw footage yesterday, he already knew her performance would be living rent-free in his head, probably forever. It had already removed all traces of former occupants, raised the thermostat to surface-of-the-sun hot, and thrown a housewarming orgy, all in less than twenty-four hours.

Once the episode aired, he expected an avalanche of new emails from Alex, who'd long ago—and with great glee—created some sort of infernal Google alert to make Peter suffer.

Their costar really enjoyed directing Peter toward fics rated E for *explicit*, ones starring Cyprian and Cassia—or, even more torturously, Peter and Maria themselves. RPF, Alex called the latter. Real-person fiction. Apparently there was a lot of it out there.

So Alex sent plenty of AO3 links, but not *only* AO3 links. Also YouTube links to fan vids that compiled every one of Cassia and Cyprian's most erotic near-miss moments and put them to extremely evocative music. Also gifs featuring the two of them eye-fucking, both on the show and in various interviews and convention panels. Also a link to the website where a Cassian shipper had posted a series of artistically ambitious and gorgeously lit photos wherein Cyprian's action figure analogue railed Cassia's in ways the manufacturer likely didn't approve, and which probably resulted in a great many dislocated vinyl limbs.

If Peter didn't like Alex so much, he'd probably have murdered the guy long ago.

That said, he hadn't asked Alex to stop.

Maria finished her banana before replying. "Of course our performances are stellar. To quote Carah once again: We're consummate goddamn professionals, bitches."

He snickered.

"But that doesn't mean Ron and R.J. won't find something to criticize." Her long, pale throat shifted as she sipped her water. "You know they've been persnickety assholes since the whole weight-loss thing our first season together."

The showrunners hadn't directed their veiled enmity toward him. Only her. And while that was good for his career, he hated how dirty it made him feel. How *complicit*.

He forced himself to meet her eyes. "I'm sorry."

Her shoulder lifted in a graceful shrug. "Better me than you. I genuinely don't give a fuck if they like me."

He kept his mouth shut, unwilling to contradict the implications of her statement. Even though he actually *didn't* care if Ron and R.J. liked him, and never had. He'd only cared whether the showrunners would fire him or damage his future career prospects. But maybe that was simply a different shade of the same guilt-muddied color.

The door to the trailer swung open. Slammed open, actually, and both he and Maria startled at the unexpected intrusion.

Ramón and Nava stomped inside, expressions thunderous. They closed the door behind them. Locked it. Stared at each other for a long, silent, tight-lipped moment, as if each was mentally urging the other to speak first.

At Maria's loud snort, everyone turned toward her.

She leaned back in her chair, stretched out her legs, and laced her hands over her belly. "I assume you're here to share our showrunners' praise? Or to tell me they're offering a retroactive raise in recognition of my hard work and unparalleled acting skills?"

"Maria . . ." Nava had evidently lost the staring contest with Ramón, because she spoke first. "I don't know whether you want Peter here for this conversation. Its outcome will affect him too, but . . . "

"There is literally nothing Ron or R.J. could say that would embarrass me, Nava. Nothing about my performance. Nothing about my personality. Nothing about my body." With a flick of her wrist, Maria dismissed that concern. "Go ahead. I don't care if Peter hears their critique."

The producer scrubbed a hand over her buzz cut. "All right. If you're sure."

"Just to be clear, neither Nava nor I agree with their feedback." The lines bracketing Ramón's mouth deepened. "We'll support whatever response you choose to make."

"Anything short of nuclear warfare," Nava added with a weak smile.

Shit. What the fuck had Ron and R.J. *said*?

Peter squeezed his nape, anxiety roiling in his gut.

"I love you both, but quit stalling." Maria's gaze turned shrewd, and she paused. "Actually, never mind. I'll bet you a hundred euro I know exactly what they told you."

Suddenly, he knew too. It was the only thing that made sense, given who Ron and R.J. were, how they likely perceived women's bodies, what they'd believe about women's core vulnerabilities, and the means they'd accordingly employ to humble Maria.

Or, rather, *attempt* to humble her. Because even after six years, they hadn't diminished her or dimmed her shine. Not even a little.

"They don't think women with body hair are sexy or appealing to viewers, so they want me to shave or wax and reshoot the part of the scene where I'm naked." Maria outright laughed then, and the sound wasn't sharp or bitter, but genuinely amused. "Because clearly, a medieval Viking shield-maiden shipwrecked on a deserted island would make hair removal a priority."

"Well . . ." Ramón's mouth twitched in reluctant humor. "Here's the good news: I didn't take your bet just now."

There it was. Ron and R.J.'s final bid to cow Maria, and do so by telling her—Jesus, now that he'd taken a moment, it made him want to laugh too—she wasn't sexy enough. Their final bit of revenge for stymying their big starvation plans. Their final attempt to control her body.

During six years of working with her, had they learned nothing?

"Perhaps Cassia took a pre-sex jaunt over to her local day spa," Nava suggested, sarcasm limning every syllable.

"No doubt." Still grinning, Maria tapped her chin with a long forefinger. "If Cassia asked nicely, I bet Venus would Bedazzle her *snippa* too. I'm certain sequins would please viewers."

That Swedish word, he didn't know. But he had a really, really good guess.

After a quiet snicker, Nava sobered. "What do you want us to say to them?"

"You already know." Maria cast an apologetic glance at the producer and director. "They won't be happy, and I'm sorry you'll have to deal with that."

"As long as you're fine, we are too." Ramón didn't appear bothered by the prospect of the showrunners' ire. "We'll gladly tell them you refused their request."

Only it wasn't really a request. It was an order. They all knew it.

That said, Ron and R.J. didn't have much power over her at this point. In reality, Peter wasn't sure they'd *ever* had any power over her.

"If they want to fire me, locate a last-minute body double, transport her to a desolate Irish island, teach her the choreography, and reshoot a good chunk of a crucial scene with her, they can have at it." Maria tipped her head in faux-contemplation. "They're already running late and over budget, though, as usual, and this is the final scene in the entire show that involves me, so doing all that for a bit of anachronistic armpit waxing seems kind of self-defeating, doesn't it?"

It was just hair. It would regrow. Literally every other actor he'd met over the course of two decades in Hollywood would promptly break out a razor in this situation, and most of the women would be waxed smooth already, no instructions necessary. But Maria's body belonged to Maria and Maria alone.

The stakes were much lower than in their first season together, of course, but . . .

Peter cleared his throat. "If Pippi walks, I walk."

Ramón and Nava turned to him in unison. The warmth in their eyes flooded him from the chest outward. And Maria's smile—

Fuck, Maria's smile.

"Really?" A jar of *sill* suddenly appeared in her palm, and she brandished it an inch from his nose. "You're going to taint your lovely gesture of solidarity by calling me Pippi, asshole?"

He shifted uncomfortably, and not because of the herring. "We both know it's too late to fire us, so it's more an empty gesture than a lovely one."

Sure, the showrunners could still badmouth him, but he now had years of high-profile, critically respected, leading-man work on his résumé, as well as a handful of awards and many, many more fans than before. His career might not be bulletproof, but it could take a few hits.

He also suspected this little incident would be the least of Ron and R.J.'s worries once *Gates*'s disastrous final season aired. And when their reputation tanked, so would their influence in the industry, so the risk to Peter's own reputation was minimal.

Besides, when it came to a woman like Maria, a smart man kept his blue cupboard as pristine as possible.

"It's not empty to me, Peter," she said with sweet sincerity. "Thank you."

The tips of his ears were on fire, and he was pretty sure that feeling in his chest was indigestion, because heartburn sounded about right.

Ramón thumped both actors on their shoulders. "I'll go tell Ron and R.J. It may take them a while to swallow their egos and admit defeat, so keep warm and relax until we get back."

As he and Nava left, a faint line appeared between Maria's brows. "I hope this doesn't cost you any future roles."

Her jar of herring had disappeared . . . somewhere. Which was quite a trick, given what she was—or, more precisely, wasn't—wearing.

"I'll be fine." He waved that concern aside. "Speaking of future roles, what do you have lined up?"

As her good friend, he should have asked long ago. But he hadn't mustered the courage before now, because the knowledge would make their impending separation feel more real to him, their time together more finite.

Then again, she hadn't asked him either. Hmmm.

"I have a few offers and some possible auditions waiting for me back in LA." With her thumbnail, she scraped away a little spot from Jeanine's counter, eyes affixed to her task. "I'm still considering them and making up my mind about my next step."

Well, that was vague as hell, especially for the Baroness of Bluntness.

"I assume you're seeing your family soon. I know you miss them."

Hopefully the visit wouldn't stretch too long, because he'd intended to use their brief gap between projects, while they were both in LA, to woo her. He also wanted to show her the house he'd bought with his *Gates* earnings, since it was his pride and joy. The touchstone he used to reaffirm everything he'd achieved, as well as everything he'd left behind forever.

He could stay patient, though. He'd already waited years. And now that she'd be living in California, they had time to settle things between them.

She nodded. "Unless shooting runs long, I'm flying to Stockholm this weekend."

So soon. So goddamn *soon*.

Fuck patience. He wasn't ready to be parted from her. Not yet.

"Right." If he traveled to Sweden while she was visiting her family and spent a few days with her there, would she welcome his presence? Or consider it an intrusion?

"What about you?" she asked, finally looking up at him. "Do you have something lined up?"

"I'm in the same position as you, mostly." He lifted a shoulder. "I have a few minor jobs booked, but I haven't decided on my next big project. I figured that could wait until we finished filming."

She made a sort of noncommittal hum. "I see."

Her gaze was oddly watchful, and he couldn't quite read her expression.

Of course, he could just *ask*. "Maria, you seem—"

Just then, the door to the trailer opened once more. This time, without an angry thud.

"Turns out, they didn't have time to wallow in pettiness. They're too busy dealing with all the other shit that's going wrong." Nava didn't even make it fully inside the door before she began talking. "Maria, you're good to go. They're pissed, obviously, but there's not much they can do about it at the moment. Peter, we made the executive decision not to mention your willingness to walk away unless it proved necessary, and it didn't. Your name didn't come up at all, so you can relax too."

Maybe it made him a coward, but he couldn't help his small sigh of relief.

The curve of Maria's lips turned smugly triumphant, and she raised her hand for a high-five with Nava, then Ramón, which they returned with enthusiasm.

Then she leaned toward Peter and raised her hand again, but not for a high-five. To clasp his own hand palm-to-palm, their elbows bent, as if they were confirming a sacred vow with a ceremonial handshake.

"And that's how solidarity works, Peter." She winked at him. "Welcome to unfettered socialism, you utter *skitstövel*."

He snorted. And in perfect accord, they smiled at each other.

Peter's E-Mail

From: AlexanderTheGreatest@umail.com
To: PeterReedton@umail.com
Subject: Your monthly roundup of smutty RPF starring YOU!

To my favorite shipwrecked Viking dude, who has, ironically, inspired fervent shipping—

This month's treasure trove of Real-Person Fiction is especially rich in delicious smuttery. Probably because the end of the series is coming soon, so fans have realized their well of inspiration is about to run dry and are taking advantage of the bounty while it lasts. (However much credit you're giving me for not elaborating on the "running dry" metaphor, IT'S NOT ENOUGH.)

Some of this month's highlights: In the first link, you'll find that you and Maria end up sea-soaked and freezing after a scene filmed on the shore, and to warm yourselves quickly, you'll need to—what else?—strip and cuddle to share body heat. As one does with one's colleagues. And then you'll go to town on various hotel room surfaces, including those that would surely not withstand your "INTENSE VIKING LUST," not to mention your "DETERMINATION TO PILLAGE" (direct quotes). Neither one of you is tiny, and most coffee tables can't withstand that kind of abuse. That's just physics.

The second link is a story where you and Maria get caught in a freak snowstorm while scouting a location for a future scene. Whereupon you escape to a convenient nearby hut, and to warm yourselves quickly, you need to—stop me if I lose you here; it's very complicated—strip and cuddle to share body heat. In the most professional way possible. And then you'll defile various hut surfaces, including those that would definitely splinter under the force of your "DESPERATE, RE-PRESSED PASSION" and "FORCEFUL CLAIMING OF YOUR WOMAN

AT LAST" (direct quotes). I'm pretty sure all that rubbing up against stone walls won't be good for Maria's back. Just FYI.

The last link is my favorite for the month. It's a three-way between you and Maria and Dolphy McBlowholeface, and it takes place entirely underwater, because you and Maria are merpeople actors or something? It's a little unclear. Anyway, Ol' Dolphy gives you a finjob at one point, and apparently inspired by your oceangoing lover, you make whistling and trilling noises when you come. You're welcome!

Well, that's it for now. Links below the signature, as always.

Enjoy!
Alex

P.S. You realize I send these links to Maria too, right? At her request, once she heard I was sending them to you? Again, just FYI.

12

MARIA COULDN'T WAIT TO HAVE A FAKE ORGASM. MOSTLY because then she'd be able to get back to her hotel suite and give herself a real one. And also maybe cry a little.

For their final take of the day—of the episode, the season, the entire series—Ramón had asked Maria and Peter to simulate sex again. Specifically, he wanted to shoot the end of their characters' long-awaited lovemaking scene one final time, starting at the point when Peter would fuck her—

No, not Peter. Cyprian.

Cyprian would fuck *Cassia* into coming one more time before climaxing himself, and they would clutch one another, panting. A few breathless moments later, they'd make eye contact and slowly smile at each other with joy and relief and pleasure and love.

And then the roar of the undead would shake their little home, and they'd realize they were fucked, both literally and metaphorically. They'd part ways for the final time.

The end.

Before this week, she'd never simulated an orgasm before, but that hadn't been an issue. It was simple enough to act out, especially for the tenth time. Only she couldn't seem to get a handle on either her body or her emotions, despite the cameras, the crew, and her determination to keep both her desolation and her horniness to herself.

So she lay beneath Peter, legs wide open and wrapped around his hips, almost entirely naked. She watched him labor mightily above her, and the pillow between her thighs absorbed most—but not all; heaven help her, not all—of the power behind each thrust. But it didn't stop her belly from rubbing against his or prevent her stiff nipples from poking into his chest. It didn't do anything to protect her from the sweet savagery of his kiss, the possessive sweep of his tongue in her mouth as they gasped and moaned against each other's lips. It didn't stop his fingers from biting into her thigh as he shoved it higher, or his other hand from cupping her cheek with a tenderness that would break her heart if she wasn't careful.

He was slick with sweat, and so was she. Real sweat, not just glycerin.

His heart thundered against hers, his pupils had blown wide, and stripes of hot color painted his cheekbones. As they'd positioned for this take, as she'd spread her legs and welcomed him between them one final time, his nostrils had flared, and she was pretty sure he could smell how hot he'd made her. How wet.

Thongs could only absorb so much. And between takes, although he turned away and donned his robe immediately, the consummate professional as always, that cock sock couldn't entirely hide his body's response to what they were doing.

Not all her moans were fake. The tears in her eyes weren't fake either.

She blinked hard, and his brows furrowed a millimeter. In an unscripted movement, he tore his mouth from hers, slid kisses across her cheek to her ear, and murmured so quietly, it was more a vibration than an actual word. So quietly even the boom mic couldn't catch it.

He said her name.

Not Cassia. Maria.

It was comfort, and it was a question. He wanted to know if she was okay.

The answer was no.

But she extracted her nails from his shoulder, sank a fist into his hair, and dragged his mouth back to hers anyway, because this was it. This was their last scene, and she wanted to kiss him as long as she possibly could, because it might never happen again. Soon they might not see each other for weeks or months at a time. Years.

The rest of her life.

He kissed her back, but his lips against hers had turned gentle, too fucking gentle, and it was *intolerable*.

So she ended it. She panted and moaned and shuddered against him in feigned orgasm, and he followed her moments later.

They made eye contact. Her eyes were dry, because she was a fucking professional.

They smiled.

Nava made a weird squeaking attempt at a roar from just off camera—postproduction would fill in a much scarier sound—and Cassia and Cyprian jerked apart, threw on some clothing, said a few final lines, and prepared to face their futures.

Their separate futures.

"Cut," Ramón called, and they were done.

It was over.

Robes. Slippers. Thumps on the back and congratulations and cheering.

She grinned and laughed as she returned hugs, and it was the best acting of her life.

Finally, she managed to slip toward the door unnoticed . . . or so she thought.

A split second ago, she could have sworn Peter was standing across the room, chatting with Darrell, but somehow there he was. Right in front of her, clasping her upper arm in one big, warm hand, his hold careful but inescapable. Studying her face with sharp, intent brown eyes. Bending down, his mouth brushing her earlobe once more.

"I'll see you tonight, Maria," he said quietly, then released her arm and stalked back across the room.

It didn't sound like a casual comment. It sounded like a vow.

And suddenly, she didn't feel like crying anymore.

She could still use an orgasm, though. Now more than ever.

"YOU'RE FLYING OUT first thing in the morning, right?" Ramón sipped his wine. "Are you packed already?"

Her attention engaged elsewhere, Maria barely heard him.

Delia's more-than-professional interest in Peter had been evident from their first meeting in the production trailer. But because the other woman was, in fact, very attentive to power dynamics and issues of consent, she'd waited until the end of filming to make her move.

They'd shot their final take early that afternoon. And now their intimacy coordinator was doing her best to coordinate intimacy with Peter.

Since the moment he'd walked into the party, a cast-and-crew celebration of both their professional achievements and the family they'd created together on this island, Delia had been fluttering around him. Touching his shoulder. Laying a hand on his arm. Getting up on tiptoes to whisper into his—

Well, not his ear. She was too short for that. More like his collarbone.

"Maria?" Ramón prompted from somewhere nearby. "Are you ready for your flight tomorrow?"

Maria wasn't a jealous woman. Not even the discovery of her ex's other life in London, complete with a pregnant wife and a mortgage, had elicited that particular emotion. Grief, yes. Rage, most definitely. Hurt and bitterness, undoubtedly.

But not jealousy. Not ever, not once in her life. Until now.

It wasn't a comfortable emotion, as it turned out. In fact, it caused the same sort of feeling in her stomach that eating dulse for all those endless takes had, so long ago. But since she didn't have a vomit bucket handy, she supposed she'd have to swallow hard and endure.

And who could blame Delia for wanting Peter? Not Maria, certainly. She'd wanted him for over half a decade now. Having spent the last week surrounded by his woodsy scent, encased in his strong arms, spread open by his broad hands and thick thighs, and brought to the brink of madness by his talented mouth, she knew exactly why Delia was panting after him.

In fact, she should salute the woman for her excellent taste in men.

And good for him, really. It wasn't as if she'd remained sexless since their one night in bed together either, although she'd come closer to celibacy in recent years than she cared to admit. She couldn't, in all fairness, begrudge him a night—or even a lifetime—in Delia's arms. She *wouldn't*.

Sure, she'd thought maybe, after filming was done, they might finally—

But it didn't matter what she'd thought. It didn't matter what had prompted her to put off making definite commitments after the end of filming. It didn't even matter how close she was to losing her excellent dinner in a convenient potted plant.

If she could stop looking at the two of them, that would probably help her nausea.

"Sorry. I was trying to remember whether I'd already arranged for a cab from the ferry to the airport." Turning back to Ramón, she offered him a cheerful, self-deprecating smile. "As long as you don't consider whether I've packed a single item in my suitcases, I'm totally set to leave. How about you? Are you heading out tomorrow too?"

"Um . . . no." A small, happy smile creased his tanned cheeks. "Nava and I intend to stay for another two weeks after everyone else is gone. Then her daughter's coming to visit us here, and the three of us will knock around Ireland for a while."

Maria's mouth dropped open.

Fy fan. How in the world had she missed *that*?

Shaking her head in delighted shock, she hauled her director into a congratulatory hug. "You sly thing. I had no idea. None."

His smile widened into a grin. "Good. That was the goal."

Across the small dining room, Darrell traced a finger down Jeanine's exposed arm as the longtime couple sipped wine and chatted with Conor. Who, even as she watched, found himself wrapped in Fionn's embrace when the chef emerged from his kitchen and leaned against his husband from behind. And at the half-cleared table, their camera op and cinematographer were sitting remarkably close together, the two women whispering quietly and playing with each other's fingers.

Carefully, she kept Peter and Delia in her peripheral vision. No need to look directly at them again. Not even to confirm her newfound theory.

"Ramón." Perhaps it was a tad indelicate, but the question had to be asked. "Is literally everyone in this room fucking except for me?"

He barked out a startled laugh, expression lit by more open joy than she'd ever seen from him before. "We are a particularly incestuous bunch, now that I think about it."

Even as Ramón spoke, Darrell coaxed Jeanine into a shadowy corner, no doubt to do something Maria had not experienced in many, many endlessly horny months.

"You're not kidding," Maria muttered.

"I thought you and Peter . . . ?" Ramón trailed off, raising a meaningful brow.

She shook her head, and the director blinked at her in seeming shock.

"I heard you laughing, even from inside the suite." Nava appeared at his side, cuddling close as he wrapped his arm around her shoulders. "What's so funny, babe?"

"Your timing is impeccable, *mi cielo*, as always." His gaze tender, he ran a caressing hand over her short, spiky hair. "Maria and I were marveling at the number of relationships created among such a small crew. There's us, of course, but also—"

"Hold on." Peter's voice suddenly rumbled in Maria's ear, and the warmth of his big body behind hers nearly melted her spine. "You two are a couple? How did I not know this?"

"Ramón and Nava are masters of intrigue, evidently." When she turned her head, his mouth was so close to hers, a simple sway of her body would have them kissing. Which would, she reminded herself, be somewhat awkward, given his hookup-in-progress with Delia. "If it's any consolation, I had no idea either."

Any moment now, he'd back away from her. Any . . . moment . . . now.

He didn't, though. Not even a millimeter. And when his eyes dropped to meet hers, they were dark and hot.

Her throat was so dry, it hurt to swallow. "Where's Delia? Are you two about to head off for the night?"

"Uh, no." His frown crinkled the skin between his eyebrows.

"She went back to her inn a couple of minutes ago. Didn't she say goodbye to you before she left?"

When she shook her head, he edged even closer to her. So close, his belly brushed against her back, and her breath hitched. Just a little. Not enough for him to notice, hopefully.

"It's a shame she had to cut her night short." According to the English idiom, she believed her pants should currently be afire. "Will you see her again before her flight home?"

The crinkles deepened. "No. Why would I?"

Wow, her stomach felt better. *Remarkably* better.

"Well." Ramón cleared his throat loudly and waited until they turned toward him. "Now that you've confirmed Delia's whereabouts, Nava and I wanted to thank both of you for making our set such a warm, supportive place all these years."

Peter's scoffing noise vibrated deliciously near her earlobe. "You two were the ones in charge. Thank yourselves."

She twisted to face him again, grinning. "That's what I was going to say."

"And if the two of us agree on something, it must be right." His fond smile made her stomach swoop, but that was still preferable to nausea. By far.

"Exactly," she said with a decisive nod.

His warm, calloused hand patted her shoulder in mute affirmation, and then it simply . . . stayed. Lingered. Cupped that curve of muscle and gently kneaded, his thumb brushing the nape of her neck.

This was—different. Peter usually avoided physical contact with her off camera, other than occasional high-fives.

She definitely wasn't complaining.

This time, Nava cleared her throat. Twice.

When Peter and Maria looked her way once more, she bit her lip for a moment before continuing. "Anyway. As Ramón was saying, we owe you a debt of gratitude. We may have theoretically been in charge, but you two set the tone. We couldn't have asked for better actors, but more importantly, we couldn't have asked for better people as our colleagues and friends."

Shit, Maria was going to miss everyone from the island. Mourn their absence like family.

"Aww, Nava." Maria flung her arms around her friend and held on tight. "I'm honored. And if Ramón ever misbehaves, let me know. I stole Cassia's ax from the set earlier today, so I can easily exact blood-soaked vengeance on your behalf."

"I'm going to miss you, you thieving, murderous bitch," Nava whispered against her shoulder, voice choked. "Please stay in touch."

"Takes one to know one, as Americans like to say. I saw you sneaking off with Cassia's hero sword." Maria swayed her from side to side. "And if you think you can shake me loose at this point, you're terribly mistaken."

"Hey. I want in on this action." Ramón sounded a bit hoarse himself. "The hugging action, not the thieving action, just to be clear."

Then he gathered both women close, Peter joined the huddle, and they were all sniffling a bit. Even Peter, although he kept tilting his face up to the ceiling and blinking hard.

"P-Peter took those torn-up leather pants of his." Maria's nose was starting to run, and she discreetly blotted it against his button-down. "They're essentially chaps at this point. I can only assume he's joining a troupe of male strippers."

"Snitches get stitches, Pippi." It was a pained grunt from her neck, where he'd buried his face at some point.

Again: not complaining.

Nava huffed out a laugh. "Ramón took a rock from the original wall you two built. It's shaped like a heart, because he's secretly sentimental as hell."

"Untrue. I have a soul of flint, stony and cold," he protested.

"You have a soul of marshmallow fluff." After one final, breath-stealing hug, Nava let go and directed a watery grin at Maria. "I'm pretty sure he's going to make everyone a scrapbook commemorating our years on this island. A mixtape too. He'll force you to listen to it while he watches your reaction on FaceTime, and when Green Day's 'Time of Your Life' starts playing, he'll sob into a pillow."

Maria shook her head. "Old people."

After she planted a kiss on Ramón's cheek, she somehow found herself in Peter's embrace again. He hugged her from behind, one arm circling her upper chest, the other her belly, while he pressed up tight against her back.

"Um, I think . . ." Lips twitching, Nava glanced at Ramón, who responded with an odd sort of snorty sound. "We should . . . go. But please make sure to say goodbye before you head for the ferry tomorrow morning. Doesn't matter how early it is."

If Peter's increasingly hard dick weren't pressing against her upper ass, Maria figured she'd be fighting tears again. But it was, which made focusing on her sincere grief remarkably difficult.

Still, she blew her dear friend a kiss. "Will do."

Then she and Peter were finally alone, and he snatched her hand and tugged her into the hall, just out of sight of the rest of the party.

His broad palm cupped the back of her skull as her shoulders hit the wall. Before her next gasped breath, his thigh pushed between hers, his free hand gripped her hip, and he'd ducked his head to whisper directly in her ear.

"It's been six years. I can't wait any longer." His lips were soft, his breath hot. "Maria, if you want me even a little, let me take you to bed tonight. Please."

She could ride that thick thigh. Grind against him until she came. It wouldn't take long, not after the way he'd pushed her against the wall. Surrounded her. Claimed her with sure, hard hands. But she had to think first. *Think.*

Sex. He was asking for sex. Not a commitment. Not a romantic relationship.

And foolishly, she was going to say yes, because she wanted him too, and not just a little. Even though it was probably a mistake— and it would definitely blur that strict line she'd maintained for so long, that stalwart barrier separating quick fucks from lovers who could offer the sort of future she needed. Not that she'd come across any of the latter for some time now.

Sex with Peter wouldn't be a quick fuck, and it couldn't truly be casual for her, not after so many years of close friendship. Their connection had long ago encompassed much more than physical desire. With the exception of her family members, she trusted him more than any man on the planet.

With her body, anyway. Her devoted friendship too.

Her heart . . .

Well, that remained to be seen, didn't it?

Maybe he could offer her what she needed in a relationship, and maybe he couldn't. Maybe he didn't even *want* a romantic relationship with her.

But she would give him the chance to show her, starting tonight. Right now.

"Maria." His mouth was a line of fire down her neck, and she lit like tinder. Her chin tipped back as she sagged against the wall, against his hold, her head swimming with each swirl of his tongue. "Say yes. Tell me I can have you."

There was only one possible answer, but—

"I still have to pack, and the ferry leaves before dawn." Embarrassingly, she was breathless, almost panting. "We won't have much time."

His sudden laugh tickled her collarbone. "It won't take much time. Not for me, anyway."

"Is that . . ." Gods above, she couldn't think with his mouth on her. Gently, she pushed him a few millimeters away and blinked up at him. "Is that supposed to convince me to say yes? Because if so, I have unfortunate news for you."

"Maria. Sweetheart." His eyes on her were heavy-lidded. Intent. Determined. "Do you really think I'd leave you wanting?"

His hand slipped beneath the hem of her dress, and a trail of bone-melting heat followed his fingers as he slowly stroked up her thigh. Her lips parted as he cupped her pussy and squeezed lightly.

"I'll make you come a dozen times before I slide inside you the first time." It was a murmur, filthy and low. "Our second round, you'll come on my cock."

She believed him. What Peter promised, Peter delivered. Pleasure would be no exception.

And unless he planned to deliver that first orgasm in the hallway, they needed to move.

"Our colleagues are just around the corner," she whispered, eyes closing as he pressed the heel of his hand against her clitoris and rubbed slowly. "I don't care, but . . ."

He lightly scraped his teeth along the ridge of her shoulder, and she arched and squirmed closer to that relentless, careful hand. "Ask me if I give a fuck."

She had to laugh. "I'm certainly hoping you'll give *me* a—"

But before she could even finish her sentence, an earsplitting shriek erupted from the dining room—was that Jeanine?—and

Peter jumped violently and raised his head so quickly, it rammed into Maria's chin.

"*Skit!*" Instinctively, she jerked away from him and clapped a protective hand over the now-throbbing bottom of her face as she gingerly checked for a chipped tooth or other damage.

A bit of blood from a nipped tongue. Nothing serious.

But the moment was gone. Hopefully not for good, but . . .

Fy fan!

13

"WHAT? WHAT DID YOU SAY?" JEANINE SHRIEKED AGAIN, before Maria's ears had even stopped ringing from the first screech.

"Fuck, sweetheart, I'm so sorry." Peter cupped Maria's face tenderly, eyes roving her features to check for damage. "Are you okay?"

Not entirely, no. She was still pretty damned turned on, and her chin and tongue hurt. But those were minor issues, especially compared to whatever had caused their hair and makeup artist to screech like a banshee getting waxed for the first time.

Maria might not know how that felt from personal experience, but she'd seen *The 40-Year-Old Virgin*. She could extrapolate.

"I'm fine, but I don't know if Jeanine is," she said, tugging Peter away from the wall.

When they rounded the corner and reentered the dining room to find out what had happened, Jeanine was still standing beside Darrell, eyes wild, jaw agape.

She was also still shrieking, hands flung wide as she stared at him. "You're *forty-fucking-nine*? How the fuck is that *possible*? You don't even use *moisturizer*, for fuck's sake!"

"Well—" he began tentatively.

"Are you sacrificing *goats*? Or bathing in the blood of fucking *virgins*?"

"Contradiction in terms," Peter muttered, brow creased as he studied the other couple.

Maria nodded. "And good luck finding a virgin around here."

Jeanine clutched a fistful of Darrell's sweater and shook him a little. "And you let me think you were in your twenties *all this time*?"

"Are you . . . are you angry at me?" He was looking anxious now. "I never actually said I was in my twenties, honey, but I'm so sorry if—"

"Angry?" Jeanine pursed her lips. "*Angry* isn't the word for how I feel."

Oh, no. Poor, poor Darrell. Frankly, Maria had expected better of Jeanine than such flagrant hypocrisy.

The big, muscular PA seemed to be shrinking moment by moment, hunching in on himself in worry and the beginnings of grief. "Wh-what *is* the word for it, then?"

"Flabbergasted. Confused." Jeanine's hands flattened on his chest. Stroked a little. "*Impressed.*"

Apparently it was Darrell's turn to imitate a stunned cod.

Then Jeanine dropped to one knee, and everyone in the room gasped.

"Darrell Watkins, you are the only man who's ever beaten me at my own game." She took his hands in hers. "I loved you when I thought you were in your twenties, and I love you even more now that I know you're a geezer."

Oh, thank goodness. They didn't have to watch Darrell get his heart broken after all. In fact, a slow, beaming smile was creeping across that bafflingly youthful face of his.

"You're still older than me, Neens," he noted fondly. "If I'm a geezer, you've got one foot in the grave and the other on a banana peel."

Her eyes rolled to the ceiling. "Shut it, gramps. I'm trying to propose."

More gasps. At the table, Ramón snatched up a napkin to blot his tears as Nava patted his back and directed a satisfied look Maria's way. *Told you*, she mouthed. *Marshmallow fluff.*

I believed you, Maria mouthed back.

Darrell was grinning down at Jeanine now, his eyes wet. "I apologize for the interruption, my beautiful Cryptkeeper. Please proceed."

"Will you marry me?" asked Jeanine. "Keep in mind that whatever Paul Rudd shit you have happening right now might not last forever, and I'm a goddamn catch at any age."

He didn't hesitate, not even for a moment.

"Yes. *Yes.*" Dropping to his own knees, he hauled her into his arms and planted a very passionate kiss on his brand-new fiancée. When he came up for air a long, long while later, he added breathlessly, "I love you so damn much, honey."

More tongue-intensive kissing followed that declaration, accompanied by enthusiastic applause and a few wolf whistles from the other partygoers. Then came several champagne toasts to the happy couple and a sort of reception line to wish them well, and everyone ahead of Peter and Maria seemed to be in an extremely chatty mood.

It was all lovely, of course, and Maria wouldn't have wanted to miss such a special moment. But by the time she was ready to leave the party again, her phone told her she now had less than five hours to pack and snatch a nap before heading to the airport.

Fuck.

Or, rather, no fuck.

"Peter . . ." Outside her suite, she turned to face him, smiling ruefully. "I'm so sorry, but—"

"It's too late. I know." He dragged a hand through his hair, mouth pressed tight. "My flight to LA is later in the day, but you're leaving first thing in the morning, and you need time to prepare."

"I do." Reaching up, she tried to smooth the deep line between his brows with a fingertip. "I wish I didn't."

The line went nowhere. "It's okay."

Despite the frustration roughening his voice, his hold couldn't have been gentler when he captured her finger and pressed a kiss on the sensitive pad. Then he gathered her into his arms, surrounding her with warmth and cedar and comfort. One broad hand rubbed slow circles on her back, while the other sifted tenderly through her hair.

It was stupid. So stupid. In all likelihood, she'd be seeing him soon in LA, unless she decided to stay in Sweden for good once she went home. And they'd definitely have another chance at a rendezvous at the next press junket or convention, no matter where she chose to live.

Still, her eyes prickled with foolish tears, and she buried her face in his neck and clutched his back, unable to muster her usual breezy cheeriness.

When his phone dinged, he ignored it. When it dinged a second time, though, he sighed and dropped his hand from her back to dig his cell out of his pocket. Only to glance at its screen for what felt like a millisecond before grunting and shoving the phone back where it came from.

That expression on his face . . . she couldn't parse the mixture of emotions there.

Asking would be nosy. She knew it. She also didn't care.

"Who was that?" She laid her palm on his shoulder and rested her cheek there. "Your agent?"

It took him a long time to answer, but she was willing to wait.

"My father," he finally said.

Oh. Well, that made sense, although she'd never gotten the impression he and his dad were close. Largely because Peter never talked about him. At all.

She made her best guess. "He's checking when your flight leaves tomorrow?"

"No. He doesn't know my filming schedule." Another long pause. "Sometimes he sends everyone in his running club photos from his latest race. I don't know why I'm in his text group, but I am, so I get the pics too. Apparently he ran a half-marathon earlier today."

Only one thing could cure an acute attack of nosiness, in her experience: finding out absolutely everything she could. "Can I see?"

Without another word, he produced his phone once more, tapped the screen a few times, and handed it to her. Keeping one arm around his waist, she took a minute to study the two photos he'd received.

In the first, a small group of older men smiled for a posed shot, all wearing pristine jerseys with the same logo. Members of the running club, she presumed, commemorating the moments before their race. The second photo was an individual shot, taken as a sweat-soaked, flushed man in his late sixties or early seventies crossed the finish line.

Flipping back to the previous photo, she found that same man. Who was, presumably, Peter's father, although that seemed rather improbable at first glance.

Slim and lean-muscled, like most natural endurance athletes, he didn't appear overly tall. In fact, he was the shortest of his group. When he stood next to his son, Peter would likely loom over him: taller, broader, more imposing. Softer around the edges.

Larger than life. Stronger than hell.

Peter took after his mother in coloring too, because Daniel was a watercolor next to his son's oil painting. His hair—pin-straight, sandy blond where it wasn't gray—lay neatly trimmed above his collar and around the ears, instead of falling in wild espresso waves to the shoulders. His pale blue eyes peered at the camera with a sort of vague amiability, rather than shining sharp with ferocious intent, near-black irises snapping with wariness.

Ample time spent outdoors had burnished both men, turning their skin golden. That was about all they had in common as far as appearances, at least upon initial examination.

An exploration of their other commonalities and differences would have to wait for another day, when she had plenty of time to devote to the task. Because Peter's past didn't seem to be an easy subject for him.

The same could be said of her, she supposed. Other than her parents and siblings, she could count on one hand the people who knew the complete history of her early childhood.

Someday, both of them might have to share more of themselves. But not now.

"Are you certain you two aren't twins?" After handing back the phone, she patted his chest. "Because you look so much alike."

The growing tension in his body dissolved in an instant, and he laughed as he tucked away his cell a second time. "If I had a dollar for every time I heard that—"

"You'd have a dollar?" Arms wrapped around him once more, she snuggled close.

"Exactly." Something soft brushed the crown of her head, and he spoke against her hair. "Maria, I have an audition in two days. But after that, if you wanted . . ."

When he trailed off, she waited a few seconds before giving him a verbal nudge. "If I wanted . . . what?"

His body subtly tensed against hers. "I could visit you and your family in Sweden. If you'd like that. If not, it's okay."

Her heart gave a happy little thump.

In her experience, people generally didn't offer to book transatlantic flights for a night or two of casual sex. And even if they did, they *definitely* didn't volunteer to meet their short-term hookup's family.

It wasn't everything she needed. But it was a start.

"Of course I'd like that, you *knäppgök*." The prickle in her sinuses had entirely disappeared, and she lifted her head from his shoulder to smile up at him. "The extra bedroom is small, but it's yours if you want it. Or there's a nice hotel not too far from our home, if you'd rather have more priva—"

Both their pockets dinged at the exact same moment.

Peter groaned. "Again?"

"If it's any consolation, I doubt it's your father this time." She paused. "Unless he hacked into your phone and got my number too. If so, I welcome further updates on his running club."

"A toddler is likelier to hack my phone than my father," he said dryly.

Without further ado, they unearthed their cells and checked the displays.

"Ron and R.J." Peter groaned again. "Holy fuck, what now?"

She didn't want to look. Hadn't she suffered enough already? "I swear, Peter, if this is another critique of my body and its attractiveness to young male viewers, I'm going to sit beside one of the showrunners at each and every damn panel and awards show, wear sleeveless dresses, and keep my arms raised the entire time, just to fuck with them."

After he scrolled through their message for a few seconds, Peter's scowl faded. "Hold on, Pippi. No need to consult Sun Tzu's *The Art of Armpit War* just yet."

Well, now she was curious again. Curious enough to threaten him with pickled herring for only a couple of pointed shakes before she put the jar away and read the message herself.

"They . . ." She skimmed their missive, then started back at the beginning. "They want us to do a last-minute press junket together? Starting in LA, with more stops to be determined?"

"Apparently." His shoulder hitched in a careless shrug, but the smile creasing his bearded cheeks belied his feigned nonchalance. "In theory, because we're the only main cast members who've already finished filming, which is true. Although that doesn't really explain the urgent need for good publicity in the first place, does it?"

"Hmmm." She drummed her fingers against her chin, cultivating a thoughtful air as she bit back her own smile. "It's all very mysterious, Peter."

"I'm sure it doesn't have anything to do with those leaked scripts."

"Those *terrible* leaked scripts," she corrected primly.

He countered, "Those terrible and *genuine* leaked scripts."

She acknowledged that point with a raised forefinger. "And our sudden press junket is definitely unrelated to how they're already getting reamed online by fans before the final season even finishes filming."

"They certainly wouldn't dispatch two of their more popular actors to combat nasty internet rumors." He offered her a smirk. "Especially since they've never acknowledged the popularity of one of those actors, because they're petty little assholes."

She nearly choked on thin air. "Peter! How much wine did you have tonight?"

In all their years together, he'd never consumed alcohol. But he'd also never criticized the showrunners so openly. Not once.

"None." He raised his brows. "I'm drunk on power. Power and freedom."

Ah. Now she understood. "They need you. More than you need them, at least for now."

"That's part of it." He inclined his head, his smile fading. "But not everything."

"What's the rest?"

His knuckles lightly stroked the curve of her cheek, leaving heat in their wake. "I'm finally free to be with you, Maria. After six years."

They weren't touching anywhere else, and it didn't matter. Gods above, those strong, careful hands could persuade her into any amount of foolishness. Part of her must have understood that since their first night together.

No wonder she'd run.

But if she now intended to let him catch her, if she wanted him to see her for who she truly was, if she was willing to risk being a fool and breaking her own heart . . . yes. He definitely needed to come to Sweden and meet her family, and it was past time she knew more about his too.

In fact, she had a brilliant way to make that happen.

When she edged back a half step from him, his brows drew together. Holding up a finger in a mute request for his patience, she bent her head over her cell, typed out a reply to Ron and R.J.'s message, and tapped *send*.

Peter's phone immediately dinged.

"What did you—" He paused, forehead still furrowed. "Oh."

She beamed up at him. "Smart, yes?"

"Yeah." Another pause, this one lengthier. His gaze firmly affixed to his cell, he didn't look up as he spoke. "Maria, I don't think Ron and R.J. will pay for us to visit each other's hometowns as part of the press junket, even if we shoot some footage for a bonus feature while we're there. And while I'm happy to see Sweden, I'm not sure a trip to Wisconsin—"

For the second time in ten minutes, both their phones dinged.

With a sigh, Peter abandoned whatever he'd planned to say.

Reading the newest message from their showrunners didn't take long. Apparently Ron and R.J. wanted to get the matter settled quickly. They were even desperate enough for good publicity to take a suggestion from her. Kind of.

"So we'll apparently be going to Sweden and Wisconsin after our stint in LA," she said, smug satisfaction suffusing every syllable. "To film a bonus feature and do more press interviews."

Slowly, his brow smoothed. "Which they claim was their intent all along, even though they only specified LA in the original message."

"Complete coincidence, I'm sure," she said.

He gave a little snort of amusement, then simply . . . looked at her.

The moment stretched like elastic, taut enough to snap.

"Earlier tonight, I wasn't sure when I'd see you again. But now we're being asked—*ordered*—to spend at least two weeks in each other's company. Day and night." He stepped into her, crowding her against the door to her suite. With the pad of his thumb, he traced the swell of her lower lip, the soft sweep of her jaw. "In LA, we're sharing the same hotel suite. Did you see that?"

He didn't seem to expect an answer, which was good. She couldn't manage to locate words. Not in English, not in Swedish. Not while his dark eyes consumed her, intent and hot, and his hands gently but relentlessly skimmed over her flesh and set it afire.

"I've been fantasizing for years." A caressing fingertip brushed the sensitive edge of her ear, and she had to lean against the solid support of the door to remain standing. "I hope you're ready."

That sounded like a challenge.

And as always, she would fight to win.

"What do you want, Peter?" Deliberately, she surveyed him from crown to toes, her gaze lingering between his legs until his dick pushed insistently against the placket of his jeans, visibly swelling under her attention. "Tell me. In detail."

He waited until she met his eyes again, and then slowly, slowly gathered her hair and wound it around his fist. A light tug, and a bolt of heat raced down her spine and between her trembling legs.

"I want my hands on you. My name on your lips, my tongue on your clit. My cock planted deep in your pussy as you come hard enough to cry." His lips curved, and it wasn't a kind expression. It was the hard smile of a Viking. A conqueror ready to pillage. "I want all of you. You have no idea how fucking much."

Over the years, she'd suspected he wanted her in his bed again. Especially since their one night together had lingered in her memory, her dreams, and her fantasies for a long, long time now, and she'd figured it had to be the same for him.

Sex that good demanded a replay. If not physically, then mentally.

The apparent ferocity of his desire still shocked her.

He was right. She hadn't realized, couldn't have conceived of him or any man wanting her that much and restraining himself that tightly for so long. His will must be . . . implacable.

Fy fan, even the thought of it made her thighs squeeze together.

"You going to let me show you, Maria?" His dark eyes studied her as he gently pulled her hair, tugging until she moaned. With pleasure, not pain, because he was so careful with her. So very,

very careful. "When you come back to LA, back to me, will you let me touch you whenever I want, however I want?"

Her response required every ounce of her faltering concentration, but she refused to surrender too much ground on such a key battlefield.

With the lightest press of her fingertips, she glided over the length of his jeans-covered erection, and he went very still. When he finally dragged air into his oxygen-starved lungs, his sharp, shaky inhalation sounded painful.

He smelled delectable, like cedar and skin damp with heat. If she licked his neck, the salt would sting her bitten tongue.

When they reached that LA hotel suite, she intended to devour him.

"The next time I see you, you can touch me however and whenever you want. As much as you want." Slowly, she smiled. "But only if I can do the same."

His fist in her hair was still so careful. So controlled. But with his free hand, he gripped the doorframe with white knuckles, clenching it so hard she wondered whether he'd rip off the wood.

Her ponytail might be wrapped around his hand. He might be looming over her, face hard with lust. But she had him precisely how she wanted him: stone-jawed, desire a hectic flush across his cheekbones, pulse throbbing hard at the base of his neck.

Desperate with need. For her.

Sadly, however, she didn't have time to oversee hotel renovations necessitated by thwarted lust, so this delicious encounter needed to end.

"That said," she added, "if you tickle me, I'll force-feed you salty licorice until you puke. Don't test me, *skitstövel*. All those long, dark Swedish winters have made me cold and ruthless."

The tension abruptly broke, as she'd intended.

He freed her hair and gathered her into his arms with a hoarse laugh. "I thought you Swedes were all about—what's that word again? Hygge?"

"That's mostly the Danes and Norwegians." She raised a brow. "But if you want to experience Scandinavian coziness, I can certainly accommodate that."

He eyed her suspiciously. "How?"

"After you vomit, I'll wrap you in a blanket." Her tone was dry enough to desiccate the entire rain-soaked island. "I imagine that would feel quite cozy."

His chin dropped to her shoulder as he laughed again, and he squeezed her in a fierce embrace. "You're mean as hell, and you'll be back in LA in two weeks. I refuse to miss you, Ivarsson."

Her hands slid down his back and over his gorgeous butt, and his cock twitched against her belly. "I won't miss you even harder."

Speaking of hard things, she should let him and his erection go. Any time now. Although, to be fair, he wasn't moving away either. And she had the definite feeling that when she finally said her farewells to Peter, she wouldn't feel like laughing anymore.

"We should seal our not-missing-each-other pact with a kiss." He raised his head and scratched his beard in contemplation. "That's the Swedish custom, correct?"

"Our daily lives revolve around the metric system, Speedos, and affirming how little we'll miss one another by kissing." Loftily, she clarified, "*French* kissing, obviously."

He almost managed to stifle his snort. "Because you're European."

"Because we're European."

"Well, then." His eyes flared with heat once more. "Consider me the newest member of the EU."

Then his mouth claimed hers, and she lost track of time. Frankly, she lost track of everything but Peter. In the end, she ran so late, he had to help her pack, and she made the ferry with only seconds to spare. There was no time for even a hurried final embrace on the dock.

But as long as she could see the horizon, there he was. Immovable. Patient in ways she was only beginning to understand. Watchful.

Waiting.

Rating: Explicit

Fandoms: Gods of the Gates – E. Wade, Gods of the Gates (TV)

Relationships: Cassia/Cyprian

Additional Tags: <u>Alternate Universe – Modern</u>, <u>Explicit Sexual</u> <u>Content</u>, <u>Fluff and Smut</u>, <u>Yes I'm Equating Fan Bros with the Evil</u> <u>Undead from Tartarus</u>, <u>and I'm not sorry</u>, <u>that said what do I</u> <u>know about apps or startups or gaming for that matter</u>, <u>nada</u>, <u>no</u> <u>research just vibes</u>, <u>this slow burn ENDS HERE AND NOW</u>

Stats: Words: 12733 Chapters: 1/1 Comments: 101 Kudos: 513 Bookmarks: 75

Floor 39
SlowBurned

Summary:

When Cassia arrives as the newest intern at God of the Sky Games, she thinks she'll be asked to fetch coffee for Jupiter, do some coding, or maybe create spreadsheets. She doesn't expect to be tasked with defending the company's newest project against angry fan bros. She doesn't expect to be marooned on floor 39 with her obnoxious fellow intern, Cyprian. And she certainly doesn't expect to have sex with Cyprian on a pile of branded koozies, but she has to admit: It's way better than data entry.

Notes:

Don't worry. No branded merch from a failed startup was harmed in the making of this fic.

———————————————

At eight o'clock sharp, my boyfriend Erik and I arrive at God of the Sky Games' main office, eager to get our first assignment as the company's newest interns. Within minutes, though, it's clear a mistake has been made, and Jupiter—the boss man himself, who frankly seems like a real dick—only wants one of us. Not two.

He turns to the burly bearded guy at the corner computer. The one who hasn't said a word to anyone, although I could swear I've felt his dark eyes on me at least once.

"Which one, lowly intern?" Jupiter smirks. "Which one will you save?"

Apparently Burly Beardo is an intern too, but for some reason he's deciding which one of us has a professional future. My guess is that Jupiter wants to fuck with his head and force a powerless underling to hurt someone, because the CEO seems like that kind of guy.

"Her," Burly Beardo says curtly, then turns back to his monitor.

I was offered another internship, though, at a rival company, and Erik wasn't. He should stay, not me.

"But—" I begin.

"Her," he repeats without letting me finish or even looking up, because evidently he too is a dick. And that's that.

Erik is escorted from the premises immediately, red-faced and eyeing me angrily, even though I had nothing to do with the decision. Great.

And then the hammer drops. Again.

"Cyprian, you and—" Jupiter looks to his long-suffering administrative assistant, who mouths *Cassie*. Which isn't right, but close enough. "—Lassie will monitor the online response to our newest project, *The Island*. You're our first line of defense against fans angry that their favorite movie hero is a woman in our game."

He pauses, looking pained. "I don't blame them. But it was the only way Juno would forgive me."

What does the company's CFO have to do with anything? Is she the woman who looks like she's trying to set fire to Jupiter using only the power of her mind?

"Anyway," Jupiter continues, "you're assigned to Floor 39."

Countless gasps echo around the room, and I hear mutterings. I can only make out a few words. *Failed startup headquarters. Abandoned. Ghost floor.*

"They won't survive it," a guy with an ironic mustache mutters under his breath.

Jupiter's voice booms, full of arrogant command. "You'll work there. Eat there. Sleep there. Until we know the game is safe, you won't leave that floor. Starting . . . now."

He gestures imperiously toward the door.

The order is draconian and definitely against OSHA regulations, but . . . gaming is a cutthroat industry, and it's dominated by men. If I leave now, word will spread, and no one will want to hire me.

Not tough enough, they'll say. *Didn't have the balls.*

So I gather my purse, take the laptop the administrative assistant offers me, and head for the door, followed silently by a brooding Cyprian, who's carrying his own laptop.

We're taken up in an elevator to Floor 39, where a set of smoked-glass doors awaits us, leading to darkened offices. Taped to the glass is a yellowed paper with curled edges reading, inexplicably, *Elephant Time!*

The doors are unlocked for us with a rusted key. Beyond them is . . . darkness. Abandoned desks and cubicles. Half-seen doors vanishing into shadows.

Is that . . . a cotton candy machine? I guess we'll find out shortly.

Once we walk inside, those glass doors shut behind us, and the lock turns.

"So . . ." I flick on the lights, then turn to Burly Beardo. "I'm Cassia. You're Cyprian?"

He merely grunts and walks away, because of course he does.

Man, what a dick.

14

WITH A SLY GRIN, THE ENTERTAINMENT REPORTER LEANED forward in her chair. "As all your fans know, you two are close friends as well as castmates. Those fans have posted popular compilations of your joint interviews on YouTube and created Twitter gifs from moments when you've stared adoringly at one another. Not just on the show, but in real life too. You've even been given a couple name: Marter, a combination of Maria and Peter."

Ah, the lead-up to one of many inevitable press-junket questions. Peter knew it well.

Any moment now, the reporter would stop tap-dancing around the topic and just ask outright: *Have you two ever dated?*

It was a classic interview question, along with a few others: What did they admire most about each other? Would they enjoy working together again? What was it like filming for so long in such an isolated place? Did they plan to return to the island at some point? What were their favorite Cassia-Cyprian moments?

At this point, they had stock answers for almost every possible query. The tricky part was keeping those answers sounding fresh and off-the-cuff, instead of prepackaged and tired.

Maria, unsurprisingly, was better at that than he was. He'd improved over time, though. And they'd both become experts in the fine art of entertaining themselves during interviews with re-lentless banter and over-the-top bickering.

Reporters might not get answers to all their questions, but they got good sound-bites. Not to mention lots and lots of visitors to their various social media channels, because people fucking loved Peter and Maria's joint interviews.

He kind of loved them too, though he'd never admit it. Just like he'd never admit to watching them on YouTube during lengthier breaks in filming, when they'd been apart so long he literally ached to see her face and hear her voice.

She caught his eye and raised a brow, silently asking whether he wanted to handle the dating question. Subtly, he tilted his head toward her in answer, and she returned her attention to the interviewer. Expression calm, she took a swig from her water bottle and wiggled her phenomenal ass in a futile attempt to find a more comfortable position on the too-hard hotel love seat. Still stiff from her long flight, no doubt.

Each time she wiggled—and she'd done it a lot; like, *a lot*—her soft, warm thigh rubbed against his. Her soft, warm, mostly *bare* thigh, since she'd chosen to wear a very short, swingy dress that day, in what he could only assume was a deliberate effort to demolish his faltering sanity.

She'd donned that dress after rushing into their hotel suite and showering that morning, all while shouting from behind the bathroom door about a late plane and heavy traffic. The hair and makeup artist and the rest of the crew had arrived while she was still drying off, so there'd been no chance to even kiss before the first reporter arrived, much less fuck.

Her flight was originally scheduled to arrive late last night, and he'd had plans for her. Very detailed, very naked plans. None of which had come to fruition, clearly. So he'd already been stewing in stymied lust and frustration, and then—

Jesus H. Christ.

Wiggle. Wiggle. Wigglewigglewiggle.

Her dress slowly crept higher, revealing more of her pale, dimpled flesh, and he wanted to tear out his hair.

Holy shit, she needed to *stop fucking wiggling*.

All that squirming, and now he couldn't find a comfortable position anywhere on their little couch either. Would it be too obvious if he tugged a cushion over his crotch?

Yeah. Probably.

Good thing the camera had been positioned to film them from the waist up, because the two of them were quite a pair. At this point, the camera op could probably see Paris, France, and Maria's underpants, and Peter might as well be headlining an ad campaign for Bulges "R" Us. Smothering a wince, he shifted in his seat, strategically placed his clasped hands over his lap, and hoped like hell his jeans placket was up to its stern task.

A split second after he fidgeted, the corner of her wide, gloss-slick mouth twitched, and he suddenly knew.

She was doing it on purpose.

That gorgeous, amazing, diabolical Swedish bitch.

"Which brings me to my next question, and it's one all our viewers are curious about." The reporter's gaze flicked from him to Maria and back again. "Have you two ever dated?"

It wasn't the reporter's fault, really. Her viewers most likely *were* curious. But so were the viewers and readers of every other media outlet that covered *Gods of the Gates*, so he and Maria had been answering the same question every ten to fifteen minutes for several hours and counting.

Actually, to be accurate, they'd been answering that question for years now. Their response never varied, and—at least for the time being—it was entirely honest.

They'd fucked, yes. They'd never dated.

"We haven't," Maria told the reporter with an easy, bright smile. "But as you said, we've been the best of friends for a long time. Peter is very dear to me."

As he knew from long experience, this was the part of the interview fans would dissect the most avidly. They'd post screenshots of her face and his, claiming they'd caught a revealing microexpression in response to the question. They'd point out the exact moment in the clip when one member of their OTP inadvertently displayed their true feelings for the other and whip up some celebratory gifs. Then they'd write some very creative and extremely filthy fanfic about what he and Maria did immediately after the interview ended.

Namely, each other.

"Although," Maria added, fingertip lightly tapping her chin, "can you truly be dear friends with someone you've basically carried for five entire seasons of a blockbuster television show? Sometimes I wonder."

Minx.

"I assume you mean *physically* carried, because as far as acting . . ." Hiking a thumb in Maria's direction, he grimaced at the interviewer and mouthed *delusional*.

Oh, she was going to pay for that insult to his considerable acting prowess. Sooner rather than later.

The reporter chuckled. "Have you ever visited her in Sweden, Peter? Maybe watched one of her theater productions during your off-season?"

"I haven't, unfortunately." As he settled back against the tufted love seat cushions, his elbow nudged Maria's ribs, in the exact spot where he'd discovered she was most ticklish. When she squeaked and jerked away, he pretended not to notice. "But we'll soon be traveling there for a few joint interviews and some bonus content for the final season."

The day after tomorrow, in fact. He'd like to say he wasn't nervous about meeting her family, but that'd be a fucking lie.

"She's told me about her homeland, of course," he said, scratching at his beard reflectively. "I look forward to my ceremonial trampling by a vindictive moose. Maria says that's how they always welcome honored guests. And if I'm not mistaken, we'll end our visit by assembling various pieces of particleboard into slightly crooked home furnishings using only an Allen wrench, all while singing the entire *ABBA Gold* playlist."

"It's the law." Maria gave a solemn nod. "No Billy bookcase, no plane ticket home. Exceptions are only made if two witnesses can certify that you sang 'Fernando' at top volume while drunk on aquavit."

"And I don't drink, so . . ." Spreading his hands, he heaved a dramatic sigh. "Wish me luck assembling my Löpblåsvädersson. I'm pretty sure Blond Pippi over here won't be much help."

"Shut it, *skitstövel*." When Maria pinched his arm, he cast her a wide-eyed look of astonished hurt. "Peter made up that word, Tonya. Ignore him, please."

The reporter snickered. "I'd translate what she just called him for our viewers, but I'd prefer not to be bleeped. If you're curious, a simple Google search will serve you well, since all true Marter fans know Maria's preferred term of endearment for Peter."

"It's not a term of endearment." Amusement lit Maria's warm brown eyes. "It's a *condemnation*. I am hereby stating to you and the entire world that Peter Reedton is the type of man who would shit in a boot. Also, possibly, in a blue cupboard."

Scrubbing a hand over his mouth, he tried to disguise his grin.

"So much for not getting bleeped." The reporter—Tonya, evidently—winced.

Maria lifted a shoulder in a desultory shrug. "I don't mind being bleeped. Not if it helps spread the word about Peter's rampant, uncontrollable boot-shitting."

The other woman rubbed at her temples for a moment. "One final question."

He and Maria both knew what was coming. Discreetly, he lowered a hand to poke the side of that tempting, bare thigh, their usual indication that he wanted her to answer. Only to jerk and cough a moment later as her surprisingly sharp elbow rammed him in the gut.

That would be a refusal, then.

"I'm so sorry, Peter." Her expression of innocent remorse should have won her an award. "My jet lag must be making me clumsy."

She patted his forearm gently, then sat back to watch him suffer.

"You mentioned the final season." Tonya paused for dramatic effect, and he bit back a sigh. "All those leaked scripts have caused quite an uproar among *Gods of the Gates* fans. Can you comment on whether those are real episode scripts?"

Maria, apparently willing to address that part of the topic—i.e., the easy part—shook her head. "We can't. I apologize."

"In that case, can you tell me more about the final season and what happens to your characters?" The reporter waved a hand. "I know you have to avoid spoilers, but maybe you can share your general reactions without giving specifics."

However little he wanted to answer, it was probably better that he address this particular question. Despite her charm, Maria was no diplomat. She hated bullshit, she could wield words like knives, and she loathed the showrunners and how their final-season scripts decimated almost all the main character arcs.

Her anger and disdain weren't new, of course. He'd known exactly how she felt about Ron and R.J. and the future of their show for a long time now.

Late one night two seasons ago, fresh from filming a particularly challenging scene and enduring yet another shitty standoff with Ron, she'd flopped down on the couch in his suite. Blithely, as if discussing nothing of great consequence, she'd told him she wanted to quit. Would have quit, if the bonds tethering her to their small island crew, to him, and to her character weren't so strong.

"Sometimes I wish I didn't care about everyone so much." She'd tipped her head back against the cushion and stared up at the ceiling, the firelight setting her hair aglow. "But even that might not be enough to keep me here, Peter, if it weren't for one other consideration."

Part of him wanted to shake her. After all that time, didn't she realize the immense privilege of working on a show like theirs? Didn't she understand how very many actors struggled their entire careers and never, ever managed to land a role like Cassia? Didn't she know that nearly every barista at every Hollywood café she'd ever visited was a would-be actor scrimping and starving and hustling for even a bit part in a doomed pilot?

He'd almost said so. Because she still didn't get it. Because she wanted to leave.

Because she wanted to leave *him*.

Then he'd looked at her. Really *looked*.

He'd spied the tiny laugh lines at the corners of her eyes. She was about to turn thirty, and it showed. Subtly. Unmistakably. Gloriously. She was gorgeous to begin with, but she'd somehow grown even more beautiful over time. He suspected that would be true until the day she passed from this earth.

But the flickering light didn't only reveal those new, adorable crinkles. It also threw the dark circles under her eyes into relief and silhouetted her slumped shoulders. She seemed—tired. Worn thin, in a way he'd never witnessed before.

Her easy, breezy cheer wasn't an act. He knew that. It wasn't all of her, though. And her confidence and talent might keep her afloat in rough waters, but that didn't mean she wasn't swimming as fast as she could. It didn't mean she wouldn't get exhausted and need a buoy sometimes.

He had to help her stay afloat. Anything, *anything*, to keep her on the show. With him.

So he bit his tongue. He kept his voice soft and mild, making sure it harbored not even a hint of the tangled emotions—fear, anger, hurt, frustration—that had rabbited his pulse when she'd announced her desire to quit. "What's the other consideration keeping you here?"

Her laugh was ragged around the edges, but it sounded genuine.

"Spite," she said. "Obviously."

When he blinked at her in befuddlement, she laughed again.

"Oh, Peter." Her hand covered his on the couch cushion and squeezed. "We both know this show is, as you Americans say, going off the rails. There aren't any more books to adapt, which means two of the most boring, self-satisfied, small-minded men I've ever met are now entirely in control of the story."

He'd figured that was why recent filming had proven especially fraught and chaotic. E. Wade's books couldn't provide plot or character guidance anymore, and the showrunners were floundering.

When Maria lifted her hand from atop his, he fought the urge to snatch it back.

"*Gods of the Gates* is going to crash and burn. So are Ron and R.J." Her smile was weary and bright and vicious. "And when they immolate their careers with their incompetent, misogynistic edgelord shit, I want a front-row seat."

Ah. Spite. Now he got it.

Her nose wrinkled, and she stared into the fire for a moment. "Wait. Do I mean edgelord or grimdark? I always get those two confused."

"Both terms probably apply," he'd said dryly, and she'd laughed once more and started to talk about the next day's scene, and the moment was over.

Outside occasional comments on the cast chat, she'd never raised the topic again. But he knew she meant what she'd said. Every word.

So . . . yeah. He should probably answer any and all questions about the final season, the same way he'd done in their previous interviews. God knew her opinion of the show and its scripts hadn't *improved* in the last two years.

Once more unto the breach, he supposed.

"The final season includes some of the most expensive and spectacular action sequences ever filmed for television, and I can't say enough about the talent and hard work of the *Gods of the Gates* crew as we shot those scenes." There. That was honest enough. "And I think Cassian fans will be very . . . satisfied with some of the developments in their relationship."

There. A little harmless insinuation, a rakish wink, and . . . done. Tonya had run out of time, and none too soon. Follow-up questions about the final season were the *worst*.

The PR rep ushered the reporter out, only to immediately usher in the interviewer scheduled for the next time slot. The guy wore glasses, a graphic tee, and squeaky sneakers. A blogger, maybe? Or a representative from an online-only media outlet?

"Hi." The twentysomething dude shook both their hands, then

settled into his chair. "I'm Carl Li, and I run the *Gays of the Gates* blog. It's lovely to meet you both."

"Likewise," Maria said with a warm smile. "I've seen your blog, and I appreciate the thoughtfulness of your posts, even those critical of the show. Representation matters, and when that representation is harmful, it needs to get called out."

The tips of Carl's ears turned ruddy. "Thank you so much, Ms. Ivarsson."

"Please call me Maria," she told him, and he beamed back at her.

Peter was pretty sure Carl would now kill for Maria if necessary, or at least provide a solid alibi while she did the deed herself.

"Um . . ." The blogger glanced down at his notebook. "I have quite a few questions. Hopefully we can get through most of them."

Peter gulped down some ice water and waited for it.

"As you may have seen, the two of you came in first and second in our recent reader poll." When Maria gave him a blank look, he hurried to explain. "It was a fun break from our more serious coverage. The poll asked: *If you had to choose, which one actor would you most want guarding your special gate?*"

"My gate really is quite special," Maria murmured. "Everyone says so."

Peter choked on his water, and she thumped his back while he coughed and tried not to consider the implications of her statement.

He couldn't argue her point, though. Her particular gate *was* the best he'd ever guarded. By far.

Having apparently missed Maria's interjection, Carl was still talking when Peter managed to catch his breath and degutter his mind once more.

"—reluctant consensus in the comments was that whether you were straight or not didn't really matter." The blogger peered at them over the top of his glasses, cheeks dimpled in a knowing grin. "Because you're secretly a couple and off the market anyway."

Here it came at last, inevitable as death, taxes, and the fridging of female characters in action films.

"Are you two dating one another? If not, have you ever dated in the past?"

At that fraught moment, as Peter attempted to muster the energy necessary to answer the question pleasantly and with sufficient verve, Maria—damn her—*wigglewigglewiggled*.

Her thigh rubbed against his, and her dress hitched upward again, to the point where he could easily see that little constellation of freckles he'd licked long ago, mere moments before he'd licked her very special, very slippery gate.

He remembered those freckles fondly. Too fondly. So fondly, his dick tried its very hardest to merge with the zipper of his jeans.

And that was when he knew for certain: He wouldn't survive this.

The coroner would declare Death by Press Junket. At the funeral, his father would note that Peter's tragic death would never have occurred if he'd attended business school, as was expected of him, instead of becoming a theater major. By his graveside, his castmates would toss roses upon his casket, sniff back tears, and tell each other, "He's in a better place now."

And by God, they wouldn't be wrong.

Texts with Maria: Two Years Ago

Peter: What's wrong?

Maria: ???

Maria: Nothing's wrong

Maria: I'm fine

Peter: That's a lie

Peter: You haven't been yourself all day

Peter: I don't think I've seen you smile once

Peter: You don't have your usual shine

Maria: My usual . . . shine?

Peter: Did I do something that upset you or made you uncomfortable?

Peter: Or did someone else say or do something?

Peter: If it was me, I apologize, and if it was someone else, tell me who, and I'll take care of it

Maria: . . .

Maria: When someone upsets me, I'm more than capable of handling it myself

Maria: But I appreciate the offer

Maria: No one upset me or made me uncomfortable, Peter, not you or anyone else

Maria: It was just a hard scene to film today

Maria: Cassia telling Cyprian how her parents died from the Plague was

Maria: ...

Peter: Emotionally intense?

Maria: Yes.

Peter: Okay. Then what can I do to help you forget about the scene?

Maria: Like I said, I'm fine, Peter

Maria: I'll just hang out in my suite and read by the fireplace, and I'll be back to my apparently shiny (!) self tomorrow

Peter: Nope

Maria: Nope?

Peter: You owe me, Ivarsson

Maria: I do not, Reedton

Peter: Did you or did you not moo at me yesterday when I was innocently drinking a bottle of water, thus causing me to jump and spray poor Ramón and Jeanine with said water

Maria: Maybe

Maria: If I did do such a thing, I'm certain it would have been very fun to watch

Peter: Pay your debts, Pippi

Maria: What do you want, skitstövel?

Peter: Hold on a minute, I'll be right back

Maria: You can't hear or see me, but I'm sighing loudly and impatiently

Maria: . . .

Maria: Peter?

Maria: Peter, did you fall asleep
or get abducted by aliens or

Peter: Hold your horses, Ivarsson

Maria: Speaking of horses, are you
terrified of them too, or just cows

Peter: I'm nobly ignoring that provocation

Peter: Anyway, Nava and Ramón are coming
to my room in ten minutes, and so are you

Peter: We're all going to watch that
Tarzan remake, so you can ogle
Alexander Skarsgard shirtless to your
heart's content

Maria: Skarsgård, not Skarsgard

Peter: Whatever, come to my room and
objectify your oddly voweled countryman
among friends

Maria: I don't know, Peter

Peter: . . .

Peter: Hold on a minute, I'll be right back

Maria: AGAIN?

Maria: ...

Maria: Gods above, you're a pain
in my very delightful ass

Peter: Okay, Conor and Fionn are coming too

Maria: ...

Peter: Fionn's making caramel popcorn
and bringing enough for everyone

Peter: With a special bowl just for you

Peter: I'm literally sweetening the
pot, Pippi, how can you resist

Maria: ...

Maria: Dammit, Reedton, you know
caramel popcorn is my fatal weakness

Peter: Of course I know

Peter: So you're coming to my room, correct?

Maria: Yes

Maria: But if we sit together, you'd better not hog my throw blanket this time OR ELSE

Peter: As a good socialist, you should be willing to share the blanket's wealth

Maria: Ah, but I've been influenced by my capitalist costar

Maria: Now I no longer see a need to address blanket inequality, however egregious

Maria: Blanket Greed Is Good, is it not?

Peter: Just get your very delightful ass over here before I spank it

Maria: ...

Peter: ...

Maria: ...

Peter: Please forget I said that. It was inappropriate.

Maria: ...

Maria: I'll do my best.

Maria: . . .

Maria: Why don't I ask Conor to get you an extra blanket too? No need to share.

Peter: Probably a good idea.

Maria: Yeah.

Peter: . . .

Peter: Yeah.

15

"YES, I SUPPOSE I DO LOOK RATHER AFFECTIONATE." MARIA peered down at the blogger's tablet, where a particularly popular gif of her smiling at Peter during a con panel played over and over. "He *is* quite a good person, if you don't consider the various ways in which he's actually a terrible person."

In all the *Gates* press junkets the two of them had endured, they'd never been asked to watch and provide commentary on gifs that theoretically revealed their undying devotion to each other. Not until this very special moment, during their last interview of the day.

Even for her, this was awkward. Peter looked ready to chew metal, despite that stiff smile splitting his dark beard. From the audible rumbling of his stomach, the chicken Caesar wraps they'd wolfed down during a hurried lunch were now a distant memory. He kept rubbing his forehead in what appeared to be an unconscious gesture, so she figured he had a killer headache too.

Not to mention his poor dick. It had to really, really hurt by now.

Late in the afternoon, in an act of gracious goodwill, she'd stopped readjusting her position on the love seat, for fear his head—either of them—would literally explode.

"*I'm* a terrible person?" His poke of her ribs was half-hearted at best. "Which one of us intimidated our entire crew by threatening to beat everyone with glass jars of pickled herring? Because I can assure you, Pippi, if I were to choose a bottled food product for bludgeoning purposes, I'd find something less smelly."

He was the only one she menaced with jarred *sill*, and they both knew it. Threats of herring-assisted violence were her love language.

Not that . . . not that she loved him. Obviously.

His brow creased as he turned to face her. "And where do you even store those jars, anyway? They appear out of fu— uh, freaking nowhere."

"Like this?"

Promptly, she produced a jar from her usual spot. Everyone else in the room visibly jolted in surprise, to her immense satisfaction.

She shook the *sill* maybe a millimeter from Peter's nose. "I could tell you, *skitstövel*. But then I'd have to kill you. By thwacking you over the head with an extremely heavy glass jar of tasty herring, naturally, in accordance with ancient Swedish tradition."

A blatant lie. She was never telling Peter where she kept the jar. It was too much fun to terrorize him.

"Then I'd eat the herring. It would taste like victory." She paused, then smiled slowly. Delightedly. "And murder. Delicious, fishy murder."

From across the room and behind the camera, the PR rep stared at her. Hard.

Maria waved.

That did the trick. Peter started laughing. Those deep furrows between his brows disappeared, and if she was reading the clock in the distance correctly—

"I'm afraid we're out of time," the PR rep told the blogger, then began politely but firmly steering him toward the door of the hotel suite. "Thank you so much for coming. You should receive the footage by the end of the week. If you don't, please contact us, and we'll make sure you get it."

After it was strategically edited, no doubt. Or maybe not, since Marter fans loved it when she and Peter went off script, which the very competent PR team had surely recognized by now.

"Thank *you*," the blogger managed to get out. "Nice to meet you both!"

Then he was gone. And in a matter of minutes—during which Peter devoured a leftover wrap or two and brushed his teeth before returning to the little sofa—the very small, very efficient crew was gone too, as was their long-suffering PR rep. The camera and a few other pieces of equipment remained in place, ready for the next day's gauntlet of interviews.

The door slammed shut behind the boom op, leaving the suite in absolute silence.

Peter said nothing. She said nothing. They simply sagged against the inadequately cushioned love seat as they gathered the energy for speech and/or movement.

He might still be hungry, his head hurt, and cheerful chattiness with strangers wasn't exactly his default setting, so he had to be exhausted. And while she was a more social creature than Peter, she'd also spent the previous night at the Stockholm airport, waiting impatiently for a flight that got delayed three separate times, then flown almost halfway across the world and raced to the hotel, where she'd had only ten minutes to shower, dress, and ready herself for an entire day of interviews.

Fy fan, she was tired.

Also horny. But mostly tired.

She'd deployed strategic squirming to work him up all day, with the full intention of tackling him like a rugby player the minute they were alone, but now . . .

A nap sounded really, really good.

Peter sort of flopped onto his side so he could face her. Expression guarded, he studied her for a long moment, his gaze skimming from her comfy flats to her high ponytail, then returning to linger on her bare legs.

His forefinger grazed the hem of her dress. "You fucked with me all day."

"I did."

No point in denial. She'd wanted him to know, hoping the realization—that her wiggling was entirely deliberate, a taunt intended just for him—would turn him on even more. And gods above, all that teasing had kept her flushed and tingling for hours.

He palmed her right leg, and his thumb slipped beneath her hem, skimming in slow arcs over the sensitive skin of her inner thigh. Her breath shuddered. Her bones turned liquid.

Her desire for a nap disappeared.

Now that they were alone, his restless lust seemed to have dissipated too, along with his headache and any lingering hunger for food. He was a man with all the time in the world. All the patience.

He watched himself touch her and said nothing.

That tiny arc of flesh under his thumb never widened. Never drifted higher. But each sweep prickled and burned, the heat burrowing beneath her skin and lapping upward with every passing moment, until it settled between her legs.

Her thigh began to tremble.

The rhythm of his thumb didn't alter. His face remained hard and still, bent to his work.

After another minute, his other hand clasped her left knee. As he guided that leg a hairsbreadth wider, he flicked her a single upward glance.

"You going to let me fuck with you?"

It was a rumble, deep and quiet. Meant for her and her alone.

Her eyelids drifted shut. "Yes."

When his thumb stilled, she managed to lift them again.

He held her gaze, his eyes dark and implacable. "Yes?"

"Please," she whispered.

His jaw ticked. "Then open up."

She spread her legs, and he exhaled slowly. Without another word, he slipped off her panties and shoes with impersonal efficiency, then stood and arranged her exactly how he wanted, his hands firm and steady and hot.

In moments, she was propped in the corner of the love seat, her left foot on the floor. The right he lifted and placed with exquisite care flat on the seat, her knee bent high and pressed against the sofa's back cushions.

Sprawled, flushed, and entirely open to him, she waited.

He stared, and his throat worked in a hard swallow.

Then he dropped to his knees.

His palm glided up the length of her left leg in a leisurely, torturous exploration, from ankle to calf to knee, then higher. At her upper thigh, though, he paused. Ran his thumb over a spot she couldn't see, again and again.

"Freckles," he murmured, then looked up at her. "Lift that skirt, Maria."

She did, centimeter by centimeter, watching his face the entire time.

When the cool hotel air washed over her pussy, high color streaked across his cheekbones, and his chest heaved. Once, twice.

She didn't stop until she was bare to the waist in front. Then she stretched her left leg out wider and smiled at him. A cat's smile, pleased and provocative.

He made a sound deep in his throat.

"*Fuck.*" Tipping his chin back, he squeezed his eyes shut. "You're the most— *Christ.* How do you do it? How do you unravel me like this?"

It was mutual. Gods above, he could undo her so easily. So quickly it was terrifying.

His eyes were still closed, his expression pained, and her patience abruptly ran out. She slid a hand between her legs and stroked. If he wasn't going to satisfy her, she could take care of herself. Gladly.

She was beyond wet. So slick her fingertips slipped over her clit with zero effort, and she dragged in a harsh breath at the bolt of pleasure.

Then her hand was batted away.

Peter's replaced it. And apparently he'd lost patience too, because he didn't tease or delay. Before the next beat of her pulse could echo in her ears, two long, blunt fingers sank deep inside her. Her body offered no resistance.

His thumb pressed against her clit.

"Ride that," he told her. "Fuck yourself on my hand."

That would be—very literally—her pleasure.

While he watched, his face flushed, his nostrils flared, his jaw stony, she rode his fingers as they bent and twisted inside her. It took a startlingly short amount of time before that familiar pressure built between her legs, and she started to shake, her nails biting into slick upholstery as she ground against that rough, implacable thumb.

Her moan echoed in the room, and he was breathing hard now too, lightly slapping her inner thigh every time she tried to close her eyes, forcing her to hold his hot stare.

"Peter," she gasped. "I need—"

He pushed a third finger inside her and circled his thumb against her clit as he bent down and nipped her inner thigh, and that was it. That was what she needed.

She bucked her hips and came with a breathless cry, her body tight and pulsing around his fingers. He watched her intently as he worked her through her orgasm, stroking her clit with light pressure while she shook against him and panted out helpless sounds of pleasure.

It was a longer, harder orgasm than she'd expected, and at the end of it, worn out and damp with sweat, she collapsed into the corner of the love seat.

A full minute must have passed before she realized his fingers were still inside her.

As soon as she lifted her head, he lowered his.

His tongue—*skit*. It was soft and relentless. He nuzzled her, licked up one swollen fold and down another, and flicked her throbbing clit so delicately she could have cried.

She reached down with both hands, tangled her fingers in his hair, and forgot herself. Forgot the world outside their hotel suite. Forgot everything but his gentle exploration and the renewed ache of arousal making her shift restlessly against his mouth.

He was patient. So very patient. But as soon as she could handle more pressure, he gave it to her.

Burying his face between her legs, he *ate* her, his mouth and tongue voracious. He licked her from slit to clit with a flattened tongue, then stabbed that tongue as deep inside her as he could. His beard abraded her inner thighs and prickled deliciously against her oversensitive flesh.

And then he started fucking her with his fingers again.

They crooked and rubbed inside her, and she was making helpless sounds as she desperately ground against his face.

When he spoke, the words were muffled against her flesh. "You want it, Maria?"

She twisted her fingers in his hair and moaned, lost.

"Then take it," he told her, and sucked her clit.

She crashed into orgasm, clenching around his fingers, against his mouth, with almost painful intensity. Eyes squeezed so tightly shut she saw stars, mouth open, she panted and came harder than she knew was possible.

"Peter." It sounded like a plea. For what, she didn't know. "*Peter.*"

He kept sucking, kept pumping his fingers, and she kept coming in little quivers and pulses. When they eventually slowed, he eased back, flicking softly over her clit until she twitched against his tongue for the last time.

Her cheeks were wet. She couldn't say whether it was sweat or tears.

When he finally raised his head from between her legs, he looked wrecked. Hair rumpled, beard soaked, face flushed, eyes wild with need.

"Gods, *sötnos.*" Reaching down, she clutched his shoulders and tried to drag him on top of her. "We can undress next time. Get inside me already."

"Won't last," he ground out, but he was already unzipping his jeans and yanking down his boxer briefs, already reaching inside his pocket for a condom. "Sorry."

She waved a hand. "Coming again would probably kill me. You don't need to last."

With effort, she managed to stay propped on her elbows, entirely so she could ogle him more easily. *Fy fan*, he was sexy. All broad shoulders and generous belly, strength wrapped in softness, with the hardest, thickest erection she'd ever seen.

It was hers. She wanted it. She didn't care whether she had another orgasm or not.

As soon as he'd slapped the condom down the length of his dick, he pulled her up from the love seat. "You're on top this time," he grunted. "Me next time."

Good. She wanted that big body over hers, just as much as she wanted to ride his cock until he shouted her name.

He sat, then gripped her waist and hauled her closer. "Come here."

She followed him down eagerly, straddling his lap. But before she could lift up to take him inside, his hands slid into her hair. Gently, he tipped her head until his forehead met hers, and closed his eyes.

She stilled. "Peter?"

His erection prodded his stomach and her own, ruddy and insistent, and he was breathing in harsh gulps, his powerful frame trembling at the effort of restraint.

Still, he glided his nose alongside hers in an affectionate nuzzle. Kissed her temple, her cheek, the corner of her mouth. Rubbed his damp beard against her neck until she squeaked.

The harsh set of his jaw softened at the sound, and he opened his eyes. They were heavy-lidded, his pupils blown with desire. Hot.

They were also *warm*.

She had to swallow past a lump in her throat.

Then he cupped her face and softly pressed his lips to hers, kissing her with unhurried tenderness. As if he didn't taste like her, smell like her. As if he weren't shaking with need.

He sipped at her mouth so slowly, so carefully. And when his tongue slipped inside, it stroked hers in playful little swirls that dizzied her.

His kiss demanded nothing and offered everything.

It was the sweetest kiss of her life.

She clutched his shoulders and let go. Let herself sink down into the moment. Let the sweetness pull her under and trusted him to keep her safe.

When the kiss ended, she smiled at him with open affection. Nudged his nose with hers. Then, rising up to her knees, she positioned him with one hand and sank down on his dick.

His groan might have been ripped from the center of the earth, and his big hands clutched her hips in a near-painful grip. But he didn't move. Not a millimeter.

"It's okay, *sötnos*." Glorying in the pleasurable stretch of his body inside hers, she rocked her hips once. Twice. "You can let go now."

"Can't. You move." He ducked his head and buried it in the crook of her shoulder, his panting breaths hot against her neck. "Don't want to hurt you."

Grabbing his chin, she forced him to look at her. To see her certainty. "You won't. Fuck me as hard as you like."

The vein in his temple was pulsing with alarming violence, but he still didn't move.

"C'mon, Peter," she murmured, then slid up almost the entire length of his cock, until he was barely inside her. "I'm a big girl. Throw me around a little."

He finally lost control.

His nostrils flared, his hands squeezed her ass with bruising possessiveness, and he shoved her back down on his dick with a snarl.

Before she even had time to gasp in pleasure, he'd begun bucking his hips, fucking her with such ferocious power that all she could do was hold on. Each impact jolted through her like a thun-

derbolt, and gods above, it even felt like lightning. Electricity arc-
ing. Power gathering.

Dimly, she heard herself panting. Clinging to his shoulders,
she arched back and spread her legs even wider, until her inner
thighs ached at the strain.

She wanted him so deep she'd still feel him in a month. So
deep he'd never leave.

"Changed . . . my mind." His gravelly words barely sounded
human. "First time . . . inside you again. You're . . . coming . . .
on my . . . cock."

He licked his thumb and pressed it to her clit, and with each
slap of flesh against flesh, the rough pad of that thumb rubbed
against her. Again and again and again, mercilessly.

He was thick inside her, hot beneath and around her, his hold
inexorable, his thumb so fucking talented, and she let her eyes
flutter shut as the pleasure built and built within her.

She was panting harder now. Whimpering. The hand squeezing her ass disappeared, only to land firm and heavy on her nape.
Using his hold on her neck, he hauled her against his chest, so
tight her breasts scraped against him with every ruthless stroke,
so tight she could barely breathe, and he claimed her mouth in a
bruising, unapologetically carnal kiss.

His lips were greedy, his tongue demanding immediate entry.
When she opened to him, he sucked her own tongue inside his
mouth, and he tasted like sweat and mint and pussy.

Then he wrapped her ponytail around his fist and tugged hard.

Without warning, she convulsed again, her body racked with
pleasure and clenched tight around his plunging dick, and he
swallowed the breathy cry from her lips.

"Thank"—he groaned into her mouth—"*fuck.*"

While she was still shuddering, he gave one last violent buck of his hips, ripped his mouth from hers, and shouted hoarsely as he finally came, the same strangled word ripped from his throat over and over again as he shook in her arms.

One word. Her name.

It sounded like a prayer.

LATE THAT NIGHT, after they'd had dinner, made love for a second time, and showered together, Maria pulled the bedcovers over both of them and flopped down on his chest.

He wheezed for a moment. "Holy shit, woman."

"You're tough." She patted one broad pec, then played with some of his dark hair there. "Suck it up, *skitstövel*."

After shaking his head at her, he twisted a bit to reach the bedside lamp and turned it off. "Cruelty, thy name is Maria."

They hadn't actually discussed whether they'd sleep in the same bed. They'd simply . . . not separated. Even though Maria hadn't spent an entire night with a lover since discovering her ex's other life in London.

It was a fool's act. Until she knew for certain he could commit to her the way she needed, she should maintain a healthy emotional distance. Keep the sex purely physical. Watch and wait and evaluate.

In the end, though, it hadn't been so much a conscious decision as an instinct. A visceral urge to huddle against his warmth and allow him to see her vulnerable in sleep, a sudden certainty that pushing him away would feel *wrong*. Obeying that reflexive conviction, she'd followed him to his bedroom, to his bed, without a word of protest.

And that was a fool's defense, making a dangerous choice and declaring it unthinking. Inevitable. Out of her control, so what could she do, really? What could she do but open herself up to someone else whose intentions she didn't entirely trust, much as she cared for him?

What could she do but offer him another piece of her heart to break?

She shifted uneasily, sliding off his chest to reach the other side of the huge bed, where her own pillow awaited, comfortable and cold.

His thick arm closed around her waist and tugged her back.

"Where are you going?" Rolling onto his side, he wrapped her tight in his embrace. "I was just joking, sweetheart. I like having you sprawled on top of me. You know that, right?"

He'd thrown one heavy thigh over her legs, so she couldn't move away. Not unless she told him to let her go.

She didn't.

"I know," she said, and pressed her ear against his chest, right over his heart.

It thumped steadily, each beat strong. As she listened, her breathing steadied, the metallic taste in her mouth melting back to mint.

"What did you call me earlier?" He sounded sleepy. "It wasn't shit-boot. Something like 'soot-no'?"

Gods above, she'd revealed entirely too much of herself today. "*Sötnos.*"

"Knowing Swedes, it still probably involves shit in some way." Soft pressure against the crown of her head. A kiss. "What's it mean?"

She bit her lip, but answered. "Literally? Sweet nose."

"Sweet . . . nose?" His body shook as he laughed. "What the fuck, Pippi?"

Loath as she was to explain herself further, she couldn't overlook the slight to her mother language. "American endearments don't make any more sense, Reedton. Grown adults call each other 'baby.' Parents refer to their kids as 'sweet pea' or 'pumpkin,' when human children are not, in fact, produce."

He fell silent for a long moment, all laughter gone.

"It's an endearment?" A quiet question as his arms hitched her tighter against him. "What's the closest English equivalent?"

She'd answer him honestly, but then she was done with the topic.

His pulse might be strong and steady, but hers was skittering unpleasantly.

"*Sweetheart*," she told him, her tone brisk and matter-of-fact. "Anyway, something occurred to me earlier."

After a long pause, he let out a slow breath and stroked her hair back from her face. "What's that?"

Okay. He was letting it go.

Her heart slowed, and she reached deep to find a genuine smile. Genuine amusement.

There it was. Her reliable companion through joy and desolation both, no matter who came and went in her life.

"We—" She snickered, and it wasn't an act. Merely a redirection. "We basically just lived out that really explicit fic Alex sent us last week. Like, almost exactly. Remember? The one where we ended a joint interview by fucking on literally every flat surface in the hotel room, including the fold-down ironing board in the closet? Which somehow didn't collapse under our combined weight, even as you railed me from behind?"

She'd applauded the author's imagination, if not their grasp of physics.

"Remember?" Peter snorted. "I have that fic bookmarked. I considered it a key source of inspiration for today's sexual exploits. Except for the ironing board bit. I wouldn't want to explain to housekeeping how it broke in half and stabbed me in the junk. Besides, they shouldn't be asked to clean junk blood, so I was trying to be thoughtful."

"Very generous of you," she said, laughing.

"I thought so." He yawned so hard, his jaw cracked. "Go to sleep, Pippi. You've got a nine-hour time difference to conquer."

He was right. If she wasn't leaving his bed, there was no point agonizing over whether she should. She needed her rest, and so did he. So after giving him a half-hearted poke for the Pippi reference, she closed her eyes and let herself relax against him.

"Good night, *skitstövel*," she said.

"Good night, *sötnos*." A tired chuckle, and he ducked his head to kiss her nose. "Well, I'll be damned. It *is* pretty sweet."

"Your pronunciation sucks," she muttered against his chest, in lieu of either panicking or crying, and he chuckled again.

They lay cuddling for several minutes, his hairy legs slightly scratchy against her own, their soft bellies pressed together, his cedar scent an ineffable comfort.

She was almost asleep when something occurred to her. "Peter?"

"Yep?" It took him a few moments to answer, and his voice was gravelly with exhaustion.

"Alex can never know we used the fic he sent as inspiration."

If he did, only the gods above knew what he'd force on them next.

If there was such a thing as sleepy horror, Peter's voice contained it. "Never. We'll never tell him." When he shuddered, the movement jostled her pleasantly. "He couldn't handle that much power."

She lifted a fist, and he bumped it to seal their vow. Afterward, his hand stroked down her spine and cupped her butt, apparently with the intention of staying there till morning.

"'Night," he mumbled.

That hot, huge hand on her ass felt good. So good she squirmed a little, which meant she rubbed up against him, caressing his entire body with her own. Breasts over chest. Legs tangling with legs. Pussy sliding over hair-dusted skin.

That felt even better.

Jet lag was weird. A moment ago, she was exhausted and near sleep. But in Sweden, it was nine in the morning, and her body didn't yet understand she'd left evergreens behind and removed to the land of palm trees and hot, unrelenting sunshine.

The time difference might explain how she could suddenly be wide awake and aching with arousal once more. It couldn't, however, explain the growing press of Peter's dick against her thigh.

With a happy little hum, she fisted his erection. Stroked up and down, tweaking the underside of the head in exactly the way that'd made him gasp earlier that night.

Now too, evidently.

She couldn't resist. "Speaking of handling power . . ."

"Sweetheart . . ." Peter groaned, but he also closed his hand over hers and helped her squeeze harder, his hips starting a slow grind. "Have mercy. There's another full day of interviews tomorrow. I'm tired, and unlike my nubile Swedish costar, I'm an old man."

When she nipped him right over his heart, her teeth didn't break his skin, but they'd sting. They'd leave a mark. "*My* old man."

He'd encouraged her to bite earlier, so she had. But not in that spot. Not until now. Her possessiveness didn't bode well, and she knew it, but she was too turned on to care. Especially when that rumble in his chest vibrated through her so deliciously.

"Yeah." A near-growl, firm and low. "Yours."

Adjusting a little, he wedged his thigh between hers, pressing higher and harder, until he could nudge rhythmically up against her clit. She closed her eyes, moaned, and tried to wriggle even closer. Gods above, she *loved* that powerful body of his.

After a few minutes riding his thigh, she was close to coming, and his dick throbbed in her hand, wet at the tip. They were both breathing hard, both sweaty once more.

"If you leave in the middle of the night this time, I swear to God I'll find every fucking herring factory in Sweden and burn them to the fucking ground," he said, then rolled her over and proceeded to prove he wasn't so old or tired after all.

Rating: Explicit

Fandoms: Gods of the Gates RPF

Relationship: Maria Ivarsson/Peter Reedton

Additional Tags: <u>Actor RPF – Freeform</u>, <u>Explicit Sexual Content</u>, <u>Dirty Talk</u>, <u>Porn with Feelings</u>, <u>Hurt/Comfort</u>, <u>When I Say I Didn't Research How Press Junkets Work I Mean I Didn't Care About How Press Junkets Work</u>, <u>Anyway Here's Wonderwall</u>

Stats: Words: 6560 Chapters: 3/3 Comments: 21 Kudos: 97 Bookmarks: 8

One Final Question
MarterForTheCause

Summary:

After an interviewer hurts Maria's feelings, years of suppressed lust boil over, and Peter has one last question for the woman he loves.

Notes:

Just to emphasize: This work is RPF. If you don't know what that is, detour to Google before reading.

I didn't research how press junkets work. I did, however, do an image search for fancy hotel rooms to take an inventory of all available flat surfaces located therein. Priorities!

———————————————

"He had no right to ask me that," Maria sniffles. "Thank you for breaking his nose for me."

He would do anything for her. Anything at all. Punching an asshole journalist is the least of it. Sure, there might be some legal hassle, but he's a star. He has people to take care of that.

He pulls her tighter and tells her, "It was my pleasure."

She goes very still against him.

"You know, I've been thinking about your pleasure, Peter," she whispers. "A lot. For years now."

This is it. The moment is here at last.

"Then I guess I have one final question for you, Maria," he says.

Her eyes are wide and wondering as she looks up at him.

"Where do you want me to fuck you first?" he growls.

"Anywhere," she breathes. "Everywhere."

They're close to the closet, and he desperately searches for the nearest flat surface as he rips off his clothes. Buttons fly everywhere, but he doesn't care. He can buy a million new shirts if he wants. Her dress comes off over her head, and there she is. Naked.

"You're even more beautiful than I imagined," he groans.

"You're so strong and hard," she murmurs. "Please fuck me, Peter. I need you."

He can't wait any longer. He won't wait any longer.

He pulls down the ironing board from inside the closet, and it's good enough.

"Turn around and bend over," he demands, and she obeys.

"Will the ironing board hold us?" she whimpers as he positions his cock.

He snarls, "I'll make it hold us. Besides, I'm supporting most of your weight with my dick."

Then he's inside her at last, and practicalities don't matter anymore. Nothing does, other than fucking Maria and locating the next flat surface to drill her into for round two.

That Chippendale-style end table should work.

16

"TECHNICALLY, I SUPPOSE ALL FISH BOUGHT HERE ARE Swedish Fish," Peter said to Maria as he pushed the grocery cart past the glass-fronted display of seafood. "Just like all massages are, by definition, Swedish massages."

Maria snorted and nudged him toward the prepared foods section with a warm hand on his back. "How long have you been waiting to share that little gem?"

"Since three-point-two seconds after I found out I was traveling to Sweden."

The stupid joke shouldn't tickle him so much, but a long day of overseas travel had left him punch-drunk, as had his visceral terror at meeting her parents for the first time at the airport. Luckily, Stina and Olle seemed perfectly nice thus far. Medium height, several inches shorter than their daughter. Both gone gray, both clad in neutral-colored leisure wear. Both surprisingly bland and nondescript, actually, for people who'd raised a woman like Maria, although they were undeniably loving toward her.

Even now, Olle reached up to sling an arm around her shoulders with casual affection as he peered quizzically at Peter. "I'm not sure what you mean."

"Swedish fish?" Stina blinked up at him, wispy eyebrows drawn together. "I don't understand."

Maria bit her bottom lip and offered zero help.

Really, of the two of them, she was the true shit-boot.

"Um . . ." He halted the cart by the deli counter and prepared to explain himself. Because the best jokes all had to be explained, right? Right. "So there's this candy sold in the U.S.—although I'm not sure it's manufactured in America, actually. Maybe it originally comes from here in Sweden or somewhere else in Europe? I should look that up."

Stina and Olle stared at him blankly, while Maria now had both lips sandwiched between her teeth and was gazing down at the tile floor.

"It's called Swedish Fish. But it's not fish." He drummed his fingers on the cart handle. "Well, actually, it is fish. Sort of, although not the ocean type of fish. It's gummy."

A choked sound drifted from Maria's vicinity.

Stina frowned at him, even as she reached to pluck a slip of paper with a number on it from a red dispenser on top of the deli case. "Gummy? So the fish comes from a lake or river and has a bad texture?"

Resting an elbow on the edge of the cart, he closed his eyes and massaged his temple. Maybe he should have suggested a nap before going grocery shopping, instead of agreeing to stop on the way home from Arlanda. But Maria's parents had wanted him to pick breakfast items he'd enjoy, and he was trying to be as accommodating as possible, so here he was. Jet-lagged and chilled—because spring had evidently not quite sprung near Stockholm—and fumbling to explain gummy fish to a pair of befuddled, bespectacled Swedes in their late sixties.

So much for a good impression. Shit.

He tried again. "I'm not explaining this well. I'm sorry. What I mean is—"

"Peter." When he opened his eyes, Stina patted his upper arm and offered him a sweet, grandmotherly smile. "I should apologize, not you. Olle and I are merely . . ."

She turned to Maria. "What's the appropriate phrase in English?"

"I believe that would be 'fucking with you,' Mamma," Maria said. "As in, 'Olle and I are merely fucking with you.'"

He opened his mouth. Closed it once more.

"Thank you." Stina nodded, then swiveled to face him again. "Olle and I are fucking with you. As we did when we warned you against openly criticizing Alexander Skarsgård, lest you be sentenced to several years' hard labor serving meatballs in an IKEA cafeteria. In reality, that's only for repeat offenders. The first time, you'd simply be forced to assemble display shelves for a month or two."

"Also when we warned you about a rampaging herd of wild Dala horses menacing the countryside outside Stockholm," Olle added. "Those are mainly found in southern Sweden."

At this point, Maria had staggered away from all of them, hiding her face in her hands, but he could hear her distinctive cackle down a nearby refrigerated aisle. She was losing her damn shit.

"Ah," said Peter politely. "I see."

As discreetly as possible, he unearthed the cheap cell he'd bought at the airport upon arrival and did two quick Google searches.

Dala horses were, as it turned out, decorative wooden horses from the Dalarna region of Sweden, hand-carved and painted in distinctive colors. And as far as the search engine knew, criticism of Alexander Skarsgård remained both legal and unpunished by hard labor in the IKEA mines.

Okay, now he believed Stina and Olle were truly Maria's parents.

"You're still fucking with me," he noted mildly.

He'd feel worse about swearing in public, but Maria had assured him on the plane that Swedes didn't object to obscenities the same way many Americans did. Although, in retrospect, he should probably Google that little tidbit too.

"We are." Olle nodded gravely, the very picture of dignity.

In contrast, Stina allowed her smile to shift from grandmotherly to openly wicked. She might not share a genetic heritage with Maria, but he'd recognize that smug grin anywhere.

"*Ja,*" she said, then tugged him down with a hand on the back of his head and planted a smacking kiss on his cheek. "Welcome to Sweden, *skitstövel.*"

SOMEONE WAS SAYING . . . something.

Peter couldn't seem to focus. He was still dazed from jet lag and a long flight aboard a crowded plane. Not to mention exhaustion from several days of incessant fucking at every opportunity. Also the brain fog resulting from a too-short, sweaty nap spent atop a very narrow guest bed, beside a radiator pumping out tropical air, covered by a stiflingly heavy duvet so he couldn't inadvertently expose Maria's entire family to freshly showered, full-frontal goodness—

He rubbed his forehead, his erratic train of thought entirely derailed.

What was with the lack of bedding, anyway? Did Swedes not believe in top sheets and blankets? Didn't they experience sleeping temperatures anywhere between Steamy Heat Requiring Absolute Nakedness and Hypothermic Huddling Beneath a Down Duvet Suitable for Antarctica?

If he'd known, he'd have packed pajamas. Or purchased pajamas *to* pack. Or, alternatively, gotten used to sleeping in boxer briefs rather than going commando.

Which raised yet more fuzzy-minded questions: Was Maria

naked right now? Was her bed bigger than his? Might she want company? And did her mattress creak too? Because if not—

Someone cleared their throat, and Peter raised his head, blinking wearily.

Oh, right. While Maria continued her own nap, he'd stumbled downstairs and found himself surrounded by the entire remaining clan of Ivarssons. Most of them were working on dinner, and he'd wanted to assist, but when he'd offered, the outraged refusals had been too fierce to resist. So now he was sitting at the large dining room table with Maria's brother Vincent, who appeared to be the family's chosen diplomatic representative to the Sovereign Sleepy State of Peter Reedton.

Vincent, who also appeared to be waiting for a response to a question Peter hadn't heard.

"Sorry. Jet lag is a beast." Peter straightened in his chair and marshaled his straggling thoughts. "Can you repeat what you just said?"

"What did you think of ICA?" Vincent didn't appear offended. "Is it very different from American grocery stores?"

Peter took a moment to blearily consider the appropriate level of honesty in his response.

Under normal circumstances, staying in the guest room of complete strangers for an entire week—as Maria had finally persuaded him to do—would necessitate a certain amount of tongue-biting and noncommittal small talk, for fear of offending his hosts. Who were, after all, feeding him, and could thus spit in his food whenever the spirit so moved them.

Plus, he didn't want her family to hate him. They were a close-knit group, maybe closer than he'd even guessed, and if they disapproved of him . . .

Well, if pitted against them, he was pretty sure he wouldn't come out on top. Not yet, anyway. So he was making a concerted effort not to be surly or silent or in any way like himself.

That said, they were Maria's family, so he figured they couldn't be too easily offended. Also, her parents had spent the entire ride from ICA to their yellow-painted two-story home outside Stockholm feeding him yet more complete bullshit about Sweden.

For example: According to Stina, sixty percent of Swedes self-identified as ABBAsexuals. Including her and her husband.

After she made that pronouncement, Olle glanced over at her and placed a hand on her knee. "Knowing me, knowing you, being ABBAsexual is the best we can do. Right, *älskling*?"

Yeah, they were smartasses through and through. But maybe Maria's siblings weren't.

Vincent, in his late thirties and the oldest of those siblings, was still looking at him, blond man-bunned head cocked. Still waiting yet again for an answer to a completely innocuous question.

Aw, fuck it. Other than a few television appearances and interviews, he and Maria would be spending a lot of time with her family, and he didn't want to pretend for seven days.

"Your checkout lanes scare the shit out of me, man." When he saw Stina gathering silverware for the table, he half rose out of his chair to help, but she waved him back down. Reluctantly, he turned to Vincent once more. "I don't mind bagging my own groceries, but I wasn't prepared for the intense *pressure*. By the time I managed to get all our stuff in the bags, two separate families were waiting for me to finish so they could pack their own groceries, the checkout clerk had stopped scanning things and was giving me a look of disdain and pity, and I think I panicked and threw an entire ham on top of our eggs."

"You did," Stina called from the far end of the kitchen.

Olle nodded, mouth grim. "Somewhere, a lone hen felt a disturbance in the Force. A century from now, historians will trace the origins of the Great Chicken Rebellion to this very incident and blame you for the carnage."

Peter could now identify the owner of the sci-fi novels stacked on the coffee table.

"And without those eggs, we'll all starve." Stina shook her head and removed a stack of plates from a white-painted cabinet. "It's a shame. I actually like one or two of you. Mostly Filip, if I had to specify."

Filip snorted and kept stirring his pot of gravy.

Astrid, Maria's younger sister, grinned at Peter as she set the table. "Mamma and Pappa didn't help you pack the bags?"

As if. "The three of them sat down on a bench to watch and laughed until they cried."

"That sounds like them. Monstrous, aren't they?" After distributing the last of the silverware, she straightened. "Rest assured, Peter, if I'd been there, I wouldn't have been laughing on the bench with them."

"Thank you, Astrid." Despite Stina's flurry of objections, he got up, claimed the plates from her grasp, and deposited one in front of each chair. "So you'd have helped me?"

"*Nej*," she said. "I'd have gotten closer and captured the whole thing on video so I could sit on a bench and laugh at it whenever I wanted."

She winked before returning to the kitchen, and he found himself laughing as helplessly as Maria and her parents had earlier in the day.

Just then, Maria herself came tripping lightly down the stairs, as fresh and energetic as someone who'd spent the entire day re-laxing at a goddamn spa. It was aggravating as fuck, frankly.

"Gods above, I needed that nap." The kiss she planted on his lips was over before he could react, and she bounced toward the kitchen. "How can I help?"

One way or another, he was stealing a longer, better kiss from her tonight. More than a kiss, if he could figure out the logistics.

"You look much better, *älskling*." Stina stroked her daughter's cheek. "Finish up the mustard sauce while I deal with the cabbage?"

Without any fuss, Maria slotted herself into the organized chaos and took her place at the counter. Beneath the short sleeves of her tee, her triceps visibly tensed as she began vigorously whisk-ing oil into a small bowlful of yellow sauce, and *Jesus*.

Those dumbbells in her Irish hotel suite obviously hadn't gone unused. Which he'd already known, and he'd witnessed countless displays of her strength before, but . . .

She was so round, so soft, sometimes he forgot.

Sitting back in his chair, he watched, rapt.

When Filip carried a steaming platter of food to the table, he lightly bumped his shoulder against Peter's in a friendly gesture. Peter jumped a little, startled out of his Maria-induced fugue state.

Before then, her second-oldest sibling had remained in the kitchen all evening, so he and Peter hadn't had much chance to talk. But from what Peter had seen, he got the sense that the rest of the family was taking turns checking on the slim, soft-spoken man, giving him searching glances and brief pats on his arm or back whenever they passed him. They didn't force him to talk; they just silently let him know they were there and they cared.

That quiet cocoon of love and protection resembled nothing

Peter had ever seen before. At least, not outside the pseudo-family Maria had gathered on the island.

What would it have been like, growing up in a home like theirs? What would *he* have been like?

After setting down the platter, Filip offered Peter a sweetly sincere smile. "Don't worry about the checkout line. We all have trouble in the beginning. The first time I tried to bag groceries on my own, an elderly woman ran out of patience, shoved me aside with her walker, and filled my final bag for me. I think she stole a package of frozen pancakes too."

"Didn't she leave you her number on your receipt?" Astrid asked with a smirk, flicking her long brown hair over her shoulder.

"Yes." Frowning, Filip adjusted his thick-rimmed glasses. "Even though I wanted my pancakes back, I didn't call her. I hope I didn't hurt her feelings."

"If you're wondering who the nice one in the family is, Peter, look no further," Vincent said, then stood, strode into the kitchen, and removed stoppered carafes of sparkling water from the refrigerator, returning to set them on the table. "Filip carries the rest of us when it comes to human decency."

Peter had his doubts.

Several times in the store, he'd watched Maria's parents unobtrusively assist other customers who couldn't reach the top shelf or the farthest depths of the freezer compartments. Maria's mom had insisted on buying Peter whatever food looked good or interesting to him—although he planned to pay them back for that somehow—and in line at the deli counter, a wailing child had forgotten his misery when Stina crouched low and played peekaboo with him, while the boy's young mother nearly dissolved into grateful tears. On their way out, Olle had gathered stray carts from the parking lot and added them to a nearby covered corral.

Their actions weren't dramatic. Just observant. Just considerate.

Astrid had washed countless dishes, carried any pot or pan she deemed too heavy for her mom, and coaxed Stina to sit down and let Olle or Filip take over the cooking at several points in the afternoon, because Stina apparently had back problems. Vincent worked for an environmental organization, and he'd drawn Filip aside shortly after his brother's arrival for an intense, whispered conversation, during which he helped dry Filip's tears and held him for a long, long time.

"Girlfriend issues," he'd murmured quietly to Peter when he'd returned to the table.

Filip had retreated to the bathroom for several minutes. When he'd returned, he'd had a freshly scrubbed face, a determined smile, and nothing but kind words for their guest.

No one needed to tell Peter about Maria's inherent goodness, obviously.

And he didn't intend to stand out as the only lazy, self-centered one in the crowd, so he ignored all of Stina's entreaties and helped bring out the rest of the food. In the end, the table fairly groaned with all the dishes Maria's family had bought and prepared. Smoked, herbed salmon with mustard sauce. The egg-crushing ham. Little oblong boiled potatoes. Sautéed green beans. A sweet dish of boiled red cabbage and apples. The inevitable jar of herring. Some unidentified type of pâté. Meatballs, because of course meatballs. Brown gravy. Lingonberry jam. A huge, curved cylinder of pale sausage called falukorv, sliced partway through and stuffed with mustard and cheese. A toasted baguette and butter.

Shortly before they all sat down to eat, Filip tugged Maria into his arms, exactly as the other siblings had after they arrived, exactly as her parents had as soon as they saw her in the airport. Like the rest of his family, he squeezed her tight and said something affectionately. Something that ended with *jag älskar dig*, one of the few Swedish phrases Peter recognized.

I love you.

Maria returned the words, face tucked against her brother's shoulder, and Peter wasn't sure he'd ever seen her look so peaceful and content.

And although he wanted that for her—wanted her happiness with an intensity he'd never experienced before, not even with his ex-fiancée—the open generosity of her family's love strung his chest tight, and for more than one reason.

She cared about him. Without question. She also had a blossoming career and several auditions waiting for her back in LA.

But for the first time, he wondered whether all that—whether he—would be enough to keep her by his side.

17

MARIA'S LONG, BLISSFUL AFTERNOON NAP HAD BEEN, IN retrospect, a truly terrible idea.

The rest of her family had already headed to bed, either in her parents' house or in their own homes. Peter had also disappeared upstairs, and the gush of water in the pipes indicated he was cleaning up for the night. In a minute or two, he'd come down, give her a kiss, then trudge back upstairs to erase those dark circles under his beautiful eyes.

She should be getting some sleep too, of course. The next day, *Gates'* PR department had scheduled interviews with local and national news outlets for Maria and Peter, as well as an hourslong photo session that would take them to various iconic Stockholm locations. It was going to be exhausting, and the more she rested now, the better.

And given how awake she felt, she might as well have guzzled Sweden's entire supply of energy drinks, then charged into one of the few Starbucks locations and started an espresso IV. She was nowhere near sleep. At the moment, she wasn't certain she'd ever sleep again.

If she were irredeemably selfish, she'd convince Peter to forgo the rest he needed and talk with her. Not because she was lonely for company in general, but because she'd pined for *him* all day, even though he'd remained no more than a few meters away from her at any given time. But she wouldn't ask him to give up yet more sleep and keep her company when he was already beyond exhausted. No matter how much she wanted him to herself for a few hours.

Dividing her attention between him and her family hadn't come naturally that day, much as she wanted him to like them and vice versa. She'd missed one-on-one time with him, missed the privacy they'd relinquished by staying in her parents' house, missed the thrill of knowing—even when surrounded by other people—that at some point, the two of them would find themselves alone in a bed and fuck like rabbits.

Her childhood bed, sadly, was not conducive to rabbitlike fucking. It was barely wide enough to fit her, and it also shared a wall with her parents' bedroom. Which had been a source of much consternation during her teenage years, because Stina and Olle still led a very active life, both in bed and out. Nevertheless, she preferred not to follow their example in this particular instance, and she would not be banging Peter in a location where her parents could provide play-by-play commentary, should they so choose.

Peter's bed abutted Filip's old bedroom, where her brother was staying until he found an apartment far from the home he'd shared with his ex. The guest bed was the same size as hers, and the old frame would collapse in despair if asked to support their combined weight.

So the two of them were fucked, yet also unfucked. They would remain so until they flew to Wisconsin next week, where they'd check into a hotel. He'd rejected the idea of staying with his father with such stony finality, she hadn't even asked for an explanation.

Fine, then. She couldn't sleep, and she couldn't have sex, but she could still entertain herself. Uncurling from her favorite spot on the couch, the corner farthest from the television and closest to the windows, she drifted toward the built-in shelves and contemplated her options.

Sci-fi paperbacks. Cookbooks. Noir thrillers. Or—childhood photo albums.

Nostalgia it was.

The album she removed from the shelf was a bit worn around the edges now, some of the photos inside not as bright as they once were, and that only made her cherish it more. Those scuffs and slightly bent pages meant the album had been well loved, pored over by her and her family again and again over the past two decades.

It contained everyone she truly needed, everyone she loved.

Although . . . that might or might not be true any longer.

A heavy, warm hand landed on her hip. "What's that?"

For such a big man, Peter could move very quietly. Without turning, she let herself lean back against him, trusting him to support some of her weight, and he wrapped his arms around her and propped his bristly chin on her shoulder. With each deep breath, she inhaled her family's usual lemongrass-scented soap and whatever product made him so deliciously cedary.

The unexpected combination smelled good. It smelled right.

She wished she believed in omens.

His feet were bare, some sort of soft-looking pants loose around his ankles, the fabric of his long-sleeved tee smooth and cool against her forearms. The equivalent of pajamas, which she suspected he didn't own. So this was a good-night hug, obviously. Not an invitation to share her childhood—not to mention her siblings'—with him.

"Are you ready for bed?" Ducking her head, she kissed a tiny scar on his lower arm, the memento of a too-sharp piece of lime-stone as Cassia and Cyprian built their home. "Is there anything you need? An extra pillow, or a nightlight?"

She was almost certain she heard him mutter, *Some fucking bedding would be nice.*

When she turned in his arms to face him, though, he only shook his head. "I'm not ready for bed yet, and I don't need anything. But I want something."

"So I can feel." She raised a brow and nudged his burgeoning erection with her belly. "While I appreciate your enthusiasm, I've considered the logistics, and—"

"I want to know what you have in your hands, and I want time alone with you, Maria. That's all." His own belly vibrated with his low laugh, and his cheeks creased beneath his beard. "Well, not all, but I'm still working on the logistics too. For now, let's see if we can find a chair that'll support us both and . . ."

He paused and shifted his weight.

"Why, Peter Reedton. My stoic, silent costar." Leaning back against the support of his arms, she tipped her chin until she could see his expression clearly. "You want to chat, don't you? Chat and cuddle. How adorable."

His scowl should have incinerated the album still cradled in her hands and propped against his chest. But it was too late. She knew his dirty little snuggling secret now.

Tucking the album beneath one arm, she stepped out of his embrace, took his hand, and led him to the chaise longue in the corner. It was another of her favorite spots in the house, perfect for reading. Wide, thickly cushioned, and upholstered with velvety teal fabric, it overlooked the small back garden, had comfortable rolled arms, and resembled an overstuffed armchair stretching out its legs.

After one good look at it, Peter closed his eyes and groaned.

Well, after that pained growl, she was imagining the possibilities too, and they were both delightful and legion. But . . .

"Let me stop you right there. Yes, fucking on the chaise would be amazing, but the door doesn't lock, and Filip is a restless sleeper." She used her hold on his hand to urge him toward the enticing piece of furniture. "Sit."

His answering grunt brimmed with aggrievement, but he put a knee on the chaise and maneuvered until the back cushions supported him and he could extend his strong legs over the elongated seat cushion. Then he spread those legs as wide as he could get them between the rolled arms and patted the space he'd created in front of him.

It was a tight fit, but with a bit of wiggling, she managed to wedge herself between his slightly raised knees and recline against his chest and stomach. His arms loosely circled her shoulders, and his chin nuzzled her cheek.

His body surrounded her. Braced her. Enclosed her in strength and softness and warmth without demanding a thing in exchange.

In the late-night stillness of her childhood home, they might have been the only two people awake in the world. Turning her head, she planted a kiss against his prickly chin, and the little hum in his throat sounded . . . content.

When he spoke, his tone was gruff but amused. "You realize we're going to need a crane to get us out of this chair."

"Worth it," she said, and propped the thick album on her belly. "To answer your question, my father made this album when Vincent went away to university. Pappa was having empty nest issues, even with the rest of us still around, so he gathered photos showing how everyone became part of the family, up through the first year or so after we arrived."

Over time, she'd seen each member of her family flip through the pages. The album served as a sort of touchstone for all of them, even as she and her siblings scattered to various spots around the world, only to inevitably return before scattering once more.

"Show me." Peter took over holding the album upright. "Tell me about your family."

Despite the quiet calm in his voice, new tension thrummed through his limbs, turning them from languid to slightly stiff, and she wanted to ask what was worrying him. But not if asking would distract from the conversation they were about to have, because he needed to know. He needed to understand the stakes for her in whatever sort of relationship they were creating, because his own stakes weren't nearly so high. Not when he already lived in LA, seemingly content to settle a good distance from what she'd gathered was his semi-estranged father.

So instead of pressing him for answers, she simply flipped to the first page.

Her mother, red hair in loose curls, in her early thirties and pregnant, a smile on her face and one hand on her belly as her blond husband wrapped an arm around her shoulders and beamed at her. With her free hand, she held his.

"Mamma and Pappa didn't meet until they were almost thirty. He'd just moved from the countryside to find factory work, and they met on the production line of our local pharmaceutical plant. They married two years later at the city hall, and they didn't know it at the time, but she was already carrying Vincent." She traced her parents' entangled fingers through the plastic barrier. "The pregnancy was fine, but things went wrong during labor, and they were advised not to have more children. Pappa was particularly devastated, since he'd always wanted lots of kids."

The only child of parents who'd died when he was in his twenties, killed at a crosswalk by a reckless driver, he'd craved—*needed*—noise and chaos and *connection*. A big family to love and raise with his beloved wife, however that family came to be.

"So no more pregnancies." Peter's thumb tapped the edge of the plastic-covered page. "But that didn't mean no more children."

She smiled. "Exactly."

Silently, they flipped through the rest of Vincent's photos, watching him transform from a red-faced, squalling newborn to a chubby infant chewing on plastic keys and a bright-eyed toddler standing on his own two feet.

A flip of the page, and there was Filip. Eighteen months of age, his black hair choppy and tousled, his brown gaze wary. Fresh off the plane from South Korea, where he'd spent his entire infancy in an orphanage.

"My parents were waiting at the gate when Filip arrived, and they fell in love with him the moment they saw him," she said.

"Well, yeah." Peter touched Filip's small, solemn face. "Who could blame them? I'm not even a kid kind of person, but he's fucking adorable. One look at him, and I'd have scooped him up and fed him ice cream until he smiled."

She had to laugh. "That's pretty much what they did. As Vincent always points out, you can actually see his cheeks get chubbier and chubbier with each picture."

Some of that was the food, but not all. His cheeks plumped when he smiled. And after a few months, when he'd settled in and grown to trust his new family, he'd begun smiling all the time. A quiet, sweet smile that looked almost exactly the same more than three decades later.

She flipped through more photos and basked in her brother's growing contentment, the happy glow that said he'd found his place in the world at long last.

"I'll be damned. You really can track the cheeks." Peter sounded tickled by that. "By the end, his face is like a little moon."

It really was. "When he shot up during puberty and lost those cheeks, my mother was devastated."

"I'll bet." He turned to the next page and took a moment to study the photo of a sleeping infant with a surprisingly thick head of brown hair, clad in green footed pajamas. "This is Astrid, right? Why is she next? You're older than her."

"She was adopted as a newborn. I wasn't. So she became part of the family before me."

Something she'd tried her hardest not to envy growing up, more or less successfully. And the last traces of longing and resentment had disappeared altogether when Astrid got older, and Maria finally understood: There were many ways to feel like an outsider, and not all of them involved family.

Most early photos of Astrid showed her playing in the sunshine, because from what their parents said, she'd always hated being cooped up indoors. It hadn't surprised any of them when she became a hiking guide after a couple of unhappy years as a hairstylist.

"Astrid was an outdoor cat from the very start," Stina would say when they were growing up, then proceed to ruffle Astrid's hair until her teenage daughter squawked in outrage and ran off, generally to her tree house.

Several pages later, Peter paused. "Hold on. Why did your sister get fewer photos than your brothers?"

"A lot of the pictures taken before she transitioned make her uncomfortable." Even though Swedes generally weren't as attached to sex-specific clothing as Americans, some of her sister's earlier outfits and hairstyles had virtually screamed her assumed gender identity. "Pappa only put in photos she approved."

"Gotcha." Peter nodded, entirely unfazed, as she'd both hoped and expected he would be. "That makes sense."

Maria tried not to tense up in anticipation of what he'd see next. What she'd have to explain to him, and what it would reveal about her.

It wasn't that she felt shame about it anymore, or blamed something intrinsically wrong with herself. Really, there was no one to blame. Over time, she'd come to sincerely believe that.

But pain didn't require a guilty party, and Maria didn't often display her vulnerabilities for the scrutiny of others. Outside her family and a couple of her closest girlhood friends, only her ex Hugo knew the full story of how she'd become an Ivarsson.

Not that knowing it had stopped him from causing her yet more pain.

After the next flip of the page, Peter went quiet for a moment. "And here you are."

There she was. Wearing jeans and a tee. Already tall for her age, solidly built, with her blond hair in neat braids by her ears. Expressionless, her stare bold and cold.

"Sweetheart." Through the plastic covering the photograph, Peter's forefinger smoothed over her girlish cheek, again and again. "I didn't realize how old you were when your parents adopted you."

"Eight." No need to belabor any of this. Just the bare facts would do. "My biological parents died in a terrible fire at a Stockholm club when I was four. It was their anniversary, and I was with a babysitter."

His finger stilled. "Maria."

No, she wasn't stopping yet. Especially not for that too-gentle murmur.

"There was no will specifying where I should go, and they were both the only children of only children, so there weren't a lot of options." Her memories of those months in limbo remained tucked so deep in her mind, even she couldn't access them. She could only assume she'd been terrified. Heartbroken. Utterly bewildered by what had happened to her family and her secure existence. "Eventually, a distant relative of my biological mother took me in for two years."

After a few months, she'd settled in. Stopped having nightmares every night. Adored their little apartment overlooking a tree-studded courtyard. Grown to love Inga, who wore her thick hair in a graying bun.

That she remembered, although not as well as what happened next.

"Her adult daughter became very ill. Cancer. My guardian"—not mother, although she'd called Inga *mamma* that last year together—"was the sole caretaker, and she couldn't meet her daughter's needs and raise a young child at the same time. Not with her own health issues."

Inga had been in her early sixties and a lifelong smoker, and her cough often kept Maria awake until late in the night. Years later, when Maria had looked her up online, she'd found both women's obituaries. The mother had outlived her daughter by only three months.

Peter's arms had tensed around her, but his voice remained as soft as the chaise's velvet upholstery. "She relinquished you?"

"Yes." If she sounded a bit brusque, so be it. He'd have to forgive her. "I went back in the system and got sent to another home a few months later. A couple in their late thirties. I was with them for over a year. She cleaned offices, and he did maintenance for some local apartment complexes. He got laid off, and she found out she was pregnant. They'd assumed they couldn't have children, so they were shocked."

And delighted, despite their financial woes. Effervescent with joy to have a child of their own blood, although they'd liked Maria fine.

But not enough to keep her.

Maria explained it to Peter the same way she'd explained it to herself so many nights in bed, a forsaken child desolate and trying to cry quietly enough that no one else would hear. "They couldn't afford two children. Even before he lost his job, they could barely pay their rent each month. So without his income and with a baby on the way, they didn't really have a choice."

A few times over the year she'd spent in their apartment, she'd overheard intense, low-voiced discussions about scraping together enough money for spaghetti and whatever fruit was on sale that week and maybe an outfit she hadn't already outgrown.

Their decision to give her up made sense. It had made sense to her even then. They were in a difficult position with no good options, and they'd chosen one. It didn't mean they were bad people.

Still, when they'd called her into that tiny, cluttered kitchen and told her their big news and what it meant for her own future, she'd been fiercely glad she'd never called them *mamma* and *pappa* as they'd said she could, never committed her heart as fully as she had with Inga. Even though her slight emotional remove had hurt the couple's feelings at times.

Maybe that was spiteful of her. But sometimes only spite had kept her functioning after they'd left her, kept her going to school and smiling and trying to make friends as she bounced from home to home, none of the placements lasting long.

"So they let you go." His chest expanded as he inhaled slowly, and his even slower exhalation tickled her cheek. "Okay."

The words might still be quiet, but he sounded like he'd gargled rocks, and the legs bracketing hers might as well have been stone.

His thumb kept whispering over the cheek of the lost, devastated, distrustful girl she hadn't been for a long, long time.

"It *is* okay," she told him, patting that restless hand.

The silence following her reassurance was absolute. So heavy it should have crashed through the chaise and the wooden floorboards below them and bored a hole deep in the earth.

His jaw began making a weird grinding noise she'd never heard before.

"Don't worry," she rushed to add. "A few months later, my parents adopted me, and they didn't fuck around. They made everything permanent and legally binding as soon as they possibly could."

As an adult, she'd understood why. They'd meant to declare in every conceivable way, both to her and to the authorities: This placement was forever. *They* were forever. Her new family would never leave her, would always want and love her, would always choose her.

And in retrospect, she'd also understood how big a gamble that decision was, because before the adoption went through, she spoke to her parents and siblings only when absolutely necessary. She didn't trust them, she didn't intend to get comfortable in their home, and she sure as hell wasn't allowing them anywhere near her heart.

She was polite and uncomplaining, but chilly and distant as northernmost Lappland. A stranger in every fundamental way.

When they adopted her, they didn't *know* her.

"But we already loved you" was her father's perennial response whenever she said so. "That heart of yours was too big to hide, no matter how hard you tried. And you tried *very* hard, *älskling*. Frankly, we were impressed by your level of commitment. It's a shame TED Talks weren't around back then, because you could have given a lecture on how to remain stone-faced and uncommunicative in the face of blatant bribery and embarrassingly effusive displays of affection."

They'd tried the ice cream trick on her too. It hadn't worked.

But that was the least of it. Gods above, Astrid had latched on to her like a tick from the beginning. And whenever her younger sister wasn't clinging to her leg, Vincent and Filip were walking Maria to school and taking her to movies on the weekends and sneaking her absurd amounts of candy. Worst of all, every one of the five Ivarssons could sense when her defenses were low and pounced immediately, like lions stalking a hapless blond gazelle who was really trying very hard not to have her heart broken yet again.

They asked if Maria would like to redecorate her bedroom, because Stina loved assembling furniture, sewing curtains, and hanging wallpaper—especially with company. If Maria wanted to learn how to bake a raspberry roll cake the same way Olle's late mother had, so he could pass on the tradition to the next genera-tion of Ivarssons. If Maria was willing to have Vincent teach her some self-defense moves, so if anyone at school ever gave her a hard time, she could make them pay. If Maria would consider playing catch with Astrid in the backyard. If Maria needed a tutor for any of her classes, because Filip would be delighted to help her with whatever subjects she found difficult.

They were fucking relentless. Despite her best intentions and considerable stubbornness, she couldn't hold the line for longer than a few months after the adoption became final.

Eventually, when they asked if they could hug her, she said yes and hugged them back.

Eventually, she started laughing again.

Eventually, the nightmares ended and she no longer woke in tears.

Eventually, she called Stina *mamma* and Olle *pappa*.

Eventually, when they said they loved her, she said *jag älskar dig också*, and her voice didn't even shake.

Eventually, she believed them when they said they weren't going anywhere, and neither was she. Not unless and until she was ready. Which she hadn't been . . . until six years before, when she'd boarded a plane for LA and committed to spending months of her life far away from her family for the first time since they'd *become* family.

Six years before, when she'd found herself in the same sauna as the man vibrating with suppressed emotion and holding her with such tense care in her parents' dark, quiet house.

All that emotion and all that care were for her, experienced and offered on behalf of the girl she once was, which felt like a different kind of embrace. Both were appreciated, but both were also needless, which he'd discover shortly.

"Turn the page, *sötnos*," she said, then planted a kiss on that very feature. "See what happens next."

His thumb stilled on her child's face, and after a moment, he obeyed.

Olle's photo choices explained more clearly than words ever could. The first page, she was cold and disconnected and lost. But a few pages later, she was smiling, posing awkwardly, giggling as Vincent tickled her, carrying Astrid on her shoulders at a Midsommar celebration, and resting her head on Stina's shoulder as her mother stroked her hair.

In the later pictures, she was never alone.

Then came the final section of photos. A few months after Maria's arrival, Filip had fastened Stina's camera to a tripod, set a timer, and raced back for their first official Ivarsson family portrait. A year later, he did the same thing. And now the album contained over twenty of those group photos, taken whenever all of them found themselves in one place.

For a long time, looking at those photos had made Maria cry. Now it only made her smile.

When Peter reached the final page, he closed the album very carefully and set it on the little table beside the chaise. "Next time, I'll ask for the stories behind each picture. Tonight, though, I have something else I need to do."

"Oh?" Maybe he wanted to sleep now?

When she twisted her neck to see his expression, it told her nothing. But his jaw still ticked with whatever emotion had brought high color to his face. The long muscles of his legs remained knotted with tension.

He was holding her very, very tightly.

Even though he'd seen the final family portraits, seen how happy she became and how happy she'd remained, his distress hadn't eased. It had only . . . shifted, in a way she didn't understand.

Until his hold around her shoulders loosened, but not to let her go.

Instead, he slid those big hands up her belly and cupped her breasts, unhurriedly thumbing her nipples to aching hardness. With his chin, he shifted her hair away from her right ear. The prickle of his beard, the heat of his breath, sent fire between her legs.

"The guest shower is pretty generous," he murmured, and licked the rim of her ear.

Resting her hands atop his, she let out a shaky breath. "Not generous enough for two people of our size to fuck."

"Hmmm." His teeth closed around her lobe, and she shuddered. "Just generous enough for me to make you come with that detachable showerhead."

Hand jobs didn't require much space either, despite the impressive size of his growing erection against her lower back. Clearly she hadn't given the matter of rabbitlike-fucking sufficient consideration, and Peter had. That kind of initiative and creativity deserved a reward, did it not?

When he lightly pinched her nipples between his knuckles, she pressed her leggings-clad thighs together. "We'll have to be quiet."

Because the water would drown out some noise, but not the volume of sounds the two of them usually made.

"I'll put a hand over your mouth," he told her.

Gods above, why did the thought of that only turn her on more?

As if in demonstration, he slid one hand upward until it covered her parted lips, and stroked the other lower, over her stomach and down farther. Wedging a hand between her legs, he palmed her pussy. Squeezed. And as promised, her breathy moan emerged faint and muffled, made private, offered to him alone.

"Up." After a final, firm stroke of his thumb over the fabric covering her clit, he let go and started maneuvering them both off the chaise.

As soon as they managed to wiggle themselves free, he snatched her hand and propelled her forward, up the stairs and into the guest bathroom.

Turned out, there was plenty of room for a detachable showerhead aimed at her clit and deployed at various intensities, because Peter was a fucking tease. Only . . .

He didn't seem playful. His intensity didn't diminish, even for a moment.

Not when he let the water drift away from where she needed it every time she got close to orgasm, or twisted the showerhead until the spray became too diffuse and gentle to do anything but provoke her further. Not when a relentless, targeted stream of water hit her at just the right spot, and he finally—finally—let it remain there until she arched and came and cried out against his hard palm, nearly collapsing against the thick arm bracing her back. Not when she shoved him against the wall, covered his own mouth, and gripped his dick exactly how he liked it, pumping him to a fast, hard orgasm.

Not even when they held each other afterward, limp and spent and waterlogged, or when he went to his knees by the sink to dry her with his own towel.

His lips remained pressed in a grim line. His intent focus on her never wavered. He kept at least one hand on her at all times until the moment they said good night. His mouth devoured hers outside her bedroom doorway, his fists buried deep in her hair, before he abruptly let her go and stalked away.

He was trying to prove something. She could recognize that much.

She wished she had the slightest idea what it was.

18

THE IVARSSONS WERE A HARD FUCKING ACT TO FOLLOW.

In hopes of delaying the inevitable, Peter had suggested flying into O'Hare and driving to his hometown instead of catching a commuter flight from Chicago to the small Madison airport. But the trip couldn't last forever, and with each mile of interstate guiding them closer and closer to his childhood home and his sole remaining family member, his hands clenched a bit tighter on the steering wheel. Even Maria's cheerful, provoking conversation from the passenger seat of the rental could no longer entirely distract him from the amorphous dread pounding at his temples.

"So you don't think the Amerikansk section in ICA was a fair representation of your nation's cuisine?" Reaching down for the controls, she sent her seat sliding back even farther and stretched out her legs with a relieved sigh. "Because it seemed pretty accurate to me."

He slanted her a look, one that told her without words: He knew she was pulling his chain, and he was allowing it only out of extreme benevolence. Or at least, that was what he meant to convey. Hopefully his growing anxiety hadn't ruined his ability to emote, because he was going to need that again when he—no, he was going to think positively; when *they*—booked new roles back in Hollywood.

His response was as dry as LA in August. "Maria, that wasteland of an aisle contained nothing but off-brand faux-maple syrup, beef jerky, ramen, and shelf after shelf of candy, much of which I'd never actually seen before."

"You forgot the Marshmallow Fluff."

The traffic had grown heavier, so he couldn't glance at her again. But a smile he couldn't see warmed her voice. That too-innocent, smug voice.

"As if that disproves my point," he told her witheringly.

"You didn't have a point, as far as I could tell." She patted her mouth over a loud, fake little yawn, an annoyingly adorable gesture he caught from the corner of his eye. "Merely a list of foodstuffs. One of which, despite all your patriotic protests, you actually purchased."

Gladly. Also repeatedly, because candy deprivation could happen to anyone at any time.

He sniffed, nose high in the air as he smothered his grin. "My duty as an American forces me to buy Reese's Peanut Butter Cups wherever I may find them. It's a lesser-known part of the Pledge of Allegiance, and doesn't invalidate my argument in the slightest."

"Fine, then. If the Amerikansk section was both inaccurate and inadequate, what would *you* add to it?" She sounded genuinely curious.

"Nonperishable items?" He thought for a moment. "Grits. Granola and cereal bars. Graham crackers. Cranberry sauce. Stuffing mixes. Canned pumpkin. Not to mention pumpkin pie spice and—"

Her snort cracked his stone face, and he smiled at the windshield.

"Now you're just naming Thanksgiving ingredients," she told him.

"I didn't hear you complaining about Fionn's turkey feasts whenever we filmed on the island in late November."

In fact, she'd pretty much licked the sweet potato casserole dish clean each time. One year, the crew briefly, hilariously nicknamed her There's Something About Maria because of the orange goop she'd unknowingly gotten in her hair and allowed to harden.

"I had no choice but to eat a lot." She poked his arm. "I didn't want to insult either your culture or Fionn's cooking."

"Bullshit. More like you didn't want to put down your herb-rubbed turkey drumstick, you Swedish ingrate."

Her laughter filled the car, and he couldn't help laughing too. When they quieted again, his knuckles no longer ached as they gripped the wheel, and his shoulders had loosened.

After so many years, he still didn't know whether she did that on purpose. At first, he'd thought not. He'd figured all that charm, all that humor, had to be effortless, because why would she exert herself to make him, of all people, more comfortable?

But now . . .

He claimed her hand from the SUV's console and brought it to his lips. Kissed her palm. Interlaced their fingers and placed them on his thigh.

Everything would be okay. So what if the Reedtons weren't exactly the Ivarssons? So what if Dad didn't know how to talk to him? So what if Peter had never figured out how to make himself understood to his father?

His awkwardness around his dad wouldn't come as a shock to her, not after she'd had to work for months to bridge the gap between him and their crew, him and their castmates. That awkwardness also wouldn't tip the balance and drive her away if she was still considering whether she should return to Sweden for good.

Or so he hoped.

He hadn't raised the issue directly, especially not after she'd just spent quality time with her adoring parents and siblings. Right now, if he told her she should stay with him, she could easily marshal so many arguments about why he was wrong, why she needed her family more than she needed him, and Maria's arguments were always, always devastating and convincing.

She played to win. She played for keeps.

And once she made up her mind, she didn't change it.

So no, he wasn't asking whether she'd stay with him, because he was scared to find out what she might say, what she might do, and she'd already left him once. He couldn't fathom how he'd survive a repeat now that he actually *knew* her. Knew her and—

Well, that didn't matter. What mattered was convincing her—without words—that she belonged with *him*. Wanted *him*. Couldn't imagine a life without *him*.

Which was what made this hometown visit awkward and terrifying, right?

Because his dad—the man partially responsible for his very *existence*—had basically lived without him for a couple of decades now. And if Maria caught a glimpse of Peter through his father's eyes, she might find herself willing to do the same.

It would destroy him. Part of him, anyway.

The part that beat only for her, and had done for years now.

The part he'd never intended to risk again, but here he was. Here it was.

Entirely hers to break.

FOR A FULL two hours, butter wouldn't have melted in Maria's mouth.

Which reminded Peter: While she was in the area, he needed to get her to Culver's for a butter burger, fried cheese curds, and a hot fudge sundae made with frozen custard, because otherwise he'd consider this a wasted visit, filmed interviews or no filmed interviews.

But in the meantime, it was bizarre to watch her be so . . . demure? Was that the right word? Cautious? Whatever it was, she was letting his gregarious father do almost all the talking and uttering polite nothings in response as she watched them both very, very carefully.

"Lovely to meet you, Daniel," she'd murmured when Peter introduced his dad. "I've heard so much about you."

A total fucking lie. He'd barely mentioned his father to her, ever, and she hadn't pressed for more information, not even on their drive to Madison.

"The restaurant you chose sounds perfect," she'd said as they headed outside town to a converted nineteenth-century stable for a traditional Wisconsin Friday night fish fry dinner. "I love fish."

She didn't even smirk at Peter or produce a jar of herring to shake in his face.

Weird.

"What a gorgeous lake!" she'd exclaimed when they rounded a curve in the SUV—because his father's small Prius couldn't comfortably fit two people as tall as Peter and Maria—and Lake Mendota came into view, blue and sparkling and so familiar his throat prickled. "How nice that you live close to the water, Daniel."

So then his dad discussed what an isthmus was, promised to show her Lake Monona later in the visit, and gave her an engaging, lighthearted, somewhat truncated history of Madison and the university all the way to the restaurant.

"It looks delicious," she'd said to the server upon ordering the baked cod, fried cod, and fried whitefish combo platter. "Thank you."

Which, of course, inspired his dad to explain the origins of the Wisconsin fish fry tradition, along with the state's other culinary idiosyncrasies. Beer brats. Cheese curds. Also the utter deliciousness known as kringle, even though Peter thought those actually originated from Scandinavia. As had many early white settlers in Wisconsin, which likely accounted for the region's affection for—ugh—pickled herring.

Luckily, his father didn't bring *that* up.

Maria had heard it all before. Earlier that very day, in fact, at a media event where she'd taste-tested various regional specialties. She didn't interrupt, though. She didn't look bored. She just nodded attentively.

And now, as the three of them ate their final bites of dinner, she was listening to his father talk about his training regimen for an upcoming triathlon with every evidence of pleasure and no attempt to change the topic, even though Peter knew for a fact she enjoyed exercise but found discussion of other people's fitness routines *boring as fuck*.

That was a direct quote.

"Fascinating." With her fork, she dolloped some tartar sauce on her remaining whitefish and teased free a substantial bite. "Do you run marathons too?"

His father nodded, a pleasant smile deepening the lines that bracketed his mouth. "Only half-marathons now. But I attended UW-Madison on a track scholarship, and while Peter was growing up, I still did marathons with my buddy Len. Even now, Len and I like to take the path around the lake and—"

Dad kept talking, and she didn't interrupt. She also didn't ask

Peter whether he'd joined the track team as well, either in high school or college. She knew he hadn't.

Instead of participating in varsity sports or student government—his father had served as class president too—Peter had joined the drama club. Because he'd loved acting from the very beginning, but also because offstage, the other theater kids let him be as taciturn and introverted as he wanted. They tolerated his silence without commentary, and without offering him mournful bewilderment in response.

His father always bought a ticket for a single performance of each of Peter's productions and always congratulated him once he'd taken his final bows. But Dad never seemed to enjoy the shows, and he never had much to say afterward.

At one time, Peter had considered that a deliberate slight. A sign of his father's disdain for what he did and who he was. As an adult, though, he'd come to believe Dad simply didn't know what to say to him. What would make him happy. What possible feedback would connect the two of them, when Peter was so different from his father. Not sociable or popular or interested in organized sports, but a quiet, creative, sometimes moody loner.

Just like his mom.

Which was why, when she and Dad had separated two years before her death, he'd lived with her. After her massive stroke, after her funeral, he might have returned to that familiar childhood ranch-style house, but it never felt like home again. Not without her.

He bent his head to his plate and ate his coleslaw, because just like his dad, he didn't know what to say, and he never had. What Peter *did* have to say, his father generally didn't understand, so it was pointless, and always had been.

Maria's knee nudged his, but he didn't look up.

"—try to keep my runs less than an hour, so I don't have to carry a water bottle." Dad squeezed more lemon over his remaining fish. "Are you a runner, Maria?"

Peter had to give credit where it was due. At least his father didn't assume fat people hated or avoided exercise, unlike many others Peter had met over the years.

"I prefer walking, generally." Her lips pursed adorably as she sipped her sparkling water through a paper straw. "At the gym, I mostly focus on strength training or use the rowing machine."

Thus all that glorious upper-body strength. When they got back to the hotel, he was going to strip her to the waist and lick a path over—

"Peter's fiancée preferred treadmills to running outside, and I never understood that," his father said, shaking his head. "Why not enjoy the fresh air?"

A more pertinent question: What the actual fuck? Why was his father talking about *Anne*, of all people?

Beside him, Maria had abruptly straightened in her chair, her thigh tensing against Peter's. He laid a hand on that warm thigh, offering silent reassurance, even as the violent clench of his jaw sent a bolt of pain to his temples.

In contrast, his dad leaned back comfortably, obviously settling in for another lecture. "I always told her—"

"*Ex*-fiancée," Peter interrupted without apology, temper edging the words with iron. "Our engagement ended over a decade ago, Dad. She has no place at this table, and no part in this conversation."

And Maria should never have found out about her like this, in front of his goddamn *father*. But fuck it all, that was on him too, not just his dad. He should have told her about his broken engagement years ago, wounded pride and instinctive reserve be damned, as soon as he'd begun to understand and trust her. As soon as she'd become the most important person in his life.

She hadn't shifted away from his hand, but she hadn't relaxed under its weight either.

Fair enough. Let this be his penance, then. An offering of pain in apology for a silence that had stretched far too long. He would tell the story of the woman who'd broken his heart in front of the man who'd done the same, and hopefully Maria would forgive him.

"I only had one serious relationship before meeting you." He waited until Maria made eye contact, and looked solely at her. "Anne, an orthopedic doctor in LA. We were engaged for a few months, a little over ten years ago."

Her expression had turned opaque, her eyes guarded. But she was listening instead of walking away from him, which was more than he probably deserved.

"Around the time we got engaged, I was cast as the lead in a big-budget pilot. Up until the last minute, it looked like we were going to get picked up, but . . ." His dismissive wave expressed it all. *You know how it goes in our industry.* "Before the show fell through, I don't think she understood how precarious the life of a working actor can be. If the pilot had been picked up, I'd have been more than comfortable, financially. Without the role, I still had enough money for rent and food, but not much extra for a wedding."

Maria's thigh twitched, and her lips pursed. "I thought doctors in the U.S. made good money. Couldn't she pay for the wedding?"

Of course she'd ask that. Of course she'd defend him.

Maria fucking Ivarsson, the greatest miracle of his life.

"Probably. But she didn't want to. Not all of it, anyway. One day, she just . . . left." His chest rose and fell on a silent breath.

"No warning. No note. No explanation. I had to find out from mutual acquaintances what happened."

At that, Maria winced. Probably because, as she well knew, another woman had also left his bed without a word or note. Six years ago, to be precise.

The circumstances weren't the same, obviously. A one-night stand didn't create the same obligations as an engagement. But . . . at least she now had a bit more context for his resentment when he'd encountered her in that LA office building the next day. Some additional explanation for why he'd acted like such a dick in that damn parking lot.

His bitterness wasn't simply about a wounded male ego. Or at least, not entirely. Her fuck-and-run had inadvertently pressed on the exact same spot as an old injury and brought it flaring back to painful life. So he'd gotten hurt, and then he'd gotten pissy.

It was that simple, and that dumb.

"She'd decided my career and life were too volatile for her. She wanted stability." He'd offered Anne his heart, his loyalty, and his future, but he couldn't promise what that future would entail. He'd understood that all along, and she hadn't. Not until it was far too late. "She wanted a guarantee she wouldn't end up supporting us both. So she broke our engagement."

A man like him couldn't meet her needs. He got that.

He didn't blame her for leaving. He could and did blame her for the way she'd done it.

"I'm sorry, Peter," Maria said quietly, her neutral expression softening with sympathy.

On her thigh, the warmth of her hand covered his. Squeezed.

It was a gesture of forgiveness and comfort offered privately, out of his father's sight. Just for the two of them. He smiled softly at her in gratitude. In—relief.

Telling her about such a painful part of his past had hurt, but now the story was in her capable, gentle hands. She'd keep it safe there. She'd keep *him* safe, and that realization was like sinking into a hot bath after a lifetime spent wading through rocky, icy shallows.

Dad cleared his throat. "I told Peter he should choose a different major for a more stable career path, but—"

"So, Daniel." This time, Maria was the one to interrupt his father, her voice bland and perfectly polite. "You said you attended university here in Madison? Like Peter?"

After a final squeeze of Peter's hand, she let him go to refill her glass with San Pellegrino, and they both resumed eating.

"Yes. It's where I worked too." His father's chair creaked as he leaned back in it. "Peter and I were based in two different parts of campus, though. I majored in accounting and worked in the bursar's office, and Peter got his bachelor's in theater, so our paths didn't cross much, even when we were there at the same time. Especially since he chose to live on campus instead of at home."

Another choice his dad had found inexplicable and argued against, although seeing Peter caused him nothing but consternation and pain.

They both knew it. Neither of them had ever said it. Not even his father, for all his facility with words.

Maria placed her fork on her plate so carefully, it didn't clink. "He graduated summa cum laude, correct?"

Peter's own fork paused halfway to his mouth. How the fuck did she know *that*?

"Yes, and I wasn't surprised. Peter was always bright, and whatever he decided to do, he did well. He could have majored in anything. Excelled at any job." His father's words sounded like praise. Almost. If you didn't hear the lament in each syllable. "But right after graduation, he left for Los Angeles, and that was it. He never moved back to the area or returned to school."

"Why would he?" Maria's head tipped to one side. "He's been a successful actor for twenty years now, has he not?"

Anyone who didn't personally know her would swear that was an innocent question, born of genuine confusion. But he knew that tone. When he raised his head from contemplation of his plate, he knew that look on her face too. And maybe a better person would have intervened at that point, but . . .

Yeah. He was who he was.

"More or less." His father's brow creased. "Like Peter said, an acting career doesn't offer a steady income. The first few years, he had to do construction work to make ends meet."

True enough. Early on, the parts Peter landed were too small and didn't pay enough. The few leading-man roles he got offered, the story usually revolved around his size, and he didn't want those parts unless they guaranteed him either a lot of money or a lot of fame. Which they hadn't, so he'd continued playing bit roles for far too long.

"Ah. So he had to supplement his acting income, like virtually all Hollywood hopefuls." Her shoulder hitched in a graceful, dismissive shrug. "And almost every single one of those hopefuls eventually gives up and leaves, or stays but never finds success. Your son is the exception, Daniel. A man who's defied incredibly steep odds and carved out a meaningful career through sheer talent and stubbornness and hard work."

Hearing that—fuck, it felt good. So good, he couldn't breathe for a moment.

His father blinked at her. "He's very talented, of course. As I've often told him, he should have been winning awards well before his role on *Gods of the Gates*."

Dad *had* frequently said that over the years. Peter would have been flattered, only the comment always sounded less like outrage on his behalf and more an implication that awards might justify his career choice.

His father best understood concrete accomplishments. Blue ribbons. Varsity letters. Diplomas. Certificates. Race times. Expensive homes. And yes, paychecks and statuettes, which was why the role of Cyprian had finally reconciled him to Peter's career. Somewhat.

The significance of years and years of steady work in Hollywood before *Gods of the Gates*, the joy of excelling at a craft he loved . . . things like that were difficult for his dad to grasp, and thus difficult to praise. And Peter knew—he *knew*—he could have made everything easier on his father. Could have tried harder to explain himself and the details of his career and its *context* in a way Dad might comprehend more easily.

But his parents had been married for a decade and a half when they separated, and despite all those years, despite choosing each other and committing to a life together in front of a minister and dozens of guests, his father had never understood the woman he'd wed, and he'd never understood why she left. If she—his fucking *wife*—hadn't managed to make herself known in all that time, what chance did Peter have?

There was a fundamental disconnect somewhere, and it was no one's fault. He got that now, in a way he hadn't even a decade earlier. Just as he could now study his father and see very clearly that Daniel Reedton had never really recovered from losing his beloved Patty.

That slight rounding of his shoulders didn't appear in photos until after she'd packed her bags and moved to an apartment across town. It only got worse after she died, once his father knew she couldn't ever come back. Same with those bags beneath his eyes and the deep lines across his forehead. Same with that awful *lost* expression whenever he stopped talking long enough for the memories to surface, or when he unexpectedly encountered a photo or heard the name of the woman he'd courted and married at the age of twenty-three.

The woman who'd left him at thirty-eight.

The woman who'd died at forty.

He'd loved her. He hadn't understood her, but he'd loved her.

Just as he loved Peter. Sincerely. Without an ounce of comprehension but plenty of pain.

"Yes, Peter should have shelves full of awards dating back to the beginning of his career. He deserved them." Maria held his father's tired blue eyes, her voice gentle but firm. "But in some ways, what he accomplished before being cast in *Gods of the Gates*, before receiving his first statuette, is more extraordinary than any award he could earn. I hope you realize that."

Across the table, Dad shifted in his seat. "Of course I do."

"Good," Maria said simply, then buttered a piece of sourdough bread. "Because your son deserves that too."

Given her trademark outspokenness, it was the mildest possible reprimand, and *fuck*, he loved her for it. Loved her for defending him so carefully, even after belatedly discovering the existence of his ex-fiancée. Loved her for attempting to bridge the yawning gap between him and his sole remaining family member. Loved her for the soft press of her body against his side, silent comfort provided to a silent man.

Loved her, period. End of sentence.

He looked again at his father's strong, slumped shoulders. His shadowed eyes. His furrowed forehead. The silent record of his grief for the woman he'd married and lost, inscribed on his body for always.

Dad hadn't gotten over her.

He wouldn't get over her.

And for the first time, Peter thought maybe he did in fact understand his father. If only a little.

Texts with Maria: One Year Ago

Peter: Have you made it home, or are you still en route?

Maria: Two-hour layover in Copenhagen

Maria: I'm in the business lounge eating cheese

Maria: It's airport cheese, but still quite Gouda

Peter: In kindness to you, I'm going to pretend you didn't make that awful pun, Pippi

Peter: Any issues at LAX or during your flight? I saw you were heading into bad weather.

Maria: Some turbulence, nothing serious

Maria: As long as the oxygen masks didn't appear, I figured we were good

Peter: . . . you thought you might need an oxygen mask?

Maria: At one point, yes

Maria: An overhead compartment popped open, so a few suitcases went flying, and our section's poor flight attendant took a header into

the bathroom door and gave herself a bloody
nose when she didn't get buckled fast enough

Maria: There was no taking off
our seat belts for a while

Peter: That's

Peter: ...

Maria: That's what?

Peter: Fuck, that's terrifying, Maria.
Are you sure you're all right?

Maria: Yup, don't worry

Maria: I got a bit frightened, but I had my birthday
present from you in my pocket, so I was protected. ☺

Peter: The four-leaf clover in resin?

Maria: Ja

Peter: You're not superstitious, though

Maria: No, not like you are

Maria: But

Maria: ...

Peter: Maria?

Maria: It was a piece of you

Maria: I held it and thought of you

Maria: You were with me

Maria: And you'd never let anything happen to me

Maria: So I was fine.

Peter: Maria.

Peter: . . .

Peter: . . .

Maria: I need to head to my gate, sorry

Peter: You still have the clover in your pocket, right?

Maria: Always

Peter: . . .

Peter: You *always* have it in your pocket?

Maria: Yes, or in my purse

Peter: . . .

Maria: I really have to go now

Peter: I clipped a photo from a magazine article about you years ago

Peter: You're laughing on a beach

Peter: You're unspeakably beautiful

Peter: A human beam of sunlight

Peter: The photo's in my wallet, Maria.

Peter: Always.

Maria: . . .

Peter: You'll text when you land?

Maria: Yes

Peter: You'll think of me if you're frightened?

Maria: Yes

Peter: Always?

Maria: Always.

19

THE NEXT EVENING, MARIA LICKED HER TWO-SCOOP CONE of mocha macchiato and had to wait for her brain freeze to thaw before continuing to eat. Ambling toward the lakeshore, his arm around her shoulders as they walked side by side, Peter appeared to be having no such trouble. His own overstuffed cone of mint chocolate cookie, also purchased at the university's Memorial Union, had mostly disappeared, and he was eyeing her remaining ice cream a bit too closely.

If he tried, she'd rip off his arm and beat him with it until he promised not to steal her food again.

Huh. Brain freeze: conquered. Apparently thoughts of justifiable violence warmed her.

After angling her cone farther away from Peter and taking another lick, she thought back on their day. "I have a question, but you'll probably mock me for it."

He frowned down at her, the very picture of wounded affront. "I would never."

"You have. You do. You will."

"Probably," he conceded, then dropped the innocent act and grinned at her. "So tell me already, and I can get to the mockery portion of our evening. It's my favorite part."

He paused meaningfully, bumping his hip against hers. "No, wait. My *second*-favorite part."

They'd made good use of that private hotel room and that wide, gloriously nonsqueaky hotel bed last night, much to her relief. One more night in her parents' house, sleeping in separate beds and giving each other quickie orgasms in the guest shower, and she'd have tackled Peter and ravished him on the narrow guest room mattress like a Viking of old, Filip's tender sensibilities be damned.

Given how desperately she wanted him, she also had no desire to pretend in public that they weren't lovers, and Peter had agreed: Whenever the media and/or fans discovered the changed nature of their relationship was fine by them.

She was hoping for *soon*, so everyone would know he was hers.

"What about our frozen custard outing last night?" Dairy products were, she now understood, Wisconsin's main claim to culinary fame. She approved wholeheartedly. "Wouldn't that rank higher than mockery too?"

"Fine, you Norse nitpicker." He crunched the final bite of his cone. "Third favorite."

"*Norse* primarily refers to Norway and Norwegians, rather than Swedes."

Brow raised, he gave her a long look. "I rest my case."

"Whatever." Over the past several years, she'd learned to love that particular English word. It encompassed dismissal and casual scorn so *neatly*. "Anyway, I wanted to ask about our taste test of famous regional foods yesterday."

The newspaper had arranged the spread and eagerly filmed Maria's reactions to all the unfamiliar items. Only to be disappointed, because a woman raised in a country that willingly consumed both *surströmming* and *lutfisk*—respectively, salty fermented herring so foul-smelling most people vomited before their first bite, and dried cod reconstituted in lye and cold water until gelatinous— wasn't going to flinch at various midwestern offerings.

A tuna noodle casserole crusted with potato chips? Delicious.

Some unidentifiable mixture of foodstuffs topped with cheese-blanketed tater tots and called a *hot dish*? No problem.

An ostensible salad that contained no actual lettuce, but rather pineapple chunks, tiny orange slices, coconut, marshmallows, and sour cream? Sure. Why not? Welcome to America!

Chocolate cheese? Well . . . the less said about that, the better. Still, it was relatively inoffensive, all things considered.

Oddly enough, the food that had baffled her was possibly the most straightforward of the newspaper's offerings. It tasted fine, but—

"Were those cheese curds supposed to *squeak* against my teeth?" She couldn't hold back a tiny shudder. "Because the sound was incredibly disturbing."

He stopped in his tracks and scowled at her. "*Yes*, they're supposed to squeak. That's how you know they're good!"

"I see," she said with what she considered exemplary diplomacy. "Then those were excellent cheese curds, clearly. Very . . . noisy."

His eyes narrowed. "Don't patronize me, Pippi."

"No, no." Her long, unhurried lick of her ice cream was a taunt, and they both knew it. "Who *doesn't* want to eat a food product that, when chewed, sounds like distressed mice were set loose in your mouth?"

"Goddammit, woman. Don't insult the jewel in the crown of Wisconsin cuisine." His attempted glare kept faltering as his lips twitched. "Besides, you'll like them fried. Especially dipped in ranch. No squeaking, just melty goodness."

"Whatever you say, Peter." Popping the remainder of her cone in her mouth, she chewed and swallowed. "By the way, you were right. The mockery portion of the evening *is* fun."

When he made an actual growling noise, she laughed, then tugged at his arm and set them back into motion. After muttering for a while about condescending foreigners, he looped his arm around her shoulders again and tugged her close as they walked.

She let the silence play out, content to enjoy the scenery and the man beside her.

After an early, extremely tasty dinner at a Nepalese restaurant located near the university campus, he'd taken her hand and led her to the Memorial Union building for ice cream, then to the shore of Lake Mendota.

The sun was beginning to set, splashing the horizon with pink and orange. Clusters of people sat on steps leading down to the water, earbuds in place, backpacks and purses by their sides. Others sprawled on the countless colorful chairs surrounding tables on a large patio overlooking the lake, chatting and eating and drinking beer.

The faint sound of live music drifted their way whenever someone opened a door to the building, but Peter drew her past the doors, past the crowds, and toward a spot on the steps where the lake lapped the shore only an arm's length away.

They sat side by side, so close their hips and thighs pressed warmly together.

"I love this place." Peter's words were abrupt, his eyes trained on the water rather than her. "Mom and I would take walks here. There's a path around the lake."

She kept her voice gentle. "Maybe we could do that before we leave."

"Yeah." His fingers played with the ends of her hair, but he still didn't look her way. "We'd come whenever I was upset. She knew I found the water"—he waved a hand—"soothing, I guess. We'd walk until I was tired, and whether I'd told her what was wrong or not, she'd hug me and take me for ice cream on the way home, even in the middle of winter. Either way, I'd feel better afterward. More settled."

Gods above, she knew so little about his past.

There was the memory he'd just shared, of course. And she knew his mom had died while he was still relatively young. Somehow. He'd reluctantly told her that years ago, and she hadn't pushed him to tell her more.

Yesterday, his father had essentially forced him to disclose his broken engagement, and Peter's revelations had explained a lot. Before then, she'd never fully understood his obvious hostility toward her after their one-night stand. Yeah, she probably should have left a note, but why so much anger when he didn't even know her?

It hadn't made sense. Now it did.

So she knew a few things. A very few things. Otherwise, his past was a void, dark and featureless, and in deference to his private nature, she hadn't tried to illuminate it.

But the moment had arrived. She had to know. She had to ask.

And if he wasn't willing to offer answers after all these years, that would tell her something important too. Namely, that he wasn't ready for a real relationship and might never be. That she should cut her losses and stop committing ever-larger pieces of her heart to him. That she should probably return to her family.

They'd reached a tipping point. Which way they'd fall—apart or deeper in love—she couldn't say. But it was time to find out.

She let the silence linger for another minute. Then she broke it.

"What was your mother like?" she asked.

IF MARIA NOTICED how Peter immediately stiffened at her question, she didn't show it.

"Because you and your father are very different from one another," she added, huddling close to his side.

At sundown, the lakeshore breeze had grown chilly. He should take her back to their hotel, where they could both get warm. Get naked. Fuck away memories of his parents and everything else he did his best not to think about or discuss.

"You don't say." His voice was so dry, Lake Mendota should've evaporated on the spot.

When she shivered a little at the next gust of wind, he tightened his arm over her shoulders, hauled her even closer, and braced himself.

Talking about his mother felt like swallowing glass. But he loved Maria. *Loved* her, and if he didn't tell her now, when would he?

"Mom was soft." The words were gruff, forced out syllable by syllable from the depths of his battered heart. "She gave the best hugs in the world."

Maria took his hand in hers, her hold heartbreakingly gentle.

"Her name was Patricia. Patty." He kept his eyes on the water. "She was kind. Creative. Hardworking. Even quieter than I am, and stubborn as hell. Dad always said she was smarter than both of us, and he was right." What else to say? "She *hated* parties and public speaking. And she loved us, but she always needed a lot of alone time too."

God, he was fucking this up. But how the hell could he adequately explain his mom to someone who'd never met her and never would, when his memories would always be those of a child? When he'd only rarely attempted to encompass her in words before, even in his own mind?

"She was an introvert, then." Maria's fingers interlaced with his warmed him in a way he couldn't entirely grasp. To an extent that shouldn't have been possible. "Like you."

He nodded, still unsure what needed to be said, and what could remain his alone for now. What he was even able to say, and what would stick in his throat.

"She worked as a medical transcriptionist, and she was good at it, even though the job bored her." Some nights across the dinner table, she'd eat in seeming slow motion. Drained and dead-eyed, with nothing to say about her day. "When I was born, she took a few years off, but she went back to her old position once I reached school age."

Even though it was killing something inside her. A child could see that. *He'd* seen that.

"Looking back, she was probably depressed, but it wasn't diagnosed at the time." Suddenly restless, he lifted his arm from around Maria's shoulders and dragged a hand through his hair, gripping a fistful at the back of his neck. "Maybe she was just generally frustrated with her life. Her work didn't interest her. Most of her closest friends had moved away and lost touch. She had a shelf full of travel books, but Dad didn't see the point of going overseas, because we hadn't visited all the nearby sights yet."

In the end, they'd just drive to the Dells again. Inevitably. Even though his mom hated water parks almost as much as public speaking.

"And when she was struggling, when she cried and tried to explain what was wrong, my father didn't really listen to her. Instead, he'd hold her close and list all the good things in her life." The story was coming more easily now. Spilling from him in a flood, unfiltered and uncontrolled and full of uprooted ugliness. "I guess as a reminder that she should be happy, because he couldn't fathom how someone who lived virtually the same existence he did could find it stifling."

Transcription work is so easy for you, he'd tell her. *And just last week, you went to lunch with Janelle, remember? You can always redecorate our house if you get bored, and we can go to the Dells next month if you need a vacation. Everything's fine, Patty. Why are you so upset?*

"He loved her with all his heart, Maria. I mean that," he added when she looked at him with open skepticism. "But empathy requires imagination, and he didn't have enough of either."

Her little nod didn't necessarily indicate agreement, but she didn't argue.

"Dad got a promotion when I was in third grade." With one last tug, he let his hair go. "With his new salary, he made just enough to support all three of us. So she quit her job and used the remaining funds from her parents' estate to start an interior decorating business."

Maria's smile was wide and bright with relief. "Good for her."

"She'd always been artsy. Creative. Coordinating fabrics and paints and furniture satisfied that part of her." In his LA home, some of her design sketches were hanging framed on his walls. One of them—the one he found most beautiful; the one he loved the most—he even remembered watching her draw at the kitchen table. "And if she was good at transcription work, she *excelled* at interior decoration."

Maria tipped her head to the side. "Did she love it?"

"That first year, she was happier than I'd ever seen her before. Smiling. Energetic."

At the time, he'd thought, *It's like someone turned up her volume.*

Over their late-evening family dinners, she suddenly had so many stories to tell, and when she spoke, her voice rang with laughter and quivered with annoyance and brimmed with professional pride. Her eyes were bright, her appetite fierce. And when he occasionally offered his own stories from school, it felt like she listened more carefully than before.

"She was . . ." What was the right word? "She was *present* with us anytime she was home, even though she was working longer hours than she used to."

"What did your father think of her new business?" Her voice was carefully neutral.

"Dad didn't get why anyone would leave a steady job with a regular salary to 'fuss with curtains and wallpaper,' as he put it, but he didn't quibble with her decision. Not—" Swallowing hard, he forced himself to continue. "Not until the economy tanked her second year in business, and she stopped getting new clients."

"*Fy fan*," Maria mumbled under her breath.

"She managed for a while, but once she'd operated in the red for a few months in a row . . ." He lifted a shoulder, as if the end of his mom's business were no big deal. As if it weren't, in such painful, terrible ways, the end of absolutely everything else too. "To Dad, there was only one reasonable solution."

"And that solution was returning to her old job."

It wasn't a question but a statement. And she was right, of course.

"He didn't browbeat her, Maria. But he has this way of framing things where it's so hard to argue with him, because everything he says makes perfect sense. You leave the conversation convinced that what he'd do in your position is the only safe, sane thing to do, and what kind of fool *wouldn't* choose the safest, sanest path?"

Her brows had drawn together in a pained wince. "So she went back to medical transcription work."

"Yes." Scrubbing his face with his hands, he sighed. "It was awful."

For a time, his mother became a ghost that drifted through their lives. Mournful. Unsettled. Rattling emotional chains only she could hear.

Cold. Untouchable. Even with him.

"There was no more mistaking her depression." That was the good news, such as it was. "She finally got diagnosed, found a therapist, and started meds. And one day, she came home from work, packed a suitcase, and asked where I wanted to be. Which one of them I wanted to live with."

"You chose her." Another nonquestion.

"Dad always said we were two peas in a pod. He had no idea how to deal with either one of us at that point, especially when I was a surly little shit." He snorted. "And Maria, I was *frequently* a surly little shit."

Her laugh rang with genuine amusement, and he found himself smiling too.

"I believe you, *skitstövel*," she said, patting him on the arm. "How did your father take you and your mom leaving?"

And suddenly, he was back to feeling he might never smile again. "When she left, it broke him, Maria. He was desperate to win her back. He gave her birthday and anniversary gifts. Hung a Christmas stocking for her on the mantel, just in case she decided to come home. He'd call and beg her to talk, beg her to tell him what he needed to do for her to move back to the house, and she tried once or twice. She really did. But what she said made no sense to him, and eventually she started screening his calls."

"What about you?" Maria's frown pinched her forehead. "Didn't he care that you were gone too?"

"I guess." Re-creating his father's thought processes had never come easily to him, to put it mildly. "I think he sort of considered me a . . . um, kind of a subset of my mom. Not something separate that he'd miss independently of her."

Her voice turned rough. Fierce with anger. "I hope you were happier without him. Both of you."

"Maybe?" Everything was in such turmoil for so long, happiness had seemed almost beside the point. "Mom would only accept enough of Dad's money to support me. I don't know why. I guess she wanted to prove something, to herself or to him. So we lived in a shitty apartment, and she still had to do transcription work. But she had more energy, and we spent more time together. She'd sketch, and I'd read. Or we'd take walks, like I said."

Now came the rest of it. The hardest part of all to talk about, which was why he didn't. Why he hadn't. Resting his elbows on his bent knees, he hunched forward and watched the tiny little waves rush in to shore, one after another.

The world went on, always, and there was still beauty in it. Even when he couldn't see that beauty. And there had been so many years when he couldn't, anywhere but onstage and on set, where he could be somewhere else. Someone else. Someone who could offer and receive uncomplicated love and appreciate the resilience of the living.

For a while, Anne had reopened the world to him, but it shut tight again after she left.

And then, six years ago, he'd walked into an LA sauna and seen a woman with hair like sunshine, eyes like warm earth, and all the strength and softness he needed so desperately.

When he reached out blindly, she clasped his hand without hesitation.

He took a hard breath. "Almost exactly two years after my parents separated, my mom died of a massive stroke at work."

Her long fingers caressed the back of his hand. His palm.

"I'm so sorry, Peter," she whispered. "So, so sorry, *sötnos*."

He cleared his throat. Twice. "Me too."

After play rehearsal that night, not knowing what had happened, Peter had watched in surprise as his father pulled into the school lot and parked, hands shaking on the wheel, and that was it. That was the end of the life he and his mother had slowly constructed, stone by stone.

Back in his old home, everything was the same, and nothing was the same. He was still a surly little shit, and Dad was still loving, befuddled, and entirely unable to deal with his son.

But now he was also entirely unable to deal with his own grief, much less Peter's.

"I went back to my dad." With his small kick, a nearby pebble splashed into the water. "And he cringed every time he looked at me."

Maria muttered something in Swedish. Probably an obscenity involving shit. "You reminded him of her."

At first, Peter had hoped that would pass, but his father never truly managed to let his wife go. Never managed to move on, if only enough to see his son as a separate being. An entirely different person, who needed him.

Or if not him, *someone.* Anyone. Any fucking person who could help Peter grapple with the rage and agony and the crippling loneliness. The desolate, gaping hole in his life that only his mom had filled.

But his father never found that person. Not in himself. Not in someone else.

And Peter didn't know how to ask for help, not when he barely talked, had no friends, and the only person who'd *ever* helped him was a pile of ashes enclosed in a decorative urn on the mantel above the fireplace. Contained safely at long last, where Dad would see her always, and she could never leave him again.

Outside of what his father considered crucial daily interactions, they barely spoke for years. Dad took care of meals. Herded him to the bus stop on time and made certain all homework got completed before dinner. Mandated showers and toothbrushing.

And that was it. That was everything.

"When he looked at me, he saw her. He couldn't stand to be around me." He laced his fingers behind his neck, gaze fixed between his feet in the growing darkness. "But he couldn't stand the thought of my moving away either."

She let out a long breath. "Maybe he didn't want to lose you too. Even in the very limited way he had you in his life."

Yeah. After all, Peter was his father's strongest connection to Patty that still existed in the world, outside that enameled urn.

"He wanted me orbiting him at a safe distance, where he could still check on me regularly and ensure I made the right choices," Peter said flatly.

This discussion couldn't last much longer. It was fucking cold by the water now that the last sunset colors had faded and allowed a few hardy stars to battle the local light pollution.

His throat ached from all this *talking*, and his fucking head ached from all the memories, all the effort of finding the right words so Maria could understand him in a way even he himself hadn't for so long. Not until he hauled his ass to therapy after *Gates'* first season of filming, his bank account finally healthy enough for him to get the help he'd needed decades before.

Maria's lips brushed his cheek, and suddenly the evening's chill receded again.

"He'd only release my college funds if I stayed here." Admittedly, UW-Madison was a world-class university, but Peter had wanted to leave Madison. Leave Wisconsin. Go anywhere he could escape the boy he'd been and the family that had fractured around him. "And he didn't agree to let me live in a dorm until I threatened to skip college entirely."

It had been Peter's first real victory. His first taste of independence. The first time in years he'd lived somewhere not haunted by ghosts that remained unacknowledged and undiscussed.

It was fucking *amazing*.

Maria sighed. "When you told him you were moving to LA after graduation, I'm certain he told you other professions would offer you steadier employment, and you should stay with him while you trained for a more reasonable career path."

He had to laugh. "Are you sure you didn't read a transcript of our conversation?"

From the start, his father couldn't fathom why he wanted to pursue acting as his profession. And when he'd heard Peter was leaving for Hollywood, possibly for good . . .

Well, Dad had made eye contact then. Panicked, uncomprehending eye contact as he listed all the very logical reasons Peter was ruining his own life and sacrificing his future.

His departure had devastated his father. Or whatever word was stronger than that, because Peter would never forget that look on his face.

"You'd have thought I kicked him in the stomach." Finally, he unlaced his fingers and lowered his hands to his lap, but only after he'd captured both of hers. "But I couldn't stay, Maria. I wanted to act more than I wanted anything else in my life, and I couldn't do that in Madison. Not as my career."

And he'd wanted out. Finally, definitively *out* from under the shadow of his father's grief and the knee-buckling weight of his own memories.

"When I got on the bus for California, I kept remembering the day Mom left Dad. I kept wondering how it felt to drive away from our house, from him, with nothing but our suitcases in the trunk, and I thought maybe I was feeling the same way right then." He swallowed. "I dropped my bags by the side of that Greyhound, walked up the steps, and took my seat, and it was like she was walking beside me. Sitting beside me. I hadn't felt that close to her in years."

Ducking down, he leaned his forehead against the backs of those strong, familiar hands. The same hands that carefully cradled sea urchins in the shallows of an Irish shore. The same hands that bled hauling stone and gleamed with nail polish at conventions. The same hands that had cupped his face last night as she gazed at him with such *fondness*, such knowing affection, like she understood him inside and out but cared about him anyway.

The same hands that now contained the entirety of his troubled, stubborn, adoring heart.

It was time to finish this story, so he could start another. This one, he hoped, had a happy ending, although he hadn't allowed himself to believe in those. Not ever.

"Like Mom, I was striking out for the unknown. Like Mom, I had something to prove to him and to myself and to the world." He kissed her knuckles. Each fingertip. Her palms, once they opened like a flower under the gentle stroke of his thumb. "But unlike Mom, I had enough time on this earth to find the partner I needed. Someone who's not just my lover but my friend too. Someone who can understand me, as well as . . ."

It was too soon. Despite all their years together, it was too soon, and he wouldn't presume to tell her the contents of her own heart. Even if he hoped he knew what they were.

But she didn't hesitate.

20

MARIA HADN'T INTENDED TO COMMIT HERSELF SO SOON.

During this press junket, she'd meant to offer sex and companionship to Peter, but not her heart. Not until she knew for certain he'd finally put her—put *them*—first in his life, above even work, and could give her what she actually needed, not just what he found easiest to offer.

If he had, if he could, she'd take some of the Hollywood roles being offered to her and stay in LA with him. If not . . . well, she hadn't wanted to think about it. But she always had another life waiting for her back in Sweden, with family and satisfying work and sex whenever that particular itch presented itself for scratching.

Not romantic love, though. Not Peter.

Until now, she'd been unsure what to do, because over the years, he *had* occasionally put his professional reputation at mild risk for her sake. But when he discussed his future, work still seemed to be the organizing principle. The central, immovable obstacle around which everything else had to bend, including the people he cared about.

But the longer Peter spoke tonight, the more her remaining qualms faded.

Here were the corner pieces of his puzzle, at long last. And now that he'd finally given them to her, she could put everything else together without much trouble.

Of *course* Peter instinctively gravitated to the edges of every group, no matter how desperately he needed companionship and affection. He'd been installed on the outskirts of even his own goddamn father's life. He was used to isolation. Used to not belonging. Used to being misunderstood, so what would be the point of speaking, anyway? Why even try to find friends?

As if that weren't bad enough, Daniel had then proceeded to make the same fucking mistakes a second time, prioritizing his own needs, his own desire for security, above helping his family get what they actually wanted. What would make his son happy, as nothing in Peter's life had since the day his mother died.

A chance to live outside his father's orbit. A profession that fulfilled him.

No wonder Peter hadn't been willing to risk the role of Cyprian. It wasn't only a long-overdue, triumphant rebuke to Anne, who hadn't been willing to risk a future with him. It was also the final, best proof he could offer his father—and maybe even himself—that he hadn't made a mistake when he climbed on that LA-bound bus so long ago. It was the highest-profile role of his career, one that offered a steady, generous income and the sort of fame that couldn't be denied. Not by his ex-fiancée. Not even by a man who wanted to deny it with all his heart, if only so his son would move back home at last and help fill part of the gaping, decades-old hole his wife's death had left in his life.

If Peter's work had been absolutely everything to him, tonight's revelations told her why.

But now he had genuine friends among his *Gates* colleagues, people who sought his company and would do almost anything for him. He had the critical respect, fan following, and financial security he'd been chasing his entire career.

He had her. Gods above, did he have her.

In time, he'd have her family too, because they adored him. After such extensive experience, it hadn't taken them long to recognize another lost, lonely soul bursting with love to give. One who'd gone far too long without someone in his life to take that love and return it in kind.

They'd adopt him. Emotionally, if not legally, and she wouldn't even put the latter past them. Filip was a lawyer, after all.

Peter's life had changed in the past six years, and he'd changed with it. Work would always remain important to him, because he loved acting, but it wasn't his entire existence anymore. His world and its possibilities had expanded spectacularly since that terrible conversation in a sunbaked LA parking lot.

He had room for her now.

She could be the new center of that world.

So here she was. Sitting by a lakeshore on a clear spring evening in Wisconsin, her hands cradled in his, the quiet shush of waves a reassurance, his warm body beside hers a bulwark against any cold that might come her way.

She now knew his past; she'd been at his side for much of his present; and she could take an informed guess as to what his future might hold. And with that new understanding in mind, she also knew what to do. Finally.

She loved him. Of course she loved him. If she'd believed she could offer her closest friend and most trusted colleague her body and all her time without handing him her heart too, she was just as much a *knäppgök* as he was.

Luckily for them both, she now trusted him with that heart.

Which meant she had nothing left to conceal and everything to share with him.

Because he loved her too, whether he'd admitted it to himself or not.

Her doubts were gone. It was time to celebrate.

"SOMEONE LIKE ME," she repeated. "I love you, Peter. You're my beloved *skitstövel*. Do you want me to find a house in Hollywood, or would you rather I stay with you?"

Celebrations and logistics weren't mutually exclusive, right? Because in approximately five days, their whirlwind press junket would be over, and they'd be flying into LA, the city where she intended to remain for the foreseeable future. Also the city where she currently had nowhere to stay, since there'd been no point in arranging for a hotel or a rental there when she might be returning to Sweden instead.

If Peter wasn't ready to live together, fine. But either way, she needed a home. One not located near Stockholm.

His lips still pressed to her hands, the man of the hour appeared to have frozen as solid as Lake Mendota evidently did in winter. He was blinking rather rapidly, though, so she hadn't killed him with her pronouncement of love. She considered that a good omen.

After a few moments, he sort of gasped against her knuckles, inhaling sharply, which was when she realized he'd actually stopped breathing for a while.

Fy fan, what a drama queen.

Carefully, he lowered their hands to his lap and angled himself to stare at her. Rather blankly, it must be said. Also, his mouth was open more than a little. The word *gaping* might go too far, but the phrase *parted lips* didn't go nearly far enough.

English could be a very imprecise language, she'd found.

"You . . ." More staring. "You want to . . . move in with me? Because you, uh, love me and plan to move to LA?"

All pronounced in the same tones one would use to say, for example, *You want to smother me with jewels and then cook me a gourmet meal before giving me a thousand orgasms? Really intense, long-lasting ones, like you'd been edging me for hours?*

Only she was the jewels, the meal, *and* the edging-heightened orgasms.

It was all very flattering.

And as long as they were having this conversation, they might as well get everything out in the open, because who knew how long it would take Peter to say it without prompting?

"Correct." Leaning forward, she planted a smacking kiss on his still-somewhat-gaping mouth. "Do you love *me*?"

There he went again. Frozen solid, other than that blinking. Or maybe that wasn't blinking, but an eye twitch? Well, either way, it was proof of life.

His lips shaped the word *yes*, although no sound emerged.

She'd been confident that would be his answer. Completely, utterly certain. But now that she'd seen it mouthed silently, she could admit that her pulse had skyrocketed in that fraught gap between her question and his response, her blood pounding so hard against her temples she'd seen sparks in the dark night.

She refused to believe, however, that the deep, ragged breath she'd just taken meant she'd been holding it until he answered in the affirmative.

No longer on the verge of passing out, she waited uncomplainingly for further, more audible communication. After a time, he cleared his throat and squared his shoulders and met her gaze with a directness that bordered on defiance. Because, for him, this admission must require untold amounts of bravery, and she should have remembered that.

She couldn't imagine he had much recent practice with the declaration. Had he even spoken those words to anyone but Anne since his mother's death?

"Of course I do," he finally said with commendable aplomb. "Don't tell me you didn't know how much I love you, Maria. How much I've loved you for years now."

His voice was stone-steady, but his hands trembled against hers. And for a moment, she regretted her boldness, even though it had earned her the words she wanted. The words she'd needed to hear so badly, but not because she hadn't realized he loved her already. Because she had to know he was willing to *acknowledge* those feelings, to her and to himself.

Unacknowledged emotion was too easy to dismiss, to set aside in favor of something more important, and the stakes for her were far too high to allow avoidance of hard questions.

She wasn't moving half a world away from her native country and her family for a man who couldn't tell her he loved her. It didn't matter how many good reasons he might have for his reticence. It didn't matter how much he *did* actually love her. It didn't even matter how much she loved him in return, and how much— how very, very much—she wanted him in her life.

Okay, so she'd had one or two remaining doubts.

But now they were all gone. Really.

He'd given her what she needed, and in return, she'd give him everything she had.

Carefully detaching her hands from his near-painful grip, she cupped his face, his beard scratchy against her sensitive palms, his eyes wary but hopeful on hers.

Her thumbs stroked his cheeks slowly. Lovingly.

Then she leaned in and kissed him. Soft brushes of her mouth against his, damp and warm and tender. Patient, because she now had all the time in the world for him.

"*Jag. Älskar. Dig. Sötnos,*" she said, punctuating each word with another kiss.

"Don't know why," he mumbled against her lips. "But thank fuck for it."

His arms slid around her then, and he pulled her onto his lap and cradled her close as he kissed her back with just as much deliberate care. He explored the corners of her mouth, sipped on her lower lip, and slipped his tongue inside, but not to claim. To coax and slide and twirl around hers until she grew dizzy with the sweetness of it all.

It felt like a first kiss.

Well, no. Her first kiss had been with Arne Gustafsson in middle school, and he'd eaten garlic salami earlier that day, and his tongue had slithered like an eel. Peter, in contrast, tasted like mint and chocolate and smelled like cedar. Furthermore, his clever, agile tongue should be bronzed, but not until after she'd had full use of it upon demand for her entire lifetime.

So this didn't feel like her first kiss.

But it was the first kiss that had offered her a future in a long, long time.

When it was over, his big, warm hand on her hip supported her as she got to her feet. Immediately, she turned around and extended her own hand, a mute offer of assistance. He took it and gave her some of his weight as he rose. Because he trusted her strength, trusted *her* enough to relinquish some of his independence and let her help.

Because he wasn't alone anymore, and he wouldn't be again.

When they made it back to the hotel room, they reached for

each other as soon as the door thumped shut behind them. They stripped off their clothes and tumbled beneath the covers, but not to fuck. At least, not right away.

Tucking her close, he smoothed his palms down her spine, her sides, her arms. Anywhere he could reach. Each time she put her mouth to his ear and whispered something else she adored about him—his sharp intelligence, his ready wit, his protectiveness of her, his stubborn determination, his undeniable talent—his hands paused for a moment, then kept sliding slowly over her bare skin until she was nearly liquid with pleasure.

"Gods above, I love you," she murmured, pressing a kiss to his earlobe.

When he buried his face in her neck, she sifted his hair through her fingers in the way that always gave him goose bumps. And when her neck grew damp, she didn't say a thing.

Some emotions needed to be acknowledged.

Others could remain private.

LATER, WHEN HE braced himself above her, head bowed so he could nuzzle against her cheek as he slid inside her body, he offered the words to her freely, unprompted, his voice hoarse and broken and fierce.

"Fuck, I love you, Maria." With his first jolting thrust, he pushed even deeper. So deep his breath caught for a moment, and so did hers. "Move in with me. Please."

"Okay," she said, wrapping her legs around those busy hips.

He paused midthrust. "Shit, if I'd known it was that easy—"

"Keep going, *skitstövel*. As they say in American medical dramas: ten ccs of dick, stat."

Her slap of his ass probably hurt her hand more than his butt, but it did the trick. He started moving again. Moving and snort-laughing.

"Isn't that, like, a tiny amount of dick?" He slipped a hand between their bodies and found her clit, his grin wide and bright. "You just want the tip?"

"Feel free to increase my dosage," she told him, and for the very first time in her life, she had a man in her bed who gave her an orgasm after they both laughed until they cried.

Good tears.

The best she'd ever had.

YouTube Comments for "More Interviews Going Off the Rails: Maria Ivarsson & Peter Reedton, Part 2"

Bea'sKnees 2 years ago

I . . . I don't understand. They're not dating? How are they not dating? Whenever she turns her head away, he's GAZING at her in total adoration. Especially right after she brings out that jarred fish and shakes it around like an inch from his nose, for whatever reason.

Which raises another critical question: Where the heck did that fish come from??? Because it seems to appear from nowhere, and I don't understand???

Gods of the Gates Forever 2 years ago

I'm not saying that Peter Reedton wants to leap up from his chair and drag Maria Ivarsson to the floor and have his bearded way with her. I'm simply saying I'm pretty sure that happened a millisecond after the camera stopped rolling, because that dude was THIRSTY for a tall, tall glass of Swedish whatever-they-drink-in-Sweden. Jeez.

DinoTheWino 1 year ago

I've never wanted someone to affectionately call me a sh*t-boot more.***
Keep living the dream, Reedton!

***Of course, before this video, I had no idea Swedes were total weirdos who called people sh*t-boots, so.

Model Railroad Guy in Reno 1 year ago

For actual derailment videos, look elsewhere. Very disappointing.

That said, if these two aren't banging, I'll eat my Lionel Lines 1668E K-4 Torpedo Locomotive. And I really don't want to eat my Lionel Lines 1668E K-4 Torpedo Locomotive. It's very valuable. Also inedible. So that should tell you something.

21

"I STILL CAN'T BELIEVE YOU LIVE IN A GATED COMMUNITY,"
Maria said as she leaned toward the master bathroom mirror and
dusted her nose with loose powder. "It's so . . . exclusionary."

Well, yes. By both definition and intent.

Peter could list all the practical reasons he'd moved to a tiny
incorporated city of less than a thousand residences perched amid
the rolling hills of western San Fernando Valley, and done so immediately after receiving his first *Gods of the Gates* paycheck. He'd
used that paycheck as a down payment on the least expensive
home for sale in the community, and he hadn't regretted it for a
moment since.

Those three gates Maria disliked kept Google's photography
vehicles from driving by and sharing images of his house with
randos on the internet, most of whom were harmless—but not
all. The guards at those gates also prevented buses of star-hungry
tourists from rumbling past his home all day as they sought out
the properties of his more famous neighbors.

Furthermore, the setting was idyllic. Almost ridiculously so.
A greenbelt and nature preserve bordered his side of the community, and his home's hilltop spot guaranteed spectacular sunset
views. Since the area had been developed in the 1950s, backyards
resembled forests, with mature trees gently rustling in the breeze,

and all the houses were different, rather than cookie-cutter clones of one another.

There were no sidewalks. No streetlights. Almost as many people riding horses as driving cars. Other than occasional helicopters overhead, whisking various musicians, athletes, and actors—and their guests—to and from nearby houses, quiet ruled this corner of the world.

But he was honest enough to admit the truth, at least to himself. Practical reasons hadn't made him choose this community, and they hadn't driven him to scrimp for five years to pay off every last cent of his mortgage.

These two square miles of LA were exclusive. Famously so, and famous people lived here. People who'd undeniably *made it*.

Every time one of those three gates opened for his SUV and he drove inside, it was like being judged by some pitiless, omnipotent being and found worthy. His heart weighed less than a feather, and all his risks and struggles had reaped their rewards, and no one and nothing could make him return to where he'd been.

That lifting gate was a concrete reminder: This community was his. This property was his. This *life* was his.

And now Maria was his too, finally, here in his home, and she loved him and understood him, and he'd never been so happy in all his life, and he was trying very, very hard not to panic.

But she didn't need to hear all that. To her, the gates weren't a sign of divine approbation. They were just . . . long pieces of painted metal.

Meeting her gaze in the mirror, he finished buttoning his shirt by feel. "I'm a private person, Pippi."

Either she was too busy with final preparations to shake jarred fish an eighth of an inch from his nose, or there were no herring-friendly pockets in that tempting little dress.

Such a shame.

"Let me rephrase." She straightened and twitched the folds of her dress until they fell into place. "I can't believe you live in a gated community whose gate is shaped like a giant oxen yoke, as if you're all humble nineteenth-century beet farmers. Even though one of your neighbors is a reality TV star with a golf course on her property, and you nearly peed yourself every time one of the cows on the island mooed at you."

If he protested that the golf course only featured two holes, because there wasn't enough available acreage for more, Maria would mock him. Rightfully so. Even though his own property barely encompassed an acre and didn't contain a single putting green.

The other issue, however, he'd gladly address.

"Those fucking cows were unnaturally large and loud, and their huge eyes brimmed with malevolence." Chewing cud and plotting murder. That was all they did, apart from occasional naps. "They were picturing pieces of my trampled corpse digesting in their four stomach compartments."

He might boast a small barn on his property, but a bovine would set foot—hoof—in it over his dead body. And given their inherent maliciousness, that might literally be true.

In the face of his remembered terror, Maria only laughed at him.

Okay, then. Time to go on offense.

"I know you Swedes like them, sweetheart, but beets?" Aiming for sheer provocation, he flicked the tip of her powdered nose. "They taste like dirt. Socialism and dirt."

As anticipated, her nostrils flared in patriotic aggrievement, and she elbowed his ribs. "Beets taste like free college tuition and universal health care provided via governmental policies aimed toward the common good." She paused. "Also somewhat like dirt. And blood."

"Aha!" Turning from the mirror, he jabbed a finger in her direction. "I knew you—"

But she wasn't done quite yet.

"Not to mention growing economic disparity, despite our largely left-wing governmental policies." Her brow creased. "Which is troubling, frankly. If anything, those beets aren't socialist *enough*."

Shit, she was adorable.

"Wow." He had to smile at her. "Those are some complex fucking beets, sweetheart."

She snorted. "Anyway, the gates are weird, but your house is great."

His smile widened as he basked in that decisive, very Maria-esque pronouncement.

They'd only arrived at LAX the evening before, exhausted from their time in Madison, so he'd waited until morning for the grand tour. Heart thumping a bit too hard, he'd guided her through the three-bedroom, two-bath, single-story ranch home, an original 1950s build renovated and refurbished over the years under the exacting eye of the all-powerful Community Association.

Unlike some of the other properties in the area, the house wasn't flashy, inside or out. From the road in front, only the home itself was visible, with its neutral gray-green wood siding and white trim, framed by a few bushes and flowers. Inside, everything had been updated but kept reasonable. He had hardwood floors; a decent-sized main bedroom, a small office, and two guest rooms; a generous living room open to a kitchen equipped with marble countertops and high-end appliances; and bathrooms that weren't huge but were pristine and modern, with more marble and sleek white tile.

After walking into the en suite bathroom and spotting the

sunken jetted tub and the glass-walled shower, Maria had offered him a slow, naughty grin. "I believe we'll enjoy ourselves in here, Peter."

He'd already considered the tour a success, even before she explored the true glory of his property: the backyard. Surrounded by the same white three-rail fencing all his neighbors had, perched atop a hill with expansive views of the undulating land surrounding the community, and complete with a large covered patio and a small, pretty pool, it was his favorite place to relax.

On days with pleasant weather, he could open the wall of glass doors leading from the dining area to the patio and let the outdoors inside even as he puttered around the house. And now that he was done filming overseas for most of the year, he might finally have time to decorate the interior and make it as gorgeous as the view outside.

His mom's sketches would serve as inspiration.

Right before her business went under, a client—her final client, as they'd soon find out—had requested a serene bedroom in the blues and greens of a calm tropical ocean. At the kitchen table, Peter had watched his mother's nimble fingers fly over her sketch pad, first with pencil, then pen and watercolors. Her nails might have been ragged, lines firmly etched between her thick, dark brows, but the corners of her mouth had been tucked into a quiet smile as she worked.

Creating beauty from nothing and offering it to others. Unable to keep it for herself.

"There it is, darling," she'd said as she laid the sketch to dry on the laminate countertop. "What do you think? Will she like it?"

"If she doesn't, she's a moron," he'd said.

Instead of—*It's beautiful, Mom. You're so talented, more talented than even you realize, and I can't find the right words to tell you how much I love you. Thank you for loving me too, always, and telling me so, even when I don't say it back.*

But he'd been so young, and he'd been a sullen little asshole, and they'd had all the time in the world. She'd had all the time in the world to keep drawing, keep creating beauty, and he'd had all the time in the world to tell her that her hugs made him believe, if only for a moment, that someone could love him and everything would be all right again. Maybe not then, but someday. As long as he had her.

The client loved her bright, peaceful new bedroom.

His mother closed her business and became a ghost.

But what she'd offered the world still existed. In him, and in that final sketch he'd had framed. The intricately drawn, prettily painted death throes of his mom's dream, now hanging over his fireplace and waiting for him to bring it back to life.

And Maria would help him do it.

His mother would have adored her. Who wouldn't?

"I'm glad you like my home." A vast understatement, but Maria would interpret it correctly. "Since it's yours too now."

For that, she planted a kiss on his cheek, then rubbed the resulting smear of lipstick from his skin.

"By the way, Peter," she mumbled, lips barely moving as she reapplied the deep rose shade, "was that an actual barn in your backyard? Because if so, I'm surprised, given your apparently deep-seated terror of murderous livestock."

One day, when a bovine criminal mastermind engineered Peter's grisly death, she'd repent her casual dismissal of his concerns. He might originate from Wisconsin, the home state of cow-loving dairy-product enthusiasts, but he was no fool.

"The barn was already on the property, and I had to have one. It's in the bylaws. Our Community Association is . . . somewhat intense." Drumming his fingers on the marble countertop, he chose to put a positive spin on things. "But we have access to a communal clubhouse, tennis courts, and a basketball court. And there are weekly community barbecues in the summer."

Eyeing him with amused skepticism, she put down her lipstick tube and raised one brow. "Have you ever gone to one of those barbecues? Even when you were in town and available to attend neighborhood events?"

Socializing in crowds? Among strangers? Without Maria to smooth his path?

Ugh.

"No," said Peter firmly.

Her lips twitched. "Another question: Do you have any actual animals in your barn?"

Peter Reedton, gentleman farmer. He tried to picture it. Imagined himself squatting beside a cow's ass, her deadly hooves mere inches from his vulnerable skull, tugging at her sensitive parts for unpasteurized milk still warm from her body.

He shuddered. "Of course not."

"Well, what do you keep there instead, if not livestock?"

"My dignity."

Maria laughed then, her unguarded, inimitable cackle that made the sun shine brighter. Which was quite a trick in Southern California.

"I can't wait to use your pool." When she tilted her head, a tendril of hair tickled her shoulder. "Can your neighbors see into that part of your yard?"

Oh, he knew where she was going with this, and he approved. Wholeloinedly.

"Nope," he said, and considered the various wonderful possibilities.

"Then I guess it's okay I didn't pack my bikini."

He'd give a lot to see that red bikini again, but after six years, she probably didn't even have it anymore. And in that case . . .

"Naked is good." After thinking a moment, he corrected himself. "No, naked is *great*. Better than great. *Optimal*."

She snickered.

"I'd have loved a pool in our yard when I was growing up. At least for the two weeks each summer the weather was hot enough to use it," she added wryly. "If all your neighbors didn't have pools of their own, I'm sure every nearby kid would be climbing the fence and sneaking into yours."

Kids. Yeah.

This wasn't the world's best moment to raise such a sensitive topic, but maybe it couldn't hurt to feel her out on the subject a little?

"A lot of people here do have children. In case that's something that interests you." He kept his voice carefully neutral. "We have a community elementary school, a playground near the clubhouse, and lots of pint-size kids in designer clothing selling lemonade at the ends of their driveways. Like, real lemonade. Squeezed from an actual yellow lemon from a tree."

Her mouth opened, then closed, and her brows drew together. *Shit.*

Unable to stand the silence, he spoke again. "Although most of 'em probably use electric juicers, now that I think about it. And fancy so-called natural sweeteners instead of plain old sugar, mixed with water from artesian wells. Ones ceremonially blessed by ghostly nuns at the ancient, abandoned abbeys where the wells are located."

Ah, nervous rambling, the refuge of those ill equipped for serious conversations.

This was what he got for talking. Silence was so much easier.

She continued staring at him for the space of a breath or two. Then she finally spoke, testing out each word with uncharacteristic caution.

"I thought . . . or maybe I hoped?" She hesitated. "Hoped is probably more accurate. Anyway, I kind of hoped you were, uh . . . past the point of wanting kids?"

"Oh, thank fuck." He exhaled in a rush, sagging with relief. "I don't want kids either. I have zero desire to take on that responsibility, especially given how hectic and unpredictable our schedules can be."

So many television series and movies filmed outside Hollywood now. Establishing a stable home for a child of two working actors would be extremely challenging at best, impossible at worst. As a former miserable kid, he wasn't going to risk perpetuating their ranks. No, thank you.

For Maria, he might have considered bending on the issue, but he wouldn't have been thrilled about it. Shit, what a stroke of good luck.

"Excellent. Happy to have the matter settled. No kids." She beamed at him and turned back to the mirror over the dual vanity. "In that case, this house has plenty of room, and we won't need to move. Unless your extremely intense Community Association—"

"*Somewhat* intense."

"—wants to force us to become actual beet farmers." With the side of her nail, she removed a speck of something from her upper cheek. Probably mascara. "I'd oppose that."

"I called the Community Association *somewhat* intense," he emphasized once more, "and if you ever tell them I said otherwise, I'll drop you in the middle of a murder of cows and walk away, no matter how much you beg me to save you. I'll make certain your funeral is nice, though. Assuming the board members don't kill me first."

"As board members of community associations that are only *somewhat intense* are prone to do." She looked down her nose at him, her tone lofty. "In English, incidentally, I believe that's called a *herd* of cows. Murder of crows, herd of cows."

"I said what I said."

"Whatever." She handed over her tube of lipstick, the final item she needed him to carry that night. "I'm ready to go, *skitstövel*. Stop primping."

He shrugged on his suit jacket, slipped the lipstick inside a hidden pocket, and ran a brush over his beard one last time, then took a good, long look at the woman in the bathroom doorway.

Shaking his head, he crossed his arms over his chest.

All his grooming efforts were pointless. It didn't matter that his beard was soft and gleamed in the slanting sunlight from the bathroom windows. It didn't matter that he'd plucked his most stylish suit, charcoal gray and perfectly fitted, from the walk-in closet they now shared. It certainly didn't matter that he'd shined his shoes to a high gloss.

He could be wearing a fucking clown costume, and it still wouldn't matter. No photographers were going to bother snapping photos of him at Alex's charity auction. Not with her nearby.

The deep blue of her dress turned her skin luminous, and the garment was almost as beautiful as she was, with lavishly embroidered sleeves, a square neck that dipped low, and a hem that flirted high on those luscious thighs. The straps of her flat sandals wrapped lovingly, possessively around her ankles and calves. With seemingly two flicks of her wrist, she'd gathered her hair into a casual bun, just messy enough to be modern, with waving tendrils framing her gorgeous face.

He wanted to kiss that lipstick off her. Rip that dress off her.

She could keep the sandals on.

"*Fy fan*, Peter." Her eyes swept over him in similar appraisal, from top to toe. "Forget the buffet. I could eat you for dinner instead."

In case he'd missed the husky invitation in that comment, her eyes flicked to his dick, hopeful and hardening beneath his suit pants. Also doomed to disappointment, because they needed to get going.

"Save that thought for approximately four hours from now, sweetheart," he said.

Taking her hand, he led her through the house and to the door. But right before they went outside, she halted and tugged him to a stop too.

Her eyes twinkled with malicious glee. "Just in case you thought I forgot about the Pippi reference from earlier . . ."

And there it was, albeit belatedly. A jar of pickled herring, shaken so close to his face he couldn't actually focus on it without crossing his eyes.

It shouldn't be scientifically possible. Was materializing sea-food from thin air a special power all Swedes shared but kept secret from outsiders?

"Now we can go," she announced, and swept out the door in front of him.

He watched the jiggle of her ass and let it soothe his concerns about the laws of physics.

A minute later, as he handed her up into the SUV, she suddenly snorted. "Oh, gods above, I just realized something."

He grunted in response, because when she was sitting down, that dress—*that dress.*

Holy shit.

The short, wide hem would fit so easily over his head if he knelt at her feet in an abandoned hotel hallway, spread those fucking amazing thighs, and licked until she gasped and shook and came on his tongue.

"You live in a gated community, Peter, where you can make the gates open at your will." Waiting, evidently, for his attention to leave her legs, she fell silent a long, long time until he met her eyes again. "You know what that makes you?"

He had no damn idea. "Wealthy?"

"God of the gates," she told him, then screeched with laughter until he was laughing too, helplessly. "Oh, *fy fan*, it's *perfect.*"

You are too, he thought, and wished for the millionth time he could banish the thread of fear woven amid all his joy. *Heaven help me, you are too.*

22

AS SOON AS MARIA AND PETER MADE IT PAST THE RED carpet and inside the upscale Beverly Hills hotel where Alex's charity auction was occurring, she stopped, clapped a hand to her chest, and took a deep breath.

"*Skit*, Peter." She closed her eyes for a moment, trying to calm herself down. "My heart is still racing. That was Lauren with Alex, right? His minder? Are you sure she was all right?"

"Yeah, that was Lauren. In the cast chat, he said he was bringing her tonight." One hand resting protectively on her lower back, he used the other to scratch at his beard, the motion twitchy and fretful. "I don't know for sure, but I saw her walking off with one of the event organizers afterward, and she seemed to be moving okay. And if she'd been seriously hurt, we both know Alex would have lost his shit entirely."

"Instead of only partially." Her weak attempt at a smile died immediately.

Alex's bellow for help on Lauren's behalf could have been heard at Stina and Olle's home across the Atlantic, and no wonder. That sickly-pale intruder with greasy dark hair had appeared out of fucking nowhere. Babbling something about red pills, he'd forced his way through the crowds and leaped onto the red carpet, apparently in an attempt to attack Alex. Only to knock down Lauren instead, when she reacted more quickly than her charge and blocked the man from reaching his target.

Maria and Peter had watched in horror from their spot on the red carpet, too far away to intervene. They hadn't been able to protect their friend or his minder. Not before the attack, and not before security dragged the man away.

When Maria sucked in a hitching breath, Peter pulled her into his arms, one big hand warm on her nape, the other rubbing her back. After a minute, her pulse no longer thumped in her ears. But when she tried to leave his arms, he didn't let her.

In all honesty, she didn't fight that hard.

"You have my phone." Because fucking designers still didn't put enough pockets in women's clothing, and she hated fiddling with a clutch all night. "Can you text him and ask if Lauren got hurt?"

"Of course." It was a low rumble, and he still didn't let her go or reach for his phone. "Shit, Maria. Thank fuck you're fine. I saw that asshole barge onto the red carpet, and I had no idea what to expect. If he'd had a gun and turned on you next . . ."

When his voice broke, he trailed off. His arms squeezed around her just a bit too tightly for comfort, and it was her turn to rub his back—which she did gladly, grateful for his own safety.

As another cluster of auction attendees arrived, he pressed one last soft kiss to her temple and pulled back, looking noticeably calmer. "Let me text him, and then we'll grab you some free booze and spend tons of money on things we'd never normally buy. I personally enjoy bidding on signed headshots of Alex, drawing terrible, terrible things on his face with a Sharpie, and then sending him pics of the desecration while he complains about how I'm a monster who's wounded him to his very soul. That's a direct quote, by the way."

The corner of his mouth indented in a subtle smile, another indication he'd relaxed at last.

"Hmmm. Evil *and* charitable. I like it." She tapped her chin consideringly. "But is the booze truly free when event tickets cost a hundred and fifty dollars apiece?"

It was a philosophical question rather than a complaint. She had the money to spend. They both did. And Alex's choice of charity, a regional nonprofit working to prevent domestic violence and help survivors rebuild their lives, couldn't have appealed to her more.

"Fine." Heaving an exaggerated sigh, he tapped out his text and slid his phone back in his pocket. "I take it back. It's not free booze; it's booze *at no additional cost.*"

He mumbled something under his breath, and it sounded very much like *you Norse nitpicker.* When she cast him a sharp look—because that was nothing less than blatant provocation, given their earlier discussion about the word *Norse*—he smiled innocently and angled his elbow in invitation.

Arm in arm, they entered the expansive ballroom. This early in the evening, they still had plenty of time to grab a drink, eat hors d'oeuvres, and peruse the silent auction items displayed on long tables at the back of the room before the live auction began. Plenty of guests had already arrived, though, chatting in small groups and clad in everything from sparkly cocktail dresses to tube tops and ripped jeans.

The tube top people were probably musicians. Even she knew that.

"No one told me I could wear a tee instead of a dress," she said as they stood in line for the open bar. "At this very moment, I could have been silently announcing *Agnetha and Anni-Frid Were Robbed* to everyone who glanced at my boobs."

He pursed his lips. "Is this an ABBA thing?"

"Yes."

"Do I want to know?"

"Probably not."

"Am I going to find out anyway?"

"What do you think?" She smiled at him, beaming with good cheer.

Now at the front of the line, he heaved another exaggeratedly downtrodden sigh and ordered himself a mojito mocktail while she requested a glass of pinot noir. And by the time they crossed the room to the silent auction tables, his reserves of ABBA-related knowledge had expanded significantly.

"—though they didn't write the songs, their voices and performances drove the success of the band, so they deserve more critical respect than they've traditionally received," she finished. "And don't even get me started on a newly divorced Björn having his very sad ex-wife sing 'The Winner Takes It All.' Even though she apparently loves that song, what a dick move, as you Americans say."

He scratched his bearded chin. "You, uh, clearly have strong feelings about this."

"I have the *correct* feelings about this," she told him, and he raised his hands in surrender.

When they reached the first table, she snorted when she saw the current bids for a two-night stay in a five-star San Diego resort and the opportunity to be a walk-on in a cult-favorite sitcom. The going price for the next item, an exclusive wine-tasting retreat in Napa, almost made her choke on the fig, honey, and goat cheese crostini a server had offered her moments before.

Which was silly, since she could afford either item. Hell, she could afford both, and the money would go to a good cause. But somehow, entering her credit card number into a charitable website's donation page and giving them that very same amount without expecting anything in return didn't feel as . . . excessive?

This was most likely a Swedish thing, much like her instinctive distaste for gated communities. So be it. In both cases, she could either compromise or find workarounds.

Although she didn't love those ridiculous, exclusionary oxen-yoke gates, she would accept them if they made Peter happy and simultaneously entertain herself by mocking them—and him—mercilessly. And the charity would gladly accept her money without a single, luxurious string attached. Later tonight, she'd visit their website.

Done. She could live with those choices.

"You going to bid on the Napa trip?" Peter asked after swallowing the last bite of his own crostini.

"If I were going to try to win anything, that would be it. But no." At the next table, a very large signed and framed photo of a sexily smirking Alex dwarfed the other offerings. She had a feeling she knew who was going to win that item. Then deface it mercilessly. "I'll just give the organization money and leave the auction items to the people who'll be happiest to win them."

He gave a little grunt, preoccupied by filling out the form in front of Alex's photo.

While he emptied his bank account to troll his friend and co-star, she kept wandering down the long line of tables. Only to hear her name shouted from across the enormous ballroom in a very familiar, very welcome, very loud voice.

"Maria! Get the hell over here!" that voice shouted again before Maria managed to respond. "Peter, what the fuck is taking you so long at that table?"

She turned and saw exactly who she'd expected: Carah, her

favorite non-Peter *Gates* castmate. The other woman was standing by a round table—one of many—at the very front of the ballroom, hand in the air to catch their attention. After checking in with Peter, who waved her off and continued scanning the silent auction items, Maria headed that way.

A very attractive woman in a suit with a skinny tie checked her clipboard before letting Maria enter what was apparently the VIP section. Approximately one millisecond later, Maria was forced to catch an entire grown woman as Carah flung herself at her costar.

"Oh my fucking God, Maria, I have missed you so fucking much," Carah declared. "It's been *months* since the last goddamn convention."

"I know," Maria managed to choke out despite her compressed lungs. *Skit.* Carah had a grip of steel. "I've been wanting to talk to you too. I have some news."

As soon as Carah let her breathe, Maria would tell her about moving in with Peter. Which would probably prompt another round of obscenity-studded hugging, since no one in the cast knew they were together yet.

"Ooooooh." Improbably, Carah managed to squeeze even harder. "Tell me, you withholding bitch."

Maria's first attempt to peel off her friend failed. But during the second attempt, she heard yet more voices she knew and loved and would recognize anywhere. So she put a bit more vigor into her next de-Carahing efforts, which procured her both a glare from Carah and the ability to turn around and hug Nava and Ramón instead.

Gods above, it was good to see them again. "I didn't know you were coming!"

"It's a great cause, and we couldn't miss the opportunity to check in with you and Peter. Your last night in Ireland, Ramón and I got the sense the two of you—" Nava looked over Maria's shoulder and grinned. "Ah. There he is. The man in question."

Peter's strong arms circled Maria from behind, and he propped his chin on her shoulder. "Good to see you again, Nava. Ramón. Carah. I intend to text all of you next week about coming to our house for dinner."

Carah's blue eyes lit with glee. "*Our* house? Peter Motherfucking Reedton, after all this goddamn time, did you finally get your thumb out of your—"

"Yes, Carah," Peter interrupted, then kissed Maria's cheek. "The two of us are together, and my ass is now entirely digit-free. Thank you so much for inquiring."

Well, *that* was an outright lie, unless he was referencing the state of his ass at this very moment, but she generously chose not to point that out.

The more truthful part of his declaration, as predicted, elicited another round of hugs, more swearing, and several disapproving stares from neighboring tables. Then the lights flickered, a signal that the more formal portion of the evening was about to begin, and everyone let go of one another and circled the table to find an empty seat.

Poor Peter sagged in introverted relief as he thumped down into the chair beside hers. But a wide smile split that dark beard of his, and he intertwined their fingers on the tabletop, where everyone could see.

"Later tonight, you *will* tell me every fucking detail," Carah whispered in Maria's ear. "And I mean that in every possible way I can."

AFTER ALEX MADE his heartfelt, impassioned case for supporting his charity, the live auction commenced. And when he urged the attendees to spend big and bid it up, they listened. If Maria thought the silent auction items were going for breathtaking amounts, that was nothing compared to what people would evidently pay to attend a series finale party with the *Gates* showrunners or what they'd spend for a fucking *car*.

Suffice it to say, he raised—as Carah put it—a shitload of money for his charity.

Afterward, crowds of people were waiting to speak to Alex, which meant Lauren knew no one at the table. So after all her tablemates filled their plates at the dinner buffet, they introduced themselves, confirmed she was uninjured, and made casual conversation. Even Peter, despite his discomfort socializing with strangers.

"Lovely to meet you, Lauren." He smiled at her, warmth in his dark eyes. "We've heard so much about you from Alex."

"I'm certain you have," Lauren said dryly. "I hope your data plan is very generous."

Apart from having the most gorgeous green eyes Maria had ever seen, Alex's short, round minder was also smart and very funny, albeit in an understated way. And then, when they were nearly done eating, the star of the evening swooped down upon the table, hustled Lauren toward the ballroom exit, and took her . . . somewhere.

"That'll be interesting to watch," Nava murmured, and she wasn't wrong.

Ramón's phone buzzed atop the table. One glance at the screen was enough to make him sigh. Meeting Nava's inquiring gaze, he gave her a tiny nod.

She groaned. "Again?"

"Sadly, yes." Leaning back in his chair, the director laced his hands over his belly and told the assembled group, "So that was my ex-wife, for approximately the thousandth time in the last couple of weeks. As soon as she heard I was in a committed relationship with Nava, the barrage of texts and calls started. Which I don't get, since we've been divorced almost a decade now, and the decision to split was mutual."

"Wants what she can't fucking have." Carah shook her head.

"We're just waiting her out." Nava patted Ramón's thigh consolingly. "Thank goddess I don't have the same issue. Dottie's been great. Very supportive of my relationship with Ramón, especially around Carlie."

"I would have expected my ex to be the same way, but . . ." He lifted a shoulder. "Like I said, I don't get it, but I've heard it's a pretty common phenomenon."

Poor Ramón. Maria couldn't even imagine how frustrating that would be, for him and for Nava too. Given the circumstances of Maria's own breakup with her only significant ex-lover, she was entirely certain she'd never know from firsthand experience.

Ramón, obviously ready to stop discussing his own woes, twisted in his chair to face Peter. "What about you? Any exes come out of the woodwork after you and Maria got together, asking you to give them another chance?"

Maria fought a wince and nudged Peter's leg with her own.

Yes, Ramón wanted to change the subject, but that was clumsy of their former director. After all this time, he should know Peter didn't share sensitive information in public. Or at all, generally.

To her surprise, though, Peter didn't seem bothered by the question.

"My only significant ex is married to a thoracic surgeon now, so the good news is that she's extremely unlikely to come calling the first time she sees me kissing Maria in a tabloid photo." Turning his head, he met Maria's eyes and . . . smiled. Not a forced or fake smile, but an expression of genuine joy. "No, I take it back. That's not the good news. The good news—the best news—is that if she'd stayed with me, I wouldn't have Maria. So I'm glad she left me. Thrilled."

A chorus of *awwwww*s greeted his declaration, and for good reason. Coming from a man like Peter, that was a public declaration of love.

Smiling back at him, she squeezed his fingers and absently rubbed at her chest, which seemed to have . . . melted, somehow?

Nava turned to her. "What about you, Maria? Any persistent exes?"

Well, that took care of the melting. Immediately.

After six years together, she still hadn't told Peter about Hugo. And maybe it was a tale better told privately, but he needed to hear it one way or another, sooner rather than later, and she wasn't embarrassed or heartbroken anymore.

Hugo's behavior didn't indicate her worth. Or, rather, her lack thereof.

As Carah would say: *What the fuck. Do it, bitch.*

A big gulp of wine, a deep breath, and Maria prepared to offer the briefest explanation possible. Hugo hadn't deserved her time then, and she wouldn't waste an extra moment of it on him now.

"Like Peter, I only have one significant ex," she said. "Hugo. He was a banker in Stockholm. We'd been a couple for two years and were talking about buying an apartment together when his company transferred him to their London office. Our relationship became long-distance."

Later, of course, she'd found out the transfer hadn't been forced on him without warning, as he'd implied. He'd asked for it. Asked to move away from her, to an entirely different country.

"A long-distance relationship is . . ." Nava's face creased in sympathy. "It's hard to make it work. I know that from very personal experience."

Hmmm. Maria had always wondered whether endless months spent apart as Nava filmed on location had broken her relationship with Dottie. She'd also wondered, however, whether her own experiences were coloring her suspicions.

Both could be true. Likely, both were true.

"Frankly, I don't see how *anybody* could make one work," Maria told her. "I certainly couldn't, anyway."

And Hugo never tried. He didn't remain faithful for even a month. Which she knew for certain, based on a single piece of evidence.

In her defense, it was a very good piece.

"Several months after he moved, he texted the wrong thing to the wrong person," she continued, and wished her cell weren't in Peter's pocket, because she wanted to capture their reaction to the next bit. "A request to the obstetrics office of Dr. Millicent Ivey that they reschedule his pregnant wife's ultrasound appointment."

Peter's hand convulsed in hers, and his dark brows snapped together so hard, he appeared to have a generously sized caterpillar on his face. Carah mouthed the word *motherfucker*, and Ramón jerked back in his chair with enough force that it scraped against the floor.

Otherwise, it was all dead silence and dropped jaws.

Fy fan. She really should have reclaimed her phone. This was *priceless.*

And to her shock, the story didn't cause her pain anymore. Not a single twinge. In fact, the whole thing was kind of . . . hilarious?

With a huff of amusement, she flicked her wrist. "Ivey, Ivarsson. It could happen to anyone."

"It happened to *you*." Peter didn't look amused. At all.

In fact, he was staring at her so hard, she half wondered if he was attempting telepathy. Or perhaps telekinesis, in hopes he could whisk her from the ballroom to somewhere more private using only the seething energy generated by his scowl.

If so, good luck to him. Her ass was planted in this seat for the duration.

"It hurt." She spoke directly to him, because she knew at least part of what that glower hid. Concern. For her. "But my family helped me pick up the pieces. And a few months later, I sent audition materials to Hollywood on a whim, figuring I could use a new setting. A new adventure."

Slowly, the severe lines of his face softened as he saw her smile and heard what she hadn't said: *Then I met you. Then you became my closest friend. Then you became my everything.*

Those snapping dark eyes turned tender, and he gave a little nod. An answering smile tipped the edges of his mouth, and it was small and sweet.

He didn't need to remove her from the crowded ballroom with the power of his mind.

The music swelling in the distance was only for them, because everyone else had already disappeared. Just like that.

"Without him, *sötnos*, there's no us. That's his only importance to me now." She lifted their entwined fingers. Kissed his knuckles. "So let's hit that chocolate fountain at the dessert display, order more drinks at no additional cost, and find out whether I can convince the DJ to play 'Dancing Queen.'"

His eyes narrowed again as he helped her to her feet. "Oh, they'll play it."

"Or you'll . . . what? Murder them?" Even as a proud Swede, that seemed a bit extreme.

"I had intended a bribe, but . . ." He lifted a shoulder. "Whatever's necessary. I've plumbed the depths of evil before. Peered into the eyes of killers. Learned their malevolent secrets, which I can now employ for my own ends."

She stopped. "You're talking about the Irish cows again, aren't you?"

"I'm talking about *all* cows," he corrected. "Now gather your molten milk chocolate and enjoy the fruits of iniquity."

In the end, the DJ did indeed play "Dancing Queen." It required only a twenty-dollar bill, rather than bovine-inspired homicide. With the ridiculous man she adored at her side, she danced surrounded by friends, and she contained no more secrets. No more hidden history. Nothing else to hold within and curl around, out of shame or wounded pride or lingering grief.

She felt light enough to drift, airborne, in the wake of Peter's laughter.

And if this—along with her family—was her reward for all her pain, all the times she'd been abandoned, all the moments she'd been set aside and watched the people she loved choose anything and everything other than her, it was enough.

More than enough.

Like Peter, it was everything.

Gods of the Gates Cast Chat: Tuesday Evening

Carah: I CAN'T BELIEVE YOU OUTBID ME FOR THAT SILENT AUCTION NAPA TRIP, ASSHOLE

Carah: talking to Peter, by the way

Carah: the rest of you are assholes too, but he's the SPECIFIC asshole in this situation

Carah: I was going to film my next food-reaction video there

Carah: I'm sure people do weird shit with grapes, but now I'LL NEVER KNOW, YOU DICK

Peter: You snoozed, you lost.

Carah: I did NOT fucking snooze!!! I had to fucking pee!!!

Peter: Then let me rephrase: You peed, you lost.

Peter: Maria, want to do a wine tasting in Napa? Because I hear people do weird shit with grapes there.

Maria: Are there spa treatments involved?

Peter: Uh . . . no?

Maria: *Can* there be spa treatments involved?

Maria: Because I like wine, but as long as I'm going on a fancy retreat, I might as well also be scrubbed and peeled and massaged thoroughly by a man named Sven who reminds me of my homeland.

Peter: Chilly and asocial?

Maria: Haha, Peter.

Carah: Told you. TOTAL ASSHOLE.

Carah: Anyway, I think we've lost sight of the most important issue here

Carah: I.e., Peter's rampant assholery toward me and how it should be punished

Maria: Peter, how many people can come to the wine-tasting retreat?

Peter: . . .

Maria: Would you be unhappy if we had company?

Peter: . . .

Peter: It's fine.

Maria: Carah, consider yourself invited. You can film yourself eating bizarre grape-based foods or get yourself pummeled alongside me. Your choice.

Carah: I'M A MODERN WOMAN, I DON'T HAVE TO CHOOSE, I CAN HAVE IT ALL

Carah: You're the best, Maria, thank you

Carah: Thank you too, Peter, I SUPPOSE

Mackenzie: I found the best kitty massage place recently, didn't I, Whiskers, didn't I

Mackenzie: Oh, Whiskers, I agree. I should get a massage too, shouldn't I?

Peter: . . .

Maria: The more the merrier, but Mac, you have to wear something not covered in cat hair for once. Especially if Alex comes, because you're killing that poor, allergic man.

Peter: Alex is coming too?

Maria: Maybe. If we don't hear from him by tomorrow, I'll email him and find out whether he and Lauren can make it.

Asha: Oh, I'm so sorry I'm in Mykonos!

Otherwise, I'd be there!

Summer: May I come? Pleeeeeease? I need pummeling too! I am pummel-deficient!

Carah: I'd fucking love that, Summer

Carah: You can share my room!

Summer: ☺

Maria: I'm so sorry you can't come, Asha. And of course, Summer. I'd love to see you!

Maria: Tack tack for the group weekend in Napa, Peter. It's really sweet of you.

Peter: ...

Peter: Yes. Sweet.

Peter: Maria, I just want to say that Benny and Björn were true geniuses

Peter: They might as well have been the only people in ABBA, what legends

Maria: TAKE IT BACK, SKITSTÖVEL

Peter: :-)

23

TWO MONTHS LATER, WHEN PETER AND MARIA ARRIVED at Con of the Gates in San Francisco, the first large publicity event they'd ever attended as an official couple, *Gates* fans lost their fucking shit.

Sure, the two of them had been spotted together before the convention. At Alex's charity auction, Peter hadn't tried to hide how he felt about Maria, and various Hollywood insiders had taken notice. And their relationship truly became public on their Napa trip, when some asshole at the winery had captured video of them making out in a seemingly private corner and posted the clip all over social media. A predictable burst of online excitement and interview requests had followed, and after that, they received a certain amount of attention whenever they explored LA together.

So people knew they were a couple. But *Gates* fans hadn't seen that up close and in person until the con. So their relationship was the talk of the event. For, oh . . . four hours, maybe.

That Friday afternoon and early evening, as they checked into the hotel, found their room, and posed for their joint fan photo sessions, he couldn't count how many con attendees used their phones to record the sight of his arm around her shoulders, or the number of times some bearded dude in an artistically tattered Viking costume shouted *Finally!* or *I knew it!* to him at top volume, or—once, memorably—*Pillage away, you lucky motherfucker!*

That guy made Maria grin. As did all the fans in tees reading VIKING? NO, VI-QUEEN or SHIELD-MAIDENS DO IT WEARING LEATHER, or his personal favorite: IF YOUR SLOW BURN LASTS MORE THAN FOUR YEARS, PLEASE CONSULT A PHYSICIAN, accompanied by a stylized drawing of Cassia and Cyprian looking long-suffering.

"Instead of a physician, shouldn't that be a script doctor?" Maria whispered right before the camera clicked, and that particular fan photo caught him choking on laughter.

It was a lot of attention. *A lot*, even by con standards.

Then Alex lost his entire goddamn mind at his Q&A session that first night. After that, most fans became too occupied either checking Urban Dictionary for the definition of *pegging* or reading all of Alex's thinly veiled sexual fantasies about Lauren and equally transparent screeds against their showrunners to pay much attention to Maria and Peter.

Normally, he'd say *thank fuck* to that, but Alex had become a dear friend and was a very good—if very impulsive—man. So Peter and Maria tried to help with damage control however they could, even before Alex vanished from the convention entirely to pursue his fired minder . . . somewhere. His disappearance caused yet another hubbub Saturday morning, when fans realized he was gone and wouldn't be attending any of his remaining sessions and panels.

And then later on Saturday, Marcus—Mr. I'm an Extremely Intelligent, Thoughtful Man Pretending to Be a Shallow Idiot for Some Reason I'd Rather Not Disclose Even After Six Years—decided to reveal both his dyslexia and the fact that he sounded like a fucking classics professor whenever he wasn't in character. In character—*as himself*—Marcus Caster-Rupp.

It was all very confusing and attention-grabbing, and that was *before* Marcus shoved his way through crowds of confused fans to interrupt his estranged girlfriend April's own session and announce his devoted love, then French her in front of a live studio audience.

Okay, to be fair, it wasn't a studio. It was a convention hall.

The rest: one hundred percent accurate.

At that point, the *Gates* fans who'd decided to skip this particular convention kept posting videos of themselves weeping in despair.

By Sunday morning, Peter already knew the audience for the last event of the convention, his joint Q&A session with Maria, was going to fall into one of two categories: They'd either slump into the hall, sagging with postdrama fatigue, or burst into the space wired as hell and waiting with twitchy impatience for the final bombshell to drop.

But he and Maria were the normal ones, and they had no earth-shattering news to share. By now, everyone knew they were together. Each of them had accepted a few smaller, short-term roles and auditioned for others, but they were both willing to wait for the right project to come along before committing to anything bigger. Especially since the longer they waited, the more time they could spend together, and they couldn't get enough.

Enough time together. Enough sex. Enough conversation. Enough privacy.

Fuck, he loved her. The thought of a life without her—

Well, he tried not to think about it. Ever. Because when he was alone and those thoughts, those sibilant whispers born of fears he couldn't seem to shake, did slither into his brain, he panicked. His pulse echoed in his ears, his breathing turned shallow and rapid, his skin flushed and dampened with sweat, and he wondered if he might be having a heart attack.

It wasn't a heart attack, though. It was a panic attack. He hadn't had them for years now, not since his days in weekly therapy, but he still recognized the signs.

In the aftermath of those occasional episodes, he always racked his brain, searching for some way to tie her closer to him. Even though she'd already moved from Sweden to be with him, and they already lived together.

He knew she didn't want kids. Neither of them did. But whether she'd accept a marriage proposal . . . that, he kept questioning. Kept debating.

Ask too soon, and he might scare her off. Ask too late, and she might question the strength of his commitment and pull away to protect herself.

The other thing he knew for certain: If he did ever propose, he sure as hell wasn't going to do it in front of a fucking audience.

So, much to the dismay of everyone in the assigned hall, there wouldn't be another bombshell of any sort in his Q&A session with Maria. None. Zero. Zip.

Or at least there *wasn't* going to be a bombshell.

Then he got the call from his agent, a mere half hour before they were due to report backstage in their hall. It wasn't enough time to go over the nuts and bolts of the offer he'd just received, but plenty of time to understand the essentials.

To keep from disturbing him, Maria had closed herself into the suite's bedroom as soon as DeShaun called. But once the conversation ended, she immediately emerged and flopped onto the couch next to him, cheerful and gorgeous as always.

Her knee nudged his. "What did DeShaun have to say? Any new nibbles or exciting scripts?"

In his daze, he barely heard her.

This was it, finally. His next big job, essentially dropped into his lap without any effort on his part. Or, as Maria might counter, no *additional* effort.

All because he'd finally proven himself to the powers that be in Hollywood with *Gods of the Gates*, finally shown them what he'd earned and what he deserved.

A lead role on a high-profile show. A fat paycheck. Guaranteed years of steady work.

Enough career stability to offer the woman he loved marriage.

"Yeah," he said slowly. "I . . . I got an offer."

She planted a smacking kiss on his cheek. "Congratulations, *sötnos*. Which part?"

"I didn't audition for it." Bemused, elated, he shook his head and turned to her. "I mean, I auditioned for a guest role on the show, but not the part they gave me. I guess they felt like they'd seen enough between that and *Gods of the Gates* to cast me."

Her beam nearly blinded him. "Even better. They obviously know your value. What is it?"

This role would cement their future together. Cement *them* together.

And the sooner he managed to get the words out, the sooner they could start to celebrate.

"Maria, sweetheart." He took her hands in his. "Remember how I auditioned for the multi-episode serial killer role on *FTI: Forensic Team Investigations*?"

She offered him a very dry look. "Since it's one of the biggest shows on basic cable and there are approximately a dozen spinoffs currently airing around the world, including in Sweden, all featuring people in white coats peering into microscopes, enhancing computer images of license plates, and becoming inadvertent targets of murderers, and I thought one of those murderers might eventually be you, yes. Yes, I remember."

He would bristle at her description of the show, but she was right, and they both realized it. The role they'd offered him wouldn't allow the sort of character depth and development he usually preferred, but an opportunity like this . . . he'd be a fool to turn it down, and when it came to his career, he was never, ever a fool.

Shit, he could barely believe it, even though DeShaun had confirmed the offer five separate times during their call. "My audition was for the original series, the one set in Seattle. Turns out, the actor who's been their lead since the beginning wants to return to films, and he's leaving between seasons. They're killing off his character, so the on-screen team needs a new head forensics dude."

He waited, and it didn't take her long to fill in the rest.

"You, obviously. Head forensics dude extraordinaire," she said brightly, and kissed him again, this time on the mouth. "Peter, that's *wonderful* news. When will you start?"

"Maybe in a month or so?" Letting go of her hands, he checked the notes he'd taken on his phone. "They film in Vancouver, apparently, so I'll need to arrive a few days before they start shooting the next season and set up a place to live there."

"Vancouver?" Her hands fluttered for a moment, then folded neatly on her lap. "I-I've heard it's a lovely city."

"Yeah. Me too. Maybe we can take a trip out there between now and when I have to go, so we can explore the city a bit." There were only a few more notes, which he reread before setting aside his phone. "The other big news is that they want a three-year commitment."

She bit her lip, her smile a shadow of its former glory. "Okay."

Abruptly, she got up from the couch to pour herself a glass of water from the bathroom tap. Her brow had creased in concern, and no wonder. The role would initially mean big changes in their daily lives.

But she didn't need to worry about any continuing upheaval. In his conversation with DeShaun, he'd made certain of that. So he got to his feet and followed her to the bathroom doorway, where he told her the rest of what she should know.

He braced his hands on either side of the doorframe. "Since the show is already renewed for another four years, we won't have to watch and wait every year to find out whether it'll get canceled in the middle of my contract."

There would be no uncertainty for either of them. Just a regular, generous paycheck, the unattainable pipe dream of almost every would-be actor in Hollywood. That dream had already come true for him once before. Twice was a fucking *miracle*.

"We'll know exactly where I'll be for all three years, so I'll rent a place big enough for two." Was the climate there anything like Sweden? If so, he'd try to find somewhere that would remind her of her homeland. A cottage with a view of evergreens, maybe. "One where you'll be comfortable whenever you come to visit."

"Have you . . ." Her throat worked, and she took another sip of water. "Have you already accepted the offer?"

He shook his head. "DeShaun is still negotiating a few things, but their initial offer was more than fair, so he thinks we can officially say yes very soon. Later tonight, he'll send me the contract and highlight the parts still in question."

"It's basically a done deal, then." Her glass clinked against the granite countertop as she set it down. "Okay."

Gently but firmly, she moved him out of the bathroom doorway so she could gather her badge and purse and slip on the lacy flats arranged neatly just inside the room.

What he'd been offered today was the most stability a working actor could provide to his partner. So why did her forehead still have that crease in it?

"You and I can look over everything tomorrow, once we're back home, to make sure there's nothing problematic DeShaun didn't already flag," he suggested, moving closer. "Just in case."

Would that be enough to reassure her? Because he wanted her as his ally from the very beginning of this project, without reservation. The two of them an indivisible team, as she'd once suggested.

Back then, he'd scoffed at the very idea of it, at the prospect of having a true *partner*, because he'd been a hurt, angry idiot. Now that kind of partnership encompassed everything he wanted, and had become the source of all his contentment.

So he needed her with him on this. By the time he left for Vancouver, he wanted them so united in hearts and minds that even a little distance wouldn't weaken the fierce connection they shared.

But maybe *that* was the source of her concern. The distance between them. The prospect of another relationship with a man she'd have to book a flight to see, a man with plenty of opportunity to find trouble if he went looking for it. After what happened with her ex, he couldn't exactly blame her for being skittish.

"Okay," she said again, and reached for the door handle.

"You know I'd never . . ." He faltered. There was one thing he could tell her that would reaffirm his constancy in a way she wouldn't be able to doubt, but it would mean sacrificing a bit of pride. "Maria. After we—from the moment we met, I haven't been with anyone else. I haven't even kissed another woman since you walked into that sauna in your red bikini and blew my fucking mind."

Her hand dropped to her side, her chin to her chest. "Peter—"

Ducking his head, he tried to catch her eye. "I don't expect you to say the same, sweetheart. I'm the one who didn't want a sexual relationship while the show was filming, so I can't and won't judge you for taking what you needed elsewhere."

At that, she looked up. Unmistakable affection shone in her warm brown gaze, even as her lips remained pressed into a tight line. And when he stepped closer again, she didn't try to keep him at a distance.

He let out a long, slow breath of relief and cupped her beautiful, beloved face.

"My point is that I would never, ever fuck around on you." Her cheeks were so soft beneath the stroke of his thumbs, but cooler than normal. Paler. "Not even if we were filming on separate continents for thirty years."

"Thirty years, huh?" Her laughter was oddly shaky, and her eyes glistened. "That long?"

"Thirty years. A hundred years. Forever."

It was a vow.

"Oh, Peter." Twisting her neck, she kissed his palm. "I know you wouldn't cheat on me."

Good. Because he would never, ever hurt Maria the way her asshole ex had.

"Then let's get this session over with and start celebrating our good news." He skimmed his nose along the side of hers and brushed his lips over her temple. "I love you, Maria."

"I know," she said as he took her hand and led her out into the hall. "I love you too."

The door to the suite they shared swung shut with a decisive thud, and her hand in his was as cold as her cheeks. Maybe colder.

He shivered but kept moving.

24

MARIA WOULD RATHER EAT DIRT THAN ACCEPT PITY FROM strangers, and she refused to reveal her vulnerabilities to anyone who'd already hurt her.

So she wasn't crying in front of a packed hall of *Gates* fans, and she wasn't crying in front of Peter anymore either, not if she could possibly help it.

He loved her. Just not enough.

It was a threadbare refrain, and it left her feeling fragile and frayed too. She was unraveling, faster and faster for every minute that passed.

Still, she smiled. Laughed. Answered questions. Bantered with Peter, because that was what the audience wanted. What they expected and deserved from someone they'd spent good money to see. If it was a nonverbal lie, it was one she needed to tell for everyone's sake, including her own.

Using every ounce of grit and acting ability she possessed, she managed to convincingly sell that lie for almost the entire session. Only to find herself telling a tattered corner of the truth at the very last minute, in response to the very last question of the very last con event, and doing so not just in front of countless strangers, but in front of Peter as well.

And that was the disastrous part.

He might not love her enough, but he *did* love her, and she loved him. He deserved her utmost care in handling this situation. He'd earned it. And even if he was hurting her, he didn't mean to, and she didn't want to hurt him. Especially not in a setting like this, because he had his own pride and his own wounds to nurse in privacy. There was no way she could forget that, not when those wounds were the very reason he was leaving her behind.

Under the circumstances, with the stakes so high, such a simple topic shouldn't have tripped her up.

"Um . . ." As the moderator glanced at his tablet, she distracted herself by studying his CODS OF THE GATES tee, which she'd never seen before. It featured a line drawing of a large fish fin-slapping Jupiter, and it was perfection. If anyone on the cast deserved to be walloped by a vengeful cod, Ian was the one. "Final question, Peter and Maria. What's happening next for you? Any upcoming roles we should know about?"

Of course he was going to ask that. It was the obvious, okay-we're-almost-at-the-end, let's-wrap-things-up question, and she had a rote, sharing-just-enough-but-not-anything-better-kept-to-herself response.

Peter answered first. "I have a few smaller roles lined up in some upcoming films. I'm especially excited about *On the Lonesome Range*, a gritty western about nineteenth-century cowboys that doesn't whitewash history, since so many cowboys were Latino or Black, or overlook the existence of female cowhands. The script is spectacular." After a pause, he added, "All that said, I hope like hell they don't put me near many actual cows, because cows are fucking terrifying."

The audience laughed, assuming he was joking. He was not, of course.

When he'd accepted the role, she'd stared at him incredulously for several moments. Then mooed at him loudly and made him jump, which she'd found very satisfying. Cows aside, though, the script had delighted him. Hopefully he'd still be able to film his part between shooting episodes of *FTI*.

Not that she'd know, because by then she'd be long gone.

At the thought, she swiveled her chair away from Peter, away from the audience, and convincingly—she hoped—pretended the terrible sound she'd made was a strangled cough, one so harsh it brought tears to her eyes and required a few sips of water before she turned back.

Peter's warm hand spread across her back and rubbed there, even as he continued speaking, and his attempt to soothe her fake cough only made things worse. Much, much worse.

When she finally faced front again, he was wrapping up his answer with a vague hint concerning his big news. "I should be able to share more information about a future television role, a significant one, soon. What about you, Maria?"

He turned in his chair to watch her answer, and something about him in that moment undid her. His slight frown of worry as he uncapped a fresh bottle of water and handed it to her. The way his knees nudged hers in a gesture that might look accidental but was not. The final, gentle pat of her shoulder before he leaned back and surrendered the spotlight to her.

The open adoration lighting his dark eyes. The pride in his posture—all puffed-out chest and squared shoulders and relaxed satisfaction—as he surveyed her at his side.

She couldn't speak for the agony of it. Couldn't think.

Fuck. Swiveling away again, she faked another cough and bought herself a few more seconds, but the time to get a handle on this was now. *Right* now, so they could walk back to their shared suite, have the awful, heartbreaking conversation coming their way, and get this initial bit of agony over with already.

"Maria, sweetheart," he murmured in her ear, one hand over the mic clipped to his collar, the other spread wide and supportive across her back once more, "are you okay?"

Another wet, violent cough dragged from laboring lungs. "I— I'm fine."

It wasn't a lie if she would be fine. Someday. Not soon, though.

Ready or not, she swung back around to see a huge roomful of people looking at her. Waiting. For something she couldn't quite remember.

She peered at them blankly, lost.

"Maria?" The moderator glanced discreetly at his tablet, probably checking the time. "What's coming up for you?"

It was a prod, gentle as Peter's hand slowly circling between her shoulder blades.

"I . . ." She wasn't unraveling. She was undone. "I don't know."

Peter's brow furrowed, his mouth pressing into a grim line, and he quickly looked at the moderator, a silent request to end the session so he could check on her well-being. But the other man was already speaking again, already giving her a helpful prompt so she could tell everyone exactly what they expected to hear. What Peter expected to hear. What she'd expected to tell them less than two hours ago.

"Well, we all figure you'll be based in LA rather than Stockholm from now on, right?"

The moderator aimed a knowing glance and a wink at the crowd, and they smiled, delighted for the happy couple onstage. The happy, committed couple who wouldn't part, not for anything.

She opened her mouth.

And somehow, somehow—found herself telling the truth. "I . . . don't know."

Only that *wasn't* the truth, was it? Because she already knew she'd be booking a flight to Stockholm as soon as she and Peter finished digging a grave for their relationship and buried it deep beneath the brown, desiccated grass of LA in July.

So far underground it would never resurface.

The rest was a babble of voices and applause and shuffling feet as the moderator did whatever he was doing and wrapped up the session, but she paid none of it any attention, because the look on Peter's face—

Mouth rounded in absolute shock as he stared at her. Forehead creased in utter bewilderment and so much pain, she might as well have knifed him in the ribs. Stricken brown eyes pleading for reassurance, for her to tell him she didn't mean it, that she'd misunderstood the question or misspoken.

He'd gone pale as death.

Then that vulnerable, open mouth snapped shut, and betrayal edged the sharp jut of his jaw. A tide of hectic color slashed across his cheekbones.

He closed down.

Expressionless, all emotion shuttered and tucked safely away, he stood. A single hard look ordered her to follow him, as if she weren't already going to do that. As if now, after all these years, she could simply walk off without another word the same way she had long ago.

Earning his trust had taken so long. So much effort.

And with three very short, very basic English words—*I don't know*—it was gone.

Her own heartbreak had required a three-word, hyphenated phrase: *three-year commitment*. Because the man she adored could apparently commit to stay among strangers for three years for the sake of a job, but he couldn't commit to stay with her for longer than three months. Not even for the sake of her love and her presence in his daily life.

She couldn't live with that. She *wouldn't* live with that, because he wouldn't be living with her, and she had other options.

Peter strode ahead of her and cleared a path through the hotel hallways, so stone-faced that not even lingering selfie-hunting fans dared flag them down, although she caught a few camera flashes along the way. Occasionally he shot a glance back, confirming her continued presence, but she hadn't gone anywhere.

When she offered someone her heart, she was never the one who chose to leave. It was everyone else who left her. Always, with the sole exception of her family.

Step by step, she followed in his wake, silent. When he fumbled for his keycard outside their suite, his hands shaking, she produced hers and slotted it in place. The sensor flashed green, and he shoved open the door with violent force.

But he was Peter, so he also held it for her, making sure she was fully inside before letting it slam shut again.

Before the echo of that slam even faded, he'd turned on her.

"*I don't know.*" It was a mockery of her voice. "What the fuck did *that* mean, Maria?"

He stalked farther into the room, off to the side where he wasn't blocking the exit. Deliberately. Because again, he was Peter.

He didn't join her in the little seating area when she carefully perched on the edge of the too-narrow armchair, though, and he didn't appear particularly inclined toward civil conversation. Fists curled at his sides, he waited for her answer.

"I—" Clutching the squared-off armrests, she tried again. "Peter, I can't . . ."

His dark eyes were pinned to her face, narrowed and mean and distrustful.

And to her shame, she began crying.

There was no passing these tears off as coughs. Not with her ragged gasps for breath and her rough sobs and her face crumpled in distress behind the trembling shelter of her hands. She bent at the waist, the ache in her heart literal and so painful she wanted to keep collapsing in on herself, tighter and tighter, until she disappeared entirely.

He'd never seen her like this before. No one had, outside her family.

It was humiliating. She hated it. Hated herself. Hated him for witnessing it from across the room, already so unbearably distant before he'd even stepped foot on an airplane.

Only he wasn't across the room anymore, because he'd somehow dragged her out of the chair and onto the couch. Onto his lap. Into his arms, which closed around her securely.

His palm cradling the back of her head, he pressed her face into his neck and held tight.

"Sweetheart . . ." It was a ragged murmur. "For fuck's sake. I have no idea what the fuck's happening here, but *please* don't cry. And i-if"—his voice wavered and broke—"if you l-love me even a little bit, even a *fraction* as much as I love you, please don't fucking *leave* me."

At that, she jerked her head up and back. "*I'm* n-not the one leaving, Peter."

"We both know that's not true." His own eyes wet, he simply looked at her, his arms still supporting her as she nestled in his lap. "I'd never leave you. *Never*, Maria."

To him, it obviously wasn't a lie. Which meant his definition of leaving didn't match hers. At all. And maybe, if she could make him understand . . .

"Then tell me something." She cupped his face in her hands, willing him to hear her. No, more than that. To *listen*, even if he wouldn't like what she was saying. "If you'd never leave me, why will I be spending most of the next three years alone?"

His head gave a little bewildered shake, his beard abrading her palms.

"But that's not leaving you. That's doing my job. *Our* job." Ducking his head slightly, he looked her dead in the eye and kept making promises, so many solemn promises, and none of them were the ones she needed. "And when it's over, or anytime I have more than a day or two off, I'll be right back by your side. Or you can come live with me there if you want. That's fine by me. I'll be making enough to support us both."

When she closed her eyes in frustration and grief, tears leaked out from beneath her lids. "I—I don't want you to *support* me, Peter. I like working. I like having a career of my own. I just want you to *stay* with me. To not *leave* me for three fucking years."

"We're working actors, Maria." His voice was very gentle as his lips captured her tears, one by one, and kissed them away in a gesture so loving, more promptly appeared. "When an opportunity like this comes around, we have to take it, because we might never get another offer that good again. Not even if we audition the rest of our lives. You know that. Please tell me you know that, after all this time."

Gods above, he still thought *she* was the one who didn't get it.

She might not have spent two decades in Hollywood, but she comprehended the nature of their profession. Its inherent instability. The challenge of career longevity in a youth-obsessed industry. The extent to which any actor's success, in the end, depended on luck and timing and privilege of various sorts as much as talent.

But she also comprehended her own nature, in a way he evidently didn't.

"I get that work is important to you, and I get why. It's important to me too, although I know you have trouble seeing that." Letting go of his face, she knuckled away her tears and tried to explain herself as plainly as possible. "But I need to be your priority. Not something you squeeze in between jobs, stowed safely away until the next time you're available."

His voice held the faintest hint of an edge. "It's not like I *want* to be separated from you, Maria."

Beneath her, his thighs had gone rigid. Steely.

He was bristling instead of listening.

"I know that. I understand why you want this role. I even understand your decision to accept the offer, no matter what it means for us." Unwilling to give up yet, she spoke carefully as his sharp eyes bored into her, demanding she concede her position, when she couldn't. Not without conceding herself too. "But I want a real home. A shared home. I won't accept spending most of my time alone after I moved halfway across the world for you. I also won't uproot myself to follow you every time you land a new role. Not even if I love you, and I *do*, Peter. More than I think you understand. If I loved you less, I wouldn't need you this much."

So much it frightened her sometimes.

He went silent. Bit his lip, thinking, before he spoke again.

A wild burst of hope made her tremble in his arms. Because his eyes had gone cloudy with concentration as he considered her words, and maybe he grasped what she was saying now, maybe—

"Is this about what happened with your ex?" His hand clenched against her back, then flattened and stroked. "Because, sweetheart, I'd never cheat on you, and I thought we already—"

He understood nothing.

"*No.*" When that emerged as an impatient snap, she took a breath and deliberately lowered her voice. "This has nothing to do with Hugo's infidelity."

His cheating might have been dramatic and heartbreaking—and, again, hilariously inept in retrospect—but even if he'd remained faithful, underlying fissures would have fractured their relationship anyway, given enough time. She saw that now, more clearly than ever.

"This discussion only involves Hugo because my relationship with him taught me I didn't want to be with someone long-distance." At the charity auction, as they'd discussed their exes, she could have sworn she'd made that point very clearly. "Even before I found out he was cheating, I was miserable, Peter. I hated that we were living so far apart."

She grasped his shoulders and squeezed, as if that would force her words into his resistant, stubborn brain and help him see who and what she truly was. Not the version of herself he hoped she was, or fooled himself into believing she was, or found easier to handle.

"I love you so much more than I ever loved him. I need you more than I ever needed him." All her love, all her heart, all her raw, aching sincerity suffused every word, and his eyes on hers softened. "And if I was lonely without *Hugo*, of all people, even when I was living a five-minute walk away from my parents' house, how do you think I'll handle being without you? A stranger in a foreign city, tucked away in your gated community without family nearby?"

Despite his half-stifled wince, she continued, relentless. "How do you think I'll feel every morning when I wake up alone, and every day spent rambling around an empty house alone, and every night I go to bed alone? For three years, Peter. Three fucking *years*. And what if they want to renew your contract? Will you turn them down, or will you stay away even longer?"

They both knew what his preference would be. His instinct.

And to be fair, it was the same preference and instinct most actors in Hollywood would have. But she wasn't from Hollywood, and she wasn't willing to put her career before her heart.

"Not all the time." His knuckles pressed against her spine, his open hands curling into fists once more. "You wouldn't be alone all the time."

He sounded resentful now. Sullen.

And both of them knew precisely why he hadn't answered her question.

"You're right. Some of our castmates live in LA. You'd visit between seasons and during filming breaks." They'd reunite with heartfelt joy, like the lovers they were—and then he'd leave her again. And again. "But I'm not you, Peter. I need people I love around me every day to be happy."

This time, there was no pause for thought before he responded.

"I spent most of my *Gates* money on the house." The words were flat, and for an actor of his caliber, that was a choice. A decision not to reveal emotion to her anymore. "For us to be financially secure, I need steady work. A steady paycheck."

His voice, his posture—everything told her he was closing down now. Digging in, just as she'd feared. Just as she'd known he would, somewhere deep inside herself, despite all her hopes. It was why she'd already mentally prepared herself to buy a plane ticket.

She'd always understood him more than he understood her. Just as, over time, she'd grown to love him more than he loved her.

Or maybe she was being unfair. Maybe differing priorities didn't mean differing amounts of love. That was how it felt, though.

The familiar crawling sensation wasn't shame, exactly. But it was related. Cold and sticky, it crept outward from her heart. Every pulse beat spread it further, the rapid thud in her aching temples a steady accusation. A chant that looped around on itself again and again.

You betrayed yourself again.

You knew who he was.

You let yourself care too much, when you knew better.

Of all people, you knew better.

You betrayed yourself again.

Further argument was pointless. She wouldn't change Peter's mind. She wouldn't change anything. She'd only hate herself more for begging.

But she couldn't seem to stop trying. "I get that you're concerned about money. But don't you think you could find enough jobs in LA, ones that wouldn't require sacrificing years of our life together? And what about our *Gates* residuals? What about the money I'll bring in from *my* work?"

So much of the film and television industry still flourished in Hollywood. It gave him options. It gave them both options. Why didn't he see that?

"What if all that's not enough, Maria?" His nostrils flaring with frustration, he shifted in tiny, restless movements beneath her. "I may not have a mortgage, but we need retirement savings, because our careers won't stay hot forever. Even apart from that, we have property taxes and Community Association dues and living expenses to cover, and they'll drain us dry if the jobs we take don't pay enough."

To her, the answer was obvious, though she knew—she *knew*—he wouldn't agree. "Then we should sell the house. Because if you feel forced to take certain jobs just so you can keep it, those gates aren't keeping you safe. They're keeping you stuck."

The yoke above the community's entrance was all too fitting. That zip code was a burden laid across his broad shoulders, keeping him in harness and hard at work.

"Peter..." She placed her palm over his heart. "Moving wouldn't change what's most important. You'd still be just as much a success no matter where you lived. Besides, I adore your house and yard, but we could own that same house with an equally beautiful view in another neighborhood, a good neighborhood, for far less money."

As soon as she'd mentioned his home, his body had turned to stone, his chest and arms hard and unwelcoming underneath any surface softness. And she loved him, but if she wanted to be held by a cold, blank-faced statue, she could go visit an art museum and alarm some security guards instead.

She slid off his lap and sank onto the couch beside him.

The instant she left his arms, he flinched. His gaze flicked down to his empty lap, then to her. Then, with visible effort, he seemed to force himself to relax. To soften his posture and his expression. Swallowing audibly, he reached out to her again and gently clasped her upper arm. His thumb stroked her bare bicep in a tender, coaxing gesture.

He spoke quietly. "Living there was my dream, Maria. Ever since I moved to Hollywood. How can you ask me to move?"

Put like that, how could she argue his point? If that community was truly his dream, and not a crutch, not a yoke, of course he should stay there. But either way, it wasn't *her* dream, and she wouldn't sacrifice herself on the altar of his ambitions.

"Taking this job is the best way to keep moving my career forward." He was still speaking, still trying to persuade her to his side, as if they didn't both know the battle was already done. "When it's over, I'll have plenty of experience on a network television set, which will broaden my appeal to casting directors, and I'll have enough savings so I can pick and choose my next project without worrying so much about money. I won't ever have to leave you again. Not for years at a time, anyway."

He said that now, but she could already see it. See him, a decade later, still taking whatever role offered him the steadiest, biggest paycheck or the biggest bump in his career, no matter how long and how far they'd be apart.

They'd be together, but she'd be alone.

"Peter. *Sötnos.*" She stroked his bristly cheek, her attempt at a smile quivering with sadness. "It'll never be enough money for you. Enough security."

Because he'd never have enough reassurance that his dream couldn't be taken from him like his mother's had. He'd never have enough proof that he'd made it, no matter what his father said or believed.

His heart was still empty, even with her in it.

She couldn't fill it. She wasn't enough. Again.

Why was she even still talking? It didn't really matter what she said, did it? He didn't understand her position, and he wasn't compromising his.

"Sweetheart." His hand covered hers, pressing it to his jaw. "You say you love me. But real love wouldn't require me to give up my dreams and ambitions."

Such a tender gesture for such a harsh judgment.

She returned the latter in kind. "Maybe so. But in that case, real love wouldn't require me to be alone when being alone doesn't make me happy."

Any remaining light had drained from his eyes.

He was still looking at her, still cradling her hand, but he was gone.

"It doesn't matter if you think my needs are irrational or foolish." One last caress of his temple, his cheek, his beard. Then she dropped her hand and stood. "I know myself. I know what makes me happy and what makes me miserable."

Slowly, his own hand dropped to his side and curled shut. Otherwise, he held himself completely still.

"Fine," he said hoarsely. "I could say the same for myself, though."

"You're telling me you know yourself too. You know what you need to be happy." When he dipped his head in silent affirmation, she offered him a final, wry smile. "Do you, Peter? Do you really?"

But he didn't bother answering. The discussion was done. And if this was a battle for their future together, she'd lost before even taking the field.

She dug in her purse for her cell. With a few taps on the screen, she booked a flight to LA and a car to take her to the San Francisco airport in half an hour.

The winner might take it all, but this loser didn't intend to leave behind her belongings. She needed to start gathering everything she'd brought to the hotel. All her other possessions—the things she'd carried to LA and deposited in his home—she could easily retrieve next weekend, while he was in Wisconsin for his scholarship event.

The busier she kept herself, the less likely she was to break in front of him again. So she bustled around the suite, checking every drawer, every shelf, every nook and cabinet and corner in their rooms, no matter whether she already knew they were pristine.

She tended to pack lightly. At least when she wasn't hauling several suitcases' worth of Swedish snacks to stymie *knäppgökar* who wanted her to starve picturesquely on film. Within fifteen minutes, her bag was full of neatly folded clothing and toiletries zipped into waterproof pouches. The items she'd need for the plane ride went into her purse: her cell, earbuds, lip balm, a quilted eye mask.

And tissues, of course. Lots and lots of tissues, discreetly tucked into a side pocket when her back was turned to Peter.

The whole time she searched and folded and packed, he sat motionless and silent.

Funny. He didn't look like a man who thought he'd won. He looked . . . hollowed out. Pale and expressionless, arranged stiffly upright on the couch, eyes aimed in her direction but empty. Like those unsettling Victorian photographs of beloved dead family members she'd once seen at a museum exhibit.

He was obviously hurting too, and she hated—*hated*—seeing him that way. But the wound was self-inflicted, easing his pain was no longer either her responsibility or her privilege, and his company in misery was the coldest comfort imaginable.

She needed to go.

The car wouldn't arrive for a while yet, but she couldn't guarantee her composure if she stayed any longer. She'd wait in the lobby, or—better yet, given the groups of fans likely still congregating in that area—just outside the hotel, behind a convenient potted plant.

Her soft knitted wrap would help keep her warm on the plane, so she looped it around her neck before donning oversized sunglasses.

It was a futile gesture. If she cried, anyone watching would notice her blotting her nose with all those tissues, and her height and build and hair were likely unmistakable to fans even without her eyes visible. But she could at least *try* to preserve her anonymity.

A good faith effort, Americans called it.

She'd always liked that phrase.

In her opinion, she'd put forth a good faith effort with Peter too, although he'd probably disagree. But his opinion shouldn't matter to her anymore, right?

She slung her purse over her shoulder. Her suitcase handle telescoped smoothly, and the bag trailed behind her to the door without a hitch.

Her breath, however, did hitch. Once, twice, a third time, as she looked back over her shoulder and prepared to say farewell to the man she'd loved far too long, far too much.

In the end, she couldn't say it. She couldn't say anything. If she opened her mouth, a sob would emerge, and if she waited any longer, her tears would spill beneath her sunglasses.

So she left their hotel room without a word. Again. Just like their first night together.

But this time, his eyes were open.

He watched her go.

GODS OF THE GATES: SEASON 6, EP. 9

EXT. CASTAWAY ISLAND - DAY

The clouds lie heavy and dark over the island, and the water is choppy, the waves becoming more violent by the minute. CYPRIAN and CASSIA stand by the shore, heartbroken, each angry and terrified for their own reasons. They are still rumpled from their lovemaking. Cyprian drags the curragh from its shelter, looking despairingly at its frail frame and thin covering.

> **CASSIA**
>
> I won't go. I won't leave you.

> **CYPRIAN**
>
> You heard the roar of the undead. Our gate to Tartarus has been breached, and no human will survive the forthcoming carnage. *Go*, Cassia.

Cassia, tears in her eyes, stubbornly refuses to even look at the curragh.

> **CASSIA**
>
> I won't let you die alone. I *love* you, Cyprian.

She grips his tunic and shakes him. He doesn't move, only covers her hands with his.

> **CYPRIAN**
>
> If you do, if you love me, you will climb into that boat and leave. Even now, you could be carrying our child. *My* child. My blood. My legacy in the world of

the living, and the only proof of our devotion that
will still exist after this day.

CASSIA

If you love *me*, do not let me leave alone. Let us
brave the waves together.

Cyprian leans down and gently kisses her.

CYPRIAN

My love is not in doubt. You are the beat of my
heart. The sun that warms me. The rain that washes me
clean. But my love for you alters not the truth, my
beautiful, brave shield-maiden. The vessel is not yet
strong enough to hold us both.

Cassia sobs, and Cyprian comforts her in his arms.
Then he positions the curragh at the shoreline and
hands her inside as she continues to weep. After one
final loving kiss, he guides the boat deeper into the
rough water and shoves the vessel out as far as he can.

CASSIA

This boat may fail. Humanity may perish. But my love
for you will remain.

She begins rowing. He watches waist-deep in the
water until he can no longer see her or the curragh.
Face like stone, he turns and strides toward shore,
then toward the cliffs, where he'll watch the woman he
loves disappear into the horizon. Where he'll meet his
destiny and his death. Alone.

25

IN RETROSPECT, EXPECTING A UNIVERSITY'S THEATRE AND Drama Department to keep a celebratory event simple and subdued was stupid beyond words.

It wasn't, after all, the Theatre and Low-Key Introversion Department.

Peter wasn't thinking too clearly these days, though. Not since last weekend, when Maria fucking *left* him after accusing him of leaving *her*. So here he was. All alone in a crowd of roughly a hundred strangers, flummoxed by the elaborateness of what he'd thought would be a pretty basic event.

Endowing a scholarship—one! just one!—didn't require this sort of fuss, dammit.

Regardless, a seemingly endless line of people had pinned him in place at the front of Vilas Hall's screening theater. They wanted to introduce themselves to him, congratulate him, thank him, remind him when and where they'd met before. They wanted to have a pleasant, lively conversation with the man of the hour.

But he had no reserves of energy or goodwill remaining after an agonizingly solitary week, and he didn't know how much longer he could pretend he did.

In his own company, he hated himself.

In other people's company, he hated them instead.

Either way: misery.

Then he saw two familiar faces standing right in front of him. And for a brief, very frightening moment, he thought he might have to excuse himself from an event thrown in his honor so no one could see him weep.

"Nava. Ramón." A single throat-clearing didn't remove the lump there, so he tried a second time, then a third. "Wh-what are you two doing here?"

Nava got up on her tiptoes to throw her arms around his neck and draw him close, and she wasn't Maria. She wasn't ineffable softness wrapped around iron strength, wasn't his missing piece clicking into place every time she pressed against him.

But she was so fucking warm, her hug affectionate, her eyes brimming with knowledge and concern for him. Ramón's own embrace included a fierce squeeze and several thumps on the back that somehow communicated both sympathy and fondness without a word spoken.

"I'm an alumna of this department too. Did you forget?" Nava's finger flicked his tie, and she wrinkled her nose at him. "But even if I weren't, we wouldn't have missed your event for the world."

He looked up at the ceiling and blinked hard.

When the department had asked for the names of family and friends he wanted to invite, he'd contemplated adding his father to the list. Because maybe, when faced with such a concrete marker of financial success and professional prestige, Dad would finally understand why his son had chosen to defy reason and escape to Hollywood. Maybe he'd look at Peter and say, at long last, "You were right. I was wrong. You had to leave, and I'm sorry."

Then, once Dad made that life-altering realization, maybe he'd say the same to the decorative urn containing his late wife, and

Peter would finally, after all these years, be able to picture his mother at peace, wherever she was now.

Only that wasn't going to happen, was it? Not ever. So Peter hadn't invited his father, because it hurt to see him.

He'd meant Maria to be his family in this room, in this moment. And she was gone too.

But here were Nava and Ramón, and he loved them. Maria had brought the three of them together and forged his initial, tentative connection to them, but Peter had earned their loyalty and affection on his own, just as they'd earned his, and he didn't love them simply as an offshoot of Maria, but because they were good, smart, kind people.

Loyal as hell too. He needed them, and they'd shown up. He didn't even have to ask.

They were his family.

They loved him.

Even without Maria.

"Oh, Peter," Nava whispered. She laid a gentle hand on his arm. "Honey."

Somehow, they'd heard. They knew what had happened a week ago at that fucking hotel.

He swallowed hard. "Don't."

It was a plea in the guise of a gruff command, and they understood that. They understood him. So they gave him a minute to get himself together without any argument or sign of offense at his tone, but Nava also didn't let him go. And for that, he loved them even more.

In this entire room, only two people truly knew him.

Turned out, that was enough.

"Thank you," he finally choked out.

"You're welcome, obviously, but you don't need to thank us."

Back on her tiptoes, she planted a kiss on his cheek. "We want to be here for you."

Before he could gather enough of his composure to respond, the lights flickered, and everyone began to settle into the rows of seats. Without even a glance at one another to coordinate their efforts, Nava and Ramón each took one of his arms and marched Peter's reluctant ass to the little dais in front of the screen, depositing him alongside a couple of official-looking people he'd met maybe twice before.

"You can do it, kid," Ramón said quietly before they left.

But they didn't go far. After maybe five steps, they sat in the very front row, directly in the middle, where he couldn't miss their presence. Nava smiled at him like a proud older sister, and Ramón gave him a little encouraging nod.

The speeches lasted far too long, especially given the modesty of his endowment: tuition and a small stipend for one in-state department major per year, enough to buy their textbooks and class materials and maybe help them pay for a dorm room.

It wasn't much. But it was enough to give another lost Wisconsin kid a chance to escape and a chance to succeed. Or, at the very least, save that kid some student loan payments.

His own speech, he supposed he delivered well. He was an actor, after all. But other than his sincere good wishes to the scholarship's eventual recipients, it was mainly bullshit.

When the applause finally ended and he could collapse into a seat beside Ramón, he let out a long, heartfelt breath of relief. Only to be confronted with his fucking face blown up ten feet high—holy shit, that never got less painful—as the event organizers began playing a collection of taped testimonials from former colleagues interspersed with publicity photos and clips from his various roles.

Those organizers were grateful to him, sure. But they were also bragging about one of their most successful alumni in hopes it would burnish their reputation and lead to more money for the department.

He got it. It made sense. It was still embarrassing as hell.

One by one, his *Gods of the Gates* castmates and crew appeared.

Marcus held forth on Peter's so-called gravitas in the least-himbotastic explanation of acting technique ever, that big faker.

Carah smirked and called Peter "the fucking master of portraying tightly restrained but intensely powerful emotion, as well as unbearable goddamn horniness with no outlet."

Alex complained, "God, Peter's the *worst*. For three years running, he stole the top spot from me in *Fan Thirst* magazine's 'Celebrity Beard We Most Want to Ride' poll. Did you know that? It was a goddamn *travesty*." He pointed off camera. "You agree with me that I should have won, right, Wren? Tell me you agree with me."

Jeanine grinned and flicked her hair behind her shoulder. "That man rocks a pair of torn-up leather pants like no one else. His thighs did eighty percent of my work for me, and that delicious beard of his did the other twenty percent. Peter Reedton. What a legend."

Ramón and Nava showed up too, and talked as a duo about his professionalism and work ethic. Then added, "Peter's one of the most quietly caring individuals we've ever met, so we were completely unsurprised to hear about this scholarship. He's not only an incredibly talented actor. He's also a very good man, and we're proud to be his friends."

After their segment ended, he glanced at the two of them, and they were smiling fondly at him in the dimly lit theater, their incandescent pride practically setting it alight.

The video went on and on. His friends were entirely themselves. They made him laugh, and if he weren't so emotionally repressed, they'd have made him cry. Again.

Between the interviews, short snippets of projects spanning the course of two entire decades played. In clips from low-budget or indie films, he was sometimes the leading man. In scenes from higher-profile movies and television shows, his roles were smaller.

All that had changed with *Gods of the Gates*. He was now considered a viable lead actor for a tentpole production, as the offer from *FTI* made clear. But that hadn't been true for long, and before tonight, he'd never seen so many of his less-prestigious roles laid out alongside each other for comparison.

Some of the early projects were ridiculous, of course, and the compilation's creator made very certain to include his justifiably infamous scene from *Creekwatch*. The one that featured Peter—"Drowning Guy #2"—nearly, yes, drowning in the titular rain-swollen creek while the lifeguard-slash-vigilante hero, played by Marcus, fought to save him wearing only a Speedo and way too much self-tanner.

"I won't let you die!" Marcus declared along the muddy shore, beside Peter's utterly still body. "Not in the same place my sister was killed! Not when I haven't yet found her killers, even though I've been looking for so very long!"

The clear and somewhat disturbing implication was that if Peter's character had chosen any other drowning location along the creek, or if Marcus's character had already imposed his spectacularly inept brand of justice on his sister's killers, Mr. Why Aren't You Giving the Victim Mouth-to-Mouth Instead of Making a Speech would have let Drowning Guy #2 become Entirely Drowned Guy #1 without a second thought.

So that clip made him laugh. It made everyone in the theater laugh, and for good reason.

But so many of his other performances still made him *proud*. The agoraphobic sculptor. The snootiest clerk at the record store, with the funniest lines of anyone in the entire cast, even if he wasn't a lead. The hostage at a bank robbery with a medical condition that would kill him if he didn't get treatment soon. The plumber in a small town, quietly romancing the shy librarian in the background of so many scenes as the main couple found their own happily-ever-after.

Each of those roles had stretched him in a different way. Tested his skills and made him better. He'd come home to his little apartment at the end of a workday and feel—satisfied. Not necessarily happy, because he was so goddamn alone. Fulfilled professionally, though?

Yes. Without a doubt.

In a bid to appeal to the masses, main characters in tentpole productions were often required to be so damn *bland*. Character actors and leads in indie films, though—they could be *anything*, because another season or a possible sequel or hundreds of millions of dollars of production costs didn't depend on their relatability. On *his* relatability.

But if he signed the now-finalized contract with *FTI* . . .

Well, there would be subplots, of course, but Maria had nailed the essential dynamic. In less than a month, he'd be just another interchangeable white guy in a white coat peering into a microscope, enhancing computer images of license plates, and becoming an inadvertent target of murderers. If he was lucky, maybe he'd have a marriage falling apart behind the scenes, which the show would indicate via a total of four minutes of footage and two fleeting indications of open grief during the entire season.

Frankly, the serial killer role he'd originally auditioned for would be more interesting to play. By far.

Why hadn't that even occurred to him before?

Uneasy, he stared sightlessly at the screen for another clip or two. And then . . . there she was.

He'd known this part of the video was coming. There was no way in hell they *wouldn't* request a clip from Maria, and no way in hell she'd refuse them. She'd probably shot the segment weeks ago but intended to keep it a surprise until the actual event.

Somehow, though, it didn't matter what he'd known or how well he'd thought he prepared himself. When her beloved face appeared, her beaming smile, her warm brown eyes sparkling with confidence and vivacity . . .

If one of those fucking enormous cows on the island sat on his chest?

Yeah. It felt like that.

He stared at her dumbly.

Her mouth was moving as she said whatever she was saying, her lips rosy and tipped up at the corners. He'd slipped his tongue between those lips. Slid a thumb across them. Opened them wide for his cock. Covered them with his palm as she came.

He'd kissed them softly, marveling at how well they fit his. How well she fit him.

Six years. Six years they'd spent together, lovers turned friends turned lovers once more. During those six years, he'd earned widespread critical recognition, won several golden statuettes, raised his professional profile to lofty new heights, scored legions of new fans, and deposited unprecedented amounts of money in his bank account.

It was success. Undeniable, profound success.

He'd tilted at a windmill and . . . won.

For those six years, that enormous stretch of his professional and personal life, he'd been happy. Startlingly, terrifyingly, consistently happy, in a way he'd never experienced before and might never experience again.

And he'd spent most of those years on a tiny fucking island off the coast of Ireland, where all the perks and trappings of his success couldn't find him or change his daily life.

On the island, as long as he had enough money to live comfortably—to buy souvenirs or pub meals or ferry rides to the coast—the excess didn't matter. There was nowhere and no need to spend it. His new ability to score lead roles didn't make much difference either, since he had little time to film said lead roles. If he had more followers on social media, that didn't change how he posted: infrequently and curtly. Which, bizarrely, had become a source of much hilarity among his fans and brought him even *more* social media followers. His golden statuettes sat on the mantel above his fireplace in LA, right below his mother's drawing. They might have kept her company, but they didn't do a thing for him from across the Atlantic. Neither did the house itself, no matter how perfectly it sat perched on some the most exclusive real estate available.

So if his long-awaited success had made him happy all those years on the island, he wasn't quite sure how.

Was it the mere *knowledge* of his success that did the trick? The prospect of how that success would, in fact, demonstrably change his life during his next filming break, between seasons, and after the show ended?

Or did he just fucking love being around Maria and their friends whenever he wasn't filming scenes for a role he found both challenging and interesting?

She was still talking on-screen, and suddenly he could hear her. More than that. He could *listen*.

"—thing I adore about Peter is that he puts as much effort and emotion into a small role as he does into a role like Cyprian," she said, leaning forward in emphasis. "Because he's a master of his craft and committed to giving his colleagues and audience his absolute best, every time. So in those movies and television shows where he remains in the background, or plays the friend or co-worker, or nearly drowns in a creek in front of the world's most dramatic lifeguard-slash-vigilante—hi, Marcus—if you pay attention, his acting is . . . brilliant. Just as brilliant as his performance as Cyprian. Every time."

Her brown eyes were soft and sincere, her gaze direct. After so long together, he could recognize her lies, and he could reckon with her truths. If he paid enough attention.

He was paying attention now.

This was the truth, as she saw it.

"Peter Reedton's work ethic is unparalleled, anyone who truly gets to know him adores him, and he's an absurdly gifted actor," she declared firmly. Almost aggressively, as if daring the audience to argue with her. As if she'd gladly take on every single one of them if they dismissed his worth, and she'd win. Of course she'd win. "He deserves all the praise he's gotten and more, and that would be true with or without *Gods of the Gates*. Our show was merely the means by which the world finally noticed what he was doing all along. In every project, big or small."

She fucking meant what she was saying. If he only played bit roles for the rest of his career, she wouldn't give a shit. She wouldn't think less of him. She'd still consider him a success, because he cared about his coworkers and worked hard and was good at his job.

Her love and appreciation for him didn't depend on accomplishments or money.

They depended on him. Just . . . him.

Motherfucker. He *was* a goddamn *knäppgök*.

On-screen, she flicked her wrist dismissively. "Still, he's a *skit-stövel*. A fact is a fact."

He hung his head. Yes. Also that.

But he couldn't help but smile, despite the acid churning in his gut, because her comic timing was impeccable. The audience was laughing too, which meant they apparently knew her pet name for him, as well as its English translation.

Correction: That *was* his pet name.

Now she didn't call him anything at all.

Cupping a hand around her mouth, she pretended to whisper to the unseen audience. "Also, Jeanine is right about those thighs. Don't tell him I said so."

Someone off camera wolf-whistled—it sounded like Carah—and Maria grinned at whoever it was, even as the theater audience laughed again.

Then her face faded to black on the screen. She was gone.

His breath shook as he dragged it into his lungs. When he closed his eyes, her afterimage flickered to life, burned irrevocably onto his retinas.

From the sound of it, the video presentation had moved on to clips of Cyprian's scenes with Cassia, and normally he loved to watch Maria's work. But—

Ramón's lean, strong hand clasped his and squeezed.

Maybe Peter should be embarrassed by how tightly he clung to his friend's hand in response, but he wasn't. He needed that support, that reassurance, as his world upended itself.

All his certainties had rattled and heaved and cracked down the middle, and there he was, standing in their rubble. Shell-shocked. Helpless to do anything but piece those certainties back together, but this time in a different way, in the right way, so they wouldn't collapse around him ever again.

He had to question everything, *everything*, he'd thought he understood about himself and Maria. And he knew exactly where to begin.

Why had he been so goddamn determined to take a role that didn't even fucking *interest* him, when he knew it would make Maria unhappy?

Yes, retirement and health insurance and living expenses required savings, but he wasn't hurting, and neither was she, and both of them had long careers still ahead, with a lot more options open to them after having starred in *Gates*. Those *Gates* residuals weren't insignificant either. And even before landing the role of Cyprian, he'd managed to support himself with his acting. He'd made a decent, if not luxurious, living. So had she.

Hell, if they got married and worse came to worst, they could always move to Sweden and let the fruits of socialism feed them for a while. For all his teasing about the Swedish system, the prospect of a guaranteed comfortable retirement and health care . . . well, higher taxes didn't actually seem that terrible a price to pay. Literally.

What happened to his mother wouldn't happen to him. To them. It couldn't.

And if he didn't need to take the role for money, why else would he accept? If he meant to show other casting directors that he could handle a leading role on television, hadn't he already done that with *Gods of the Gates*?

He wasn't trying to prove anything to the Hollywood influencers and power players. That was just an excuse. He simply hadn't wanted to admit the truth to himself or anyone else. Not even

Maria, the one person who'd probably understood that truth long ago, without his having to tell her.

Because if he admitted it, he also had to admit that he still cared what his father thought of him, after more than two decades of estrangement, and he didn't want to care. Caring made him feel like that helpless child again, unable to make his dad even *look* at him, much less understand him and his choices.

It was pathetic, and he hated himself for it, and the realization should probably send him back to therapy for a while. But it was the truth.

He was still trying to prove he was worth something.

He was still trying to prove he'd been right to leave.

He was still trying to prove things that shouldn't have needed proving in the first place. Even if they had, twenty-one years of staying afloat in Hollywood—no, *thriving* in Hollywood—and six years of creating a new, tight circle of loyal, loving friends should have *already* proved them. To his father. To himself.

So why was he still listening to his dad's voice in his head?

And if he didn't have to prove anything to anyone, what kind of life did he actually *want*? What would make him genuinely happy?

Did he even know?

Because he'd told Maria he did. He'd told himself and her and everyone else that he'd dreamed of having a multimillion-dollar home in an exclusive gated community from the start. That he'd always yearned for high-profile, well-compensated roles on shows like *Gods of the Gates* and *FTI*.

But that was a lie too. When he'd moved to LA, he'd simply wanted to make a living doing projects he found worthwhile.

He'd wanted love as well. He'd needed it, *ached* for it. Love and friendship and a family.

And over the course of six glorious years, Maria had given them to him, one by one.

Before she'd begun her quiet but relentless campaign to connect him with his colleagues on a personal level, he'd been respected in Hollywood. Considered hardworking and professional. But no one especially liked him, and why would they? How could they even claim to *know* him, when he barely said a word to them off camera?

People had known he was a good actor. They hadn't known whether he was a good man.

That question still didn't have a definitive answer, did it?

Because when Maria, the woman who'd lit his lonely life and filled it with joy and companionship, had told him what she needed, what would make her happy, he'd heard her.

But he hadn't listened.

Just like his father.

Maria hadn't just told him once, either. She'd told him multiple times in multiple ways. At Alex's charity event, when she'd shaken her head and said she didn't know how a long-distance relationship could work for anyone. On the island, where she'd woven a disparate group of people into a loving, supportive community, a very real sort of family, and not simply because he'd needed that family and maybe everyone else had too. *She'd* needed it.

She'd told him with all those regular, lengthy FaceTime calls with her siblings and parents, so many he'd marveled at the likely cost of their data plans. Even before he'd met the Ivarssons in person, only an idiot could have missed how important family was to her existence.

Then he *had* met them. And for the first time in his life, he saw how a functional family could work. How everyone could repair chinks in each other's armor, always knowing their own vulnerabilities would be shielded in return whenever necessary. How affection could be freely offered, and needing that affection wasn't a source of shame or weakness. How people with very different personalities could still respect and appreciate one another.

He also saw how comfortable and content Maria became when the people she loved surrounded her. Then she'd sat surrounded by *him*, cradled in his arms, between his legs, and literally opened the most painful reaches of her past to him in the form of a family photo album. The stories she told, the pictures she showed him, had exposed her vulnerabilities so starkly, he'd sat stunned behind her, touched and terrified and shaken to his core. Because from that moment forward, she was trusting him to shield those vulnerabilities, to keep her safe, in the same way she trusted her family—and no one else in the world. Just the Ivarssons and . . . him.

That first photo they'd taken of her would haunt him for the rest of his damn life.

The little girl in the plastic sleeve looked like Maria. Sturdy. Tall. Same features. Same hair. But the Maria he knew sparkled and shone, lit from within by joy, by warmth and humor and confidence and a determination to confront the world on its own terms without ever losing herself in the process.

Any light in the photo of that child came from the camera flash or the sun. Not from her. There wasn't a single spark of warmth in her shuttered expression or those hard, suspicious brown eyes.

She was a young Medusa, powerful and angry and weary of a world that hurt her and hurt her again for no reason, and the chilly boldness of her stare should have turned that world and everyone in it to stone. But it didn't.

So she'd turned herself to stone instead, because stone couldn't grieve.

Except in the most basic of ways, she looked nothing like the

Maria of today. She looked, in fact, much like Peter had in photos until approximately six years ago.

If she got him in a way no one else had, maybe that was why. She'd been a version of him once. Unlike her, though, he'd had no Ivarssons in his life to insistently chip away at his veneer, then return him to the world protected by something far warmer than stone. At least, not until Maria Ivarsson arrived at an LA sauna, wearing only a small red bikini, and cracked his impenetrable facade before she even began trying.

The little girl in the picture wasn't his Maria. Not yet. Her cold eyes were a silent testament to that, and to all the betrayal and loss she'd already endured at eight years old. Once he'd heard her story, he'd seen it written in her picture.

That story and that picture had broken his heart.

But he *still* hadn't understood. Preoccupied by his own needs, his own desires, his own demons, he still hadn't fucking *understood*.

Maria might not be a child anymore, but that child still existed within her somewhere, and she remembered all too clearly.

One after another, the people she loved had left her alone among strangers.

And he'd intended to do the same. For a job he didn't even fucking *want*.

If he'd ever loathed himself more, he didn't remember when.

In that convention hotel room, she'd *sobbed*.

He'd failed to listen, informed her that he intended to re-create the worst horrors of her life, and then fucking *raged* at her when she'd balked. So there she'd been, perched uncomfortably on a too-small upholstered armchair, bent over and huddled in on herself, hiding behind her fucking *hands* as hoarse, broken sobs wrenched from her throat and convulsed her body.

Because of him. Entirely because of him.

He'd done that to the woman he loved more than anyone and anything in this world.

And even then, she'd kept trying to explain to him how she felt, what she needed, again and again, in different words, using different arguments, hoping he'd get it. Finally, finally get it. But he simply couldn't comprehend how the life he wanted—told her he wanted; thought he wanted; tried to convince himself he wanted—would make her miserable, even if she loved him. Which she did. Only a fool would claim otherwise.

His father should be proud. His boy had grown up to be just like him.

If his mother could have seen him in that hotel room, what would she have thought of him? Why hadn't he been listening to *her* voice in his head all these years? Because Dad hadn't understood him, hadn't known how to love him in a selfless way, but she had. And if he'd thought about it, he'd have known exactly what she would have wanted for him.

Not prestige or fame. She didn't care about that. Not an expensive house, clearly, since she'd willingly abandoned their spacious family home for a dingy apartment and never looked back.

No, she'd want him to have creative work he found satisfying and a partner who loved him as he was and would help him be the man he needed to be.

That was all. That was everything.

And he'd already had it. Then let it walk out the door.

He hoped his blue cupboard was never this soiled again. Digging it out was going to require one hell of a shovel, and Maria might never agree that he'd gotten it clean enough to earn her forgiveness.

But he had to try.

When the screen went dark and the lights in the theater came on again, he barely noticed.

Applause. Another short speech. More applause. More small talk. Handshakes. Exits.

Then it was over, thank fuck, and Nava and Ramón walked him to his car. He embraced them. Promised to call and visit soon. Thanked them for coming. Then drove away.

He hoped like hell they'd caught the sincerity of his gratitude, because he quite frankly had no idea what he'd said to them. Logistics had been occupying his entire brain, and making pleasant conversation wasn't exactly his forte at the best of times.

But he'd make it up to them back in LA, and when they needed *his* patience and forbearance, he'd offer it. Gladly. It was what families did.

He knew that now. Thanks to Maria.

26

FOR SOMEONE WHO HADN'T LIVED IN PETER'S HOME ESPE-
cially long, Maria had spread out to a surprising extent. Somehow, without her noticing, her belongings had scattered to every
room in the house, and that was before she'd even shipped all her
stuff from Sweden.

Good thing she hadn't finalized those arrangements yet. She
wouldn't exactly have been able to ring up the barge in the middle
of the Atlantic and tell it to turn around.

Still, the packing process was going to take longer than she'd
hoped. Every minute she spent in Peter's house was another minute she spent miserable, unable to distract herself from her grief
in the setting where they'd spent most of their time as lovers. So
she was moving as fast as she could, but the whole endeavor would
take about two hours, probably. Which was an hour and a half
more than she'd prefer.

At least the man himself wasn't anywhere nearby. Since she'd
helped him make the arrangements, she knew he'd planned to
check out from his Madison hotel Sunday morning to head to the
airport and board his flight to LAX.

It was only Saturday, and after spending another night at
Carah's house, she'd left bright and early to drive to his home and
remove all traces of their brief life together. So even if he got sick

of socializing and left early—and odds were good he'd do just that—he still wouldn't make it back before she was gone, no matter whether it took her a half hour or two hours to pack.

Besides, no way he'd come if he knew she was there. And he did, because she'd texted him to ask for permission to enter his house, even though she'd still had her keys and remotes and everything else that allowed her access to his life.

Fine, he'd texted back yesterday evening, an hour or so before the alumni event.

One word. Nothing more. Because he was Peter, and because he was pissed and hurt.

Oddly, though, he'd written her again close to midnight and used a somewhat wider selection of his vocabulary. Text me when you get there and before you leave, please.

The *please* was weirdly polite. And why did he care when she came and went? Maybe it was an alarm company thing? Or he'd revoked her permission to enter the stupid community gates, and now he'd need to make an exception?

Or maybe he just wanted to be very, very sure she was gone before he came home. If so, fair enough. She wanted the same thing. So she'd obediently texted him upon arrival without expecting to hear back, because what else was there to say, really?

But as she gathered up all her elastics, clips, and other hair supplies from both bathrooms, her phone dinged again, and gods above, did he want her to fucking record her packing process so he could ensure she hadn't stolen anything, or—

Oh. It was Ingrid, her agent. Not Peter.

After reading the text, Maria obediently FaceTimed Ingrid so they could discuss the movie script her agent had received the evening before. The project had a great director attached, a woman Maria had wanted to work with for a while, and an award-winning cinematographer interested too. The story was a suspenseful woman-on-the-run movie with a romantic arc—the main character's computer-genius best friend–turned–more—and absolutely no reference to her size.

Again and again, she'd used her moments in the media spotlight to advocate for more films starring fat people that had nothing to do with fatness. Superhero movies starring fat people. Erotic movies starring fat people. Romantic comedies starring fat people. Period films starring fat people. Gangster movies starring fat people. Spy movies starring fat people.

Suspense movies starring fat people.

Like this one.

Apparently, the director planned to film in Iceland, a setting Maria found absolutely breathtaking. The project would require three months of shooting, more or less. And if her agent's opinion could be trusted—and it could—the story might as well have been written with Maria in mind. So unless the script itself failed to impress her, she wanted that part.

Which would require three months. Three months of shooting. In Iceland.

And she'd have wanted the part even if she and Peter were still together.

She dropped abruptly onto the oversized, ridiculously comfortable couch in his great room and told her agent she'd call back later in the day. Because . . .

Skit. There was no use in denying it.

She'd fucked up. Not entirely. Not in the essentials, not in the decision she'd made to walk away, but her own blue cupboard was far from pristine at the moment.

There were nuances to her position, and in her panic and grief and hurt, she'd considered and explained exactly zero of them to

Peter. Three years spent mostly apart would still destroy her, so his insistence on accepting that *FTI* role still meant the end of their relationship.

Three months, though?

It would hurt. But she could handle that length of separation, if either one of them found an amazing role they truly wanted to accept, rather than just a role that paid well.

Fy fan. No, she was still fucking up.

If Peter wanted to take a role simply because it paid well, and he needed the security of a huge financial cushion and an expensive house in a gated community after what had happened to his mom, after what his father had done to him, who was she to judge?

They both had pasts. Because of her past, she had needs other people might not, and she'd drawn a boundary to protect them and herself as well. Because of his past, he had his own idiosyncratic requirements for happiness, and he should be able to fulfill those without criticism too. As long as meeting those needs didn't mean hers went unmet.

Her therapist had once said Maria's tendency toward all-or-nothing relationships would come back to—as Americans liked to say—bite her in the ass one day.

Well, no.

Because Kerstin was a therapist, she'd tilted her head before noting with complete neutrality, "When it comes to sex and romance, you only seem open to relationships that fall into one of two very distinct categories: absolutely everything you ever wanted or casual sex. I'd like to hear more about how that choice is serving you."

Sometimes, she kind of wanted to slap Kerstin.

Even when Kerstin was correct. *Especially* when Kerstin was correct.

But her therapist would still agree that Maria had the right—no, the *imperative*—to walk away from a relationship that would leave her miserable, and three years of separation from her partner would do just that. Maria knew Kerstin would say that, because they'd had an emergency appointment earlier in the week, and Kerstin *had* said that.

Well, no.

Not exactly that. Not in those words. Again: therapist.

"Do you have any uncertainty about whether that amount of time apart from Peter would make you unhappy?" she'd asked. And when Maria had shaken her head and swiped at her cheeks with a tissue, Kerstin had simply said, not without sympathy, "Then let's talk about the coping skills you've been employing."

So yes, Maria had fucked up in the particulars, but not in her overall decision.

Maybe someday she'd apologize to Peter for those particulars, once the thought of seeing him again at various cons and awards shows and press junkets stopped nauseating her.

Time to keep packing.

But as soon as she rose from the couch, the front door slammed open, and she jumped at the loud thud, her chest squeezing in instinctive panic as she swung toward the entry. Only to find Peter, breathless, brows drawn tight, racing through his own door at a sprint.

He skidded to a halt just inside the house and stared at her.

She stared back.

He said nothing.

She said nothing.

Bewildered, she glanced out the open door to see his SUV parked crookedly in the street in front of his house, his right front bumper buried in one of the bushes lining his yard. And if she wasn't mistaken, he'd left the driver's-side door open.

Gods above, what had happened? And why wasn't he saying anything?

"Is . . . something wrong? Did I set off an alarm? Or do you need me to leave so you can deal with . . . whatever's going on?" She swung a hand toward the leafy bush now decorating his SUV's bumper. "I'm not quite done packing yet, but I can come back later in the—"

"No."

One gruff word. Zero explanation.

She waited for explication that didn't come, waited some more, and then lost patience.

"No . . . what? I can't come back another time?" Her hands on her hips, she glared at him. "Because really, Peter, I need to—"

"No, you didn't set off an alarm. No, I don't want you to come back another time." He stalked closer to her, step by step. "No, I don't want you to leave."

Another two steps, each one eating up enormous amounts of hardwood flooring. Another.

"Ever," he finished.

His eyes devoured her, raking her from sloppy ponytail to slippered feet, then back again. He was wearing a wrinkled suit for reasons she couldn't even begin to guess, his shirt unbuttoned at the collar. His wavy mane looked like he'd dragged his fingers through it a million times, and his hands were fisted at his sides so tightly his knuckles were white, and—

And she didn't understand any of this.

"What . . ." *Skit*, this was cruel of him. He should *not* be looking at her that way, with so much heat and need and *affection*, not when she'd told him exactly why she had to go and shown him in such an unmistakable way how much leaving would hurt her. "Peter, why are you even here right now, instead of Madison?"

"Ramón and Nava were there." He clarified, "At the event."

"I'm glad," she said slowly. And she was. Just entirely befuddled too, and entirely miserable and increasingly angry. "Okay, the next time you're out, I'll come by and—"

His face softened. "If they'd known I'd see you so soon, they'd have sent their love."

When she'd intended to stay here in Los Angeles, the four of them had made plans, but . . .

She swallowed, her ire swamped by grief. "I miss them."

And since she was leaving for Sweden at the end of the week, she'd continue to miss them for a long time to come. Maybe forever.

"I know." Lips pressed tight, he just . . . looked at her. "I know you do."

Her rage rekindled in a heartbeat.

He had no *right* to speak so gently to her, as if he understood how she felt, when he didn't understand at all. If he did, if he cared as much as that loving tone implied, she wouldn't be packing her fucking belongings, would she?

Fisting her own hands, she bit her lip.

She wanted to scream at him, to slap at his chest and shove him farther away from her, almost as much as she wanted to sob, and she would do none of it. *None*. Because whatever this was, whatever he wanted from her, the torture would be over soon, and she refused to humiliate herself yet again.

His eyes met hers directly. Unflinchingly. "You love them, and you want the people you love nearby, so of course you miss them."

Her breath hitched, and she wanted to turn away. But she didn't.

Maybe they couldn't be together, but at least . . . at least he finally seemed to comprehend what she'd tried to tell him so many times, in so many ways. At least part of it.

And that was something, wasn't it? To part with his understanding rather than his anger?

"Sweetheart." Raising his hand, he softly thumbed away a tear on her cheek. "It hurts more than you show, doesn't it? To have everyone from the island suddenly gone their separate ways. To have your family so far from here."

If she spoke, her voice would waver. Tremble like her fists. So she didn't speak.

But it was true. All of it.

And she'd never told him. Because there was nothing he could do about it, and because even with him, even during the best of their times together, she'd hated revealing that parts of her skin were so thin, they could bleed at the tiniest injury. That parts of her heart were so fragile, they could snap under a featherweight of pressure, in the space of a single beat.

So how did he know? What exactly had happened in the last week?

"Ramón and Nava will be back in LA soon, probably later today. They'll want to see you, and I know you need to see them." Then he gave his head a violent little shake. "Anyway, the event was . . ."

After brushing away a tear from her chin, he took another step closer, until he filled her vision so entirely, the rest of Los Angeles ceased to exist.

"It explained a lot. To me. About me. About you too, I guess." His dark eyes searched hers. "And right after it ended, I went to my hotel, packed, and drove directly to O'Hare in the middle of the night so I could catch the first flight to LAX in the morning.

I hoped you'd still be packing when I made it back, and I was worried if I told you I was coming, you'd leave, so . . . here I am."

Dazedly, she blinked up at him, too shaky and afraid to ask . . . why? Why *was* he here?

"Coach sucks," he declared. "It was the only option. So I could either have flight attendants ram service carts into my legs or use my knees to palpate the kidneys of the guy sitting in front of me. I decided he looked like someone who could use a deep-tissue massage, although I'm not certain he'd agree."

Forced into speech, she sniffed. Hard. "Deep-organ, more specifically. If it involved kidneys."

"Norse nitpicker." His lips curved in the sweetest, smallest smile she'd ever seen him give anyone. Then he sucked in an enormous breath and cradled her face in both hands. "Okay. Enough avoidance. Here's what you need to know, so I can find out what *I* need to know."

Her heart was thudding so hard, she—gods above, she might not survive this.

If she had to walk away from him still, *again*, it would break her. Fucking *demolish* her. Crush her into so many damn pieces, she might not ever manage to put herself back together.

"I texted my agent from the plane and turned down the *FTI* role." He lifted a shoulder, the very picture of nonchalance, and all she could do was gape at him. "Turns out, I have no interest in enhancing photos of license plates to a scientifically impossible extent while possessing precisely one overriding character trait."

At any other time, she'd laugh at that very apt description. But right now, she had no mental bandwidth for humor, because what he'd just said sounded like Peter *bending*. Rethinking, instead of digging in further.

And she wished it were enough. But it wasn't.

Because what happened when the next big role appeared on the horizon, one he actually found interesting and worthwhile? Would turning down this first offer only delay the inevitable?

She didn't want six more months with Peter, or two years, or even a dozen, before she had to walk away and savage her own heart yet again.

She wanted forever.

"Here's the more important bit, though." Tipping his head, he rested his forehead against hers and wiped away yet more of her tears. "Even if I did truly want the part, three years would still be too long to spend away from you. Because I'd miss you terribly, which I know for certain, since even a week apart felt like fucking *dying*. And because you need me here, and I need you happy. I need you with me. I need you mine, Maria. I love you so much. I'm . . . *hollow* without you."

She sobbed out loud, the sound a tearing ache in her throat, an explosion of unspeakable relief mixed with stomach-churning dread. Because all the gods *help* her, what if she'd misheard or somehow gotten it wrong? What would she do then? How would she survive it if she truly believed he'd handed her everything she wanted, but she'd fooled herself yet again, betrayed and broken her own heart *yet again*, when she fucking *knew* better?

What if she had to watch him leave her? Stand there and try to breathe while he set her aside like an unwanted gift?

His own eyes grew wet, and he shuddered against her with his next breath.

"Sweetheart, please. Fuck, please don't cry. Not over me, not *ever* again. I can't take it." His voice was hoarse now. Ravaged. "I wish I'd gotten my head out of my ass sooner. I'm so sorry I hurt you."

She squeezed her eyes shut and tried her best to believe, but it was so *hard*.

"You were right. Baby, please listen to me and stop crying." He buried his fingers in her hair and curled them into possessive fists, and she sobbed again, harder, because he wasn't leaving her, and he wasn't letting her leave either. "You were right, and it'll be fine. We'll be fine. We'll be *great*. There are plenty of movies and shows that film in LA. They might be smaller roles, some of them, but they'll be enough to keep us afloat, with our savings and residuals."

But staying afloat wouldn't pay his property taxes or Community Association fees.

"The h-house . . ." she managed to choke out.

"Is a fucking chunk of wood and stone." The anger roughening his tone wasn't for her, she knew. He'd turned all that raw emotion, all that frustration and rage, against himself. "It's not more important than you. Nothing on this motherfucking *planet* is more important than you. Not work, not this house, not this neighborhood, not some stupid bullshit from my past."

Okay, but he was in the middle of accommodating stupid bullshit from *her* past. He wasn't being fair to himself. A few deep breaths, then a few more, and she managed to calm down enough to say just that without another round of hysterical weeping getting in the way.

Flattening her hands on his chest, she took a final shuddering breath and stepped into his body. "*Sötnos—*"

"I have nothing to prove to my father, or to casting agents, or to anyone. Except you, Maria." His fists tightened in her hair the slightest bit, and the tug spiked lightning down her spine. "However long it takes, I'll prove that you can trust me."

Fy fan, for a taciturn man, he certainly could talk a lot.

His words were such a balm on her aching heart, though, and she let them soak in. Let herself relax her vigilance, stop fighting the immensity of her love for him, and—believe.

"I'll never leave you," he told her, a vow as solemn as any she'd heard in a church. "I'll never set you aside. I'll never betray your faith in me. I'll always listen when you tell me what you need. And I'll always, always, want you. Please trust me."

Peter, the proudest man she knew, was pleading with her. Pleading *for* her.

She couldn't stand it.

So when he finally took another breath, she seized her moment. "I do. I *do* trust you."

The desperation furrowing his tired face didn't diminish, so she kept talking.

"You don't lie to me." Even when it would have behooved him to do so, because he'd sometimes been a real dick in their early days together. "You've *never* lied to me. Except when you pretended very unconvincingly to be sick all those years ago. And even then, you're normally such a fantastic actor, I have to believe you intended to get caught."

"Not consciously. I'm just really bad at faking things off camera." His lips tipped upward the tiniest bit, then flattened again. "But yeah, on some level, I probably wanted you to know I was trying to keep you safe. I've loved you for a long, long time, Maria."

"I could say the same." She stroked his chest. "Peter, you're being too hard on yourself. If you need to have a lot of money tucked away or feel better living in this zip code, so be it. I can deal with that, as long as you're with me."

His eyes brightened, and the heart thundering under her palm slowed a fraction.

"I owe you an apology too." Brushing a kiss over the wrinkled fabric beside her hand, she rested her face there for a moment. "Right before you arrived, I was thinking about how long a separation I could actually handle, and I think . . . I think several months would be okay. The time it would take to film an average movie. So you'd have work options outside Hollywood too, at least once a year, and so would I. It doesn't have to be all or nothing, and I'm sorry I didn't realize that earlier and tell you so."

The solid warmth under her cheek shifted as he exhaled slowly.

She raised her head, studying the softening lines of his beloved face. "I might go visit my family if you'd be gone that long and I wasn't working on my own project. Or I could come stay with you and explore wherever your shoot is based."

"I'd love that. But if you need to be in LA while I'm on location, I'll come see you whenever I can, for as long as I can—and if you land a role that'll keep *you* away from home for long, I'll come stay wherever you're filming whenever I'm between jobs. That's a promise." Ducking down, he slid his nose alongside hers in a sweet caress, although his voice remained decisive. Hard with resolve as he laid out his plans for meeting her needs and making her happy. "And we'll only accept work outside LA if and when we both agree it's okay. Either one of us can say no for any reason, no explanation needed. Deal?"

If she knew she could always say no, would she find it easier to let him go?

Probably. But even if she didn't, he'd understand.

The relief of it . . . it felt like floating. Like being washed clean.

"Deal," she said, fighting yet more tears. "Gods above, I love you more than I can express in English *or* Swedish."

Pushing up, she pressed her mouth to his in a tender, brief kiss that tasted like salt and elation. When she settled back on her heels, though, he still had his fists in her hair and fear in his eyes.

"Does that . . ." His throat worked. "Does that mean you're coming back to me?"

"Yes." Of course. Hadn't he been listening?

He inhaled shakily. "You're not leaving?"

"I never want to leave you again, *sötnos*." Another quick buss on the lips, this one hard. An adamant claim on the man she adored. "Not as long as I draw breath on this earth."

"And you love me as much as I love you?"

"More."

Finally—*finally*—he smiled. "Not scientifically possible, Pippi."

"Whatever." Normally, she'd brandish a jar of *sill* in front of his nose in retaliation for the Pippi crack, but even she had to admit—reluctantly—that not all moments were herring-appropriate. Including this one. "Any more questions?"

Because she'd really like to leave the uncontrollable-weeping portion of the morning behind and move on to the make-up-sex portion, and she suspected Peter would also appreciate that transition.

"One more." Gently, he unwound his fingers from her hair. Then dropped to his knees.

Oh, good. He'd read her mind.

She laughed. "Peter, you *knäppgök*. You never need to ask if you can go down on me. The answer is always going to be yes. *Always*."

"I'm not—" Ducking his chin to his chest, he huffed out a laugh. "Only you, Maria. Only you would mistake a heartfelt declaration of love and proposal of marriage for an inquiry about licking your pussy. Shit."

A . . . proposal of marriage?

He wanted to be her husband?

Slowly, a smile spread across her face. *Nej*, a *beam*. Because while many committed Swedish couples didn't care whether or not they ever legalized their union, she was still—sorry, Kerstin—very much an all-or-nothing kind of person when it came to love.

She didn't give a fuck about weddings. But marriage? To Peter?

The sooner, the better.

Really, she'd have thought Peter couldn't improve upon his performances the previous times he'd sunk to his knees in front of her, but bravo to him. As Jeanine would say: *Peter Reedton. What a legend.*

Still, she knew of one way to make this particular knee-sinking occasion even better.

"Are offers of marriage and oral sex mutually exclusive?" Reaching down, she slid her fingers through his hair in the way that made him shiver every time. "Because if not, I'm saying yes to both. Just to be clear."

He only seemed to hear half her answer, sadly.

"You'll—you'll marry me? It's not too soon for you?" Why on earth he sounded so shocked, she'd never know. "I'd have asked weeks ago, but I didn't want to scare you off."

She snorted. "I think you can safely say I'm not afraid of commitment, Peter. I'd make you my husband right this second if I could."

The last traces of fear shuttering his eyes vanished, leaving only love and piercing joy. His expression, his posture—everything about him seemed to open. To bloom.

There wasn't a hint of wariness left.

Peter knelt before her, unprotected and unafraid.

"I'm sorry I don't have a ring," he said with the sort of adorable, uncharacteristic earnestness that was going to earn him a good amount of time spent on her own knees in the near future. "I was in a hurry to get here before you left. And if you said yes, I thought you'd want to choose it yourself."

He truly did know her very, very well.

Bending from the waist, she used her fingers in his hair to guide his mouth to hers in a lingering, sweet, unhurried caress.

Not a claim anymore but a declaration: that they had all the time in the world. That she trusted him with her softness, not just her strength. That, like him, she wasn't worried or wary any longer, because he was hers, and she was his, and both of them were too damn stubborn to let go of what they loved.

Then she ended the kiss with a flick of her tongue against his, because her love encompassed softness, strength, sweetness, *and* fierce need. *Heat.*

"We'll choose my engagement ring and yours at the same time." It wasn't a request. "I know it's not standard for men, but I want everyone lusting after your thighs and dying to ride your beard to know you're taken."

She paused. "And speaking of beard-riding . . ."

After all, he was *right there.* And it had been a *week.*

He shook his head, lips twitching. "My greedy Swede."

"You're complaining?"

"No," he said, and grinned openly. "Bragging."

Then he yanked down her panties and leggings in one swift, strong tug and set a new standard for knee-sinking excellence. Because whatever Peter did, he did with unshakable commitment.

And since he was currently doing *her* . . .

Well. Enough said.

Texts with Maria: Thursday Afternoon

Peter: You've broken me, Pippi

Peter: Shame on you

Maria: ???

Maria: I'm delighted, of course, but further explanation would still be useful here

Peter: Am I or am I not the man who acted like a jackass and let you leave me because I was determined to take jobs that would keep me away from you for months or years on end

Maria: Yes, obviously

Maria: If one of us is behaving like a jackass, I think we should always assume it's you

Maria: That general rule has stood me in good stead thus far

Peter: And are you or are you not the woman who said she'd miss me terribly if I were gone for too long

Maria: I believe we both remember the incident clearly, Peter, thanks so much for reminding me of that very happy day

Peter: If all that's true, if we're remembering things clearly, then why am I here on location in NYC and fucking miserable after two fucking weeks apart while you're blithely doing your own thing in LA and seem happy as can be

Peter: YOU BROKE ME, WOMAN

Peter: SHAME ON YOU, I WAS IN MINT CONDITION

Maria: ...

Maria: Of course I miss you, sötnos, but work helps, and seeing our friends helps, and I've FaceTimed my family a lot too

Maria: I wouldn't say I'm happy as can be, but I'm okay

Maria: So if you're trying to get me to admit that I'm struggling by pretending YOU are, please don't worry

Peter: Sweetheart, I'm not trying to do anything but tell you I miss you like fucking crazy

Peter: I don't care whether you're fine

Peter: Well, I do, you know I do, but what I'm attempting to say is that I don't want a several-month separation more than once a year

Peter: Whether you can handle it or not, I can't

Peter: I may be a broken shell of a man, but I'm YOUR broken shell of a man, and I need you near me

Maria: Want me to fly out tomorrow evening for a quick visit?

Peter: No

Maria: No?

Peter: I already booked my flight to you, Maria

Peter: I'll be there tomorrow night

Peter: If you have time to pick me up from LAX, please do, I need to have you in my arms as soon as I possibly can

Peter: I love you.

Maria: Jag älskar dig också, Peter.

Maria: Your blue cupboard is gleaming right now. You know that, right?

Peter: :-)

EPILOGUE

EVERY TIME HE AND MARIA VISITED ALEX AND LAUREN, PEter had to marvel anew.

Holy fuck, they lived in a fucking *castle*. With a moat. And stables. And *turrets*.

And somehow, the whole ridiculous structure managed not to especially stand out among its Beachwood Canyon neighbors, since all those homes—estates—boasted different architectural styles. As his SUV wound up the twisting mountain roads, he'd paid particular attention today. He'd spotted a sprawling Spanish colonial home, a few midcentury modern houses, starkly modern properties with endless walls of windows, as well as a tree house that had evidently consumed vast quantities of steroids.

No gates. Some tourists. Plenty of personality.

Several for-sale signs.

During a cast chat last week, there'd been a lot of discussion about how settled all of them were—or weren't—in their current homes. And before long, it had become clear that most of his costars, or maybe all of them, intended to move closer to Beachwood Canyon. Even Marcus, who lived with April in San Francisco, had expressed interest in either renting a guesthouse near Alex or investing in a second property.

Over the years, the cast had become more than professional

colleagues. They'd become dear friends. In a very real way, they'd become a family. Other than Ian, because fuck that guy.

During the entire texted conversation about homes and guest-houses and possibly moving en masse to Beachwood Canyon and its surrounding neighborhoods, Maria hadn't written a single word.

Neither had he.

That didn't mean he hadn't been thinking.

Yesterday, when he'd quietly emailed Ramón and Nava about their living arrangements and inquired as to whether Beachwood Canyon might suit them better, he'd thought more.

And now, as he sat sprawled on one of Alex's oversized sofas with Maria tucked close and so many people they loved milling around them, he was thinking yet again.

"Shut up, assholes, I want to make some toasts before the episode starts!" Carah shouted from across the large den. "Get your drinks and take your fucking seats!"

As they'd agreed to do months before, the cast—minus Ian, naturally—had gathered to experience the series finale of *Gods of the Gates* together, in privacy, where they could rail and lament and cackle gleefully to their hearts' content. And now, after a group takeout dinner, they were all claiming comfortable spots in front of Alex's huge television, ready to watch the forthcoming literal and character-arc carnage.

After a few toasts, evidently.

"To my darling Summer, whose Lavinia spinoff is going to be the biggest goddamn hit StreamUs has ever had," Carah called out, lifting her glass of champagne in Summer's direction. "Guaranteed blockbuster, babe."

Startled, Peter studied Carah more closely. He wasn't certain he'd ever heard her say *my darling* in such a caressing way. And come to think of it, hadn't Carah and Summer shared a room at that Napa outing?

Maria glanced up at Peter and raised her brows.

"Thanks, hon," Summer said, smiling sweetly.

Carah moved to stand beside Summer's armchair. "No offense, Marcus, but I never understood why Dido went for Aeneas when she could have had Lavinia instead."

Then Carah ducked down, cupped Summer's jaw, and gave her former on-screen rival a long, enthusiastic kiss as a chorus of whistles rose to a deafening din.

"I take full credit for this," Alex announced to the room at large from where he lay on the couch, his head in Lauren's lap. "I knew sending them that consentacles fic where Lavinia lovingly rails Dido with her tentacle before they swim off to Greece or wherever would do the trick."

After one last stroke of her—new? Or just newly revealed?—girlfriend's cheek, Carah straightened as Summer beamed up at her.

"To Alex, my *Unleashed* cohost and beloved asshole." Carah raised her glass again. "Stay chaotic, my friend. And pray Lauren continues putting up with your annoying ass, because that patient bitch deserves either some fucking hazard pay or sainthood."

Lauren's voice was as dry as the Santa Ana winds. "As my first miracle, I managed to convince him not to send a bouquet of fish-shaped helium balloons to Ian's house tonight, along with an oversized banner congratulating him on seven years of successfully endangering the world's tuna population."

When Alex smirked up at her provokingly, she lightly tugged on a lock of his hair.

"To Asha, our very own Jane motherfucking Bond!" Cheers broke out as Carah hoisted her glass high. "I can't wait to watch you fuck your way through most of Europe's male population in between speedboat chases and murdering people in creative yet bloodthirsty ways, you talented bitch!"

"Correction, my dear Carah." Asha's smile was wicked. "Not *just* the male population."

The two women high-fived.

"I'm singing the theme song." Asha's boyfriend tugged her onto his lap. "Although they're objecting to my lyrics for *Octodicky*. Apparently there were focus group complaints."

After pausing a moment to stare at him, Carah shook her head and spun to face Mackenzie.

"To Mackenzie and Whiskers, the *New York Times*–bestselling coauthors of the first-ever memoir written through cat-human telepathy: *Here and Meow: A Cat's Life*." Another raise of her glass, this time directed to where Mackenzie cuddled Whiskers on her lap. "May your telepathic connection remain clear, your sales brisk as fuck, and your self-grooming habits unshared, unless Mac unexpectedly needs to raise money from fetish videos."

"Thank you, Carah. We're so grateful to—" Stopping suddenly, Mackenzie lifted her cat so they stared at each other face-to-face. "What's that, Whiskers? You want to hear the lyrics? Because you're wondering how Teddy wrote a catchy song about a villain with eight penises?"

To be fair, Peter imagined they were all wondering that. Why not the cat too?

Asha's boyfriend shrugged. "Sure. I'll sing it for you later, Mac— er, Whiskers. I think you'll be surprised by the poignancy of the chorus."

Alex sneezed violently enough that they all jumped. After blotting his nose and eyes with a tissue, he cast Whiskers a narrow-eyed glare. Discreetly, Lauren passed him an allergy pill and a glass of water, which he guzzled before tugging her down and whispering in her ear.

Whatever he said, it turned her cheeks pink and her smile uncharacteristically giddy.

Knowing Alex, it probably involved pegging somehow.

"To Marcus." Carah's smile turned soft. "My closest colleague for so many years, and my dear friend. May you find roles and projects that make you proud as hell, and may your adaptation of the *Aeneid* blow away every single fucker who sees it. Also, may you avoid media questions about whether it's a fix-it fic in film form, because it totally is, dude."

"Since you and Summer are starring in it, it'll be amazing." Marcus poked April in the ribs, but it didn't stop her from laughing at him. "And it's not a fix-it fic in film form, per se. More . . . uh, an exploration of Aeneas's character that hews a little more closely to Virgil's work than *Gates*. For instance, Dido will not call herself a *crazy undead bitch coming for Aeneas's ass* before setting fire to his fleet of ships."

Truly, capturing Virgil's tale more accurately shouldn't prove too challenging.

Carah might be disappointed by that accuracy, however. When she'd filmed the fleet-burning scene, she'd enjoyed herself immensely.

ALL DEATH AND NO AENEAS MAKES DIDO A PISSED GIRL, she'd texted in the cast chat, if Peter recalled correctly. HEEEEEEEEEEERE'S PYRO DIDO!

"Also, April, my good bitch . . ." Carah saluted the redheaded geologist. "Thank you for helping Marcus be his best fucking self. One might even say: You rock."

A chorus of groans rang out.

"We literally just came from this amazing rock and mineral warehouse in Vacaville," April cheerfully admitted. "There's no shame in my geology game."

"Really?" Alex sat up a little, brows raised high. "That's all it took? For both of you?"

A few seconds passed before everyone got it. Then Lauren smacked his arm, and April, normally an unflappable scientist, blushed a little as she glanced at Alex and giggled. *Giggled*.

Marcus scowled at his BFF and tugged April tighter to his side.

Carah rolled her eyes. "It's a good thing you're hot, Woodroe."

"Wren agrees." With a wink, he lowered his head back to his girlfriend's lap.

Determinedly, Carah turned away from him. "To Maria and Peter, the last of our main cast. Or, rather, the last of our main cast who isn't a tuna-obsessed asshole with what appear to be tiny biceps on top of his biceps."

Peter could almost feel sorry for Ian. Perhaps he *would* have felt sorry for him—if Ian weren't, in fact, a tuna-obsessed asshole who'd alienated the rest of the cast and lorded his ostensible status over the crew. But he was, so Peter wouldn't shed any tears for the guy.

"Maria, everything I've seen about your next movie makes me want to get in line right fucking now. Woman-on-the-run flicks are my motherfucking *jam*." When Carah leaned forward, she and Maria fist-bumped. "And I can't tell you how goddamn happy I am that you're here in LA for good, my most vicious of bitches."

"Me too." Maria directed her effervescent smile toward all their friends before meeting Peter's gaze for a long, speaking moment. "There's nowhere else I'd rather be."

A message to everyone, but also to him in particular.

As she knew, he still worried about her distance from her family. Because that distance was a sacrifice, and one she'd made for him and him alone, no matter how much she genuinely adored their castmates. And she'd never made him feel guilty about it, but he wanted her to have absolutely everything *she* wanted, and it hurt that he couldn't provide that for her.

But he could do better. He *would* do better, and it started tonight.

Carah continued, "Peter, my beardy bro, you've been racking up the goddamn wins lately. That lead role in *Young MacDonald* is the part you were fucking born to play, dude. I mean, a surly but sexy city-guy veterinarian newly arrived in a small rural town? With his own farm? *Score.*"

He would agree. Mostly. Except when it came to all the fucking *cows*, Jesus Christ almighty, *so many fucking cows*.

But he loved the character of Jack MacDonald, and the series mainly shot in LA, so he supposed he was willing to risk death by malicious trampling. Best of all, the pilot had already been picked up, and they were guaranteed at least one full season.

If they got a second season, maybe he could convince the writers that Young MacDonald only liked chickens or sheep or *anything*, really, *anything at all* other than fucking *cows*.

It would also help if Maria would stop fucking *mooing* at him at unexpected moments, then cackling in delight when he jumped out of his skin. And whenever he suggested afterward that her blue cupboard or her boots might be a tad shit-filled, she only laughed harder.

The Danes had been right all along: Swedes were a cruel people.

"Your other huge win, of course, is that fine piece of Nordic ass at your side." Carah's appreciative wolf whistle was low and long, echoed by others in the room, and followed by cheers and applause. "How you were lucky or clever enough to drag that gorgeous Valkyrie to the altar, I'll never know, but congratulations, Peter. Well done, you sneaky fucking beardo."

He hadn't actually dragged Maria to an altar, although he would have, as needed. Instead, immediately after his proposal, they'd scheduled a civil ceremony and gotten married as quickly as the law allowed. Which Carah and everyone else in the room well knew, since they'd all attended. As had Ramón, Nava, and Maria's entire family. Not his father, though, who'd been unable to make the trip on such short notice, and Peter had been more than okay with that.

He didn't consider himself especially clever either. Carah's *gorgeous Valkyrie* bit, though? And the part about him being lucky?

Entirely, breathtakingly, joyously correct.

Apart from all the mooing, obviously. That wasn't lucky. That was annoying as hell. Which was why he planned to debut his new T-shirt tomorrow, the one reading BENNY AND BJÖRN: TRUE GENIUSES. And below, in slightly smaller print: WERE THERE OTHER MEMBERS OF ABBA? I DON'T REMEMBER ANY.

She was going to lose her fucking mind.

Payback. She'd learn.

"And finally," Carah began, an evil smile curling her lips, "to Ron and R.J., our—"

"Wait." Peter stood, hoisting his bottle of sparkling lemonade high. "One last toast before you eviscerate our absent showrunners, please. To Carah Brown, aptly known as both our caringest and swearingest cast member. The true star of *Unleashed*, obviously"—he ignored Alex's outraged, overly dramatic, entirely feigned gasp—"and the most loyal colleague and friend we could ever have. Here's to you, you complete fucking bitch."

Carah took a proud, grinning bow as the rest of them applauded.

"Thanks, Peter. I guess you aren't a total asshole after all. Only most of one. Like, ninety percent or so." Carah winked at him, then raised her champagne glass one more time as he reclaimed his spot next to Maria. "As I was saying, here's to Ron and R.J., wherever they might be."

"Not on social media or a con panel, I can tell you that much," Summer murmured.

Carah snickered, then kept going. "After years of critical fawning and various amazing job opportunities, this has been a tough few months for them. They've been pulled from directing *Star Fighters* and cut from other high-profile projects. Eviscerated online for startlingly terrible and slapdash scripts, as well as bizarre, rushed, and/or unsatisfying plotlines and character choices."

"If people thought the rest of the season was bad . . ." With a sigh, Marcus ran a hand through his gleaming, perfect hair. "Just wait until everyone sees tonight's finale. Holy shit."

"Ron's been the subject of several recent investigative pieces about misogyny on *Gates'* set, and I know someone in this room is responsible," Carah declared. "I just want to say, whoever you are: I fucking *love* you. I would offer to have your babies in gratitude for your exemplary service to humanity, but I don't want any. My ovaries are more like no-varies."

Surreptitiously, Alex turned his head slightly on Lauren's lap. Just far enough to catch Peter's eye and exchange the most infinitesimal of nods.

Yeah. It could be said that Alex still held a very deep, very well-founded, very rage-filled grudge when it came to Ron's behavior toward Lauren. Peter was pretty certain his friend would take that grudge to his goddamn grave, in the same way Peter was pretty certain gravity would continue to exist.

It could also be said that Peter had provided Alex a safe way to indulge that grudge. And that Peter had drawn on his own hidden complement of rage to exact justifiable vengeance.

If the showrunners hadn't shaken Maria's confidence, hadn't broken her spirit or harmed her body or made her question her own worth and beauty, it wasn't due to lack of effort on their parts.

They'd tried to take advantage of her. Tried to break her.

Tried and failed.

Maria had her vulnerabilities, as he well knew, but Ron and R.J. had never managed to locate them, thank fuck. She also knew how to protect herself and her interests, and she'd done so capably, with very little help from Peter.

But he wasn't the same man anymore, and he'd happily assume some risk to avenge the woman he adored. So, yeah, he'd used his contacts to give anonymous interviews a few weeks back. Shared damning memos and emails. Discreetly recruited Alex's assistance, because Alex still wanted payback and always would. He'd burn down the world for Lauren, even if Lauren didn't want him to.

Peter got that now, in a way he hadn't even a few months before.

Carah was still speaking, because the list of misfortunes visited upon the showrunners in recent months was long and varied and uniformly delightful.

"—my absolute favorite part," she was saying, her entire face alight with glee. "Let us not forget—let us *never* forget—how Ron and R.J. traveled to Maria and Peter's island to shoot footage for a bonus feature, and then decided to pay a visit to Dolphy McBlowholeface, despite all the locals' warnings. And how they tried to ride her, because they're assholes, and she immediately smacked the shit out of both of them and broke Ron's nose and gave R.J. a black eye. And how it was all caught on film by said locals, who promptly posted the video online, where it will live forever and ever, a-fucking-men."

For a minute, they all silently reminisced about that golden moment in their lives, exchanging nostalgic, satisfied smiles as they mentally revisited all the hilarious Twitter memes.

He and Maria had spent countless hours huddled on the couch that day, scrolling and chortling. "I always knew Dolphy was my life coach for a reason," she'd told him.

"According to Whiskers, that was the best day of his entire life," Mackenzie said now, a serene smile on her lovely face. "Even better than when he got that kitty massage and pedicure."

"Next year, we should celebrate Dolphin-Smacking Day together," Alex said lazily. "Or if we're all too busy exchanging presents and cooking a feast, we can always schedule something for Dolphin-Smacking Eve instead."

Asha made a note in her phone's calendar.

"Here's to Ron and R.J." Carah raised her glass one final time. "You've been fucking around for a long time now, assholes. Welcome to the *find out* portion of your career."

"I'll drink to that," Summer said, rising from her chair and linking her free arm through Carah's. "Gladly."

Obligingly, Peter rose too, and they all clinked bottles and glasses while enjoying the delicious schadenfreude.

Then the big moment finally arrived.

"It's about to start!" Carah cried, and rushed for Alex's remote.

Peter settled back, ready for the carnage to begin.

Not ready enough, as it turned out.

"WAS THIS FILMED during a supernova? What the actual fuck?" Marcus muttered, shielding his eyes with his flattened hand. "You can't even see me ascend to immortality. It's too damn *bright*."

"Maybe they wanted you to look more godlike." April squinted a bit. "But it's kind of hard to tell whether you're consuming ambrosia or a white-hot chunk of the sun."

Sprawled once again on Lauren's lap, Alex lifted his head and studied the scene thoughtfully. "Sorry you had to achieve immortality during a nuclear explosion, dude. Better luck next time."

Summer patted Marcus's arm consolingly, while Carah pointed at the screen and cackled. Asha and her boyfriend were making out, and Mackenzie had covered Whiskers's eyes and angled the cat away from the too-bright footage.

Peter's scenes with Maria had already come and gone, he could barely determine what was happening on-screen, and there would be plenty of time ahead to survey the wreckage of their godforsaken series finale, so he turned away from the television and ducked his head to speak directly into Maria's ear.

"How would you feel about finding a house near here? In Beachwood Canyon?" he whispered. "Would you like that?"

She didn't have to say a word. Her face lit to such an extent, the glare should have outshone whatever atrocities were occurring on the enormous television screen.

Her eyes searched his. "No gates, *sötnos*?"

"No gates."

"No guards?"

"No guards."

"No yoke?"

"No yoke."

Just the people they loved nearby and within easy reach, equally supportive through success and failure, joy and sorrow. Equally appreciative of Maria's and Peter's own support through the unpredictable tumult of a Hollywood career.

Living so close to her dearest friends, Maria would bloom.

So would he, as he now understood.

"You're sure?" Reaching up, she cupped his cheek. "You won't miss your house?"

No, he wouldn't. Because it was still *his* house to her, after all these months, rather than *theirs*. Her phrasing wasn't intentional, but it was a telltale sign of a larger problem, and he'd intended to find a solution to that problem for a while.

Now he had.

He'd missed a lot of things in his pre-Maria life. Love. Family. Friendship.

Compared to that? A house was absolutely fucking nothing.

He tilted his head, resting his forehead against hers. "I'll have you, won't I?"

"Always," she said. "Forever."

"Then I won't miss anything," he said, and smiled at her.

"Next year, I think we should try to one-up last summer's Con of the Gates. More surprises. More drama. More internationally televised references to pegging."

Someone had paused the show, and Alex was speaking to Marcus, who surveyed his best friend with a complicated expression on his mobile face, a familiar mélange of horror, resignation, affection, and amusement.

All of them had seen Marcus aiming that particular expression at Alex before. Many, many times.

He spoke very slowly. "I . . . don't think that's possible, Alex."

"Pessimist." Alex waved that aside. "What's the quote? 'Life finds a way'?"

"That's not life," Carah said, then tossed back a handful of mini pretzels and kept speaking with her mouth full. "That's you, our resident fucking chaos demon. *You* find a way."

Alex shrugged, unoffended. "Same diff."

"Also, please note that when life found a way in that particular movie, people got fucking *eaten*." Her voice emerged garbled by half-chewed pretzels. "And not in the good way."

Lauren claimed the remote.

"I'm going to restart the show now, before Alex experiences any more strokes of terrifying genius." Without even looking at him, she held up a hand as his mouth opened. "And no one wants to hear what a genius you are at stroking, Woodroe. Put a sock in it."

"Spoilsport," he muttered, even as he gazed at her profile with undiluted adoration.

When she unpaused the episode, there were several involuntary yelps at the excessive *brightness*. Luckily, though, that scene ended moments later, and the battle for Tartarus and all of humanity recommenced.

His most pressing problem now solved, Peter settled back on the couch and prepared to watch more miserable people dying horrible, pointless, badly scripted deaths.

But he wasn't thinking about death. Not really.

Right now, he was more concerned with life.

He might miss his mother every remaining day he drew breath in this world. He might never find a way to connect with and forgive his father. His career might founder as he grew older, or if he fell out of favor in Hollywood. His bank accounts might slowly empty.

But with Maria cuddled against his side and their friends sprawled all around, bickering and embracing and snickering in petty glee—

"Stop hogging the footstool, *skitstövel*," whispered the woman who owned his entire heart. "Or I'll trick you into eating salty licorice again and laugh at you as you gag."

She would too. Maria didn't make idle threats.

"Swedish shrew." He pressed a kiss to her temple. "Why do I love you so much?"

"Because I'm amazing. Obviously." Twisting her neck, she looked up at him consideringly. "I suppose it doesn't hurt that I love you too. Even though I'm forced to carry around an extremely heavy jar of herring at all times to keep you in line."

His scowl was so fake, even a child could have spotted the lie.

She patted his bearded jaw. "You're welcome."

Then she turned back to the television and claimed more of the footstool.

Turned so she couldn't see it—because only a fool would encourage her—he let a grin spread across his face until his cheeks ached.

Yeah. With Maria snuggled under his arm and so many people he loved less than a dozen steps away, even a stubborn, surly pessimist like him was forced to admit the obvious.

It was unexpected but true.

For the first time in his life, he—*Peter Reedton*, of all people—believed in happy endings.

He had to. He had no choice.

After all, he was living one, wasn't he?

ACKNOWLEDGMENTS

LEFT ON MY OWN, I WOULDN'T HAVE FINISHED *SHIP Wrecked*. A year into the pandemic, I wasn't precisely in tip-top shape as far as mental health. Even opening up a Word document felt overwhelming some days. (Most days.)

Every moment I wavered, though, help inevitably appeared.

When I couldn't decide on the book's setting, Emma Barry told me about the Aran Islands and then—entirely unasked—created a freaking *PowerPoint presentation* about her trip there, which was both Peak Delightful Nerd and exactly what I needed to visualize Peter and Maria's small, windswept filming location. When I got 30,000 words into the story and knew something was wrong, she read over what I'd written and patiently helped me figure out where I'd erred and how to fix my mistakes. When I finally completed my draft, she read it again, and both Susannah Erwin and Therese Beharrie read it for the first time. Their confidence in the completed story allowed me to believe I'd accomplished what had once seemed impossible: Despite my ongoing depression, I'd managed to write a book I loved, and one full of all the humor and joy I wanted for my readers.

The times when I lost momentum along the way, Theresa Romain FaceTimed. Therese Skyped. Mia Sosa, Susannah, and so many other friends emailed and DMed and asked what they could do to help. In the end, even when I spent weeks at a time socially isolated and holed up in my Swedish apartment, I was never alone.

I was never alone for another reason too: My family did everything they could to support me as I wrote, even when all they could really do was keep loving and encouraging me. Which was, of course, precisely what I needed from them. Mr. D, Little D, and Mom: I love you so much.

And that's not even taking into account all the other people who made this book happen! I was gifted with not one, but two amazing editors for *Ship Wrecked*. Elle Keck's enthusiasm for the story and willingness to talk through it with me inspired me each day I wrote, and her love for my draft buoyed me more than I can express. I will never be able to thank her enough for her belief in me or the attention and care she gave my books. Elle, I hope every day at your new job is full of joy, because you deserve that and so much more. When Elle left, Nicole Fischer stepped in, and I am so grateful to her for the thought and care she devoted to my story. I can't wait to work with her on my new series. :-)

Nicole was incredibly patient as we worked through the process of creating the most gorgeous cover imaginable. For that cover, of course, I also owe a huge debt of gratitude to Leni Kauffman, my illustrator, and Yeon Kim, my cover designer. Between the two of them, they *slayed* this cover. I couldn't be prouder to have my name on it, for so many reasons.

Everyone else at Avon was absolutely amazing as well: Eliza Rosenberry, Amanda Lara, and Holly Rice were kind and efficient and enthusiastic and basically everything an author could ever want in a publicity team. DJ DeSmyter was so responsive and simply a delight to work with. Someday we'll end up at a bar together and make a toast to Avon's first-ever preorder campaign involving strap-ons! (As I write these acknowledgments, he does not yet know what I have in mind for *Ship Wrecked*'s preorder campaign, and I hope he's ready for possible illustrated nudity.) Also, all my gratitude to Laura Cherkas for being so thorough and careful in my copy edits.

Then there's Sarah Younger, my indefatigable, stalwart, incredible agent. Thank you, Sarah, for putting my well-being above any other consideration, without hesitation. Thank you for having my back, always. Thank you for believing in me and my work, and thank you for demanding more for me than I'd ever demand for myself. I am so lucky to have you in my corner, and I know it.

And finally: Thank you to all my readers. Please know that I am grateful for you every day. Every. Single. Day. ♥

ABOUT THE AUTHOR

OLIVIA DADE grew up an undeniable nerd, prone to ignoring the world around her as she read any book she could find. Her favorites, though, were always, always romances. As an adult, she earned an MA in American history and worked in a variety of jobs that required the donning of actual pants: Colonial Williamsburg interpreter, high school teacher, academic tutor, and (of course) librarian. Now, however, she has finally achieved her lifelong goal of wearing pajamas all day as a hermit-like writer and enthusiastic hag. She currently lives outside Stockholm with her delightful family and their ever-burgeoning collection of books.

Have you read the other books in Olivia Dade's fan fiction–inspired series? What are you waiting for?! *Spoiler Alert* (Marcus and April's story) and *All the Feels* (Lauren and Alex's story) are both available now, wherever books are sold.

ALSO BY
OLIVIA DADE

Olivia Dade bursts onto the scene in this delightfully fun romantic comedy set in the world of fanfiction, in which a devoted fan goes on an unexpected date with her celebrity crush, who's secretly posting fanfiction of his own.

"It's a path of self-discovery, healing and growth, punctuated by scorching chemistry, whip-smart dialogue and sidesplitting humor."

—*WASHINGTON POST*

Following *Spoiler Alert*, Olivia Dade returns with another utterly charming romantic comedy about a devil-may-care actor—who actually cares more than anyone knows—and the no-nonsense woman hired to keep him in line.

"An absolutely witty, swoon-worthy, behind-the-scenes romp! Delightful from beginning to end!"

—JULIE MURPHY,
#1 *New York Times* bestselling
author of *Dumplin'*

DISCOVER GREAT AUTHORS, EXCLUSIVE
OFFERS, AND MORE AT HC.COM.

AVONBOOKS

HarperCollins*Publishers*